The Finest Stories of Sean O'Faolain

By Sean O'Faolain

NOVELS
A Nest of Simple Folk
Bird Alone
Come Back to Erin

SHORT STORIES
Midsummer Night Madness
A Purse of Coppers
The Man Who Invented Sin
The Finest Stories of Sean O'Faolain

BIOGRAPHY
Constance Markievicz
King of the Beggars
The Great O'Neill
Newman's Way

TRAVEL
An Irish Journey
A Summer in Italy
An Autumn in Italy

CRITICISM
The Short Story
The Vanishing Hero

PLAY
She Had to Do Something

TRANSLATIONS
The Silver Branch

MISCELLANEOUS
The Irish

SEAN O'FAOLAIN

The Finest Stories of
Sean O'Faolain

An Atlantic Monthly Press Book
Little, Brown and Company • Boston • Toronto

Third Printing

The author wishes to thank the following
for permission to reprint material which first
appeared in their pages: the *Atlantic Monthly;
Commonweal; Kenyon Review; New American Library; Tomorrow* (copyright 1948 by
Garrett Publications, all rights reserved); *Yale
Review.*

ATLANTIC–LITTLE, BROWN BOOKS
ARE PUBLISHED BY
LITTLE, BROWN AND COMPANY
IN ASSOCIATION WITH
THE ATLANTIC MONTHLY PRESS

*Published simultaneously in Canada
by Little, Brown & Company (Canada) Limited*

PRINTED IN THE UNITED STATES OF AMERICA

To My Wife

Foreword

I MUST, if only in self-defense, tell the reader of this volume that
it opens with three stories from my first book of stories, *Midsummer Night Madness,* and that although I have chosen them because I
like them very much they contain things that make me smile today
— and, yet, I have been unwilling to rewrite them. I should like to
explain why. They belong to a period, my twenties. They are very
romantic, as their weighted style shows. I should have to change
my nature if I were to change the style, which is full of romantic
words, such as *dawn, dew, onwards, youth, world, adamant* or *dusk;*
of metaphors and abstractions; of personalizations and sensations
which belong to the author rather than to the characters. They also
contain many of those most romantic of all words, *and* and *but,*
which are words that are part of the attempt to carry on and expand
the effect after the sense has been given. Writers who put down the
essential thing, without any cocoon about it, do not need these *ands*
and *buts.* The thing is given and there it lies; whereas the writer
who luxuriates goes on with the echoes of his first image or idea.
His emotions and his thoughts dilate, the style dilates with them,
and in the end he is trying to write a kind of verbal music to convey

feelings that the mere sense of the words cannot give. He is chasing the inexpressible. He is interested mainly in his own devouring daemon. He is, as I was in my romantic twenties, drowned in himself. French writers, on the other hand, often spoil their stories by adding too much analysis in their obsessive pursuit of clarity at all costs. Hemingway is the real man. He writes short sentences because with his genius for seizing on the essential he can also seize on the simple image to convey what he wants to say. If we sometimes think that he is saying something obvious that may well be because only a man of genius can see and say what, once he has seen and said it, we flatter him by thinking of as obvious.

When I was in my twenties I did not know from Adam what I wanted to say. I had no grasp at all of the real world, of real people. I had met and mingled with them, argued with them, lived with them, shared danger with them. They were mysteries to me. I could only try to convey my astonishment and delight at the strangeness of this bewildering thing called life. Besides, when I wrote "Fugue," my first successful story, in 1927, I had come out of an experience which had left me dazed — the revolutionary period in Ireland. Not that it was really an experience as I now understand that word. It was too filled with dreams and ideals and a sense of dedication to be an experience in the meaning of things perceived, understood and remembered. I perceived all right, I remembered all right, but it had all been far too much to understand; especially the disillusion at the end of it all, for, as few people who are not Irish now remember, that revolutionary period ended in a civil war, and civil war is of all wars the most difficult for its participants to understand. Besides, as I found myself yesterday making a character in a novel I am writing say, "It's a terrible and lovely thing to look at the face of Death when you are young, but it unfits a man for the long humiliation of life."

I suppose that is why those early stories were full of romantic boss-words like *dawn*. At that time if you said *dawn* to me my mouth would begin to dribble, like Faulkner whenever he thinks of the word *avatar*. *Dawn* is not a prose writer's word. I doubt if it is any longer a decent word for even a poet to use. It is a sounding word, a rhetorical word. Words like that are all right for Frenchmen. They are able to use rhetoric as if it were not rhetoric; we are not. (The other day a producer said to me, "I'm doing a French play. Every time one of the characters makes a speech I want to make him stand with his back to the audience. Otherwise he seems as if he were about to take off in an airplane.") But those first stories I wrote were all the time trying to take off in an airplane. "Fugue," as the reader will note, ends up with a Pegasus leap into verse. It is a very lovely story. I wish I felt like that now. And it is so much easier to be romantic if you are romantic by nature, and so much more cozy. Anyway, all this is just to explain why I have not rewritten these early stories. I dare not. It would be a lie. A story is like a picture, caught in the flick of a camera's trigger, that comes nearer and nearer to clarity in the bath of hypo which is the writer's blend of skill and imagination; he trembles over it as the bleach trembles and wavers over the sensitive halides of the film, waiting for the final perfection of his certainty, of his desire. Then the experience, complete or incomplete, is fixed, forever. You can rewrite while you are the same man. To rewrite years after is a form of forgery.

My second volume of stories, *A Purse of Coppers,* appeared after I had more or less come out of the daze. I came out of it by writing myself out of it in a novel, *A Nest of Simple Folk,* and a biographical study of a beautiful Irishwoman, a romantic guerrilla, Constance Gore-Booth, later Countess Markievicz. The biography was slight and groping, but it helped me to get all those romantic figures into some sort of perspective, and myself along with them. I could grin a bit at my solemn self and at my solemn countrymen. I hope a certain adjustment and detachment shows itself in the stories that follow "A Broken World." Naturally, of course, I still did not know what was happening to me or what I was doing. Writers never do. For instance, a friend suggested to me that "A Broken World" was my unconscious reply to Joyce's wonderful story, "The Dead." I certainly did not consciously mean any such thing; but I can agree that what with the snow over Dublin, and the suggestion that Ireland is not dead but sleeping, as against Joyce's feeling that Ireland is paralyzed by its past, one could, I suppose, say that the stories contrast the attitudes of two different generations. After all, Joyce grew up with a strong distaste for Ireland.

But I do not think I had adjusted myself properly until my next volume of stories, *The Man Who Invented Sin* — if even then. Anyway, by the time I had more or less adjusted myself to the life about me, it suddenly broke in on me that Ireland had not adjusted herself to the life about her in the least little bit. Irishmen in general were still thinking about themselves, or rather, in their usual way, double-thinking or squint-thinking about themselves, in terms of *dawns,* and *ands,* and *buts,* and *onwards,* and *dew,* and *dusk,* while at the same time making a lot of good, hard cash to the evocative vocabulary of *tariff, tax, protection, quota, levy, duties* or *subsidies,* meanwhile carefully compiling a third and wholly different literary style (*pious, holy, prudent, sterling, gorsoons, lassies, maidens, sacred, traditional, forefathers, mothers, grandmothers, ancestors, deep-rooted, olden, venerable, traditions, Gaelic, timeworn* and *immemorial*) to dodge more awkward social, moral and political problems than any country might, with considerable courage, hope to solve in a century of ruthless thinking. This ambivalence, once perceived, demanded a totally new approach. I have been trying to define it ever since. For, as long as we were all in a splendidly romantic-idealistic fervor about Ireland we could all write romantically, or idealistically, about Ireland, as Sean O'Casey did. (He is sometimes called and probably thinks himself a realist, but he is actually the biggest old romantic we ever produced.) Or if we were all being realistic we could write in the realist tradition. But for any kind of realist to write about people with romantic souls is a most tricky and difficult business, even when he is a Stendhal gifted with a lovely irony, a Chekhov holding on firmly to the stern morality of the doctor, a Turgenev informed by an intelligent humanism, or an E. M. Forster blessed with a talent for quiet raillery. If one has not some such gift the subject is an almost certain pitfall. (Think of what happened to Hemingway with his romantic colonel and *contessina!*) But when it comes to writing about people who, like the Irish of our day, combine beautiful, palpitating tea-rose souls with hard, coolly calculating heads, there does not seem to be any way at all of writing about them except satirically or angrily. Once a writer's eye gets chilly about their beautiful souls he becomes like the only sober man at a drunken party, and the only decent thing for him to do then is either to get blind drunk with the rest of the boys (all singing in chorus, "I'll take you home again, Kathl-ee-een") or else to go home and scrub himself clean in a raging satire on the whole boiling lot of them.

The reader may recognize a few mildly tentative efforts in this direction in the last few stories in this book. They started out to be satirical; they mostly failed dismally to be satirical; largely I presume — I observe it to my dismay and I confess it to my shame — because I still have much too soft a corner for the old land. For all I know I may be still a besotted romantic! Some day I may manage to dislike my countrymen sufficiently to satirize them; but I gravely doubt it — curse them! However, as D. H. Lawrence said, one's passion is always searching for some form that will express or hold it better, letting none of it leak away. And one is always searching for different forms, since otherwise one's passion would have the same form from birth to death, which would merely mean that one had got stuck, or given up, or agreed to compromise on some easy formula somewhere along the line, and that would be premature death, since not to change is to die though still apparently alive.

One thing I find very chastening as I look at this gathering of short stories: the thought that although I began writing in 1927 — that is, really writing, writing well — and have since written lots of other books (far too many of them) all I have to show for all those years by way of short stories — or, at least, all I am content to show — is some thirty titles! One thinks of writers like George Sand pouring out volume after volume while — as Colette observed, enviously, wondering how on earth she managed it — never once neglecting a love affair, never missing one puff of her hookah, never denying herself any experience that came her way.

I think of the time when I wanted to be another Balzac! I saw myself scribbling away madly while the printer's devil stood by my desk picking up the pages of genius and running off with them to the printing press while the ink was still wet. I must have been *very* young then. When I got down to the business of writing I found that half the art of writing is rewriting, and I would be happy if I achieved two hundred words of lapidary prose in a day. (Imagine, dear reader, that you see me shrugging.)

I know now that four fifths of Balzac's sixty-odd volumes are far from being works of genius. Would all that Stendhal churned out fit into an eight-foot shelf? Would all of it that is worth while fill a two-foot shelf? Story after story by Maupassant is journeyman stuff. I can now reread only the Chekhovs that I have ticked off on the contents pages. And can anybody living, other than some rare student, lay his hand on his heart and say he has read all of George Sand? I have learned in my thirty-odd years of serious writing only one sure lesson: that stories, like whiskey, must be allowed to mature in the cask. And that takes so much time! Oh, dear! Why do they tell us in our youth that there are twenty-four hours in a day, seven days in a week, and fifty-two weeks in a year? Balzac, indeed! I

shall be content if half a dozen, if even three or four of my stories
that have taken thirty years to write are remembered fifty years
hence.

SEAN O'FAOLAIN

Dublin

Contents

CONTENTS

The Finest Stories of Sean O'Faolain

Midsummer Night Madness

FOR a second I looked back into the city, down through the smoke at the clustered chimney pots and roofs on whose purples and greens and blues the summer night was falling as gently as dust, falling too on the thousand tiny beacons winking and blinking beneath me to their starry counterparts above. It was just on the curfew hour and the last few laggard couples went hurrying past me, their love-making ended abruptly for the night, lest the Tans in their roaring Lancia patrol cars should find them conspicuous on the empty white streets of the city. Then, mounting my bicycle, I turned to the open fields and drew in a long draught of their sweetness, their May-month sweetness, as only a man could who had been cooped up for months past under one of those tiny roofs, seeing the life of men and women only through a peephole in a window blind, seeing these green fields only in the far distance from an attic skylight. I left the last gas lamp behind, and the pavement end, and rode on happily into the country.

Yet, though the countryside was very sweet to me after all those months among the back yards, I was worried and watchful lest I should run into a chance patrol or raiding party. I kept listening, not to the chorus of the birds, not to the little wind in the bushes by the way, but nervously to every distant, tiny sound — the chuckle of a wakeful goose or hen in a near-by farmyard, or the fall of water coming suddenly within earshot, or some animal starting away from the hedge where I surprised its drowsing heavy head. Once I halted dead, my grip tight on the brakes, when a donkey brayed suddenly and loudly as if he were laughing at the intense quietness of the night. Fallen hawthorn blossoms splashed with their lime the dust of the road, and so narrow were the boreens in places that the lilac and the dog rose, hung with wisps of hay, reached down as if to be plucked. Under the overhanging trees I could smell the pungent smell of the laurel sweating in the damp night air. And all about me the dead silence of the coming night, the heavy silence, drowsy with the odors of the night flowers and the cut meadows, unless a little stream trickled over the road and my wheels made a great double splash as they crossed it.

I was on my way to the townlands of Farrane and Kilcrea, to see why to all appearances the local battalion had been completely inactive for the last three or four months. That portion of my task I did not relish, for I had known and been friendly with Stevey Long, the commandant, ever since the chances of revolution threw us together. Still, I should be free of the open fields for a few days, and there was enough romance left in the revolution for me to be excited at the thought that I was to stay at a house I had known and wondered at since childhood; I might even see and meet, if he were still alive, its strange mad owner whom as children we thought more terrifying than any of the ogres in the fairy books — old Henn of Henn Hall.

I could hardly credit that he was still alive, for even when we were very young my mother always spoke of him as "that old divil of a Henn." And an old devil he was, living up there all alone, in what she used to call his "rooky-rawky" of a house, never married but always in a state of marriage with some woman or other. He began, I could well believe, with women of his own class, officers' wives from the barracks at B——, or Cork, or perhaps with what we used to call "horsy women" from some neighboring or English hunt. But, judging by his later life, he cannot have been overparticular at any time in his choice of women, and many a tinted London trollop must have walked his fields, looking in utter boredom at the gulls flying after the plow or the rain hanging in the bare trees, until finally, like all her predecessors and successors of many years, she in her turn cursed Henn and his hall, and Ireland and all belonging to it, and went back gladly to the flickering city lights and the back streets, and the familiar loved smells of gaslit theaters and stuffy hansom cabs. A man who lived by the things of the body — women, wine, hunting, fishing, shooting.

My mother often told us how as she and a crowd of schoolgirl friends were returning from their first Communion one cold autumn afternoon they entered his fields to take a short way by the river to their homes, removing their new shoes and stockings as they always did when they left the high road. They came on Henn — and he was a grown man then — standing in his pelt by the river, ready for a swim. She used to shudder as she told how he chased them, and they ran from him, screaming with fear, throwing away the new shoes and stockings as they ran, their legs all torn on the withered rushes of the bog and the furzed hedgetops, not daring to look back to see if the naked "madman" were catching up with them, until, as she said, they had left his fields "forty miles behind," and panting and exhausted they ran into their homes. Henn must have been delighted with his frolic, and I can see him, running back for his swim, his long legs and his long neck, that gave him the nickname of Henn's Neck, cutting through the air as he ran. He must have been especially delighted when in the late evening the fathers and brothers of the children came looking here and there timidly for the little blue or red socks and the black shoes. It was only one of many such escapades that spread the name and legend of madness that clung to him through his life. We needed few such warnings to avoid him and his estate. We used to say to each other, somebody's warning half understood, that if Henn caught a little girl "he'd salt her," and we went in mortal terror of him and his salting for years. We used to say that he had wires hidden under his fields and if you crossed even one of his ditches bells would ring up in the hall and he would come galloping on a white horse with his hungry hounds to salt you.

It was a wonderful old house to look at, sitting up on its own high hill, its two gable chimneys like two cocked ears and all its empty windows gazing wide-eyed down the river valley — very tall, with a wide door whose steps curled down and around like mustaches. The façade was a pale rain-faded pink at the end, but it was often called The Red House, and if it was ever really *red* it must have been visible for miles to anyone driving westward to Crookstown along the valley, following the little river and its dark line of woods. Yet, as I tried to recall it now, only one impression remained, for we came into the city when I was quite young and there I soon forgot the hall. But at least two or three times afterwards my father took me on an unusually long walk in that direction, and each time when he returned he said to my mother, "We could just see The Red House up the valley beyond Kilnaglory"; and each time she said, "Glory be to God, I wonder is that old divil alive yet?" and told us all over again how he chased them in his pelt when they were little children.

One of these walks was on a soft wintry day with packed clouds threatening to drop rain every minute, and the Lee and the Bride in flood, and the tall bare beeches with the rooks' nests in their tiptops swayed and swung in the hard wind. The roads were muddy in places and there were many potholes full of rain or liquid dung and they were all wrinkled in the breeze and the flooded river ran frothing and brown by the very edge of the road. Off up the sodden valley, high on its rounded hill, sat Henn's house, and it was really more red than pink that day because of the rain, and as we looked

at it one solitary window showed a light. At the same time the
cold yellow sky behind it was turning to a most marvelous red as of
blood, and the scarlet light blackened every leafless twig and tree
trunk that stood against it and every ditch and scooped riverbank,
and lastly the road and the very sky itself became swarthy, and
there was light only in the waves curling the river and the potholes
of the road. When the solitary window shone, my father said, "That's
old Henn." I pictured him as an old man with a beard and long
claw-hands half into the glowing ashes, so that I said, "I think, Father, it's going to be thunder and lightning," and he looked and said,
"It might," and to my joy we turned our backs on Henn and his
house and faced for the lights and the crowds and the shop windows
of the city.

Really, I am sure, that was not Henn; he would have been down
at the bridge head with his rods and his basket and his gillie. But
whenever those same winter rains streamed down the curtainless
windows now, would he not have to stand watching, back bent —
if indeed he still lived — shivering in the bay, and return to crouch
sadly — not so far removed from my childish picture of him — over
his perpetual summer-to-summer fire?

You may pity him as I tell you of him, but I, riding along the
darkling lanes that night, had nothing in my heart for him but hate.
He was one of the class that had battened for too long on our people.
I was pleased to think that if he lived he lived only in name; that if
he had any physique left now he would need it all to attract
even the coarsest women. No London light-o'-love would be at-
tracted to his ruin of a house now for other reasons; the farmers'
daughters for miles around would shun him like the plague; and
even maids who came from a distance would not be in the place a
day without hearing all about him from the neighbors. Perhaps the
traveling tinker-women would have to suffice? But, thinking of the
big Red House, with its terraced lawns, and its cypresses and its
yews, and its great five-mile estate wall, all built by the first Henn,

the founder not only of his line but of an industry — glassmaking, and long since disappeared from Ireland — I could not believe that even such a house would fall so low.

As I came to a crossways where my road dropped swiftly downhill the tenting chestnuts filled the lanes with darkness, and under my wheels the laid dust was soft as velvet. Before I took this last turn on my way I looked back the road I had come and saw upthrown behind the hill the distant glow of the city's lights, a furnace glow that made me realize how near and how far were the roofs and chimneys I had left. But as I looked I saw, too, how the clouds were gathering like pale flowers over the inky sky and even as I dropped silently downhill the first drops beat the fronded layers above. On my left, high as two men, rose the estate walls that had once kept the whole countryside at bay, but could not now (gapped and crumbling) keep a fox out or a chicken in. I passed two great entrance gates sunk in the weeds. Then the pale ghostlike pillars of the third gate came into view across a gap in the tunnel where the rain was beating down the dust, gradually changing its pattering blows for the hissing sound of a real downpour. Head bowed I raced across the unsheltered patch and edged my bicycle through the creaking gate and was just abreast of the little Gothic door of the lodge when it swung open and a woman stepped suddenly through the laurels and caught my arm, saying roughly and passionately as she did so:

"Stevey, why did you go away? Henn was down again tonight. Stevey, I . . ."

The rain beat down on us, blotting out stars and moon alike.

Then she saw her mistake, and dropped my hand.

"I'm sorry," she said. "I thought . . ."

I laughed to put her at her ease.

"You thought I was Stevey Long."

She turned and went back to the door and seeing me, from there, look after her she cried out roughly:

"Go on!"

And because I was slow in moving for all the falling rain, she cried again:

"Go on about your business! Go on!"

"What a rough creature!" I was saying to myself as I began to wheel my bicycle up the avenue, when I heard her steps behind me. She beckoned and drew me back into the shadow of one of the sheltering trees beside the little house, leaned insinuatingly close to me, fingering my lapel, and said in a hollow mannish voice:

"You know Stevey Long?"

"Yes, of course, I do."

"Are you the boy he was bringing to the hall to stay?"

"Yes."

"He told me about you. You know him well, don't you?"

"I know Stevey for a long time."

"He told me you were in jail with him once."

"Did he tell you that? I was. Oh, yes! Stevey and I had many a bout together."

She paused. Then in a low, trembling voice she said, "Do you know his girl?"

"His girl?"

"Yes. He told me all about her. He said you know her too. Tell me . . . where is she?"

Her voice was strained against the leash. I did not want to be caught by her country trickery, and I looked into her face by the light of the little window, from eye to eye searching for the truth. Seeing me hesitate she caught my arm fiercely.

"Tell me!"

"Why, I suppose you are Stevey's girl," I bantered.

"Tell me, boy! She sent him letters to jail, didn't she? Oh, for Christ's sake, go on and tell me!"

She had me by the two arms now, her full bosom almost touching mine, so close to me that I could see the pouches under her eyes, her mouth dragged down wet and sensual, the little angry furrow between her eyebrows. The wind shook the heavy leaves of the chestnuts and as they scattered benediction on us the light from the little Gothic window shone on these wet leaves, and on her bosom and chest and knees. For a second I thought her blue apron drooped over her too rich, too wide hips. Since I did not speak she shook me like a dog and growled at me as fiercely as a dog.

"I don't know," I said. "She just sent letters to us, to Stevey, of course, and cigarettes and fruit and things — that's all. I don't know!"

She threw me away so that I all but stumbled over my bike.

"I knew it was true," she moaned. "I knew it was true when they said it."

"But anyone might write him a letter. . . ."

"He denied it. He denied he ever got a letter from her." In open country it is surprising how the voice sometimes echoes. Under those trees her voice resounded so that I feared she would be heard up at the hall or down in the village. "The liar! He's going to marry that wan. That's the wan he wants. The shcut! And look what he's going to do now!"

Her great bosom rose and fell in rage.

"Do?" I asked. "What is he going to do?"

"Who'd mind Henn? I ought to know. But Stevey! With his grand talk! He said *he'd* never harm me. But I won't marry him! I won't marry him! I won't! I won't!"

And she turned and ran into the lodge, leaving me with the feeling that this hall and estate and countryside had an unpleasant, real life of its own, a life that would spoil for me the few days of quietness that I had been dreaming of this last hour as I cycled between the hedgerows. I scarcely noticed that the sudden summer shower had ceased as I made slowly up the mossed drive, dark with unpruned trees and black laurel. Everything here too seemed to send up its sweetness into the soft wet air, even the weeds bursting through the gravel, and when I came to the front of the house the great dark cypresses in the wet failing light were plumes of billowy smoke against the sky. I was now on the terrace before the hall, and as I looked down into the valley to where the sound of the waters of the Bride rose murmuring through the air purified by the shower, I almost expected to see the old libertine come floating up like a specter or a long-legged ogre through the hills.

I found my way, as I had been instructed to do, to the rear of the house and in by the servants' quarters to the great kitchen. The pale still light of a candle on the table filled the room, and at the foot of the table beneath it was a basin of dusty milk. Before the embers an old sheep dog yawned and stretched his legs. I sat down by the fire and, glad of the rest, began to try to understand what it was that so troubled the girl at the lodge, with her passionate raging outburst against Stevey, and her cry, "I won't marry him! I won't marry him!" But almost on my heels I heard the sound of feet mashing the gravel outside and she came into the kitchen.

"Put on some turf, boy," she said at once. "And blow up the fire."

As I laid on the brown peat and sat by the side of the machine turning its handle she began to lay the table for my supper. Then we heard somebody else approach outside, and with a sudden shake of her fist to me by way of warning, she opened the door to Stevey. To her he gave a mere "Hullo, Gypsy." To me he gave a cordial "Here we are again," and he shook my hand several times and told me how glad he was to see me safe and sound.

Sullenly the girl broke in on us with, "Put the kettle on, Stevey, for the boy's supper," and sent me out to the rain barrel for water. I rose and went, and as I passed the window, there she was struggling out of his arms like a wild animal. When I returned she was again by the table, and he was bending down over the fire, swinging the great iron kettle forward on its crane to be filled. I lay back in the old basket chair and watched him move silently about the kitchen, finding everything where he expected to find it, his fair flock of curls all about his neck and brow like a mountainy sheep, his knees flinging apart at every step as they always did, and his hangdog head and his rounded shoulders more slouched then ever.

Since they would not speak to one another I began to ask random questions: the name of this or that townland; whether this or that family were still alive; and they answered civilly enough but would never talk a word to one another.

A nice companionable house I have come to! I was grumbling to myself; and a nice pair of quarrelsome suspicious lovers! And I was wondering if I should really have come to this house at all, or if I was to have any pleasure in my few days of freedom, when suddenly Gypsy broke silence to say that a lorryload of Tans had gone past two hours ago on the valley road, "roaring," she said, "with the great venom and the drink," shooting over the thatch of the houses in the village; they had killed a child and gone on without a thought, laughing at the terror of the villagers. At that Stevey burst into a terrible profane rage, but he caught my eye and fell silent. He knew my thought — if he had not been so inactive for the past four months the Tans would not be roaring their way so daringly through his territory now.

"Did anyone come to warn me?" he asked.

"Aye. The girl of the Mullinses." And she added, "The boys are wild tonight."

I wished Stevey would turn to see me looking at him. I had something to go on already and I was looking forward to my talk with him when the girl would leave us to ourselves. But his mind began to wander from the Tans and he began to hum moodily to himself like a man with something gnawing at his brain, until, at last, unable to keep silent any longer he came out with a very casual, "Was, eh, was Henn down tonight, Gyp?"

"He knows what he'd get if he came."

At once everything changed. Stevey burst suddenly into a wild roar of song, his old favorite, the barcarole from *Hoffman*. He echoed it through the empty house. Even Gypsy gave me a wry smile as she bade me sit up to supper.

"By God, John," he cried at me, "we'll give those bastards of Tans something to think about. Won't we, girl?"

And he caught her up, whirling her into a corner of the room so that she screamed with sudden delight and in mock fear of his rough hands. Stevey drew a long comical face at his stupidity, and she smoothed herself down and said she was all right, and so they sat in a corner of the huge fireplace while I, with my back to them, ate my salted rashers and my country bread and butter.

"Eat up, there, John," he said; and then I felt they were kissing secretly.

"I am ready for it," I said.

"That's the man," said Stevey, and they kissed again and she giggled to herself, and turning I found her tousling his already wild mop because he was making too free of her where she sat on his knee.

"She has great titties, John," said Stevey coarsely, and she slapped his face for that, and as I went on with my supper I heard him kiss her in return. So they made their love in the dark corner, shamelessly, until I was almost finished and ready for Stevey, and then they rose suddenly and left me, to walk, as they said, down to the village now that it was so fine in the heel of the day. Stevey waved me aside when I wanted to detain him, saying the night was long and tomorrow was good too. I was alone in the hall, listening to the corncrake at his last dim rattle in the meadows and the doves fluting long and slow in the deep woods.

As I lit my pipe and smoked under the shadow of the fireplace I began to feel that I should not have come to this house at all. True, it was safe enough because it was the home of one of the "garrison" people, one of those thousand unofficial blockhouses of the English on Irish soil, the last place to be suspected of harboring a rebel. But with Stevey's girl in the same house, this was not a suitable place for the investigator of Stevey's shortcomings. I chewed crossly over this for a while, until, as when I came along the road, the quietness and the peace gradually drove it all out of my head.

The city, I thought, would by now be as empty as if it had been deserted, the Lancias booming along the naked streets, their search-lights shooting down the dark lanes and the side alleys, and the funereal *tramp-tramp* of the patrols taking with them from every door they passed its heavy sigh of suspended fear. All this Stevey had escaped. Not for him as for us, for months on end, the sight of a rusted roof in a city back yard, the stale odor of airless bed-rooms. Strange to think that one could work better in that sort of a room than where the walls were deep in grass, and the springtime rain green-dripping from the trees into water butts and cupped flowers.

The great front door banged, its echoes thundering, and steps clanked in the front hall. Another door opened and was closed again. The night had settled down about the hall, seeped into the woods, calming the doves. Only the old tireless corncrake kept up his ceaseless cry. A door opened again. Steps shuffled along the passage and halted; then an old man's voice coughed and called wheedlingly:

"Gypsy?"

Again the old voice wheedled, now almost at the kitchen door:

"Is he gone, Gypsy? Are you there, my pretty?"

The shuffling came nearer and the stick-tapping and coughing, and Mad Henn stood peering at me around the candle flame. I knew him at once by his long collarless neck and his stork's legs and his madman's face beaked and narrow like a hen. He wore a little faded bowler hat cocked airily on one side of his head, and over his shoulders and draping his body a rug. He had the face of a bird, mottled and bead-eyed, and his hair, tawny in streaks with the glister of oil, had one lock at the back that stood out like a cock's comb.

As he looked at me for a moment he pulled the loose flesh of his throat and scraped with one finger the tawny scum about his lips as if he were trying to remember whether he might not have asked

me to come there or had some business with me that he had forgotten. I stood up awkwardly.

"Gypsy is gone for a walk with Stevey, Mr. Henn," I said.

"And who might you be, young man, if I might ask a polite
question?"—his eyebrows working up and down with irritation
and the strain of having to speak.

"I . . . I'm a friend of Mr. Long's."

He sniffed so that a drop fell from his beaked nose.

"Mr. Long," he muttered in scorn. "So you're another one of 'em,
are you?"

"I don't quite understand," I said, and mentally cursed Stevey for
not having arranged things better. For the old fellow began to
pound with his heel on the floor and his legs and hands twitched
for rage so that I expected him every second to turn me out of his
house at the point of his stick.

"I suppose, I say," he piped sardonically again, "I suppose you're
another one of our new patriots? Eh? Eh? I suppose you think you
can walk into any man's house and sit on his armchair and drink
his liquor? Eh? And threaten him if he protests against you for a
cad and a bully? Eh? You're another of 'em, are you?"

He held a decanter in his right hand; it was filled with dancing
liquor. I thought it best to humor him.

"I beg your pardon, Mr. Henn," I said as humbly as I knew how,
for I did not want a quarrel with the old devil. "I'm sorry if I
have intruded. But I didn't mean to. I think I have made a mistake
—and I'll try if I can find the servant, or find Stevey, that is . . .
wherever they are . . . just now."

It was a very undignified speech, but it seemed to strike the old
man with astonishment.

"Ho?" he said. "This is a new one! Quite polite in fact. You're
not very long on the road, young man," he added with an air of
bitter experience.

"That's all right," I said, as I turned sullenly to go.

He halted me as I laid my hand on the door latch. Where I was going to I did not know.

"Here! It is all right. Your apology is perfectly all right. Don't go, boy. Don't you go."

At the word *here* I noticed how tenderly he said his *r's* — *here,* and *your,* and *perfectly.* It was the last bit of blazonry he preserved, marking him off for all his degradation as one of the conquering race.

We looked at one another silently; then, in quite another tone, as coolly and politely as if he were speaking across his decanter in a club:

"Will you have a drink?"

I looked at him in surprise.

"Come along. I should like to talk to you. You are the first of your kind that I have met who seems to have any bit of education. We'll have a whiskey and soda. Will you join me?"

I returned, largely because I did not know what else to do; and our feet went clanking on the hall flags as if the whole house were a vault, and indeed there was everywhere a musty smell of rooms long abandoned or never tended. His drawing room was just as I expected, a good room but like a ragged tramp. At the farther end was a great superfluous fire and standing by it he poured me out a jorum of whiskey in a glass whose crevices were brown with the encrustations of years, all the time peering at me around the side of a pink-bowled oil lamp whose unshaded light made everything look even more drab and dirty — the bare uncarpeted floor, the fine marble fireplace mottled and cracked, the china cabinets with broken glass and no china in them; and I remembered the look of the yards with their rusted churns and staveless barrels, and everywhere the fur of mildew and green damp.

"Here! Drink that," he said, pouring himself another glass and throwing it off at a gulp, raw. "That's the way to take your liquor. I suppose you'll empty the siphon in yours, eh? Hum! If you didn't have a revolver stuck in your back pockets what would you young fellows have over us? Oh, you're stronger — but have you more grit? Let me look at you."

As I stood up for the drink, he peered at me.

"Ah!" he wailed. "There's only one thing I regret, one thing I've lost, and that's clear eyes. The whole year is all like foggy autumn to me. I see the trees and the woods as if they were clouded in mist. It's a great blessing. I go out on a fine evening like this evening and it's like an evening in winter to me when the light fails at four o'clock in the afternoon and every hill is a valley and every tree is twice as far away."

His streaming eyes strayed to the caverns of the fire, but the flames shone dully in the milky cataracts of the old fading pink-shot pupils.

"Why are you in this business, tell me?" he asked of a sudden.

"I believe in it," I said.

He threw up his hand in disgust.

"I believed in things once," he said. "I had ideas about the people, the people on my land. I thought I'd get them to do things with their land — I was ready to help them with loans and advice. I'd tell them how to drain it, how to grow more variety of vegetables, how to make money out of their gardens selling the produce in the city, and how to make better butter and keep their eggs clean. . . ."

He sniffed a long sneer at himself and pulled his throat and looked absently into the fire.

"Look at them today. As dirty as ever, as poor as ever, as back-ward as ever, and I suppose they blame people like us for it all. If they had my land they'd know how to farm it, they think. But why haven't they done anything with their own? Why? Why?"

He was a hot-tempered old fellow, flying into a temper at a sec-ond's warning.

"But you're a city boy, you know nothing of the people. It's people like us who know Ireland. We belong to it — we who've grown up on the land and know it and the people on it."

"Your people were merchants," I said coldly.

"They made their money on bottles," he said, reaching for the whiskey. "And I've spent their money on bottles," he added with the air of a man who has often made the same joke and grown serious over it. Then as he began to pour the liquor out tremblingly he turned savagely on me. "And who makes glass in Ireland now?" he wheezed. "When we stopped, why didn't somebody else take it up? They could make lovely glass in Ireland at one time. It might have became a great, a distinctive national industry, and everywhere you'd see the men blowing the glass into lovely shapes. People would be coming from abroad to see them. I've seen them as a lad. *Pouf!* And there you had a globe of glass. Shining, colored, glowing. Oh, no! Oh, no! What do we see in the shop windows now?" he cried, leaning forward and baring his rotting, easily moved teeth. "Cobblers! Yah! A race of cobblers. That's what we are — a race of cobblers! They hadn't it in them. They hadn't it in them!"

I saw for the first time how deep the hate on his side could be, as deep as the hate on ours, as deep and as terrible.

"Oh, that all began two centuries ago," I cried back at him. "It was the union with England that ruined us and our industries. Can't you see that? It ruined you. It ruined your glass business. Aren't you part of Ireland as much as us?"

"Ach! It's always the same. This ruined us, and that ruined us, and the other ruined us. I tell you I'm ashamed to be called an Irishman, and in fact I'm not an Irishman. I'm a colonist — a planter — whatever you like — one of those that tried to come and do something with you people. Why didn't the people fight for their rights when they had a parliament?"

I tried to answer, but he wouldn't let me, spilling his liquor all over the hearth in his rage.

"I know what you'll say. But look at the Welsh, and look at the Scotch. They haven't a parliament and they have prospered. What's to stop us from making our linens and our woven silks, from weaving patterns into them like the Italians and the Slavs? Where are our crafts? What can we show? What have we ever done? Except dig ditches and plow fields? Why haven't we stuffs, yes, stuffs, stuffs, stuffs, of our own — stuffs" — how he spat it out! — "that any woman would love to fold around her body, stuffs she'd love to feel against her flesh? Colored, brilliant, delicate stuffs?"

And he began to rub his little hands down his thighs.

"Oh, fantastic!" I said, and leaned back from him smiling.

"Ah, there's your revolver man talking! But it could be done. Or why don't we export bulbs or cut flowers like the Dutch and the French and the Channel Islanders?"

"It's impossible. The climate."

"Pah! It's on our side. The Gulf Stream would do it."

"The Gulf Stream?"

Mad Henn!

"Yes! It warms our southern shores. You can grow acacias in Kerry in the open air in midwinter." (A rush of delicate *r*'s here.) "I've picked London pride on the mountains in early March. Jasmine, lilacs, fuchsias . . ."

"Fuchsia isn't a cut flower," I taunted. "Nor a bulb!"

He twitched in every limb, dashed his glass into the fire, banged the hearth with his stick, and stuttered all the rest he had to say to me:

"It grows, it grows, I tell you it grows wild in midwinter. In the open air. You're a damned obstinate young fellow. And wallflower, lily of the valley, freesia, gardenia, arbutus, mignonette. All sorts of delicate ferns. A marvelous, but a lost, opportunity. These things will bring them in more money than potatoes. But they tread on them. It's so silly, really, because it's just like treading on gold."

"But the people are farmers."

"What are the Germans, the Dutch, the Belgians? Ah!" (It was a long-drawn-out "Ah!" of sweet memories.) "I know the people. You city fellows don't know them." Then his voice fell. "I know their women."

He rubbed his little hands again and tapped me on the knee.

"I know every sort of woman: English women, French women, Italians; I've even known a Russian woman. The Russians are like the Irish, you know. But too stubborn and too obstinate and too proud. Prouder even than the Irish. And not one of them all can equal the Irish woman — of the right sort. But they're airy. You have to bind them down with a brutal religion or they'd fly over the fields from you. Don't you feel that too, eh?"

And he cocked his hat even still further over on one ear and laughed a little elfish laugh of delight and his loose lock behind almost curled like a drake's tail. He poked the embers with his stick. He filled my glass in spite of me — delighted like all old bachelors whose club days and dancing days are done to have anyone at all who will talk with them.

"Ah! Yes," he sighed as he poured my whiskey, "the women are all right. So lovely and plump. Muscular from the fields. Arms . . . right!" (He molded them with the bottle in his hand.) "Breasts like tulips. Lovely! Lovely! But you don't know. You only know the city. The city! Puh! I wouldn't give that much for a city woman."

I threw off his whiskey neat.

"Why shouldn't I know the country?" I said. "By damn, but I do! As well as you, better than you. I know their women. Many a mouse I moused with their women. What's more than that, I was born in the country and born right here in this townland. My mother was born and is buried and my grandmother and all her people before her down there in Kilcrea churchyard. I lived in the townland of Farrane myself as a child and my father lived there before me."

I thought he shrank into himself at that, pulling down his long neck like a snail or a tortoise at the approach of danger.

"What's your name?" he asked quietly.

I told him.

"I remember your mother well," he said. "She held land from me. And I remember your father. He was stationed at Kilcrea. I met him first at an eviction on my land. They shoved a red-hot poker through the door at him and he caught it; and, by God, he pulled it from them, so he did. A fine man."

"I remember that," I said, quiet myself, too, now.

"No, boy, no," he said sadly. "That was a long time ago."

"Oh, but, I do well," I cried. "I remember the bandage on his hand."

"Not at all," and he smacked the stick on the side of the marble fireplace. "This was a long time ago. Forty years or more. Forty years or more" — and as he said it his eyes strayed, rheum wet, from me to the fire and back to me again as if he were trying to see my father in me and those dead years that were gone from him forever.

"Where is he now?" he asked.

"He's dead," I said.

"Ah, and is he dead?"

"Yes."

"And your mother?"

"She is dead," I answered quietly.

"Ah!"

He looked into the embers. They glowed faintly in his all but sightless balls — a quietness more than the night fallen on him secretly and unexpectedly. Just then a step resounded on the hall flags and the door opened and in came the dark, muscular Gypsy, behind her Stevey, slouching as ever. He did not see me. He gave the old man a low "Good night." Henn did not reply, but he raised a feeble hand and took the girl's fingers in his palm. His was as tiny as hers. The fire shone pink between his bony fingers, ridged with the veins and threaded with the thousand wrinkles of age. As their eyes met, his lean neck curved up to her lovingly.

"Have you had a nice walk, pretty?"

"Yes, down to the bridge at the pub."

Before him how delicately her lips said *down,* with a voluptuous

upward curve at the corners of her mouth so that they swept into
her cheeks as the curved initials on his ring swept into the gold.
Her sullen eyes went soft. In this light she almost looked beautiful.
His hand wandered over her arm as he asked the next question: a
question as familiar as Sunday. She smiled as she replied.

"Was there anything rising?" he asked.

"Down by the bridge they're leppin'," she said.

"It's the breeze. There's always a breeze fluting down that side of
the valley."

Stevey laughed loudly at them both, and his voice was rough and
coarse beside the rich voice of the girl and the cultured voice of the
old man.

"Leppin'? Rise? Rise, how are you! That was me spittin' when
she wasn't looking."

"Oh, then, there was a rise," she cried. "I saw their silver bellies
shining as they leaped."

"Ooh!" mocked Stevey. "Bellies! Naughty word! Ooh!"

Henn gripped his stick until it trembled and his knuckles strained
the skin white. He snapped at Stevey.

"If the girl says there was a rise, there was. Aren't you enough of
a gentleman not to contradict her?"

But his voice trembled as if he were half afraid of his own daring.
In a second Stevey was in one of his violent passions.

"I don't want any English pimp to tell me what to do or not do
with the girl, or any girl. Mind that!"

Henn's hand shook, and all his legs as he pulled himself up on
his stick, taller when he stood than any of us, his bent back
straightened, made gigantic by the great shadow that climbed the
wall behind him. I could see what a man he was in his heyday,
what a figure on a horse, wielding the rod from the top of a rock,
a wiry, bony giant. There was almost majesty in him as he pointed
his trembling stick to the door and faced down to Stevey with:

"Leave my house, sir. I'll not be bullied any longer by you — not
an hour."

"And I'll leave it," cried Stevey, "when and only when I choose. I'll not be ordered by *you*. Who the hell do you think you are ordering? Do you think you can order *me*? Ho, and but let me tell you, Mr. Alexander Henn, I'm *staying* here."

I could see he had taken drink while down at the pub, and the devil was in his eyes; he skipped across the hearth by the side of Henn and flopped mockingly into the chair the old man had just left. Then he stretched out his hand for Henn's glass on the mantelpiece, and wiping the side of it on his coat sleeve raised it in mockery of the old man. There was silence for a second and then Gypsy laughed, and the laugh cut through Henn. He raised his stick and lashed at the hand that held the empty glass in the air, and as the splinters fell I leaped, Henn thrusting his face across my arm into Stevey's face, Gypsy barely holding back Stevey's fist before it crashed into the old rheumy, half-blind eyes. Henn was all but weeping for vanity, for that laughter of the girl at his age and infirmity. All he could say between his sobs was, "You young ruffian. You ruffian. You ruffian. . . ."

I thrust Stevey back. Henn turned to me.

"This young woman. If anything should happen to her, which God forbid . . ."

"Oh, you hypocrite," cried Stevey, turning to the empty air for somebody to appeal to. "Oh, listen to that! God! God forbid! Oh, the hypocrisy of it!"

"Yes, yes, yes," I appealed and implored Gypsy to take him away and pushed him from us, and the girl dragged him, and pushed him, and persuaded him out of the room. She was entirely cool as if abuse and quarreling and coarse talk were nothing to her. I put the old man in his chair and filled a glass for him and left him and found Stevey sullenly akimbo on the top of the steps. He was ashamed, I felt, to have played his heroics opposite me and I thought he might not have quarreled with old Henn if he had known I was there. I stood beside him without speaking until he said he was sorry he had broken out like that since it would ruin my chances

of staying at the hall. I could not tell of what else he was thinking, but I was thinking to myself, Where shall I go now? For I
could neither remain in the hall nor go with Stevey. My hopes of a
quiet, serene night were vanished. We stood in silence and looked
down into the night. A frightened bird fluttered in the woods; a star
fell in a graceful, fatal swoop, vanishing in mid-air as if a mighty
hand had scratched the sky with light.

Biting his nails, Stevey said, "Tell Gypsy I want her."

I went back to the drawing room, where the girl and the old
man stood by the window.

"Stevey wants to talk to you," I said; and when she went tramping wearily, heavily, from the room I looked at Henn and he
looked back at me and neither of us spoke. As I looked away again
through the shining window I could see the old man's eyes fixed
on me. At last I buttoned my coat about me and turned to him.

"I suppose I'd better be going," I said.

"Going? Where are you going?"

"I don't know really, but . . ."

"Hum! You were to stay here, I take it, eh? Another uninvited
guest?"

After a long hesitation I answered, "Yes — I was. I was. I may
even stay in your hay barn yet, for all you know. Good night," I
concluded. "I'm glad to have met you."

"No, boy. I won't say good night. And you won't stay in my
hay barn, because I have none. Stay where you intended to stay.
Even though you didn't choose to ask me, stay. If not for your
own sake, for your father's and mother's sake."

He rose and went slowly and feebly to the door, his half-emptied
bottle in his hand.

"Could I stop you," he said, "if you wanted to stay here a month?
Stay! And be damned to ye!"

"I won't," I said.

He turned to me at the door.

"Please do stay," he pleaded, nodding his head many times to encourage me. "Stay, stay, stay."

He was maudlin with the excitement and the liquor.

"Will you stay?" he asked again.

I looked out into the dark. I thought to myself, It must be near to eleven or midnight.

"Thanks very much," I said; and being satisfied he waved his bony hand, slipping his bottle into the great pocket of his swallow-tailed coat. Then he turned and went, his little hat perched on one side of his head and his rug trailing after him on the uncarpeted floor.

I sat by the table and looked about me again: at the tablecloth like a gypsy's shawl, at the dusty lace curtains dragged to the ends of their poles; and everything my eyes fell on mocked him and his desires. Lovely woven silks, he had said. And woven linens? And stuffs such as women might love to feel? And such strange flowers and bulbs as the Dutch and the Channel Islanders grew, freesia, gardenia, mignonette? What a liar, I thought; and bitterly I was pleased to end the triad, calling him (as the farming folk had called him for fifty years) a lunatic and a libertine.

Gypsy returned. I told her I was staying in the house, and once more she went and returned. We heard Stevey's steps vanish down the drive, and then silently she took a candle and lit me upstairs to bed. As we went I asked her what her name was, and she said:

"My name is Gammle."

"Indeed," I said, thoughtlessly.

"Why *indeed?*" she asked, halting in her step and looking at me.

"Nothing," I said. "It's just a strange name."

I did not tell her I was thinking that the name was well known in North Cork for a tinker tribe, in Charleville and Doneraile and the borders of Limerick and up into Clare.

"Good night," she said, and left me in a great, empty, musty room, the bed all tousled and the bedclothes soiled, and yellow. I lay down as I stood. To the sound of the branches of the trees tapping on the bare window I dozed and slept.

I awoke, wide-eyed of a sudden insomnia, to the rusted, wailing drone of an old phonograph in the room below me. By the light of the moon I looked at my watch; it was past twelve o'clock, an hour when cities begin to live and the fields are fast asleep. It reminded me of the years when I had lain awake for hours listening to late parties singing their way homeward before the war and curfew sent us all to our beds. I would be awake again now until the dawn broke. Rising peevishly I went to the door, opening it in time to hear a new record begin its nasal introductory speech: *This is an Edison Bell recawrd; number one seven nine nine; songs from the awpera of Dawn Giovanni by Mozart.* And then through the hollow-sounding house the stifled music of one of the loveliest of all operas; and humming with the singer, or rather behind the singer, came old blear-eyed, maudlin Henn's cracked and drunken voice:
"Batti; batti . . ."
I bade sleep good night, and dragging on my pants sat on the edge of the bed, my coat about my shoulders, smoking a cigarette. I watched the branches beating on the panes, the laurels shivering and shining in the tangled garden beneath my window, the Bride rain-laden far below glinting between its gall-black alders under the starry sky.
"Questo é il fin di chi fa mal. . . ."
The pair and their song died slowly. Then silence fell. Henn kicked his enamel chamber pot until it rang. Croaking and humming the love song he shuffled out on his landing. I leaned over the banister and watched him stumble down the stairs, out of the house, onto the graveled drive and out of sight into the dark.
One by one I began to hear them — those innumerable, inexplicable sounds that are to be heard at night in a house when all

the casual day sounds are still; timbers that stretch and contract, little insects that make a great creaking noise. I pulled on my boots and went down to the open door and out on the avenue and down towards the cottage in the track of Henn. Here a chill wind was blowing last year's leaves high in the air, but near the lodge where the drive fell sharply down to the gates under the trees clawing their high ditches dust lay in soft whispering drifts — soft and white as snow under the moon, so soft that as I stood by the little deserted lodge peering curiously in through one of the windows I might have been a rabbit or a fox for all the warning I gave anyone who might be inside. A shaft of wavering light lay thrown across the tiny hallway from another room. There they were, Gypsy and Henn: she with her skirt drawn above her knees, an old coat over the warm skin of her bare shoulders, toasting her shins to a little flickering fire — Henn, as he did the first time I saw them together, holding her fingers in his palm and leaning forward over her round knee to see into her eyes.

I watched the unequal pair looking at one another long, silently, seeming not to say one word to each other, her dark head bowed sidelong to his lips, her fallen lashes on her cheeks; he, with a smile foolish yet tender sagging his quivering mouth apart, his old hat cocked forward on eyes that streamed their water to his cheeks. And yet, though he was old and decaying, and she warm-fleshed, white to her teeth, full of the pride of youth, and — Henn was right — her breasts like tulips fully blown, if anything too magnificently full, he could, for all that, raise his hand now with so much languid grace to feel their roundness, hold the precious globe for one moment, so lightly, so fondly on his fingers before his withered hand fell as if in despair into her lap, that finer women than Gypsy might well have smiled, as she smiled now, with head turning slow from that flattering gesture of the epicure, with long slow-drawn sighs at the uselessness of such praise from him.

To which of these men, I wondered, had she given herself?

With her hair dragged on the ridge of her chair and her head falling lower and lower on her bosom until her eyes were caught in the embers of the fire, she permitted him to move aside her skirt, ever so little, from her bare knee, and caress it with his withered hand as softly as if it were swan's-down, caress it even after the glow of the fire shone on her eyes drowned in tears, caress it while she sat rigid with misery, her moans breaking out in trembling waves to the whispering night outside. And yet not one word from Henn; only as if hoping that his old hand could quiet her childlike sobs, he caressed and caressed and looked and looked doglike into her face.

I could not bear those doglike eyes of the old libertine, nor those sighs and sobs of the young girl. Stumbling away from the light of the little window and out of the creaking gate I found myself walking on and on under the tenting chestnuts in the windy dust-blown lane, up and along the highway I had come that evening, too moved to return and sit alone in my unkempt bedroom in the hall. Suddenly country and freedom seemed a small thing under this austere darkness, with that pair, heavy with one another's sorrow, down in the weather-streaked decaying cottage.

With the memory of those drooping mother's breasts and that large mother's belly on the young girl, and the look of pity on the old libertine's face, I find myself walking aimlessly on and on; until across the black valley there rises a leaping yellow flame, and through the night air on the night wind the crackle of burning timber.

The flames through the trees were now flickering like a huge bonfire. Running down the lanes toward Henn Hall I could see from time to time as I ran the distant outline of windows, a gable end, a chimney silhouetted against the glowing air. At the lodge the little light was still shining in the window. Without looking through I knocked and knocked until padding feet came along the floor and the girl's voice said:

"Who is it? Who's there?"

"A fire!" I cried. "What can we do? Across the valley, a big house." And in my excitement I cried out, "Where's Mad Henn?"

She answered through the door.

"He's not here. Isn't he at the hall?"

She opened an inch or two of the door and looked out at me with frightened eyes.

"Whose house is it?" she asked.

"I don't know. It's straight over the river — straight across there."

Holding her clothes about her body she stepped to the corner of the lodge and looked across at the blazing house.

"It's Blake's," she said. "We can't do anything. They may come over here. Where's Henn?" she asked then, suddenly terrified.

"I thought he was here."

She stared at me, astonished, yet full of cunning that was mingled with fright for Henn.

"Isn't he at the hall?" she insisted nervously.

"Maybe," I stuttered. "Yes, I suppose he *is* at the hall."

"Did you try?"

"I was out walking," I said.

"Walking!"

There was a pause.

"What time is it?" she asked.

As I peered at my watch, saying, "It's well after one o'clock," I could see her eyes looking at me with fear and suspicion, and having spied on her I was ashamed to look up. Then, slowly, I understood why she was watching me in that way. She thought that my coming there that night, a man "on the run," had something to do with this burning house, that I had caused it, as a reprisal, an act of revenge, and that in some way Henn too would suffer by it, and that Stevey, probably, had been the man who carried it out. Such reprisals were as yet rare in the country and it had never occurred to me that this was one until I saw the fear and distrust and hate in her eyes.

"A nice time for walking," she said shortly, and raced down the slope of the ditch and up to the hall and there she knocked on the heavy hen's-head knocker until the countryside resounded and even a dog, somewhere across the fields, began to *bark-bark* at our *knock-knock-knock* on the echoing door. I tried to explain myself.

" 'Tis why I came to the country — to sleep. I get insomnia. So I got up and came out."

"How did you get out? Henn keeps the key in his room."

"The door was open."

There was no sound from the house.

"My God," she moaned, "what's happened to him?"

Then in her fear and rage and suspicion she turned on me, a tigress robbed of her mate — and even in that instant I remember saying to myself, Oho! So it's Henn, is it?

"Where is he?" she cried. "What did ye do with him? Christ blast ye all, what did ye do to him?"

Her voice was echoed by the stony face of the house, thrown back into the fields and echoed again and again by the barking dog.

"I know nothing about him," I said angrily. "He's probably dead drunk. Knock him up."

And I clouted the hen's head until my hand ached. Not a sound but the dog over the fields, now thoroughly aroused, and the crackling of the flames across the valley, and, within, the old sheep dog howled mournfully.

The girl caught my arm in fear.

"It's the dog crying before somebody dies."

"Is that a window?"

"Is it the I.R.A. that burnt it?" she asked, looking up and then over her shoulder.

"I know nothing about it. How can we get in?"

"It's for the child the Tans killed. Ye've done something to Alec! Ye've surely done something to Alec!"

We found a little scullery window open. I clambered in and let her in at the front door. We climbed the dark stairs, the dog flopping along behind, and up to his room. We found him in his bed, snoring on his stomach with the weight of drink, his nightshirt crumpled above his bare knees, and on his head a fluff-laden night-cap of scarlet wool. Ashamed of the sight of him with his dirty toes and the engrimed creases across the base of his neck and halfway up his skull Gypsy shook him madly into a gasping wakefulness, straightened his cap on his head as if he were a child, and covered his shoulders as he sat up in bed looking about him at the angry waving light like a picture of Juan in hell.

"Are you all right?" she asked.

"I — yes — I'm all right. But . . ."

"Look." She pointed, and he looked.

"My God!" he cried. "Totty Blake's."

His eyes bulged as he looked, and trying to master himself he shambled across the floor to stoop in the open window in his shirt.

"Oh! My God! My God!" was all he could say, and then, "Do you hear them? Do you hear the noise?"

"The flames?" I said.

"No! The rooks. They'll never nest there again. They're ruined with the heat."

And he began to tousle his cap and sank on his knees crying like a child. Gypsy stood over him where he knelt.

"The Blakes will be likely coming here for the night."

He stood up at once like a hardened toper, and turned to us.

"Go down," he said, "and lay the table for them, and set the fire going. And you, boy, go, like a good fellow, and give her a hand."

Gypsy went. I thought he was unable to look after himself and tried to coax him from the window.

"I'll stay here," I whispered. "It's cold, you know. You must dress now. I'll help you. Come on."

He flung my arm aside, peevishly.

"Am I a child?" he roared.

I left him in a palsy of trembling, dragging his nightshirt over his head, rump naked, fumbling for his clothes by the pale light of the candle and the fluttering light of the burning house.

In silence we set about blowing the seed of fire on the hearth into flame, and I dipped the kettle in the dark water of the butt and the crane swung it slowly over the fire. The false dawn of the fire and the distant rooks cawing with fright had awakened the doves and all the birds on this side of the valley and the night was sweet with their music. From time to time as we passed from kitchen to parlor with ware or food we halted to look at the fire that sometimes seemed to have died away and sometimes flared up more madly than ever before. There Henn joined me and we waited there, wondering if the Blakes would come or if we should go back to bed and try to sleep out the end of the night. At last he drew me into the room and filled out a drink for himself, while I yawned, dry-eyed for lack of sleep.

"I don't know where else the Blakes can go," he said. "Though if there was another house within three miles of them they'd rather die than come under my roof. I'm sorry for his two tits of sisters, though."

"Only two women?" I asked wearily.

"Philamena and Agatha. Two sour tits. And the captain, their father. That's all that's there. Oh, but Philamena *is* a sour bitch. I chalked that very word on the door of the church about her when I was six — got whipped for it too. And she never spoke a word to me after. And I gave Agatha a penny at the age of eight if she'd let me swing her so high that I could see her drawers. They never let her see me after that. I once went," he said, throwing back his liquor, "I once went to church to a Handel service, and I had to run out of it when I saw the two virgins singing away *'To us a child is born; to us a son is given.'* Ah!" he snarled. "They're sour titties. Vinegar for milk they have. Sour and old and virginal."

He was getting angry with them, I could see.

"They'd just raise their hands in horror at a girl like . . . at a girl that would, that would . . ."

I stood in the corner of the window watching the sparks rising and falling endlessly like fireflies, silenced as one is always silenced by a raging fire, to think of calamity on one's doorstep.

"Gypsy," says Henn, suddenly rising and going to another window, "Gypsy was sick tonight."

"Bad?" I asked sleepily.

"Bad? Not yet."

"Not yet?"

"That's what I said. Didn't you hear me?"

"Yes."

He came shuffling over to me on his stick.

"The girl is ruined," he said, peering into my eyes, that filled with shame as he looked at them.

"What do you mean by that?"

"Gypsy is going to be a mother."

I answered his stare.

For answer I looked angrily over the valley at the house. What did it matter to him what I thought? What would all the country think when they heard it? Another servant of Henn's — it was an old story — about to bear a child.

"I'll not be blamed," he cried and his tubes were hoarse with passion. "I am not to be blamed."

"What does the girl say?"

"How does she know?"

And he went back to his glass and his fire.

Up the avenue in a shadowy mass, singing and shouting, came the incendiaries, Stevey at their head, ready for anything, drunk with whiskey and triumph. Had it been six months later, he could safely have burned half the houses in the district and we should not have dared, nor cared, nor had the time, nor even wished in the heat of passion — for things grew very hot by then — to question what he did. But tonight I ran to the door determined to thwart him. He faced up the steps and shouted for Henn, Henn the whore,

Henn the cock, the Henn's neck, and all about him shouted with him out of the dark.

"Henn! Henn! Come out, you whore! Henn! Come out, Henn!"

There was a glint of a revolver in one man's hand as I ran down the steps and faced up to Stevey.

"What rotten sort of soldier are you?" I shouted at him.

"What do you mean?" he cried.

"Is that what you call soldiering?" I shouted into his face, pointing across the valley at the burning ruin. For an instant he looked at it, and then to his men and at me.

"Aha!" he shouted. "We burnt the bastards out, didn't we, boys? And damn right well they deserved it."

They shouted it back to him, their memories full of the days when their people died of starvation by the roadsides and the big houses looked on in portly indifference.

"And we'll burn Henn out," cried Stevey, and made a drive for the steps. I caught him and swung him about while Henn hung over the iron railings and croaked down at us:

"If I had a gun! Oh, if I only had a gun!"

"Shut up," I shouted at him. The crowd was nasty enough without this.

"Oh, for a gun!" he persisted. "Just for one minute . . ."

"Go in, blast you," I shouted at him while Gypsy tried to drag him from the steps.

"You're fine fellows! Oh, you're great fellows," I taunted them. "You haven't, between the lot of you, fired a single shot in all this district for four months. Unless you shot a sitting hare or a tame fox. It's what you'd do by the look of you. And now you go and burn a couple of women out in the middle of the night. Oh, you're grand soldiers entirely. You cowardly mob!"

"You keep your tongue quiet," from Stevey. He was a head higher than me.

"I'm here to talk to you," I said, "and I'll give you and your men

my talk now, if you want it. Let me tell you you have the repu-
tation of being the tamest commandant . . ."

He flew into a passion at once and drew his revolver at me. At
once the country fellows skipped between us. They didn't at all like
this business of drawing a gun on one of their own. They began to
mutter and pluck at Stevey, and to signal me to hold my peace.
But I knew my man.

"Now, now, Long!" they muttered. "Be aisy now, Long."

"You won't bully me," I said. "Why don't you use your gun on
the Tans?"

He turned to them.

"Are you going to be stopped by a city caffler?"

And to me:

"We know what Henn is."

"What am I?" croaked Henn, who was still grasping the railings,
with Gypsy trying to persuade him to come in.

"What did Henn ever do to *you?*" I asked.

"Aye, what did I ever do to you?" gasped Henn, hoarse with excitement, sweeping his little hat off his head and leaning down over
the railings like a man giving a speech. "What did I do to you?
What did I ever do to you or yours?"

"Aha!" Stevey shouted up to him. "You whore master" — and I
thought he'd blow the old man's brains out. "What do *you* know
what's mine or yours?"

Utterly beyond himself he pointed with his gun at Gypsy, and
shook his fist in the old man's eyes.

"Look at that girl. What did you do to her? Answer that or you'll
not have a house by morning."

Then quite without warning the rest of them turned and raced
over the lawn into the surrounding night. Only one waited to pluck
Stevey by the arm and whisper:

"It's the Blakes. They're coming. Come away out of this. They'll
know us."

"I don't care about the Blakes," said Stevey, too intent on having his way with Henn that night to care about anything else. "Ask him!" he said to me. "Ask him what did he do to that girl? Ask him that!"

"Stevey, Stevey," implored the girl as she tried still to induce Henn to move.

I dragged Stevey to one side as Henn, who had also seen the Blakes come up the drive swaying with the weight of the bundles they bore, stood down on the steps to meet them, his hat in his hand like an ambassador or a prince receiving his guests, his head like a gander's head, jigging up and down as he bowed them in; and as the two old maids came timidly up to him, peering here and there in their fear, and the portly captain, their father, brought up the rear, peeping over their shoulders because he was almost as blind as Henn, they all looked more like frightened ganders and geese than human beings able to look to themselves. They clustered together on their way up the steps, Henn wheezing about not being "quite up to the tiptop of readiness," and saying, "You have me at a disadvantage, Miss Blake. But come in. A cup of hot tea, now. A shot of Martell's, Captain? Most regrettable! Terrible! This way, now. Allow me. This way. That's right — there we are. . . ." And so into the hall with his visitors.

When they were gone the dark figures gathered about us again.

"I'll make that man marry the girl," said Stevey under his breath to me, "or I'll burn this house to the very ground."

"We'll burn him out," they growled, the lust for destruction in their blood.

"He'll marry the girl, or he'll have no house over his head by morning."

"But the man is eighty if he's a day," I implored, "and the girl is a mere slip of a girl. Is she twenty itself?"

"Well, he ruined her," said Stevey up to my mouth, as if he would force the words into it.

"I do not believe it," I said.

Another shower had begun to fall by now, growing heavier drop by drop, dimming the starlight and shimmering dark about the distant fire. Stevey waved his hand to his fellows.

"The city fellows are a lot of help to us," he said. "But I'll show you. I'm not going to stand here all night in the rain talking with you."

He rushed past me up the steps and into the house with his mob after him. I managed to stop him at the door of the drawing room and we parleyed there for a while, whispering angrily as we peeped through the cracked door. There, where fifty years ago he had leaned across the shining walnut to his lights-o'-love, smiling quizzically down on them from his swan's neck, approving the painted lips, the tilted eyebrows, always gracious to them, however cynical, perpetually on the smile, only leaning back from his scandalous whispering when the butler laid a new course or refilled his glass — there, now, he offered his smoke-tainted tea to the two silent, miserable old maids.

"Oh, yes, do drink a cup of tea, Miss Blake," and he puffs out his cheeks to encourage her. "Just one?"

"Thank you. I don't believe I really want one, Mr. Henn."

"Oh, just one cup. Just one."

They sat straight-backed and unbending, trying hard not to keep looking over the valley at their ruined home. They looked at the soiled tablecloth, the unequal ware, the tarnished silver, or at one another, or at the old captain, their father, who sat sucking his brandy, heavy jowled and heavy bodied, by Henn's fire. They looked at Gypsy, who, careless of her ungainly, ungirlish shape, danced superfluous attendance on them, full of pity for their misfortune, glad to be in the presence of real ladies even for an hour.

So they were sitting when Stevey burst out of my grip into the middle of them, calling on Henn so loudly that they almost screamed.

"Henn," he said, "we want you."

"Don't go, Henn," said the captain at once, as if he felt as much for his own sake as for Henn's that it was better they should all cling together now.

"What do you want now?" stuttered Henn.

"I want you to come too, Gypsy," said Stevey.

"Oh, Stevey, Stevey," said the girl, utterly ashamed before the company.

"Come on, Henn," bullied Stevey. "Or will I tell my business here?"

"Out with it," says the captain.

"One minute now," pleaded Henn.

I thought it best to get the matter over, and went up to the old man and whispered that it would be best to come. I could not keep those fellows in hand for him any longer.

"Don't go, Henn," said the captain again.

"No, no," said the old maids, with the same thought as their father in their minds that even Henn was better than nothing in their extremity, homeless as they were at this hour of the morning.

He rose and went into the kitchen and Stevey and Gypsy and I after him. There he turned and faced us, looking down over us all, even over Stevey himself. Stevey returned his glare. The girl sat with her head in her hands by the fire. I looked at the rain spitting on the dark window. When Stevey had finished, all Henn could say was, "You liar, you liar!" And all the girl could do was weep and say, "My misfortune. My misfortune. My misfortune." Even when I went to her and put my hand on her shoulder she only burst away from me and cried to let her alone, let her alone in her misfortune; for God's sake to let her alone in her misfortune; and sat at the table hiding her face in her hands, shaken with tears.

"You liar!" muttered Henn.

"I'm no liar," cried Stevey.

The girl wept with renewed shame that no man would own her. Henn looked at her and said very gently to me:

"Supposing I won't marry her?"

"No harm will come to your person," I said, and faced Stevey on that.

"Your house will go the way of Blake's," said Stevey, and faced me on that. "If not tonight, tomorrow night, and if not then, the night after. But if I have to wait a year to do it, up it will go."

I shook the wretched girl by the shoulder.

"Do you want to marry this old man?" I cried into her ear. She gave no reply.

"Speak up, Gypsy," said Stevey. "You will marry him, won't you? You said you would."

She said not a word now.

"I'll not marry her," said Henn.

Stevey had cunning enough to play his last card.

"Then tell your Blake friends to get out of this house, if they have sense. Or, I'll do it."

Henn stopped him at the door.

"Don't! Don't do that!"

And thereupon he sank into a chair with a sudden dizziness, and I had to hold him up from falling sidelong to the floor.

"Gypsy," I said, "get a sup of whiskey."

"Alec!" she said, going to him, and he took her hand, her little hand, in his when she stood by his side and said his name. "Alec! Will I get a sup of brandy?"

There was silence for a few minutes, with only the noise of the rain cat-pattering against the window and the three of us over Henn. At last he began to whisper through his fingers, and I leaned down to hear him.

"Will she marry me?" he was whispering while the spittle dropped like a cow's spittle between his fingers to the flagged floor.

"Now!" cried Stevey triumphantly. "Gypsy! Will you have him?"

In her deep man's voice she replied:

"And who else would have me now? Since others won't — others that have their own life and their own plans and plots?"

And seeing that the old man was not in need of help she went out of the kitchen, holding her stomach in her little palms, murmuring as she went:

"I will, if he will."

I pushed Stevey before me from the kitchen and leaving Henn to himself we drove the rest of the chaps before us from the hall, into the darkness, now rain-arrowy and old. From the great front door I watched them go tramping down the avenue and as I, too, turned to go upstairs to my bed I heard Henn, back in the drawing room, trying once more to play the host with his smoky tea and his patched ware. I wondered as I tramped upstairs if he was thinking that, with this young wife, he might begin life again.

From my bed I heard the summer downpour drip about the house and occasionally spit down the chimney on the damp papers stuffed in the grate, tainting all the room with their sooty reek. Not until late noon did I hear another sound, and then it was the birds singing and the croaking corncrake and the doves in the high woods, and when I rose the whole house was radiant with sunshine reflected from the fields and the trees. There was nobody about the house but Gypsy. The Blakes had gone since early morning. Henn did not leave his bed for several days. Stevey I could find nowhere and the local men said he was gone into Kerry, swearing he would only return to make Henn keep to his promise. Two days I waited for him and searched about for news of him, and then I called a meeting of his battalion and replaced him by a new commandant.

One evening I left Henn Hall as I had come, but before I went I visited Henn in his room to say good-by and I found him sitting over his fire, drinking punch and reading an *Anglers' Annual* of thirty years ago.

"Be careful of yourself, boy," he warned as I turned to leave him.

"Oh, yes," I said. "I'll be careful."

"Do you believe Long's story?" he said then, leaning forward to me.

"I have no cause," I parried, "to believe or disbelieve anybody."
He leaned back and stared at the fire.

"Anyway," he said after a while, "I'm going to marry her.
She's as good as the next, and better than some, even though she *is*
only a tinker's daughter. Besides," he added proudly, "if it's a boy
'twill keep the name alive."

As if he were a Hapsburg or a Bourbon.

One night two months or so later we heard in our back-yard bedroom that a strange pair left Cork for Dublin that afternoon on the
mail express, all their dozen or so of trunks and bags labeled forward to an address in Paris. The woman, in a massive hat with a
scarlet feather, had flaunted her way to her carriage; the old man,
her husband, hobbling and shuffling along behind her. His traveling coat almost completely hid him, its tail touching the ground, its
coat collar up about his ears, and so weak did his eyes appear to be
that even in the dim filtered light of the station he had cocked his
hat forward over his eyebrows and shaded his eyes with his withered hand as he walked. But I found it too painful to think of him
with his scraps of governess French, guiding his tinker wife through
the boulevards, the cafés, the theaters, seeing once more the lovely
women gay in their hour. Anyway, we had more serious things to
think of then.

Fugue

THE clouds lifted slowly from the ridge of the mountains and the dawn rim appeared. As I stooped low to peer over the frame of the little attic window I whispered to Rory that it was pitch dark; and indeed it was far darker than the night before when we had had the full moon in the sky. Rory leaned up on one elbow in bed, and asked me if I could hear anything from beyond the river.

The damp of dawn was everywhere. It softened the lime gable of the outhouse beneath me, it hung over the sodden hay in the barn and, like the fog and mist last night under the blazing moon, it floated over the rumbling river to my right. I could imagine the flow taking strange courses in its flood, swishing in this neither dawn nor day nor dark through all the alders and the reeds and the rushes and, doubtless, covering the steppingstones that we hoped would give us an escape to the mountains beyond.

So I whispered to Rory that I could only hear the water falling in the weirs, and tumbling out of his bed he called a curse from Christ on the whore of a river that was holding us here to be plugged by the Tans for a pair of Irish bitches.

As I peered, standing in bare feet on the timber floor, I recalled last night with a shudder. We were retreating from Inchigeela by the back roads and we two had lost ourselves in the barren and rocky place they call the Rough, a difficult place by day and almost impassable by night. We had tramped up and down and up and down until I felt my eyes closing as I stumbled along, and scarcely had the energy to push back my bandolier when it came sliding around my elbows. Rory, a country fellow, seemed tireless, but my shirt clung to my back with cold sweat. The fog lay like a white quilt under the moon, covering the countryside, and black shadows miles long and miles wide stretched across the land. Up and down we went, the fog growing thicker as we stumbled into boggy valleys, our feet squelching in the sodden turf, and fear hovering round our hearts. Earlier in the evening before the night fell, I had heard a noise before us in the lag, and had clicked a bullet in my rifle breech and fallen flat, but Rory swore at me and asked me in amazement if I meant to fight them. After that I had no guts for anything but to get away from the danger of an encounter, to get across the river and the main road before the dawn, and up to the higher mountain on Ballyvourney beyond. So we trudged on and every natural night sound terrified us, a bird's cry, a barking dog with his double note, *bark-bark,* and then silence, *bark-bark,* and like that now and again the whole night long from one mountainside or another. People say the most lonely thing of all is the bark of a dog at night, but to us the most lonely sight was the odd twinkle of a light, miles away, one dot of light and all the rest of the land in darkness, except for the moon in the sky. The little light meant friends, a fireside, words of advice, comfort — but for us only the squelching and the trudging that seemed never to end, and maybe a bullet in the head before the morning.

Once only we rested when Rory lost all patience and flung caution to the wind to light a cigarette in the hollow of his palms. I stretched out on the sodden moss — God, how restful it would be to sleep there for an hour or two — and tried to keep awake by watching the

coming of the red glow in his palm every time Rory drew in a
fresh puff. The moon was a few nights from full roundness, and I
thought it looked like a jolly wench laughing at us both, and the
missing segment like a bonnety tam cocked on the side of her fat
head. The devil would look after his own, Rory was saying, blast
them, two again' twenty, we couldn't fight them. Rory pulled me up
and we went on, and I cursed Rory for not knowing the lay of his
own countryside and he cursed me for a city snot that had no business out here in the mountains. Then we heard the cattle plunging in
the boggy hollow beneath us, and we plunged ahead ourselves down
a sharp descent where the river must have cut its way centuries ago:
down we went sliding and running until the heavenly sight of trees
broke against the sky and the dark mass of a house against them.
Rory knew it for Dan Jamesy's house and we hammered with our
rifle butts on the door, anxious only for sleep, and food, and the
sight of friends. From an upper window she called to us and Rory
spoke his name. Used to this sort of thing, and pitying us, she came
down, barefooted, her black hair around her, a black cloak on her
shoulders not altogether drawn over her pale breast, a candle blown
madly by the wind slanting in her hand.

Rory had dressed himself while I peered out at the wall of
mountain before me, and slinging his equipment over one shoulder
he went down to eat something before we faced the river and the
road — both half a mile away now. I followed him in a moment
and found the old woman of the house and a little boy seated on
the settle, his eyes wide with interest, hers full of uneasiness at our
being in her house, a danger to her sons and husband. The young
woman who had opened the door the night before stood like a
statue before the wide fireplace, her bright arm bare to the elbow,
and — curious gesture — her hand on the crown of her head as if
to keep in position the hair brushed and close-combed around her
skull like a black velvet cap shining in the firelight. She smiled at

me as I entered, but I was too anxious to smile back. Rory asked her many questions about the encircling troops, and she replied, looking down at his ruddy earnest face, that some lorries had passed by an hour ago, and when he asked about the river she said that it had risen over the stones and could not be crossed. She stooped down to reach the teapot, keeping one hand on her hip as she poured the tea: before the hour was out I recollected how she looked at me while she poured me out a cupful, and at the recollection I felt just as when I saw, the night before, an odd, twinkling window light heading a deserted valley full of moonlight and mist. Stooping again she replaced the pot and went to sit on the other side of the little boy, and laying one hand on his knee spoke to him.

"That fir Tom brought last night has no fire in it."

" 'Tis a bad fire, God bless it."

"Get a good log, now, Jamesy, will you? Will you?" The little fellow looked at us only, and said, "I will," but he did not stir. The old woman broke in irritably:

"Wisha, Jamesy couldn't."

"Indeed, Jamesy is a great man, isn't he, Jamesy? Imagine Jamesy not to be able to carry a baulk of fir! Will you, Jamesy?"

But Jamesy sat with dangling legs watching us eat and she rose and with easy steps went out: the old woman stirred the wood fire; one of the sons handled my revolver with dull curiosity, and another fumbled in a rope loft over Rory's head and replied that another lorry was gone by. We prepared for the river and the road, on our guard, not so afraid as when the night was all around. I went to the door to see if it rained, and stood looking into the dark archway of the stables and at the dark hollows under the thatch — nowhere else could I see the soft, silent fall. As I looked at the dark archway she appeared in it with an armful of logs and raised her head towards me and smiled once again, and then she approached, pulling her blue apron over her head to protect her from the rain. Her smile tortured me. Then Rory and the old man of the house came out and went towards the stables, arguing about a horse to carry us over the flood, and I followed them, and we came at last to where the river was tearing madly over the drowned stones.

As I sat behind the old fellow on his white mare, clasping him firmly about the waist, and trying to keep my eyes from the swirling water that tore the gravel from the unsteady hoofs, I saw from the corners of my eyes the drops that splashed up and flashed in the sun as they fell again on the prancing knees and the brown water. I saw at the identical moment the young woman in the blowing wind of the night, and her looks at me twice, thrice that morning. I longed for an end to this vagabond life, longed for I dared not think what; but there was in it the scent and light of flowers and the scent of woman and her caresses. She had looked at me as if we had between us some secret love: not one woman in ten thousand will look so at one man in as many thousand, perhaps not one in all his life, never more than one I would have said a day ago, and now one such had looked at my eyes and I thought at once of the evening glow of the city streets when the sun has gone behind the tallest houses, when the end of the day is near, and the canyon-alleys are suffused with dusk and slow-moving lights: when men waken from the sleep of day and returning in upon themselves think of love, and the darkness where love is, and wander out from the city to the dark fields.

Rory had forgotten that he must not look down and he fell side-wise on the horse's back, and when he reached the opposite bank he began talking of his foolishness and never ceased reverting to it the whole day. He looked down, you see, he looked down into the flood, he forgot, man, he looked down, and, by God, if he hadn't looked, but he looked into the water, he knew he shouldn't — wasn't it I myself was telling you not to look at the flood, but whatever happened I looked down. And, cripes! When I did . . . To have peace for my own thoughts I told him that he had but little talk the night before; but he did not heed my jibes, and chattered on, glad of the

morning and reckless about the last mile between us and the foot-
hills. He was a little bellied fellow, his mouth like a crack across a
potato, his cap distended by a cane hoop just like a plate on the top
of his head. He had pinned a colored miniature of the Virgin to the
front of his queer cap, and when in the mood, his talk bubbled from
him in anything but a virginal flow. How he had sworn at me yesterday when he sighted the enemy troops, and I could not see at all
the tiny khaki figures below us on the lower slopes!

"Do you see them?" he had cried with equal stress on each word
after the manner of his dialect. "Christ, can't you see them?" he had
shouted in rage, saying it as if it were spelled in two syllables, Chi-
rist. "Will you look at them, Christ, will you look at them when I
tell you?"

I used to wonder at his affection for me in spite of such failures.
In better mood now he jabbered on while we made our way up
against the sprung wind and a hilly place. At last we heard the in-
cessant knocking of a threshing engine on the bald summit in front
of us, and we made our way to it. Up here the wind was a storm,
and it blew the chaff about the sky like yellow snow blown before
the wind. First the blue slate roof, then the white walls of the house,
the yellow stack of corn, the stone-wall fences of the fields, and at
last the little black engine jumping like a kettle on the hob, while
all the time the men swung their arms to and fro in labor: soon we
were among them, telling one group after another of the night's
and day's adventures. Rory gabbled between every pant after his
climb, telling about the horse and how I could not see the little
gray figures when they came around us the evening before. From
where we stood, the Rough looked like a flat plain and the distant
mountains like hunchbacks in a row. I watched the whole country
change with the shadows of the flying clouds, listening to the engine,
with its disyllabic knocking, ceaseless since morning, and the wind's
cry, and Rory shouting above it all.

"There was the bloody mare in the middle of the river, I'm not in the habit of horses, you know, a man that was used to horses wouldn't mind, but I wasn't in the habit of them and I never was, and what did I do and the bloody mare there in the middle of the river, what did I do, what did I do? The thing I did! What should I *do,* I ask you, but look down at the flood, so look down at the flood I did. I looked down and only for the lad got a grip of me I was down. Cripes, I was. I was! If I would only not look down at the flood, you see, but I looked down, and by Christ!"

Here Rory began to shake in his excitement, too moved to be articulate.

The chaff was always driving away before the wind, and now and again someone would look up and around at the sky and say to the man whose stack was being threshed in this communal fashion of the mountains:

"Maybe it will hold dry."

The other would look up and around and say:

"Maybe it will. It might then. It's a strong wind."

Then they would set to work again, piking and tossing the broken sheaves and we moved down at last to the road.

The road twisted eastward behind the rocks, and nothing but the tops of the telegraph poles showed where it ran after that. It was bare and empty, so we ran for it, crossed it, and in another moment Rory was crying that a lorry was coming around the bend. Hearts leaping, we doubled our pace and fell upon our bellies in the moss, squirming around like legless things to face the road. In a moment more the shots began to whine away over our heads, and I saw two awkward figures firing at us as they ran: I fired wildly in reply until my bolt jammed, and then rolled away into a hollow that by the fortunes of war lay behind me: thereupon I ran through the rocky place, through the bracken and the bog, more madly than ever in my life before, and raced for such a lengthy spell that when at last I fell helpless upon the ground my breath pumped in and out painfully and my heart beat against my side like a thing trying to leave my body. I heard the shots still ringing and the bullets whining high up in the air, flying no doubt in a great parabola so that I fancied I heard them thud when spent into the soft earth, their curve completed.

When at last they ceased and our hearts returned to a normal beat we had come to a little low-flung wood of birch and rowan, the silver bark peeling black stripes horizontally from the birch, the red berries of the rowan wind-blown on its delicate branches. Gray rocks covered the interstices of the trees and the sun fell sometimes on the rock to warm the cold color: a stream twisted through the rough ground and its sound was soft and bass, and up on a sudden promontory silhouetted against the sky was a single figure who was working in a series of vigorous thrusts on a spade. We remained in the little wood for many hours, listening to the bass viol of the falling water, to the wind pulling at the larchtops and shaking the tender rowan, and sometimes listening with attention to the drumming of a lorry as it passed in and out of earshot in the near distance.

Excited by danger, and by the beauty of this calm place, the falling stream beside me, the trees moving all around, I began to think again of the young woman in the black cloak who had become aware that I too lived just as much as anyone she had hitherto known at church or fair. I saw her always as she had come to us in the night, her black cloak hanging heavily against her skin as she led us to the quiet kitchen and the dead embers on the hearth. Surely life had a less miser purpose in this encounter than in the thousands of thousands of meetings when men cross and recross in towns and country places? Time and again they had appeared barren and futile, but rather than believe them fruitless, rather than feel as a spool revolving in a shuttle, I had lived instead in the unrest of a chessman fingered by a hesitant player. Now sloth of mind, as sometimes before, drew down my heart to the beauty of this life, and in this little birdless wood I began to dream. When the stream had carved itself a majesty, passing barges and lights on the barges would ride the brown smoke of the evening air, each crossing the scurrying wake of waves from swifter hulls to disappear slowly through the dusk while men sat on each deck and smoked in content with life, and recalled all the dead among my acquaintances who have suffered too willingly the futility of life. There is an owl in the Celtic fable who had seen each rowan as a seed upon a tree, and its length seven times fallen to the earth and seven times over raised in leaf; it had seen the men whose bones were washed from these boulders when the rain was rounding them to pebbles from seven hundred times their height this dropping evening; it had seen the men for whom the promontory above me was a bottomless valley and the hollow place where Rory and I sat was a high mountain before the Flood. Such an owl called out of the dusk at me and its cry filled me with age and the peace that comes when we feel the wheels of the passing years turn so slowly it is almost complete rest. I dozed as I lay — life stopped for me while my eyes swayed and fell.

But Rory, his mind whirling, sang of passionate life. He sang the song of the old Newgate murderer, the song found scrawled upon his Newgate cell after they hanged him and buried him. How eerie to see him ghosting like this in Ireland, his disjointed spine rattling. Rory, not aware that before the night had fallen death would have got him, too — his body plugged full of English lead — sang cheerily:

> My name is Samuel Hall, Samuel Hall,
> My name is Samuel Hall, Samuel Hall,
> My name is Samuel Hall,
> And I've only got one ball,
> Here's my curse upon you all,
> God damn your eyes!
>
> I killed a man 'tis said, so 'tis said,
> I killed a man 'tis said, so 'tis said,
> I hit him on the head,

With a bloody lump of lead,
And I laid the bugger dead,
                              God damn your eyes!

I did not heed the words, but the sense, entering my mind, broke
my dream. Looking up I saw the west grow cold and saffron as if
the threshers of the morn, reduplicated in valley after valley, had
blown a storm of corn sheaves against the falling cape of night. A
score of birds fulfilling their ancient ritual flew homeward in forma-
tion: as they passed into the blazing sun I dropped my eyes again to
the stream, but while I had turned away it had changed to silver
against the dark stones. Dusk was dropping upon us secretly and
we must move on to some house where we could sit before the
flames and doze before a chimney wall browned with soot and invading rain and sleep quietly while the night passed by.

We tramped ahead, keeping to the back roads still, but quite without fear now that we were so many miles from the enemy, and at
last, high up among the hills, walking in the reaches of the wind,
we came to the little roadside house that was shop and post office in
one, and we sat there wearily by the fire.

The land was cold and windswept here, and the few elms that
stood outside, landmark for many miles around, were torn by the
wind like the clouds in the sky. Rory was to stay here for the night,
but I had to move farther on, so I sat by the fire waiting impatiently for the cart that was to carry me part of the last few miles to
supper and bed. At the end of the kitchen the old carter was whispering across the little counter with the woman of the house; the
young daughter of the house stood beside them lighting an oil lamp
that hung from a beam overhead. Presently the two gray pates were
lit from above. The glow fell on the unpainted counter, plain as
when its planks first arrived from the town of Macroom twenty
miles away and were flung on the kitchen floor for the admiration
of the little fat woman with her little fat baby. The glow fell on the
soiled and mutilated bank notes, on the silver and copper coins, on

the blue sugar bags and the dun surfaces of the remainder of Saturday night's groceries. I waited while they talked in a secretive whisper, perhaps over the account, perhaps about their old-wives' gossip of the countryside. Perhaps they were wishing us wandering guerrillas farther on and wishing the fighting at an end lest their houses be burned over their heads. Outside in the windy night the old horse was tethered to an elm, its head bent low and its eyes heavy with sleep like a Buddha's. I sat by the fire and raked in the ashes with the muzzle of my rifle.

I felt it would rain heavily tonight though the wind was getting stronger, and once again I thought of the girl in the black cloak; but already she had slipped many miles into the things of the past, and in another day she would have slipped wholly from my mind not to be recalled unless in some odd place at some odd time when I would wonder about our strange encounter, and in sentimental mood wonder if she ever asked a comrade where I had gone, saying that I was a nice boy, perhaps more than that. She had been at such a door as this in her mother's arms. She would stand there again in one, two, three years' time bidding farewell to the very last mocking couple of her bridal party, and, looking at the sky with her young husband, see the coming of the rain and lock and latch the door upon it, and returning to the dying fire would hear the first drops fall on the warm core, and the rising howl strip the elms; he would draw her toward him and she, feeling her youth passed forever, would weep softly and secretly in the dark and then smile for her first ungirdling. What lovely weavings the old Weaver thinks of, as if all will not fray away in the end and moths rise from the eyes of his dears. Even storms crumble at the end in dust.

I heard Rory chant some passage from a hedge-school memory, and turning I saw the young girl of the house watching him, ready for a burst of laughter at the end.

"This," chanted Rory, "is a man, the beauty of whose eloquence and the wisdom of whose conversation are balanced only by the impeccability of his character and the noble qualities of the mind wherewith God has endowed him, for it is abundantly clear to me," continued the emperor in a graver tone, "that wherever the original refulgence of the human mind is neither adumbrated in its infancy nor adulterated in its maturity, the unique powers of the will of man must inevitably produce in every individual, no matter in what clime he has been born, nor under what star he has first seen the light of day, if only he be true to what is right and turn from what is wrong, the genius of an Alexander, the oratory of a Cicero, the wisdom of a Solomon, or the sublime skill of a Leonardo da Vinci, as the case may befall."

The little bellied fellow finished with a breathless rush, and turning to the girl clapped his hands and clapped her hands with his in applause at his own performance.

I found that this child was to accompany me a little way on the road. We snuggled into the back of the cart and sat shouting our farewells as it jolted away from the two yellow squares of light and from the figures crowding the open door. Then as we entered the spacious dark, silence fell on us three. I stretched back on the floor of the cart listening to the braggart storm. I felt young and willful under its breath; I loved to hear its impotent whine: off behind the ridge of mountain through which a pass had been cut maybe five centuries ago by roadmakers rotted in the grave there came the great spreading light of the moon. We were following the direction of the racing clouds, flying beyond us in the sky. My eyes were beginning to close with the rough swaying of the cart when suddenly the child clasping my hand said:

"Are you afraid of the pookas? I am!"

And fell upon my breast and laid her head by mine and I put an arm around her and we lay so, jolting along under the stars and the driving fleeces overhead. Presently I left them, and the old cart was soon out of earshot.

Jogging on through the dark, my thoughts wandered at will. I pictured the bed where I would sleep. I had slept in so many hundreds that it might be any size or shape, but I chose from my set of images one bed most suitable to the stormy night. It was the marriage bed of the peasants, made of plain wood, closed on back, side and top, and only the front left open, and that sometimes covered by a curtain on a string. It was like a beehive with a flat crown and sloping roofs, shallow at head and foot, so that a man could stand in comfort only in the middle of the bed. The storm might howl for all I cared, the rain might drench the stooks and fill the yards with pools of dung; the windows might rattle — I would sleep the night through and wake to find the skies clearing in the morning. I was hungry for food and sleep, and in this bed I would lie for a while thinking over the day's happenings, trying to find a scheme for things in the true dreamer's way, a scheme into which everyone would fit as by nature, the woman of the cloak, the little girl, myself, the dead husband, the carter, the crowds that meet and remeet, as it seemed aimlessly, blindly — and all these would jumble in my mind and quaint combinations occur and confuse me, and my reasoning fall under the sway of interweaving images and sleep come secretly with her hood.

At last the bright square of window light slid into view, quartered by the crucifix framework, and I found the causeway to the door and groped my way to it after the window vanished in its own recess. I played blindman's buff with the door and at last with outstretched hands I stumbled against it and grasped the latch. Fire flames, a settle, and maybe a white cloth and something to eat other than dry bread and tea with goat's milk. I lifted the latch and looked in: a young woman stood with her back to me stiffened in a posture of surprise as when I first fumbled at the door, but, relaxing and turning when I spoke, touched her soft hair and bade me enter: it was the young woman of the morning.

"Is there e'er a wake here?" I asked, seeing the lone kitchen, my voice trembling as I spoke.

"Devil a wake then!" She was smiling at me again.

"Ye're very quiet then," I said, looking around at the clean-swept kitchen, and then at her skin like a boy's under its first white down.

" 'Tis quiet, wisha," she answered, making way for me as I moved to the settle. I asked if there would be room for the night, and she said there would be and welcome.

"And a bit to eat for a hungry man?"

"Surely, if you don't mind waiting for just a moment or two."

I wanted to ask how she came before me to the hither side of the country twelve long miles away from last night's hostel. I flung aside my bandolier and raincoat; I laid my rifle and pack and belt in a corner. She went to the end of the kitchen and I heard the splash of water and the paddling of hands, and when she returned to me by the fire, wiping her fingers, they were rosy when the apron fell. She half knelt before the fire to blow it with a hand bellows, and as she worked her body formed a single curve, one breast on one knee, and her arms circling the knee while she worked lustily at the bellows. I could see the little wrinkles at each corner of her lips — laughter wrinkles, maybe?

"Are the old people in bed?" I asked.

"Yes." Her voice trembled, I thought.

"And the rest? Where's the rest from you?"

"There's nobody else. Tom, my brother, is on the run in Kerry." I leaned back on the settle and the flames crackled into life.

"Well, you must be very lonely here all alone."

"I have got used to it," she answered, patting her hair with the fingers of her hands: how soft it looked! Then she stood up and began to spread a white cloth on the white table, and then to lay a milk jug, a cup and saucer, a sugar basin, a pot of jam.

"Do you live here?"

"Yes."

"But you're not always as desolate as this — surely?"

"Desolate, just as you say; this is a lonely district, you know."

"Well, it's not so bad at all now," said I. "I shouldn't mind if I lived here — the mountains and the valleys . . ."

She halted in her step and faced me: the little mouth was gathered into a hard white button of flesh.

"You would soon tire of these mountains! The city, though, that's where I'd like to live. There's company there, and sport and educated people, and a chance to live whatever life you choose!"

She had put two eggs into a little black pot of boiling water, and the water bubbled and leaped around them with a hissing. A blast of wind came down the chimney and drove a cloud of fire smoke into the kitchen. We sat silent and presently went to the table and she poured me red tea to drink and I cut the brown loaf and plastered it with butter and jam, and ate greedily. She sat before the fire, and I asked her why she did not like the district, but she only looked at me and said nothing. I asked again, pleading that I wished to know, really and truly. She answered:

"Because this farm is bare and high. The land is poor. And this downland has a northern aspect."

A heavy drop of rain fell on the fire — the storm was howling. I saw the sea of discontent and unrest that these words were born of, saw the drizzling rain and no sun shining on it, saw her looks steal round her to this farm and to that and back from them to her own home. Another gust of wind blew the smoke around her and she turned away from it and clasped my knee to prevent herself from falling from the low stool.

"You'll be choked," said I, and her eyebrows stirred and she smiled at me. I laid my palm on her hand and thought of the whole livelong day I had spent, the rick that must be threshed before the wind fell, the carter jogging through the wet night, the sea of darkness outside the door. How many days could I live without a complete revolt! I spoke earnestly.

"It's a cruel country to have to live in."

She spoke kindly to me then.

"I think you are honest," she said.

"Do you think that?"

"I think you *are* honest. *Really* honest," she said again.

Looking at her soft eyes, and at her soft hair, my eyes wandered down to the first shadows of her breasts: she caught my glance and looked down at her warm bosom and then at me and she smiled. As I moved to her I saw the little broken corner of her tooth; I had no word to say; so I sat beside her before the leaping flames and put my arms around her and felt in the cup of my hollow palm the firm casque of her breast. Smiling at me as a sick woman might smile upon a doctor who brought her ease from pain she slipped my hand beneath her blouse to where I felt the warmth of her skin and her warm protruding nipple, and I leaned to her for a kiss.

A rush of feet came to the door and the little girl from the road-side house flung it wide with a cry to me to run, to run; Rory was shot dead; they were coming west for me! I bundled up my equipment, ran in a flash through the open door into the dark night, and raced on and on — stumbling and falling and going I cared not where but away from headlamp lights flashing to the north. When I fell into a panting walk I was like a man who has been listening to music the livelong day and after it his mind is full of strange chords, and ill-recollected they torture him with a sense of something lost. On my bare head the rain fell heavily and aslant, now and again it was blown into my face by the wind, and the clouds totally blotted out the moon. Full of terror for such a death as I knew Rory's was I filled every house with armed men, fierce men to whom killing was a little thing and torture but little more, and my imagination and the stories I had heard drove me blindly on through the sodden night. I trudged a way through the pathless bogs and tore through briery dikes: all that night I found no shelter from the lashing rain and I met not a single tree in leaf: long after midnight I saw a little glinting window leap suddenly out of the dark about a mile away, and as I thrust away from it, away to safety, into the rain, the memory of its light tortured me as the memory of cool winds must torture the damned of hell. At last I came on a lonely ruin on the mountain, three walls, and I lay on the lee side of it while the rain dripped on me from the remnants of its eaves.

When I awoke, a dim radiance lit the falling haze, but whether it was the dawn or the sinking moon or any hour past three or before three I could not say. No sound was to be heard: no living thing moved: no bird stirred the wet air: the falling haze made no sound. I rose chattering and trembling, and my feet plashed through the wet earth and the drowned grass, and when I halted there was quiet. I crossed a little stone wall and one of the stones fell with a mighty sound. I might have been the last human creature to crawl to the last summit of the world, waiting until the Deluge and the fortieth night of rain would strain him upwards on his toes while the water licked his stretched neck. Yet everywhere they slept sound abed, my dark woman curling her warm body beneath the bedclothes, the warmer for the wet fall without, thinking if she turned and heard the dripping eaves — that the winter was at last come.

> Cold till doom!
> The storm has spread.
> A river is each furrow on the slope,
> Each ford is a full pool.
>
> Each lake is a great tidal sea,
> Each pool is a great lake,
> Horses cannot cross the ford,
> Nor two feet.
>
> The fish of Ireland are wandering,
> There is no strand upon which the waves
>   do not pound.
> Not a town is in the land,
> Not a bell, not a crane's whining cry.
>
> The wolves in the wood of Cuan cannot rest,
> They cannot sleep in their lair:
> Even the little wren cannot shelter
> In her tiny nest on the side of Lon.

Keen wind and cold ice
Have burst upon the little world of birds.
The blackbird cannot shelter its side
In the wood of Cuan.

Cozy was our pot upon the nook,
In the crazy hut on the slope of Lon:
The snow has crushed the wood,
And toilsome is the climb to Ben-bo.

The ancient bird of Glenn Rye
Is grieved by the cold wind:
Her misery and her pain are great,
The ice will get into her throat.

From flock and from down to rise
Were folly for thee! Take it to heart.
Ice heaped on every ford,
Wherefore I say "cold till doom."

Down below me in the valley I heard an early cart; the morning wind, light and bitter, sang occasionally in the key of the flooded streams. The dawn moved along the rim of the mountains and as I went down the hill I felt the new day come up around me and life begin once more its ancient, ceaseless gye.

The Patriot

IT was doubtless because of the inevitable desire of man to recapture the past that they went to Youghal for their honeymoon. Their friends expected them to go at least to Dublin, if not to London or Paris, but they both knew in their hearts that they had spent the gayest days of their lives in this little town, and so, as if to crown all those early happinesses, to Youghal they went, like true voluptuaries deliberately creating fresh memories that would torment them when they were old.

Across there on the little stone promenade, when they were as yet little more than girl and boy, they had met for the first time. She was on holiday with her sister; he had come with his aunt for the day. In the train they had met Edward Bradley, his former teacher, and Mr. Bradley had walked about with him (in spite of his aunt) for a few hours, and given them tea. He had been flattered, he remembered, because old Bradley stayed with them so long, and afterwards he pretended to Norah that Mr. Bradley was really a great friend of his. Off there at the end of the promenade they had sat, the three of them, because his aunt was too old to walk far without a rest, and as they sat there Norah and her sister came and

60

halted opposite them to lean on the wall. A liner was passing slowly, almost imperceptibly, along the horizon and everybody was looking at it, and his aunt was asking him to tell them — he was young, God bless him, and had the better sight — was it two funnels or three it had. He had stood up, pretending to look at the liner, but he was really trying to look at Norah's black hair and her jet-black eyes without being seen, growing irritated because he and she could not be there alone, and growing more irritated still because he saw that she too was trying to look at him without being observed, turning her back frequently on the sea to look, as it were, up over their heads at the crowds on the cliffs, curving herself backwards over the wall and standing on her toes as if to show herself off to him. In the end her sister drew her away as the ship became too faint to be seen and Bernard became so disconsolate and silent that his aunt plucked at him and said:

"What on earth's wrong with you, Bernie? Are you tired, or what is it?"

But Mr. Bradley cocked his eye at him and winked without his aunt seeing. Old Bradley was a cute boyo, he had thought, and flushed because he felt he had been observed. After tea he and his aunt were alone again, and she, who had been so sweet to their companion, was now abusing him roundly for a firebrand who was leading all the young men into wild politics. "Some day," Bernie defended, "that man will be Lord Mayor of Cork and then you'll sing a different song," but she would have none of it and as he just then caught sight again of his dark girl in the distance and wished to walk on and catch up with her he did not argue further. Alas! His aunt got tired once more, saying that the tea was like a load on her stomach, and they had to sit on another bench. His dark vision passed out of his sight and he felt she had merely floated before him and he would never meet her again.

When he did meet her again it was several years after and she was again on holiday in Youghal, and it was only by degrees they realized they had seen each other before. On this occasion he was an Irregular guerrilla — doubly a rebel — seated high up on a lorry, with his rifle across his back and his coat collar turned up, and his cap thrown back and upwards from his forehead to let his curls free to the wind. Seven other lorries were roaring along behind him through the streets and as they tore their way under the old clock archway, there on the pavement, smiling up at them, and waving her green handkerchief to them, was the loveliest dark-haired girl he had ever seen. Their lorry halted just beyond the arch to wait for the troops marching in from the railway, and he alighted and by virtue of being a soldier was able to approach her on the pretense of wanting matches or cigarettes. By the time the troops came into the town they were in a little teashop, and he was flirting away with all the bravado in the world. As the men passed outside, four by four, they sang their rebelly songs, waking, as he said to her, the ghosts of old Raleigh, who had once lived there, and of the stiff Earl of Cork from his tomb in Christ's Church, and the ghost of every Elizabethan sailorman who had cast a rope ashore by the crumbled quays they could see through the rear door of the shop, edging with their fallen stones the glittering blue of the bay.

There were descendants of those sea dogs in that town still, she told him, for having come there year after year on her holidays since she was a little child she knew Youghal as if she had been born there. She chanted the names to him, the Merricks, the Gurneys, the Boyles, the Brisketts, and at each name he swaggered his cup on high to curse them, so that it was a profane litany that finished their tea.

"The Yardleys too," she said, laughing at him.

"God damn them forever!" he swashbuckled.

"Of course the Townshends are Cromwellians," she smiled.

"Damn them forever!" he cried again.

Her eyes wandered to the bay. A brown-sailed yawl was floating past on the blue water as gracefully as a yacht.

"Isn't she lovely?" she cried, flushing with the delight of it.

"Not as lovely as you," he bantered.

"Oh! Come and watch her," she invited, and away they went.

When he found his way to the abandoned military barracks they had taken over, it was late night — discipline was a joke in those days — but he did not sleep for many hours, standing at the window of the deserted messroom watching where the moon poured down across the face of the shimmering ocean, into the little harbor. It lit up as if it were day the shouldering furze-bright hills, and the white edge of motionless surf at the base of the distant cliffs, and every sleeping roof in the town clustered beneath him.

It was curious that it was there in Youghal, too, that same summer, that Norah had first met Edward Bradley. There had been a public meeting in the market place while the guerrillas held the town and one of the chief speakers was Bradley. That day he had spoken with a terrible passion against England, and against the Irish traitors who had been cowed by her, and his passionate words caught and flared the temper of the people so that they cheered and cheered until their voices echoed across the smooth surface of the water into the woods beyond. Bernie had cheered like the rest where he stood beside Norah, proud to be that man's friend. After the meeting the three met, and the teacher, flushed with his success, walked between them along the tumble-down quays. He found that he knew Norah's people quite well, though he had not seen them for many years.

"But I'll call on them often now," he said, looking at Norah, and he began to take her arm, and then he remembered Bernie and he took his arm — like a grandfather, Bernie had said, jokingly, to him, and was angry with himself for saying it, for a deeper blush crept over the face of the older man and, halting, he had said:

"Maybe I am too old to be walking with the like of ye," and cocking his eye at the girl again he had laughed, half bitterly as Bernie thought, and with a "God bless ye, my children," turned and walked away. Wasn't he a very nice man, Norah had said, and stood looking after the teacher so long that Bernie almost thought he was going to be jealous; but he had not thought long of it. It was a warm autumn day, and so clear that they could see across the channel where the hay garnered in for the winter had left white patches on the clovered meadows. Tempted by the fields beyond they had rowed slowly cross the bay to spend the afternoon on the other side. The geese had cropped the grass of the foreshore until it was as close and clean as a golf course, except where a few odd straws lost to the granary lay strewn about and, with them, cast up by the tide, bits of reedy sea wrack, and here and there the dark gray droppings of the fowl. The air was so rarefied that as they crossed the low stone walls on their way into the oak woods the stones fell with a gurgling sound like water, and far away the ocean boomed deeply into the crannied rocks. They had gone deep into the woods to lie there while the misty darkness fell, bringing in the night wind a little rain, to lie there in their deep love as still as corpses, as still as fallen leaves. They returned late at night to the town whose yellow windows, bright across the channel, spoke to them of sanded floors in quayside pubs and the first fires before the winter.

But before that week was out the town was abandoned and Norah had to stand under the shelter of the old town walls watching the great barracks smoking against the fading sky and the distant mountains, themselves so faint that in their grayness they blended and were lost in the darkness and the smoke.

It was the way of that guerrilla life that for months on end a man never even thought of home or friends, and for months Bernard wandered among those gray mountains to the north of Youghal, as aimlessly as, and, he used to feel, more uselessly than, a lost sheep. Once only did he use his rifle in those seven months of guerrilla life and that was when sniping from fifteen hundred yards a village supposed to contain enemy troops. He slept in a different bed each night and never ate twice in succession from the same table so that most of his time was spent in going from place to place in search of food and rest. He did so less from a sense of danger than a sense of pity towards the farmers who had to feed and shelter him and his fellows, never thinking that as all his fellows did as he was doing, it saved nothing to the flour bin lying lightly on the loft, or the tea caddy on the high mantelshelf, emptied almost daily.

The days scarcely existed for him, the weeks flew over his head as unnoticed as birds homing at night, until as a human being he almost ceased to be, enveloped by the countryside as if he were a twig, a stone, an ear of corn. And then, without the slightest warning, as suddenly as the breaking of a thundershower, he remembered how lovely Youghal had been, and Norah, and he hated to look up at the cold and naked mountains. It was late February with the rain falling as by the clock, and for a month they had been hunted through it, day and night. Thinking of that and thinking of the summer his memory began to work on him like a goad. All about him on the night he thought of her, sitting along by the embers of a turf fire after the family had gone to bed, the mountains lay black and silent, wet as if they had been dipped in the sea. Overhead a white path of stars more clear in the washed air than if there were a frost abroad. Out there, too, he felt, was danger; he was listening so intently that he almost leaped when a little cricket chirruped in the dark warmth of the hearth. He feared even to stir, so great a noise did every movement make — almost as great, it seemed, as the resounding *drop-drop* of the leaking thatch beyond the door.

In his pocketbook he had her one letter, reminding him of that little wood where they had loved:

I went specially to Youghal to see our wood again. The autumn is over it and over all the land. The days are shortening, farmers are threshing, thatching turf-ricks, digging potatoes, culling sheep from their flocks to barter in fair and market, fields are decaying with grief for the loss of their fruits, and grief is a brown and withered hag, nuts are ripening, blackberries are rotting, holly berries are reddening, leaves are dropping yellow. Mists cover the mountains like a hooded cloak, gray rocks ooze tears of desolation, green ferns on the hillside are withering, and purple heather is turning gray. Birds are silent, winds rustling in denuded boughs. In Youghal tourists are departed — no more the hum of the motor, nor the flash of fashionable attire. In my little hotel Mrs. M—— is resting and knitting, K—— turning over stacks of *McCall's Journals* and *Home Gossips,* the serving-girl is considering her return to her mother's home, P—— L—— wearing her shoes "going aisht and wesht," B—— twinkling with gestating jokes, and R—— counting the takings of the season. Norah is at the moment writing to Bernard; at other moments? — thinking, reading, peering into a dimly lit future. . . .

He smiled at that letter, so full of life as it was. Then he thought of the night outside and went to the door. He could hear the streams swirling down the dark *leaca* and as he listened their roar mingled with the desolation of the silence, and he wished passionately to be away from so lonely and cruel a place.

Three miles across the hills, in a little fishing hotel by a mountain lake, was the headquarters of the division. There, he hoped, he might get money — a few shillings would do — to help him on the road home, and maybe they would give him a clean shirt and collar, and a better hat and trousers than these guerrilla rags that, up to now, he had been flaunting as with a deliberate joy in their torn dirt. Above all he might meet Edward Bradley there. For he too had been hiding for several months in the mountains, not daring to stay in the city for fear of arrest. He felt he wanted to talk to somebody like Bradley, someone who would persuade him that this struggle of theirs was not hopeless, that all their humiliation of poverty and hunger was not, as he had long since begun to feel, a useless and wasted offering. Quietly he unbolted the door and stole through the yard into the sodden starlight.

It was midnight when he saw the lake below him and to his surprise every window in the little hotel was lit. He approached warily, alert for a sentry's challenge, an enemy patrol — he might, he knew, be shot as easily by either. But he continued to walk unaccosted past the sleeping farmhouses and the great strewn rocks until he came to the lakeside edge and the lighted windows. Inside the steamed window the room was filled with armed men, smoking, drinking, arguing in groups. He recognized the faces of three or four officers. There was the adjutant with his eyes swollen with too much drink and too little sleep — it was common knowledge that he lived like that. By the fire was Boyle, a great black-faced commandant from Kerry; under the lamp in the largest group he recognized Tom Carroll from East Cork — clearly a meeting of the officers of the division.

He entered unchallenged where a group of men were lounging in the dim candlelit hall. Three officers strode out of the room — it was the dining room — with empty glasses in each hand, returning gingerly when the glasses had been filled to the brim with black stout or porter. He saw the quartermaster coming out of the kitchen with a pair of black pint glasses dripping their froth about his wrists. He went over to tell him how dangerous it was to leave the back road unguarded. The quartermaster only growled:

"Well, what are you doing here then? Go up yourself and sentrify it," and passed on.

The column captain came out from the bar with a tray of divers-colored glasses and to him also Bernie told how the north road was unprotected. But the captain flew into a rage and glared at him over the tray.

"I've told off six men, there, to go," he said, jerking his head at the loungers in the hall.

One of them spoke back at him, a fellow with only two walrus teeth above and below in his gums.

"We won't go. Why should we go? Ye're all dhrinking. Why don't we get a dhrink?"

"Go into the kitchen and get it," said the captain.

"Where'll we get the money?"

"Ask the quartermaster."

"Damn the quartermaster."

"I want the quartermaster," said Bernie. "I want a couple of bob to get home."

The loungers scoffed at him in a loud chorus, and Buckteeth called him Sweet Innocence. Two more joined them, swaggering in their belted and ragged raincoats, out from the glow of the dining room into the dark hall. As they came they deliberately crushed against the captain's tray, all but upsetting his yellow and purple argosy. With a curse at them he raced like a waiter balancing his tray into the dining room, returning to grab Bernard and put him standing in the between passage outside the dining-room door.

"Stand there, you," he growled. "And let nobody into this room unless he has business there."

The loungers cheered.

"Will ye go up, for Christ's sake," the captain implored them, "to the north road and watch it or the whole division will be caught?"

"Oh! It's always deh division, aw!" piped up a little fair-haired sprat of a boy from the foot of the stairs. "What about deh men, aw? Dere's never any talk about deh men?"

"For God's sake, get us a drink, Jim," appealed the man with the walrus teeth.

"Go on, Jim," joined in three or four more. They seemed to have no sense of pride left.

With a sudden air of intimacy the captain stepped into the middle of them, bending his neck right and left among them like a pecking hen.

"Go in," he said, "and take it. Say the quartermaster will fix it up. They'll never know in the hotel."

Buckteeth turned away in disgust.

"No! They feed us, and they sleep us," he said, "and we're not going to soak drink from them as well."

"Well, I have no money for you," complained the captain.

"Deh quartermaster have buckets of it," declared Fair Hair.

"*Buckets* is deh word," sneered a tall man in spectacles from his dark corner at the door.

They laughed at the word in spite of their anger: it measured the quartermaster's thirst.

"Well, I can do no more for ye," said the captain in a temper, and left them.

Bernie stood where he had been placed by the dining-room door and everybody passed in and out without paying the slightest attention to him. The quartermaster, already flushed with drink, returned to fill his glasses once more, and timidly Bernie touched him on the shoulder.

"Well? Are you here still?" said the quartermaster.

Bernie had not the courage to face the refusal of a loan so he asked instead for cigarettes. The quartermaster thrust a package into his hand.

"Here," he said. "You fellows do nothing from morning to night but bum and soak for cigarettes. Why don't ye do something?"

As he passed by, a piece of black and white paper fluttered gently to the ground in his wake. Bernie picked it up. It was a hundred-pound note. For a moment he thought of rushing out to his fellows in the hall and waving it in the air before their eyes; for another moment he thought of using it himself to get home. Then he realized he could not steal money like that, and even if he did nobody would change so large a note for them or him. As the quartermaster returned he tapped his arm once again. A wave of whiskey belched into his face as the fellow turned on him and stuck his potato nose into his face. Bernie held up the note, saw him look stupidly at it, without a word thrust it into his vest pocket and stride into the dining room with his dripping glasses. What a hopeless sort of army they were, Bernie thought, and he made up his mind that he must at all costs go back into the city out of these mountains where they did nothing for month after month but eat the substance

of the people and lounge over the fire like sleepy dogs. Things were
still happening occasionally in the city. If he could rest for a while
and see Norah, he would become invigorated by her and be of some
use again. Suddenly there was a great stirring in the room and the
captain returned to tell him to close and guard the outer door.
Bernie did not have the energy to tell him that all this was foolery.
Instead he begged a match from him and lit a cigarette and leaned
into the corner of the passage to think. He had waited so long he
could wait now another couple of hours until the dawn.

By the glow of the lamps in the room beyond the passageway he
read Norah's letter again, scarcely hearing the talking and arguing
rising hotter and hotter at the meeting, though he faintly gathered
as he read the letter by the dim light that they were considering the
whole military situation in the south and that some were for laying
down their arms at once, and others for fighting on. He was hardly
interested. He was thinking only of the summer that was gone and
of every little incident of his last meeting with Norah in the woods
beyond the bay at Youghal. Gradually the discussion in the room
changed to an argument about men and ammunition and money
and as the voices fell his thoughts wandered freely to the brown-
sailed yawl they saw floating past the frame of the restaurant door,
the sun shining on the blue and white sea in its wake and the curling
foam at its bows. He remembered how he had whispered an old
song to her as they lay among the leaves and to himself he hummed
it over again:

> O beloved of my inmost heart,
> Come some night and soon,
> When my people are at rest,
> That we may talk together;
> My arms shall encircle you
> While I relate my sad tale
> That it was your pleasant soft voice
> That has stolen my heaven.

The fire is unraked,
The light extinguished,
The key is under the door.
And do you softly draw it.
My mother is asleep,
But I am awake.
My fortune is in my hand
And I am ready.
I will go with you. . . .

He heard Edward Bradley's voice addressing the meeting. Why he should be there he did not know, for he was not an army man. Afterwards he told Bernie that because he was older than anybody there they wanted to hear what the politicians had to say. He was imploring them not to lay down their arms — far better to be defeated, at a blow or by degrees, though that would be slow and terrible for them all. As on that day at Youghal his passion carried the meeting with him and they cheered him loudly when he finished. When he came into the passage he was flushed and trembling, and when he saw Bernie he drew him with him out into the hall and, because the loungers were still there, out into the cool air by the side of the lake. A sedge of broken reeds had been washed ashore by the storms, reminding Bernie of the sedge of sea wrack on the foreshore across Youghal bay, but across the lake the mountain streams made a ceaseless desolate moaning, and a night mist was blowing in their faces so that they had to shelter in the darkness of a gable wall. He told Bernie how terrible things were all over the country and Bernie told him what he knew of the state of the men among those hills, all of them weak and scabby and sore, not a penny in their pockets, not a pipeful to smoke, nothing to do from one week to another but run when danger approached, never together, badly led, beaten all but in name.

"And in this hotel," said Bradley, "the officers taking their breakfast at six o'clock in the evening and drinking in the dawn."

Suddenly Bradley said:

"Do you hear at all from that girl now?"

"What girl?"

"The girl in Youghal."

"A long time ago. I got a letter."

He hated to talk of Norah. It was as if she were a secret part of him and he would not bare it.

"She is a very intelligent girl," said Bradley.

"Yes," said Bernie as if he were not really interested, but he felt his breath come in heavy waves.

"Oh, yes!" said Bradley. "I saw a good deal of her before I came out here. I stayed at her house for safety several times before I took to the hills. A very nice girl."

Bernie shivered, his blood turning over in his body, but it was not from the cold.

"Well, I'm leaving in an hour or two," said Bradley. "This place won't be safe for twenty miles around after the news of this meeting gets to the military."

In the hall the candle was guttering out, but the loungers still remained. To say something to them as he passed in Bernie told them what Bradley had said of the conditions about the country and of the officers in the hotel.

"Puh!" taunted the tall bespectacled fellow. "And what does he do himself but hang over a book in the comfort of the hotel fire from morning to night?"

Bernie returned to his position in the passage. He was sick of these tauntings and tale bearings. He wondered how a man like Bradley could remain out there where he must hear them and notice them day after day. If Bradley chose he could go back to hide in the city any day — there would be many people glad to receive and shelter him, and Bernie wished he had asked for the loan of half a crown and a clean collar and tie. He must see Norah again, and the city, and his people, and friends. The quartermaster was talking now, in a thick but fierce voice.

" 'No surrender' must be our cry," he was saying. "I'd rather be shot any day than surrender. Let those that are tired of the fight go into the city and surrender!"

He peeped into the long room. One lamp was guttered low to a smoking circle of red wick. The other glowed like a yellow ball through the skeins of smoke woven in heavy layers from table to ceiling. Beer bottles and empty glasses were everywhere. The men were yawning and stretching themselves, some talking among themselves, paying no heed at all to the speaker, and the chairman was drawing idle circles with a pencil on the table before him.

Somebody silenced the quartermaster with a question and by degrees the talk fell again to a drone as they discussed men and money and ammunition. He leaned back into a corner of the passage and while he thought of the road home, of every wind and turn in it, of every side road and back road he could take, he fell into a doze where he stood. He awoke to hear Boyle from Kerry cry out in a fury at somebody:

"Let them that want to rat, do it. Myself and John Jo Sheehan will hold Kerry anyway. Won't we, John Jo?"

The meeting seemed to be ending. Sheehan was standing huge against the window with his back to them all; in spite of the lamp, black-shouldered against the pale glimmer of the dawn hanging over the mists on the lake outside. In taunting and utter disbelief he cursed over his shoulder at Boyle.

"Hold Kerry, how are you? You and Kerry may go to hell!"

The meeting broke up in laughter, men standing and talking in little groups, edging around their chief to discuss private questions of their own. It seemed as if they would never come out and Bernie sat on the ground to sleep. The first few officers leaving the room poked his stomach with their boots in mockery of their sleeping sentry. He made his way out to the kitchen, where the loungers were strewn asleep on the settle, the table, on chairs or about the floor near the gray embers of the fire. He rolled a porter barrel in from the bar and sat on it and through the sounds of the departing officers, horses stamping, carts trundling out, searchings in the dark for last drinks, calls and farewells, he slept in the corner of the cooling hearth. When he awoke the morning had come and the loungers were, like him, shivering together over the grate, where Buckteeth was blowing the seed of fire into a fresh sod of turf. Seeing him open his eyes they asked him:

"Well? What was deh end of deh meeting, aw? Are we to go home or stay here? Aw?"

"Fight on!" said Bernie.

They looked at him too tired to mock the phrase.

"Stay here, he means," said Buckteeth. "Stay bloody well here."

Bernie shared his cigarettes about and they smoked in silence while the fowl awakened by the echoing crow of the cock began to clatter and suckle in the rain water of the yard, for the rain was now darkening the window, pouring straight down into the dung-filled haggard. Looking out at it Bernie saw again the mist hanging in the woods of Youghal, and Norah running down the slip to the ferry, her black curls swinging as she ran. Their hunger began to stir in them, but they could not find a scrap of food in the house — it had all been eaten by the crowd just departed. In their search they found the quartermaster snoring on the sofa of the dining room, a roll of bank notes hanging from his pocket. At once they grabbed them, sharing out the smaller notes, leaving the twenty-fives and the fifties and the hundreds, but as they argued over the division the quartermaster awoke and in a fury he demanded the money. Buckteeth, who held the fistful of notes, showered them over the furious man's head, and while he clambered under the tables and the chairs to collect them they mocked at him. Beside himself with rage he cursed them for lazy, useless louts and rushing off to tackle his horse and sidecar in the yard he left through the blowing rain while in a crowd they cheered him from the door. But money would not buy them food and they went about draining the ebb of porter in every glass, then wandering over the hotel from floor to attic to see what they could find. There was not a soul there but the people of the house sleeping heavily after the long hours of work the day before, so they returned to the kitchen to wait.

At last the girls of the house came down the ladderlike stairs, their legs thrust bare into their dung-covered boots. They sat on the settle by the fire, bowed over their knees until their mother followed.

"A bad morning, Mrs. O'Rourke," said Bernie to the mother.

She stood by the low window and looked sadly at the rain.

"Isn't it a bad morning, thanks be to God?" she sighed.

Not a word of reproach was said, or of inquiry about the meeting, or of complaint at their long labor. The girls sat looking at the fire or out at the rain. There was nothing for them to eat, and nothing to do on such a wet day. The mother began to scrape the bins and the bags for flour and when the boy of the house came in he milked the cows. The dough was dampened with spring water and fresh milk. It was kneaded and shaped and put into the bastable while they all looked on. Through the open door they could see the rain splashing the causeway outside and a duck poked his eye in by the jamb. Buckteeth spat at the cocked eye and the duck clattered out, but nobody laughed. The bastable was over the fire and they had all turned to it to watch while the cake baked. While they waited six other men came to the house, sodden with rain, arm and thigh and chest, searching for a breakfast and news of the meeting, but when they found the others before them they moved on patiently to the next farmhouse a mile off. They said they must be in Millstreet, twenty miles away, before night. Then they would walk on into Limerick along the Feale. For Limerick, they declared, bare and open though it was, was safer now than Cork. One of them, a Kerry lad, had no socks and his feet were torn by the bare leather of his boots. He had no overcoat, his very shirt clung to his back with wet, and he coughed ceaselessly. The woman of the house took pity on him and asked him to stay, and when he heard the others argue that Limerick was a far more dangerous place than Cork he sat down wearily by the fire and began to cry, telling his companions between his tears that he was afraid to go on with them and would hide here among the mountains. All the while Buckteeth and the others looked awkwardly at him. They offered him cigarettes and tried to cheer him by assuring him that this place was as safe as a house, and while he and they drank the scalding tea and ate soft hot cake the girls searched him out a pair of socks and a dry, if torn, shirt.

But while they ate they were less sure about the safety of the glens and they argued and argued as to what they should do next. The Kerry lad could say nothing but "We must hide. We must hide in the holes of the mountains," and the little fair-haired city gamin kept whining plaintively "But where are our officers? Where are our officers from us now? Aw?" At intervals the boy of the house assured them again and again that it was madness to stay there another day with the valleys filled, as he said, with "people taking the heels from one another with the news of the meeting to the military in the next village." So when the rain lightened they scattered, some going to the north, one declaring that the safest thing was to skirt the village to the east, and Bernie found he had lost courage to attempt the journey home. Tomorrow he would go, he thought, and with Buckteeth and Kerry, as they christened him, he went up among the cliffs in search of a cave to hide in. The boy of the house, though he kept assuring them it was madness to stay there, showed them a dump that had been made in a cleft between the rocks, a gravelike place dug out of the earth and covered with a sheet of corrugated tin and hidden by stones and withered brushwood. There was barely room for the three to lie in this dark, damp tomb, but as Kerry implored them to go into it at once, they lay down there, shoulder to shoulder, peering up and out all day long at the gray spears of the falling rain.

At dark, in spite of their hunger and the cold, they slept. They slept past the rising of the sun, past the late morning, and all the while it rained and the whistling of the rain seemed to lull and keep them asleep in spite of encircling danger. They were awakened by the shattering echoes of machine-gun fire and the impact of hundreds of bullets tearing at the rock above their heads. When the first volley ceased, the echoes carried its *rat-a-tat-tat* across the clifftop to where another echoing air seized upon it and reduplicated it fainter and fainter into the heart of the mountains before it finally died into silence. There was such a long interval that it seemed as if everybody were listening to that last faint replication so high up and so far away. Then they heard the shouts below them:

"Come out! Come out, ye snipes! Come out or we'll bomb ye out. Come out!"

These cries were echoed, and then a brief silence followed. The next minute the gun seemed to tear the tin roof from over their heads where they crouched helpless, their faces to the clay. They had placed their boots to dry, the night before, on the ledge before their dump and these now shot in on their foreheads torn to pieces by bullets. Again the echoes were reduplicated to the farthest uttermost glen and again the shouts came, mingling with those echoes and their own that followed after.

"Yeer last chance! Ye whores! Come out!"

The Kerry boy began to weep again.

"O God!" he shouted. "Leave us out. Leave us out."

"Throw down yeer guns," cried the echoing voices below.

They did so, and Buckteeth, tearing a sleeve from his shirt, raised it before him as he crawled out into the rain. Below them was a score of sturdy green-clad riflemen and in a minute the three were among them, shivering with fear and excitement — broken, timid as children.

They passed through Youghal as prisoners, standing high on a lorry, conspicuous in their rags, and as it roared its way under the old clock archway, there across the wind-blown bay Bernie glimpsed his woods shrouded in mist, growing, as it seemed, out of the gray green bay. Never did anything seem so definitely past to him as his summer flirting under those trees. It might have happened to him in another life, it might have been something he read of in a novel, so distant did it seem.

They drove him to Cork that night and there he remained in prison until the winter was passed and another winter had come again. Norah wrote to him many times while he was in jail — at first briefly but kindly, sending him gifts as she might to any other prisoner, later on long letters at greater length, as to a special friend. After a while she brought herself to reproach him for his long silence of that lonely winter, a winter in which she had tried hard, and vainly, to be, as he had been, forgetful of the sweetness of their summer and autumn love. It was Christmas when he received a letter from her confessing how miserable and unhappy those months had been, and he was glad of the confession though it was a torment to him to be reminded, in the place where he was, of his foolishness when he had been free. When she wrote that Edward Bradley often stayed with them, and spoke kindly of him, it was a double torment — that worst torment of all prisoners — to think what lovely things life could have given him, too, if he were out in the world and part of it. When he was freed he was very ill and weak and the doctor ordered him to the sea and he went, as a matter of course, to Youghal. It was February again, just a year since he had passed through it as a prisoner, and the woods and the bay were again shrouded in haze, but because Norah came to see him, and walked with him there, and showed him the rain in the cobwebs among the branches, and — it was so mild there by the sea — an early celandine hiding under a root, he thought those woods even more beautiful than they had been almost two years before when they watched the red globe of the autumn sun sinking behind its black branches.

Small wonder then that they should come back to the little seaside town for their honeymoon. It was Easter and late in the spring

— the fifteenth of April had been Easter Sunday — so that the catkins' furry paws were already raised to the sun, and the long tails and the tiny wet noses of the lambs protruded from the red and blue creels rumbling in to the lamb fair. The yellow furze was ranged high against the blue sky along the slopes of the hills, and over the surface of the sea beneath there was a cold layer of air that made the waves break with a brittle noise such as one never hears in the soft, dead heat of summer. They went about that first day, their wedding day, noticing everything with new delight — the spears of green grass shooting through the dead fields, the primroses and the violets clustered near the gray stones in the ditches, the beech buds swollen red, the patches of hawthorn green lighting the withered hedges.

The long country lanes were empty; they had the ocean to themselves. The summer visitors had not yet even thought of coming and all the length of the old stone promenade was bare. They even felt a delight in the shuttered windows and the bathing boxes nailed up since last autumn. On the sands stretching for miles in front of them, lost in the end in the spume of the incoming waves far off in the distance, they saw only a sandpiper or two strutting by the skirts of the spreading sea, or peewits in their swoop turning as if to command on their white bellies, then turning again on dark wings, low over the thunderous waves. When they lay under an early blossoming blackthorn high above that singing sea and in the long silences of love gazed over the empty horizon, or back at the clustered smoking chimneys on the farther shore, Bernard felt, and knew that his young wife felt, that if another gull should wheel through the blue air, another distant lamb call out to its dam, their cups of ecstasy must overflow and roll upon the ground. They crossed back then, as of old, to the points of light that marked the town through an early sea haze and sought out that little restaurant where so long ago they had cursed the Elizabethans and the Cromwellians, and there they had their tea, watching back through the open door at the rear of the shop the channel darkening with the fall of night. As they ate they suddenly saw beside them a little green poster bearing that day's name and date. They read it with interest:

SINN FEIN ABU

A Public Meeting
will be addressed
in the Town Hall
at 7 P.M.
by
EDWARD BRADLEY

"Shall we go?" asked Bernard.

It was almost the hour as they made their way down the wandering side lanes that led to the wharves and the town hall. There, hidden deep in the crowd, they stood by an open window through which they could see the ever-present channel and the waters of the bay. The gaslights in the hall hummed like flies, huge green luminous flies that had floated in from the half night outside, so blue and lovely where it sank down, darker and darker, over the masts and the brown sails of the fishing smacks in the harbor, and far in the distance the peaked mountains that Bernard knew so well. It was so lovely to watch the hollow night fall outside, and through it now and again a green light climbing up a mast, and to turn from it to the pale pink-washed green-lit room within, that they paid but little heed to the speakers until their friend the teacher rose.

The years between that night and the day in the market square had not dulled his eloquence, and though his temples were gone quite white now — premature for his years — the terrible passion of the man blazed iike the fire of burning youth. Yet as he talked the lovers did not join in the cheers of the audience. The night had fallen now and nothing showed beyond but the eyes of green or red on mast and poop. The mountains had vanished. The far woods were gone. They barely heard the lapping of the bay. As by one thought they moved quietly out through the cheering crowd into the darkness. But, shyly, they did not go back directly to their hotel. Wrapped in their own silence and the silence of the night they wandered about the quays or in and out among the lanes as if prolonging the night to the very last moment. The meeting was over before they returned to their hotel, and the lights of the houses in that street, and doubtless of every street in the town, were gone up to the second story. When they entered their room they saw that the pale light of the gas lamp outside the window fell on the high old-fashioned ceiling and from there glimmered down on the wide, carved bridal-bed, and needing no other light they used none. Across the street was another row of sleeping houses, and beyond that the bay, widening to the ocean, and when they stood without stirring they could hear the low boom of the waves on the cliffs and across the bar. As they undressed, the faint hum of a motor rose in the distance and approached along the street.

"Bernard," she whispered.

Over his shoulder he could see her pale body in the dim light, but where he stood by the window with one hand raised to draw down the blind his eyes fell on the passing car. He saw the white hair of their orator friend, the old bachelor, the patriot, driving out of the town into the country and the dark night. The hedges would race past him; the rabbits skip before his headlights on the road; the moths in the cool wind would fly round his flushed face and his trembling hands. But that wind would not for many miles cool the passion in him to which he had given his life.

"Bernard," she whispered again, and her voice trembled a little.

He drew the blind down slowly. The lamp shadowed the framework of the window on it. Slowly he turned to her where she gleamed even in the dark.

A Broken World

"THAT'S a lonely place!" said the priest suddenly. He was rubbing the carriage window with his little finger. He pointed with the stem of his pipe through the window, and the flutter of snow and the blown steam of the engine, at the mountainy farm to his right. He might have been talking to himself, for he did not stir his head or remove his elbow from its rest. He was a skeleton of a man, and the veins of his temples bulged out like nerves. Peering I could barely see, below the pine forest of "The Department," through the fog of the storm, a lone chapel and a farmhouse, now a tangle of black and white. Although it was the middle of the day a light shone yellow in a byre. Then the buildings swiveled and were left behind. The land was blinding.

"Aye!" I said. "It is lonely. But," I said easily, "sure every parish is a world in itself."

He grunted and pulled at his cherrywood pipe and kept looking out the window at the whirling dots of white.

Then, without looking at me — looking down at the flap of my trousers, instead — he leaned forward, one bony hand gripping his left knee, and his elbow resting on the other knee so that he might still hold and smoke his pipe in comfort. I could see that he spoke less for the sake of conversation than from a desire to instruct me, for he seemed to get no other pleasure out of his talk.

"That used to be a credo with me, too," he said, "that every parish is a world in itself. But where there is no moral unity there is no life."

"Moral unity?"

There were ten notes in the wind, boom and whistle and groan and sigh. Listening to them I hardly heard him. The snow had stopped.

"Yes." He was cock-assuredly positive. "Life is a moral unity with a common thought. The *compositum* of one's being, emerging from the Divine Essence, which is harmony itself, cannot, unless it abdicates its own intelligence and lives in chaos, that is to say, in sin, be in disunity with itself. Since society, however, is an entity composed of many members, life becomes a moral unity with a common thought. You can see that?"

"Yes."

He went on, while I wondered if he was a professor in some seminary trying out something he had been studying. He enunciated his ideas with indrawn lips. That gave him a hellish, pedagogic look. The glare outside turned him into marble.

"In places like that you have a broken world, and there is no unity."

In spite of this abstract way of talking the next thing he said showed me that he was not a professor.

"Let me give you an example of what life is like in those isolated places," jerking his head. "When I was ordained my first parish was a lonely parish in the County Wicklow. From my presbytery window I could see the entire coast, a long straight beach, miles to the north, miles to the south, with a headland at each end stuck out into the sea. By the sea it is marsh. Then comes the first wave of highland around villages like Newtownmountkennedy. The land isn't bad on those hills, though it isn't what you would call really good land. They grow good turnips and potatoes and mangolds; the greens are not bad; but they cannot grow wheat. You need a good marl bottom for wheat. I was a young man then, and keen, so I studied these questions."

(Whatever else you were, I said to myself, you must have been a bloody bore.)

"Look!" he said, pointing through the opposite window.

A vast white plain, level as a sea, mapped with black hedgerows, all diminishing in size, spread away and away, maybe twenty miles, to a much lower range of mountains.

"My parish was in the same relation to that good land as these mountains here" — nodding over his shoulder — "in relation to that plain. That is to say, it was mountain bog, reclaimed by much labor, but always badly drained. Last of all, beyond me, was the utterly, miserably" — his voice was almost oratorical here — "wretched moor. Miles and miles of it on the plateau of the mountaintops. The native tribes lived as freebooters up there as late as the end of the eighteenth century. It was wooded then, and untouched by any road. Then, in ninety-eight, two so-called military roads cut it across and across like a scissors. They were fifty miles long, and straight as rulers. By the way," he asked suddenly, catching me looking idly out through the window, "were you ever in County Wicklow?"

"Oh, no, Father," I replied, as suddenly. I forced myself to attend. Just then my eye caught the eye of an old farmer seated opposite me in the carriage; he was midway on the same seat as the priest, and, so, near enough to hear everything. A pool of water had gathered around each boot. Spits starred the dry patch between. Seeing me look at him he took from his mouth, with his entire fist, a bit of a cigarette he was smoking, and winked at me. Then he put back the cigarette and contemplated the priest's face with an air of childlike wonderment. At that wink I began to listen more carefully. Evidently my priest was a local "character."

"They are remarkable roads," went on the priest. "Well, the people of my parish were all poor. The interesting thing about them is that there were two sets of names — either the old tribal names, like O'Toole or O'Byrne or Doyle, or foreign names like Ryder, Nash, Greene, Pugh, Spink, Empie, Gascon, Latour."

A little smile took the corners of his mouth as he said those names; but he never raised his eyes.

"The Greenes and Ryders and Pughs, and the rest of them, were soldiers who long ago trickled down into the houses of the poor, intermarried there, and became poor themselves as a result. However, they brought the people respect for law and order. Or, if you like, they knocked the last bit of rebel spirit out of them."

"Interesting!" I said, politely. I was beginning to enjoy the joke, for I could see the old farmer getting cross, and at the end of that last bit he had spat out his butt end of cigarette.

"But the middle land, the good land, remained in the possession of the big people who never intermarried. When I went there to take over my duties I looked up the history of these wealthy people in *Debrett* and *Who's Who*, and *Burke's Landed Gentry*."

His palm became an imaginary book, and with his pipestem he followed the lines and pretended to read:

"'Lord Blank, family name of Baron Blank. Fifth baron. Created in eighteen hundred and one. Lieutenant of the Seventeenth Hussars. Married Dorothy, oldest daughter of, let's say something like James Whipple Teaman of Grange House, Dilworth, Dorsetshire, you know the kind of thing. Succeeded his father in nineteen-eighteen. Educated at Eton and Sandhurst. Address, Grosvenor Square, London. Club — Travellers' or Brooks's. Recreations? Oh, as usual, hunting, shooting, fishing, racquets, riding.'"

Again the thin smile. The farmer was gob-open.

"My parishioners were their stableboys, gate-lodge keepers, woodmen, beaters, farmhands, lady's maids, et cetera. *They* were always intermarrying. *Their* bits of farms, reclaimed from the furze, were always being divided. I've seen people live on a bit of land about twice the size of this carriage."

The farmer leaned forward, listening now with great interest. Our three heads nodded with the jolt of the train.

"Then there was emigration. In the five years I spent there I had one solitary marriage. I had sixty schoolchildren on roll when I went there. I had thirty-five when I left. Last year I heard they were reduced to eleven, and five of those were all one family. No wonder the county is full of ruins. You come on them in scores on scores, with, maybe, a tree growing out of the hearth, and the marks of the ridges they plowed still there, now smooth with grass."

"Begobs, then, they're here too, Father," said the old farmer. The priest nodded sideways to him and proceeded:

"I liked the people. They were clean, hard-working, respectful. Too respectful — tipping their hats to everybody. They were always making what we call 'the poor mouth' — a mendicant habit of centuries, I suppose. They gave me no trouble, except for two things. They had a habit of writing anonymous letters, and I couldn't stop it. They were at it all the time. They wrote them to one another."

He paused. I prompted him.

"The other thing?" I asked.

The farmer leaned closer and closer.

"The other thing?" he said irritably to his pipe bowl. "In every one of these cabins they earned money by taking in boarded-out children — children unwanted by poor parents, or simply illegitimates. There was hardly a cottage without one, two, or three of these stranger children. They were well looked after, and the people often grew so fond of them they wouldn't part with them; and, I suppose, that was a nice trait too. But the point is that the only fresh blood coming into the county was . . . Well — a curious county, as you can see, and the morals were a bit curious too. However, that's enough about them."

And he had at least enough sense to go no further with that.

"Well, there you are. That was my parish, and you can't say it

was a world in itself. It was too incomplete. Too many things left
out. The human dignity of men is always impaired when, like that,
they're depending on other people who can make or break them.
They weren't men. They were servants. That's the whole of it."

"But did that make their lives lonely? You said they were
lonely?"

For the first time he looked up at me. The veins on his temples,
swollen from holding his head down, throbbed with relief.

"I didn't say *they* were lonely."

His eyes wavered sideways to the farmer. I easily followed him
over the hiatus when he jumped to —

"One day, after three years without stepping out of the parish, I
decided to see if the neighboring parish was any better." (When I
heard the personal note come into his voice I wished the farmer
was not there; as it was he kept to his cold, factual description.)

"Do you know, the contrast was amazing! When I climbed down
to the valley and the good land! And it was the trees that made me
realize it. Beeches instead of pines. Great, old beeches with roots
like claws on the double ditches. The farmhouses, too. They were
large and prosperous with everything you might expect to find
in a sturdy English farm — barns, ducks in the pond, thick-packed
granaries, airy lofts, a pigeon croft, a seat under an arbor, fruit
gardens.

"All that was good. But it was those beeches that really impressed
me. They were so clean and old, not like the quick-growing pines of
the mountains — dirty trees that scatter their needles into the shoots
of the houses and block them up three times every winter."

"Oh, they're buggers, Father!" agreed the farmer earnestly.

"I climbed lower still and came to the gates of the houses where
the gentry used to live."

"Used to?"

"Used to. I should have expected it, but somehow it hadn't occurred to me. It's funny how we all forget how time passes. But
there they were — the gateposts falling. The lodges boarded up.

Notices, *For Sale*. Fifteen years of grass on the avenues. You see? 'Owns ten thousand acres in Ireland. Address, Grosvenor Square, London.'"

The pipestem traveled across the palm.

"I met an old man who took me down one of those avenues to see the ruins of a big house burned out during the troubled times. It was a lovely spring evening. The sky was like milk. The rooks were cawing about the roofless chimneys just like the flakes of soot come to life again. I spotted a queer little building at the end of a cypress avenue. The old man called it 'the oftaphone.' He meant octagon. It was a kind of peristyle. He said, 'The Lord'—just like that—'The Lord used to have tea parties and dances there long ago.' I went into it and it had a magnificent view, a powerful view, across the valley over at my mountainy parish, yes, and beyond it to the ridges of the mountains, and even beyond that again to the very moors behind with their last little flecks and drifts of snow. They could have sat there and drunk their tea and seen my people—the poor Ryders, and Greenes, and O'Tooles—making little brown lines in the far-off fields in the plowing time."

"They could! Oh, begobs, Father, so they could!"—and a mighty spit.

"Or at night, of summer evenings, they could have sipped their brandy and coffee and seen the little yellow lights of our cabin windows, and said, 'How pretty it is!'"

"Begobs, yes! That's true!"

If anyone entered the carriage then he would have taken us for three friends, we were huddled together so eagerly. The priest went on:

"'They must have had good times here, once?' I said to the man who was with me. 'The best, Father!' says he. 'Oh, the best out. The best while they lasted. And there were never any times like the old times. But they're scattered now, Father,' says he, 'to the four winds. And they'll never come back.' 'Who owns the land now?' I asked him. 'They own it always, but who wants it?' says he. 'The people here don't want it. They'd rather live in the towns and cities and work for wages.'"

"That's right," said the farmer, as if we were really discussing his own county. "Begobs, you're talking sense now, Father!"

" 'The land was kept from them too long,' says he. 'And now they have lost the knack of it. I have two grown sons of my own,' says he, 'and they're after joining the British Army.' "

"Begobs, yes!" said the farmer, leaning to catch every word; but the priest stopped and leaned back.

The white, cold fields were singing by us. The cabins so still they might be rocks clung to the earth. The priest was looking at them and we were all looking at them, and at the flooded and frozen pools of water divided by the hedgerows. By his talk he had evoked a most powerful sense of comradeship in that carriage, whether he meant to or not: we felt one. Then, as quickly, he proceeded to break it.

"Well?" I asked eagerly. "Well?"

"Why, that's all!" said the priest. "I came back from my voyage of exploration much refreshed. Much improved in spirits. You see, I had extended the pattern of life of my own poor parish. I saw how, how — I mean, how the whole thing had worked, hung together, made up a real unity. It was like putting two halves of a broken plate together. As I walked up another one of those hill roads on my way home I passed more prosperous houses — smaller houses this time, what you would call private houses. They had neat, green curtains with fine, polished brassware inside on the polished mahogany. And through another window three aluminum hot-water bottles shining on a dark hall table, signs of comfort, as you might say. . . . Yes! I had completed the pattern. That parish and my parish made up a world, as neither did by itself, rich and poor, culture and . . ."

"But," I cried angrily, "where's your moral unity? Your common thought? It's absurd."

"Oh, yes! I realized that even before I got home. I just tell you the thing as it happened. But they in their octagon and we in our lighted cabins, I mean to say, it was two halves of a world. . . ."

The farmer was looking at us both with dull, stupid eyes. He had lost the thread of the talk.

"Yes, I suppose so," I agreed, just as lightly. "But now that the gentry are gone, won't the people, the mountainy people, and so on, begin to make a complete world of their own?"

He shook his head. The farmer listened again.

"I refuse to believe they won't," I said.

He shrugged his shoulders.

"And is there no possible solution, then?" I asked him.

He was looking out of the window, his poll to the farmer. He rolled up his eyes under his brows — a warning look — and faintly indicated the man behind him. Then he actually began to laugh, a cold, cackling laugh, an extraordinary, inhuman kind of laugh that ended in a noise like a little groan.

The train slowed up, and we were in a station, and he was gathering his bags. He got out without even saying "Good day" to us, and his face was coldly composed. A manservant, touching his cap, took the bags. The stationmaster touched his cap to him. The porter receiving the tickets touched his cap to him. The jarvey, who was waiting for him, bowed as he received the bags from the manservant. Black, tall, thin, and straight as a lamp post, he left the lit, snow-bright station with every downlooking lounger there bowing and hat touching as he passed. When I turned away, the train was moving out, and the old farmer, in his own place, had lit another cigarette.

"Do you know his Reverence?" I asked — as irritated as somebody from whom a book has been snatched before the end of the tale.

"Oh, aye!" said the old man, and he added, without interest, "He's silenced."

There was a touch of dread in that word, *silenced*.

"What did they silence him for?"

"Politics."

"Oh? He was too extreme?"

"Aye!" Still without interest.

"A clever man?"

No answer. His mind had gone to sleep. I looked at him in annoyance.

"What kind of ideas had he? I mean, what did he want?"

"Begobs, I dunno."

Then he added, as if it was a matter of no importance:

"He wanted the people to have the land."

"What land?"

"The land. The gentry's land."

I leaned to him eagerly —

"But isn't that what ye want? Isn't that what the whole trouble is? Isn't that what the government wants?"

"Aye. I suppose it is, you know? But he wanted it to be a sudden business."

"They didn't silence him for that?"

"Maybe they didn't. Ach, he's odd. Sure, he took ten or twenty foolish young lads and, one night, he thrun down the walls of Lord Milltown's estate. He started some sort of a league, too. He's odd. God help him."

"What did he want to do with this league of his?"

"I dunno. It was some kind of faddy business. He wanted halls . . . and . . . some kind of halls he wanted. Halls. I dunno what he wanted 'em for. Ah, he's a decent poor man."

I tried another line.

"I suppose it's true for his Reverence — ye have a hard time of it up here on the poor land?"

Puffing at his ease he was looking idly at the passing fields. A woman and two small boys, crushed into the doorway of a cabin, waved to us. He looked, and when they were gone his eyes were still fixed, seeing whatever passed beneath them with equal interest — or disinterest?

He tilted his head, but he said nothing. I made one last effort to shake him from his lethargic mood — possibly, most likely indeed, the mood in which he spent the greater part of his life.

"You know," I said, warmly, "I think I'd die in this lonely place. That priest is right!"

He looked at it, and scratched his ear, and said:

"Aye!" And then, suddenly, he added a second "Aye!" — and then, when I thought he was finished, he actually added, "I suppose 'tis quiet," and relapsed into indifference.

Angrily I burst out at him:

"But, damn it all, don't you mind, or is it that ye don't want to stir, ye're too damn lazy to stir?"

He took the butt end from his mouth, and he looked at me, and by the way he looked up and down at me, I was hoping he would say something bitter and strong. But his stare was childish, and the eyes wavered, as if he was very tired. He just dropped one last, vast spit on the wet floor, snuggled into his corner, and went to sleep under his hat.

In his sleep he was as motionless as a rock; but you could not say he was "like a rock" because he was like nothing on earth but himself, everything about him was so personal to him. Unless, because he was so much a random accumulation of work and season and all that belongs to the first human that was ever made, I chose to say, as I glared at him snoring in his corner, that time and nature had engendered something no more human than a rock. So I thought, as the dusk drew down, and the wind moaned in many keys, and the snow blew horizontally and stuck to the edges of the window. It was as if we two might have been jolting into a blank, beyond either sleep or night, and I wanted to get up and kick him. I felt that if I did he would only moo.

We halted at several stations, with their one or two silent white-shouldered figures. He slept on. I was just wondering if I should wake him when suddenly, at a station, identical with every other station, as if some animal magnetism in the place stirred him, he rose and stumbled out. He did not speak. He did not raise his head to see if it was his station. He saluted no one. Anyway, there was no one there but a muffled porter who silently waved a lantern over his head. As we moved off he was trudging in the middle of a road that glimmered with its own strange afterglow, passing between a row of pines whose sheltered sides were red and raw as with the cold. He was exactly like an old black mongrel loping home.

So I was left with the pool of water on the floor, dark under the carriage light, and the snow crumbling into the corners of the windows outside, and beyond that only the light leaping and falling along the hedges. And in another two hours or so, when I got out, the carriage would be racing along, empty, through the night — three bits of separateness, the priest and the farmer and myself, flung off it like bits of the *disjecta membra* of the wheel of life.

For those two hours I tried to refute the talk of that priest, thinking that he had merely spoken out of the snowy landscape, which above all other conditions of nature is so powerful to make life seem lonely, and all work futile, and time itself a form of decay; or thinking that, had it been the green-dripping spring or the hot summer, we might all have shown different and more happy sides of our worlds; or thinking that the thin cheeks and the throbbing nerves of the man were nothing but the sign of twenty years of self-corrosion, and that even when he was a young man in his first parish, his heart must have been so bitter and vain that, like a leech, it began to destroy everything to preserve itself; or thinking that because of it he had joined us for a few moments until we seemed to crouch over a fire, and then deliberately scattered us and left us with his pox. But, though that might be all true, I could not deny to the wintry moment its own truth, and that under that white shroud, covering the whole of Ireland, life was lying broken and hardly breathing. His impress remained even when the train swished slowly into the city, where the arc lamps sizzled in the snow, and the sounds were muffled, and through every street a sharp, pure wind blew down from the Wicklow hills. Once their distant convex gleamed, far away, beyond the vista of a street. There were few people abroad, and as they walked against the wind with huddled backs they, too, seemed to be shrouding something within them that slept, and barely palpitated, and was hurt by the cold. What image, I wondered, as I passed through them, could warm them as the Wicklow priest had warmed us for a few minutes in that carriage now chugging around the edge of the city to the sea? What image of life that would fire and fuse us all, what music bursting like the spring, what triumph, what engendering love, so that those breasting mountains that now looked cold should appear brilliant and gay, the white land that seemed to sleep should appear to smile, and these people who huddled over the embers of their lives should become like the peasants who held the hand of Faust with their singing one Easter morning? Perhaps it was foolish to wish for such an image — so magnificent that it would have the power of a resurrection call? Yet, there are times, as when we hear the percussion of some great music, or when we feel the shriveling effect of the cold wind and snow, that leave us no other choice but to live splendidly, or gather up at least enough grace for a quick remove.

The train could be heard easily, in the rarefied air, chugging across the bridges that span the city, bearing with it an empty coach. In the morning, Ireland, under its snow, would be silent as a perpetual dawn.

The Old Master

WHEN I was younger, and so, I suppose, in the nature of things, a little more cruel, I once tried to express John Aloysius Gonzaga O'Sullivan geometrically: a parabola of pomposity in a rectangle of gaslight. The quip pleased everybody who knew the reference — it was to his favorite stand, under the portico of the courthouse, his huge bulk wedged into the very tall and slender doorway.

I said *gaslight* because John Aloysius rarely came to work before the afternoon, when they lit the gas in the dim entrance hall, and its greenish, wateryish light began to hiss high up in the dome. There he would stand, ten times in the afternoon, smoking, or watching the traffic, or gossiping with some idling clerk. He had a sinecure in the fusty-musty little law library, a room no bigger than a box. He used to say, in his facetious way, that he left it often because he exhausted the air every half hour.

As the assizes came to us only four times each year, and the library was rarely used between the sessions, he was not hard worked. He was always at liberty to practice at the bar, but he never did —

he was a bachelor without attachments and he had a small private income.

The last time he took up his stand in the doorway was the Tuesday of the week the Russian Ballet came to town. That day he became a next-to-permanent feature of the portico. He wanted to talk to everybody about it, until we were sick of the sight of him.

Higgins, the doorkeeper, got the brunt of it; he also got a relay of John A.'s best Egyptian cigarettes. Peter Cooney, Secretary of the Poor Law Guardians, got the remnants — invited specially to drink coffee with John Aloysius in the library, and look, for the thousandth time, at his naughty prints of Ingres's *La Source* (the naked girl with the pitcher), or Fragonard's *The Swing* (the shepherdess-lady being swung much too high above the gentleman in silk knee breeches and ribboned shirt). They were good listeners, the one because he had nothing else to do, the other because he liked the coffee — it was good coffee, ground in a special little French hand mill, and flavored with a fine liqueur brandy — and because, too, he loved the romantic flavor of the tiny library with its books stacked to the ceiling, and he really admired John Aloysius, and thought him a most cultivated man, and a most refined man — even if he did tell smutty stories and had a bad name with the women.

To Higgins, the doorkeeper, John Aloysius would say — with the cigarette poised before his mouth, and the fat little finger cocked in the air — "Higgins, I am outshone. Up to last night, Higgins, I was the sole particle of color in this diminutive jakes of a town. I alone brought color and culture into this kraal that goes by the name of Cork. But I am honorably outshone. Russia has eclipsed me."

That was his regular way of talk. And if nobody took it seriously, nobody took it comically, either. For he always talked with a slightly cynical air, an ambiguous kind of self-mockery, and he never smiled. God alone knows if ever he said to himself, in the silence of the night, "John Aloysius Gonzaga O'Sullivan, you're a sham!" Such men have no life but their own drama, and if you had dared say that to him he would probably have replied, "Is it not as good a life as another?"

"Look at this courthouse, Higgins!" John Aloysius would go on. "Look at it! I have seen the Lord Chief Justice enter this building between files of cuirassiers with shining breastplates, uplifted sabers, snowy plumes. A vision of scarlet and ermine, Higgins. But that was in the good old days, before these yahoos from the heath, these bog trotters of Gaelic Leaguers, these bagmen, these Attacotti, these tin-pot patriots with the smell of dung on their boots, set the grass growing on the streets. But now, Higgins, what do we see? We see Justice arrive in a bowler hat and flannel bags. My God, Higgins! It's a symbol. And I am left! I am left! I am left, Higgins, like an old master, lying forgotten in a deserted mansion."

"Aye, aye, sir!" Higgins would respond, like the old Navy man he was.

And John Aloysius would pat his third and hairless chin, and tip his deep-bayed collar, with the tips of his pink fingers, and, in disgust at the changed world, fling his cigarette on the mossy steps of the courthouse, lingering for a second to watch some ragged-pants pick it up — his jewel flung in largess. Then he would stalk away, his great torso swaying like a young elephant from side to side, and he would bid Peter Cooney come to the library, and, lolling in his armchair, take up the tale again.

"Cooney, that fellow Higgins is a boor, a gun-room lout, a deck swabber. Why must John Aloysius Gonzaga O'Sullivan associate with such offal? Can you tell me that, Cooney? You, at least, however ignorant, have been to the ballet once — you have made your obeisance to that loveliness of which these, and these" — indicating the naughty prints, at which Cooney would be trying hard to look objectively — "are but the whispering echoes. Think of it, Cooney! Russia is at our doors — the greatest civilization in the world, crushed under the elephant feet of these yahoos of Bolsheviks, these hairy moujiks from Siberia, these Circassian Huns who never knew what beauty was — that Russia is come to our city. And what happens, Cooney? Pwah! The swine do not even smell the pearls. Last night — a first night — the theater — you saw it yourself — was *empty!*"

"O, bejaney, John A.," Peter would mumble, " 'tis a bloody shame."

"My dear boy, we are shamed before the civilized world. How can I lift my head again in London? Or in Paris? The name of this city will stink in the nostrils of every artist in Europe. St. Petersburg comes to Cork — for so, in my dreams, I sometimes call that lovely city, and think to see again her lovely streets. . . . And Cork ignores her. The Nevsky Prospect, Cooney; the sleighs on the Voznesensky; the Gorokhoyava Ulitsa, lit from end to end by the rising sun! (It runs due southeast, Cooney.) The Neva frozen and glittering! All that! And Cork ignores it!"

(That was typical John Aloysius — he devoured travel books to the point of believing himself that he had traveled the world.)

"Cooney! Will you tell me why do I live here? Why does John Aloysius Gonzaga O'Sullivan live in a sewer? You say nothing? I know why. You are saying to yourself, 'But what an error!' you are saying. 'Surely,' you are saying, 'the sewers of Paris, as compared with this chamber pot of a town, are as translucent Pierian spring?' And you are quite right. My boy, you show great intelligence."

And so, having smoked Peter, and eased his own heart, off with him again to Higgins, and back again to his office, as restless as a hen with an egg, all that Tuesday afternoon, waiting until he should be seated again in the stalls, in his starched shirt and his tails — the only man, he was certain, who would dress for the event.

He knew he would be rubbing his paunch around and around, in an ecstasy, watching the limbs twine and untwine, the waves of *Les Sylphides* advance and retire, the heads nod, the knees rise, the arms upflinging. . . . In his library he blew little secret kisses at his vision. As he dressed he promised himself, 'fore God, that he would go around after the show to the stage door and congratulate them in person. He might even take one of the ladies to supper. . . . He trembled at the thought. . . . And he knew that he was the only man in all Ireland who had the wit and grace to do it — the only man left in all Ireland with a sense of beauty . . . the old master deserted in the abandoned house.

What a phrase! "The old master on the walls — silent and dignified — while the bailiffs belowstairs drank their gin. . . ." As he walked to the theater he polished the phrase, and he swayed on his hips like a young elephant.

Nobody knows if he said all that, but we can well infer it from what happened. For at the door of the theater John Aloysius got a shock. He heard his name pronounced in full at his elbow — "John Aloysius Gonzaga O'Sullivan," spoken in a cold, malicious voice. Turning, he saw two men looking at him, one with a scornful frown, the other sheepishly. The frowner held a notebook in his hand and he was writing down the name. The other, of all people, was his satellite, Peter Cooney.

"What may this be?" stormed John Aloysius.

Cooney blushed and fidgeted, but the other spoke up.

"We're taking down the name of every man who enters the theater tonight."

He was a fine, healthy young man, with red, high cheekbones, blue eyes, a soft mouth. John Aloysius recognized him; he was a doctor named Quill.

"And for what purpose, in the name of heaven?" asked John A., with a sick feeling beginning to crawl around his stomach.

"We think it's an indecent performance," said Quill.

John Aloysius looked where he pointed and saw a little procession of young men marching around the square; among them were, also, some young women and boys. One man carried a placard which said:

Men of Saint Mark
We Have Them Marked!
DOWN WITH IMMORAL PLAYS!

He thought quickly of his job. It was a nice job. But it had to be renewed by the county council every year, and that was sometimes a delicate business.

"Dear me," he said, and for Cooney's benefit he tried to say it as facetiously as possible. "And is it as bad as all that? Have you, I mean to say, have you seen the performance?"

"I wouldn't be seen supporting it," said Quill.

Cooney was restive. He drew John A. aside.

"To tell you the gospel truth, John A.," he said, wrinkling up his nose apologetically, "Dr. Quill can say anything he likes, but it's the way I *couldn't* be seen supporting it. I'm in this all on account of Canon Paul. As you know, what he says goes. But take my advice now, John A., and let it alone. 'Twill be better for you."

"And do you mean to stand there," stormed John Aloysius, "and admit to me that you are such a craven wretch . . ."

"None of that," threatened Quill, turning on them like a flash. "Mr. Cooney has made up his own mind and you can make up yours, too, and as a matter of fact, I'm sure Mr. Cooney doesn't really approve of this performance at all."

It was on the tip of John A.'s tongue to abuse them both. As he caught the flaring lights of the foyer, the gold paint, the smell of the theater's musk, like burned toast, he wanted to ask them if they realized that all the loveliness of Russia was behind those doors, to talk of the Gorokhoyava Ulitsa lit from end to end by the rising sun. He even thought of arguing that the ballet is, by nature, anticommunistic. Rage swelled his neck. He thought of ten bad words to call Cooney — a moujik, a pimp, a blister, a PILE . . .

"I see," he said. "Dear me. I must think it over."

As he walked away from the door he heard the wretched Cooney say, "Cross out that name. Mr. O'Sullivan is with us."

He felt he would choke, or cry. He went around the corner, and to a small newsboy who tried to sell him a paper he said all the ten bad words in a rush. Then he bethought himself and walked quickly to the stage door, casting many glances behind him as he entered. He presented his card and a florin to the doorkeeper, and was finally shown into the dressing room of the dancer who did the part of the Rose in *Le Spectre de la Rose*. The room was full of excited men and women, all talking in loud voices at the same time.

"I have come, sir," said John Aloysius to the dancer, "to congratulate you, and to protest on behalf of my city against these disgraceful scenes outside. I do not wish you, sir, to form the idea that this city is an ignorant city, or a boorish city. It is a most cultivated center of the arts. It always was. I am but one of thousands who feel that your ballet is a glorious thing, and, if I may say so, an uplifting thing."

The dancer was a small, lithe Lithuanian named Rachmanoff. He was no Nijinsky. Where Nijinsky would have hurled himself through the window, ten feet through the air, onto a mattress held by four scene shifters, poor Rachmanoff jumped like any man. He was thirty-eight — near the end of his race as a dancer, and he was touring the small cities of the world, trying to lay up a little store of money against the time when he would dance no more. Eagerly he interpreted to the others, as they crowded around them to know what it all meant. John Aloysius saw the glowing lips and colored cheeks of the girls, their bare arms, their white backs, and smelled the scent of the powder. He felt the air in the musty dressing room grow quick, as when lightning is about to explode the sky.

"It means so much to us," pleaded Rachmanoff. "It will ruin us. Last week in Sheffield we did not do well. And *Cardiff* — you remember *Cardiff?*" He turned to them all, and they all groaned the word *Cardiff!* "Who are these young men?" implored Rachmanoff.

"They are young fools," said John Aloysius. "In fact, they are mere scum! In fact, they are the lowest of the low! As a matter of fact, they're really . . . what you might call, revolutionaries. That's what they are!"

"Not Communists?" begged Rachmanoff.

"Worse than Communists! Perhaps you might call them Fascists. Or Nationalists. It's very complicated."

"What can you do for us?" pleaded the little dancer, and the girls put their white arms around John A.'s shoulders and peered at him beseechingly, as if he were their savior.

"Pay no heed to them," said John Aloysius, feeling the scent fume through his brain. "I am a lawyer. There are ways and means. To-morrow night, I, John O'Sullivan, guarantee it, they will be swept off the streets. I can only apologize for them now. As an old master, as one of the very few old masters, left on the walls of modern times, from the great eras, my friends, as you are of those great eras, I speak, so to speak, and I apologize for them. They will be swept from the streets like the dust before the wind."

Then, hearing the singing of hymns outside the windows, and fearing the young men might come in and find him, he dragged himself away, followed by their beseeching eyes, their pleading smiles, their looks of fear and doubt. His heart was thumping as he left them. But he felt justified. He had given these yahoos their answer. The old master, so to speak, had leaned down from the walls, reproved their ignorance. . . .

So thinking he found himself at the front of the theater again. The procession had swollen to twice its size. Crowds of people were watching it circle round and round. Seeing them all, John Aloysius felt his resolution ebbing away. Suddenly he heard his name spoken again; this time it was Canon Paul, a lean, hollow-browed man with spectacles. With distaste John Aloysius noticed that the glass of the spectacles was dusted with little grains, and browned in the crevices of the frame.

"Mr. O'Sullivan," said the canon, "Dr. Quill has told me how you refused to support this wretched business when you heard of our protest. That's the spirit. I'm so glad you are with us. Only three men have gone into the theater — and, believe me, Mr. O'Sullivan, we'll teach them a lesson."

"Why," muttered John Aloysius, "I mean to say, it's . . . I was thinking . . . after all, it's all right for . . . adults, don't you think, Canon?"

"Ah, but it's the bad example, Mr. O'Sullivan. That's what counts. The young people must be given good example."

"Quite so," said John Aloysius.

"And now, Mr. O'Sullivan, we're going to start. We'll march through the city. Come with me."

Gently but firmly he took John Aloysius by the arm, saying something about the value of educated men, and about ending this sort of thing, and before he could get out of it John Aloysius found himself beside Cooney in the procession with a hymnbook in his hand.

"Now, men!" shouted the canon.

At once John A. imagined himself standing out and denouncing them all. What a great story it would be! And while he thought of it the procession shuffled off and he had to march with it. He saw the crowds fall in behind, marshaled by stewards. They were singing. Cooney was bawling in his ear like a trumpeter. In his white paunch, he himself was the most conspicuous of them all, he was so big and fat, and his tall hat stuck up in the air.

The canon fell in by his side and smilingly urged him to sing. Then as the procession circled around towards the drawn doors of the theater he saw the dancers clustered inside, overcoats over their shoulders, peering out, and they were gesticulating madly and pointing directly at him. He tried to hunch down his shoulders, and bend his knees. He took off his hat. But that looked as if he were trying to put more gusto into his singing, so he put it on again.

"Sing up, Mr. O'Sullivan," urged the canon, singing away himself right into his ear (as Cooney did on the other side), and banging his breviary to mark the time. Viciously John Aloysius sang.

"*Hark,*" he piped.

"Out with it," from the canon.

> "Hark, hear the sound
> Those blessed strains are telling . . ."

"Fine," said the canon. "Louder!"

> "Of that new life," sang John Aloysius,
> "When sin shall be no more. . . ."

They debouched out of the square into the principal street. Crowds gathered on the curbs. Old shawled women bobbed to the canon, and said what a grand man he had with him.

"Somebody is waving to you," cried the canon.

It was Higgins, the doorkeeper, waving cheerfully from the curb. John Aloysius looked sideways out of his pince-nez and bawled away at the hymn, pretending not to see him at all. Presently the canon said:

"We're going to hold a protest meeting in the grand parade. You'll say a few words, of course?"

John Aloysius groaned. Sweat clamped his dress shirt to his back. He felt he was going to assassinate the canon, pull out his lean neck the way you pull the neck of a hen. He saw, down a side street, a little green iron building. Pointing shyly to it, he excused himself to the canon, dived from the ranks, and, with his tails in the air, raced down the street and took refuge inside the privy.

As he turned into it he saw Cooney racing after him.

"You vomit!" cried John Aloysius, mopping his brow inside the building.

"The canon wants you to speak!" protested Cooney.

"I have a colic," said John Aloysius. "A bad colic. I get them often," and he began to unfasten his vest. "Go away, you scoundrel, you . . ."

"But the canon!" cried Cooney.

"I'll follow after you," said John Aloysius. "Go now, please go. It's so embarrassing. I'll join you in five minutes. I swear it!"

Unwillingly Cooney went. There was an old man there, too. He had a belt across his knees. John Aloysius peered out.

"Wha's all the singin' about?" grunted the old man.

"Some damn yahoos!" said John Aloysius. "Clodhoppers! Protesting about something or other! Saying something is immoral."

The old man grunted. John Aloysius decided it would be safer to join him. They were now sitting side by side.

"All nonsense, of course," said John Aloysius. "As one of the old world — an old master — left by the tide — as you might say . . ." He peered out carefully and saw the procession pass the end of the street. "They know nothing. The beauty of the world. The grace of the human body. All lost on them."

The old man grunted. John Aloysius looked at him in disgust. He lit an Egyptian cigarette and thought of the white arms of the dancers.

"The rhythm of the human form," he murmured. "Lost to them. Its life. Its color. Know nothing. Never will."

The sun streamed down diagonally into them. It was September and it had the softness of spring in it. Far away they heard the singing, the clear voices of boys and young women rising through the air, and they were — though John Aloysius hardly thought so — also springlike and clear, sweet as a shower through sunlight.

"The Gorokhoyava Ulitsa," murmured John Aloysius.

The voices sang:

> "Though our hearts be wrapped in sorrow,
> From the hope of dawn we borrow
> Promise of a glad tomorrow,
>   All through the night."

John Aloysius was left alone. The sun faded, but he was afraid to stir. He heard the sound of cheering. He formed the phrases he would use tomorrow to denounce Cooney. "A man of no courage. I, at least, made my protest. Spoke my mind. To the dancers. Defended beauty." It grew darker, and the soft voices rose again in another hymn. He stole away, wandering down devious side streets, polishing his invective, swaying as he went.

In the end he never said a word to Peter Cooney. He got his death of cold out of it, and within two weeks pneumonia had him whipped. But the strange thing is that, somehow or other . . . John Aloysius had a good time . . . amused everyone . . . enjoyed life . . . but nobody ever thought of him as anything but a free, public show while he was alive, and we only began to think of him as a human being when he was gone.

I wonder is there any wrong or right in that? Or is it, as John would have said, that one kind of life is just the same as another in the end?

Sinners

THE canon, barely glancing at his two waiting penitents, entered the confessional. From inside he looked wearily across at the rows of penitents on each side of Father Deeley's box, all still as statues where they sat against the wall, or leaned forward to let the light of the single electric bulb, high up in the windy roof, fall on their prayer books. Deeley would give each about ten minutes, and that meant he would not absolve the last until near midnight. "More trouble with the sacristan," sighed the canon, and closed the curtains and lifted his hand towards the slide of the grille.

He paused. To banish a sudden restiveness he said a prayer. He often said that prayer — an Aspiration Against Anger. He had remembered that on the other side of the grille was a little serving-girl he had sent out of the box last Saturday night because she had been five years away from confession and did not seem to be a bit sorry for it. He lifted his hand, but paused again. To add to his difficulty — for it was no help to know what, under the sigillum, he must pretend not to know — he had just been told in the sacristy by her employer that a pair of her best boots was missing. Why on earth, he sighed, did people reveal such things to him? Did he *want* to know the sins of his penitents? Was the confession being made to him, or to God? Was it . . . He lowered his hand, ashamed of his irritation, and repeated the prayer. Then he drew the slide, cupped his ear in his palm to listen, and saw her hands clasping and unclasping, as if her courage was a little bird between her palms trying to escape.

"My poor child," he said, ever so gently, dutifully pretending to know nothing about her, "tell me how long it is since your last confession."

"It's a long time, Father," she whispered.

"How long?" To encourage her he added, "Over a year?"

"Yes, Father."

"How much? Tell me, my poor child, tell me. Two years?"

"More, Father."

"Three years?"

"More, Father."

"Well, well, you must tell me, you know."

In spite of himself his voice was a little pettish. The title "Father" instead of "Canon" was annoying him, too. She noted the change of voice, for she said, hurriedly:

" 'Tis that, Father."

" 'Tis what?" asked the canon a shade too loudly.

"Over three years, Father," she prevaricated.

He wondered if he could dare let the prevarication go; but his conscience would not let him.

"My dear child, how much over three years is it?"

" 'Tis, 'tis, Father, 'tis . . ."

The canon forestalled the lie.

"My dear child, how much over three years is it? Is it four years? And would you mind calling me *Canon?*"

The breathing became faster.

" 'Tis, Father, I mean, 'tis more, *Canon,* Father."

"Well, how much? I can't make your confession for you, you know."

" 'Tis a bit more, Father."

"But how much?" broke from the canon.

"Two months," lied the maid, and her hands made a flutter of whiteness in the dark.

The canon almost wished he could break the seal of the confessional and reveal to her that he knew exactly who she was, and how long she had been away; all he dared say was:

"I suspect you're telling me a lie."

"Oh, God, Father, it's gospel truth."

"But" — the canon tapped the cushion — "there's no use in telling me if it's not the truth. For God's sake, my poor child" — he controlled himself — "maybe it's five years?"

" 'Tis five years," admitted the maid in so low a voice that he barely heard it.

He sighed with satisfaction. He straightened his hair on his forehead. Then he leaned nearer to hear her sins, nearer and nearer until his ear was pressed against the lattice.

"Now," he warned, "that is a long time, my child. But, thank God, you have come back at last. You must try hard to remember all — all — your sins. Let me help you. My poor little child! Take the first commandment."

But when he heard the shudder of her breath he knew he had made a bad mistake; she would be seeing a long list of broken commandments before her and she would slur over many of her sins in order to shorten the ordeal.

"I mean to say," went on the canon, annoyed with his own stupidity, "that is one way of doing it. Do you wish to make your confession that way?"

"Yes, Father."

"Very well."

"The first commandment . . ." She stopped in confusion and he realized that she did not even know what the commandment was.

"Did you ever miss Mass on Sundays?" he helped her out, although his knees were beginning to dance with impatience.

"Oh, never, never in my whole life."

"Good. Did you ever swear? Take the Lord's name in vain?"

"Tututut!" said the girl in horror at the very idea.

"Did you ever disobey your parents, cause them pain in any way, give back-answers?"

"I have no parents, Father. Mrs. Higg — my mistress got me from the orphanage."

"Ah! Well . . . er . . . lies? Anger? Have you told lies, or given way to anger?"

"Wisha, I suppose I did, Father. I suppose I told a little lie now and again."

"How often in those five years? On an average? I mean, is it a weakness you have? A habit?"

"God help us, Father, I don't tell many. I only tell 'em when I do be afraid."

"Well, we will say you told lies occasionally. Now the sixth commandment. Have you ever sinned in thought, word, or deed against Holy Purity? The opposite sex, for example. Have you ever misbehaved in any way with men?"

"Oh!" gasped the maid, and her voice thickened.

"Stealing?" prompted the canon, and he waited for her to say that she had stolen Mrs. Higgins's boots.

"I never in my life, Father, stole as much as the head off of a pin. Except when I was small I once stole an apple in the nuns' orchard. And then they caught me and gave me a flaking. And they took the last bite out of my mouth."

"You never stole articles of dress?" threatened the canon, and he suddenly realized that there were only three very unlikely commandments left. "Clothes? Hats? Gloves? Shoes?"

"Never, Father."

There was a long pause.

"Boots?" he whispered.

Suddenly the girl was sobbing violently.

"Father," she wept, "Mrs. Higgins is telling you lies about me. I hate that wan. I . . . I . . . I hate her. I do. She's always prying and poking and prodding at me. She took me from the nuns five years ago and she never gave me a minute's rest. She calls me low names. She tells me I can't be good or wholesome to come out of an orphanage. She is picking at me from dawn to dusk. She's an old bitch . . ."

"My child! My child!"

"I did take the boots. I took them. But I didn't steal them. Sure I haven't a boot on my foot and she has lashings and leavings of 'em. I was going to put them back."

"My child, to take them is the same as to steal them."

"What does she want them for? But she's that mean. Her own daughter ran away from her two years ago and married an Englishman who's half a Freemason. The poor girl told me with her own mouth, only last week, how she's half starved by that husband of hers and they have no money to have a family. But do you think her mother would give her a penny?"

The girl sobbed on. The canon groaned and drew himself up to ease his chest. He could hear the wind whistling up in the roof and he could see the long queue on each side of Father Deeley's box, all still as statues in the dusk of the aisle. Seeing them he groaned again as much as to say, "What's the use? They all deceive themselves. They all think everyone is sinful but themselves only. Or if they say they are sinners, and feel it — it only lasts while they are in the church. Then they go out and are filled with envy and pride and they have no charity." He leaned back.

"My child, my child, my child! For five years you have stayed away from God. If you had died you would have died with that mortal sin on your soul and gone to hell for all eternity. It's the law of the Church, and the law of God, that you *must*, you *must* go to confession at least once a year. Why did you stay away? Look at the way your mind is deformed so that you can't even recognize a sin when you commit it. Is there some sin you haven't told me that you were ashamed to tell?"

"No, Father."

"Didn't your good mistress send you to confession at least every month during those five years?"

"She sent me every week. But it was always of a Saturday night. And one Saturday night I didn't go because I wanted to buy a blouse before the shops shut. Then it was six months before I knew it and I was afraid to go. And, anyway, sure what had I to tell?"

The canon waved his hands weakly and with great sarcasm he said:

"Did you *never* commit a sin?"

"I suppose I told a lie, Father. And there was the apple in the nuns' orchard."

Furiously the priest turned to her, determined to wring the truth from her. In her compartment he heard Lady Nolan-White, his second penitent, coughing impatiently.

"My dear child, you simply must have committed sins during those five years. Be honest with yourself. Come now! Look! Take the most common sin of all. Have you, ever, had what we, vulgarly, call a . . . er . . . call a — boy?"

"I had — once — Father."

"Well, now!" He rubbed his forehead like a man in a great heat and he strained towards her as if he were struggling with her demon. "You were, what do we say . . . er . . . walking out with him?"

"Yes," panted the girl. "In the back lane."

"Well, what shall we say? Did, what do you say, did, er, did any intimacy take place with him?"

"I don't know, Father."

"You know what it is to be immodest, don't you?" cried the canon.

Her breath was panting in and out. She said nothing. She stared at him.

"My poor, poor child, you seem to have small experience of the world. But we must get at the truth. Did he — did you — did either of you ever go beyond the bounds of propriety?"

"I dunno, Father."

Loudly the canon expelled his breath. He was becoming exhausted, but he would not give in. He rubbed his hair all the wrong way, which gave him a wild look. He took off his pince-nez and wiped them.

"You understand plain English, don't you? Now, tell me, tell Almighty God the truth of the thing. Did you ever allow him to take liberties with you?"

"Yes, Father. I mean, no, Father. We were in the lane. No, Father. We didn't do nothing. Nothing much, I mean."

"Five years," moaned the canon, and he hammered his thigh with his first. "And nothing to tell. What kind of Christians . . ." He determined to make one last effort — just one more effort. "Did he ever touch your body?" he asked bluntly.

"No, Father. Well, I mean — no, Father."

Seeing that she was beginning to whimper again he threw up his hands.

"All right, child," he said gently. "Say your Act of Contrition and I'll give you Absolution."

"Father," she whispered, her eyes black through the grille, "I was in bed with him once."

The canon looked at her. She drew back. He leaned away and looked from a distance at the crisscrossed face behind the grille. Then he began to smile, slowly expanding his mouth into a wide beam of relief.

"My child," he whispered, "did anyone ever tell you that you were a little deficient in the head? I mean, you weren't very smart at school, were you?"

"I was always at the top of the school, Father. Mother Mary Gonzaga wanted to make a teacher of me."

"And," growled the canon, now utterly exasperated, and dancing his knees up and down on the balls of his feet like a man in the agony of toothache, "do you kneel there and tell me that you think it no sin to go to bed with a man? Who," he added casually, "isn't your husband?"

"I meant no harm, Father," she palpitated, "and it's not what is in your mind at all, for we didn't do nothing, and if it wasn't for the thunder and lightning that terrified me, I wouldn't do it at all. Mrs. Higgins was down in Crosshaven with Mrs. Kinwall, that's her daughter, and I was all alone in the house, and I was afraid of the dark and the thunder, so Mikey said he'd stay with me, so he stayed, and then it was late and I was 'fraid to be by myself in the bed, so he said, 'I'll mind you,' so I said, 'All right, Mikey, but none of that,' and he said, 'All right, Madgie, none of that,' and there wasn't any of that, Father."

She stared at the canon, who was blowing and puffing and shaking his head as if the whole world were suddenly gone mad.

"It was no harm, Father," she wailed, seeing he did not believe her.

"Once?" asked the canon shortly. "You did this once?"

"Yes, Father."

"Are you sorry for it?" he demanded briefly.

"If it was a sin. Was it, Father?"

"It was," he roared. "People can't be allowed to do this kind of thing. It was a serious occasion of sin. Anything might have happened. Are you sorry?" — and he wondered if he should throw her out of the box again.

"I'm sorry, Father."

"Tell me a sin of your past life."

"The apple in the orchard, Father."

"Say an Act of Contrition."

She ran through it swiftly, staring at him all the while. There were beads of perspiration on her upper lip.

"Say three Rosaries for your penance."

He shot the slide to and sank back, worn out. From force of habit he drew the opposite slide and at once he got the sweet scent of jasmine, but when Lady Nolan-White was in the middle of her confiteor he waved his two hands madly in the air and said, hastily:

"Excuse me, one moment . . . I can't . . . it's all absurd . . . it's impossible . . ."

And he drew the slide on her astonished, beautiful, rouged face. He put on his biretta, low down on his nose, and stalked out into the aisle. He parted the curtains on Lady Nolan-White and said:

"It's quite impossible. . . . You don't understand it. . . . Good night!"

He stalked up the dim aisle, and when he met two urchins gossiping in a corner he banged their little skulls together, and at once he became disgusted with himself to see them cowering from him in fright. He passed on, his hand under the tail of his surplice, dancing it up and down. When he saw two old women by the great Calvary, rubbing spittle into the Magdalen's foot and then rubbing the spittle to their eyes or throat, he groaned out, "Oh, dear, oh, dear," and strode on towards Father Deeley's box. There he counted heads — fourteen penitents on one side and twelve on the other — looked at his gold watch and saw it was a quarter past eight.

He strode back to the center compartment and flung aside the curtains. Out of the dimness the warm, cherubic face of the young curate looked at him — a pink Italian saint. Slowly the glow of spiritual elevation died from his face as the canon's insistent whisper hissed down at him:

"Father Deeley, it won't do. I assure you it's absolutely impossible. Half past eight and twenty-six people yet to hear confession. They're just deceiving you. They want to gabble. I am an old man and I understand them. Think of the sacristan. Electric light, too! And gas going until midnight. The organization of the Church . . ."

And so on. All the time he kept stretching and relaxing the mechanical bow of his genteel smile, and he spoke in the most polite voice. But Deeley's face grew troubled, and pained, and seeing it the canon groaned inwardly. He remembered a curate he had once who played the organ every day for hours on end, until the parish-ioners complained that they couldn't pray with the noise he made; the canon recalled how he had gone up into the loft to ask him to stop, and the curate had lifted to him a face like an angel, and how within one half minute it had become the face of a cruel, bitter old man.

"All right, Father Deeley," he said hastily, forestalling protests. "You are young. I know. Still, you are young . . ."

"I am not young," hissed Deeley furiously. "I know my duty. It's a matter of conscience. I can sit in the dark if you are so mean that you . . ."

"All right, all right, all right," waved the canon, smiling furiously. "We are all old nowadays. Experience counts for nothing . . ."

"Canon," said Deeley, intensely, putting his two fists on his chest, "when I was in the seminary, I used to say to myself, 'Deeley,' I used to say, 'when you are a priest . . .' "

"Oh," begged the canon, cracking his face in a smile, "don't, I beg you, please don't tell me your life story!"

Whereupon he whirled away, his head in the air, switching on and off the electric light of his smile to penitents he did not know and had never seen in his life before. He found himself before the high altar. He saw the sacristan standing on a stepladder before it ar-ranging the flowers for the morning, and he thought it would be well to apologize to him for Deeley's late hours. But the sacristan kept turning a vase round and round and round, and at last he realized that the little man was cross with him already, was deliber-ately delaying up there, and would not come down until he was gone.

Sighing, he went away, and after writing some letters he realized that his stomach had ceased to belong to him and would be out on its own devices until morning, like a hound that escapes from its kennel. Wearily he took his hat and cane and decided to take a long walk to calm his nerves.

It was a tender night of floating moonlight, cozily damp, and it soothed him to look down on the city and see the roofs as white as if there were frost on them. More calm, he returned home. The river was like milk. The streets were asleep. He hummed quietly to himself and felt at peace with all men. The clocks of the city chimed at one another in a good-humored mood, slow and with silvery, singing echoes. Then he heard a woman's voice talking from the high window of a cement-faced house, and he saw that it was Mrs. Higgins's house. She was in a white nightdress.

"That's a fine story!" she cried down to the pavement. "Ha! A cockalorum of a story! Wait until I see the canon. At confession, indeed! Wait until I see the nuns! Oh, you jade! You unfortunate poor sinner!"

He saw the little girlish figure cowering down in the doorway.

"Mrs. Higgins," she wailed, "it's gospel truth. The canon threw me out again. I told him all sorts of lies. I had to go to Father Deeley. He kept me half an hour. Oh, Mrs. Higgins," wailed the child, "it's gospel truth."

"Aha!" prated the nightdress. "But you're a nice thing. Wait until I tell . . ."

The canon felt the hound of his stomach jump from the kennel again. His entrails came bodily up to his neck. He marched by, blowing and puffing.

"Oh, my God!" he whined. "Have pity on me. Oh, my God! Have pity on me!"

He turned towards the dark presbytery deep among the darkest lanes.

Admiring the Scenery

FROM between the little wayside platforms the railway shot two shining arrows off into the vast bogland where they vanished over a rise that might have been imperceptible without them. It was just before sunset in early spring, a soft evening of evaporating moisture and tentative bird song; for the birds seemed to be practicing rather than singing, twirling and stopping, and twirling and stopping, and when the bold thrush rolled out a whirl of sound he might have been mocking all the other eager, stupid little fellows, like the bullfinch or the tits, who had not yet learned their songs.

The three men, leaning on the wooden railing along the platform, looked at the blush of the sun on the last drifted snow of the mountains, and though every rail was cut into an A shape on top, uncomfortable for arm or elbow, they found it restful to lean and look over the bog, speaking hardly at all. They had been walking all day and now were dog tired. They were waiting for the last train to take them into the country town where they all three taught in the diocesan college.

The priest stood in the middle, a young man, too fat for his years, with drooping lids, puffed lips, and a red face as if he suffered from blood pressure. The same features on another man might have suggested a sensual nature, but there was in his heavily lidded eyes a look that was sometimes whimsical and sometimes sad, and that look, with the gentle turn to his mouth when he smiled, gave him the appearance of a man who had gone through many struggles and finally solved his problems in a spirit of good-humored regret. So, now, as he pulled at his pipe and looked down into a cold bog stream that flowed beneath them, his chin and his piggy jowls rested on his Roman collar, expanded around his little mouth as if he might at any moment break into a little, silent chuckle. Only, you might have felt, those tired eyes would not even then have changed: they would have mocked his own smile.

On his left, carrying the haversack, was a small dark man, with a slim small body and a button of a head and clipped dark moustaches. The main thing about him was that he did break occasionally into sudden talk, and when he did he banged the hard railings repeatedly or lifted his two fists in the air and slapped his forehead. He did all these things, suddenly, when he cried out:

"Why on earth is this ten-thousand-times-accursed station three miles from the village? What's it here for at all? My God, what a country! What — is — it — for?"

"To take us home," said the third man, and the priest's belly shook a little, too tired to expel laughter.

There was nothing remarkable about this third man except that he had handlebar moustaches and a long black coat and a black hat that came down low on his forehead and shaded his melancholy face; when he spoke, however, his face was gentle as the fluting of a dove. There was nothing resigned about him; his oblong face was blackberry-colored where he shaved and delicate as a woman's where he did not. His eyes were lined with a myriad of fine wrinkles. They were cranky, tormented eyes, and his mouth was thin and cold and hard.

"I know," cried the small man. "It's some bloody czar that did it.

Some fool of an undersecretary long ago or some ass of a flaming lord-lieutenant who took a ruler and drew a line across Ireland and said, 'That shall be the route of the new railway!' God, what a flaming country!"

"I wonder," said the sad man, Hanafan, in his slow voice, "do the common people ever admire scenery?"

"Now that's very interesting, Hanafan," cried the small man across the priest's chest. "That's a most extraordinary thing. I often thought of that. Isn't that a coincidence!"

"Well," said the sad Hanafan, blushing modestly. "it's a common enough idea, you know."

"Of course they do," said the deep basso of the priest.

"But do they, do they, do they?" shouted the little man, hammering the railing.

The priest nodded, never taking his eyes from the stream or his pipe from his little mouth.

"How do you know?" demanded the small man, leaping backward and whirling his head left, right, and up in the air, as if the answer were a bird.

"Why wouldn't they?" grunted the priest.

"I know what you mean," interrupted the small man, and he wagged his finger into the priest's face. "I know. I met men like that. Our gardener at home, for example. I'd say to him — he was an awful old drunkard — he'd be lying of a hot summer's afternoon under an apple tree — a lazy old ruffian — 'Grand day, Murphy,' I'd say. 'Oh, a grand day, God bless it,' he'd say, 'and isn't it good to be alive?' But that's not admiring the scenery," went on the small man. "It's not being *conscious* of it. It isn't, if you understand me, projecting the idea of the beauty of the scene, the idea, into one's own consciousness. Is it, now, Hanafan? And that's what you mean by admiring the scenery."

"Well," said Hanafan, and his words were like prize pigeons that he released one by one from his hands, "I don't know. I'm not sure I mean that."

"Then what the hell *do* you mean?"

"If a man said to me," went on Hanafan, in his downy voice, " 'I do be sometimes sitting here, Mr. Hanafan, enjoying the cool of the evening,' I'd say that that man was enjoying the scenery even though he might not know he was doing so at all."

The priest nodded. The small man looked contemptuously at Hanafan, who now began to quote from Gray's "Elegy" in his round, womanly voice, all the time looking sadly at the warmth of the sun fading from the distant grains of snow, and the mountains becoming black and cold:

"The lowing herd winds slowly o'er the lea . . ."

"I know, I know," interrupted the other, but Hanafan went on quietly:

"The plowman homeward plods his weary way,
And leaves the world to darkness and to me."

"You see, I feel," he said, "that the plowman responded to the sense of the end of the day, and the way the fields were all gentle, and dark, and quiet. Just like that bog there . . . is . . . all . . ."

His voice died out.

"Ah, damn it," said the small man in disgust, "that has nothing to do with it."

"It has, Mr. Governey," murmured the priest. "In a sense it has."

"Every man," cried Hanafan, aroused with such vigor that the other two glanced at him, "lives out his own imagination of himself. And every imagination must have a background. I'll tell you a queer thing. It's about the stationmaster in this station a few years ago."

The priest nodded and chuckled aloud.

"He was nearly sixty-five," said Hanafan. "And he was married, and had a grown-up son in New York, and a daughter, a nun in South America."

"I sent her there," said the priest. "A nice poor girl she was, God rest her."

"Did she die?" asked Hanafan, and when the priest said, "Yes," he fell silent and forgot his story until the other teacher reminded him crossly.

"Yes," said Hanafan. But, again, he stopped because the station porter came out with two oil lamps, one of which he put into the frame of the standard near them.

"It's a grand evening, Father," he said as he turned up the wick.

"Is she late again?" asked the priest, and the porter looked up the line at the signal, and said:

"Aye, she's a trifle behindhand, I'm thinking."

He got down and drew a great silver watch from his corduroy vest and held it up to the setting sun, peering through the yellow celluloid guard.

"She's due, bedad. Ah, she'll be here in a quarter of an hour all right."

The small man groaned and said, "What a country!" The other two looked up at the lamp and then away, and Hanafan said:

"Isn't it dark!"

The porter had walked away.

"Well," resumed Hanafan suddenly, "this old stationmaster! His name was Boyhan. He thought he had a great voice for singing. He was stationed at Newtown and he used to come and sing in the choir with us. That was before your time, Mr. Governey. And he sang in the parish choir. And he'd have sung in the Protestant choir and the Wesleyan choir and the tin-hut choir if they let him. There was not a concert in Newtown that he wasn't the head and tail of it, and he always sang twice and three times, and it was all they could do to keep him from giving encores all night long. For," sighed the teacher, "he had no sense and the people used to make a hare of him. He couldn't sing any more than I could. He had a small little voice, a small range too, but it had no strength or sweetness; there was no richness in it."

The teacher said these words, *strength, sweetness, richness,* with a luscious curl of his thin lips around the fruit of sound. His eyes widened. Clearly he was seeing nothing but the old stationmaster. Earnestly he went on, a small glow on each cheek:

"That was all right until they shifted poor Boyhan to this Godforsaken place. And if Newtown is a lonely hole, this is the back of beyond. At the same time they started the new broadcasting station in Dublin and Boyhan conceived a great ambition to sing there. He formed the idea that some day or other a passenger would be on his way to Dublin, or from Dublin, and he would hear him singing and say, 'My heavens, who is that with the grand voice?' And he would make inquiries — some director or government official — and stop the train and seek out Boyhan and say to him, 'What's the meaning of this neglect? Why haven't you been asked to sing over the radio?' Then there would be paragraphs in the newspapers about Discovery of Great Irish Baritone, and Romance of a Chance-heard Voice, and so on.

"The result of this was that whenever a train rolled in, Boyhan used always to come out of his office singing. He'd be singing little trills up and down the scale, or a bar of 'The Moon Hath Raised Her Lamp Above.' He was known to all the passengers and, sure, they used to be looking out for him. And there he would always be, rubbing his hands and pretending he was doing his do-sol-mi-do just for delight and jollity.

"Well, one hard, moonlight night in December, I was here, like this, waiting for the last train back to Newtown. The snow was white on the hills. It was blazing. There wasn't a sound but the wind in the telegraph wires. The clouds were in flitters, in bits. I well remember it. A rich night. A deep, rich night, and no harm in the winds, but they puffing and blowing."

Again Hanafan's cold thin lips sucked the sound of those words, *rich, deep,* and his eyes dilated under his black hat with the image of his memory. His eyes were not cranky now, but soft and big.

"I was here with a — a — I was here with a — a friend."

He stopped for a second. The small man's eyes pounced on him, observing at once his strange embarrassment. He glanced at the priest, but he had lowered his face and his mouth was clamped. In that hesitant second he saw at once a piece of Hanafan's secret life revealed, a memory of something known also to the priest; the thought of a dead friend — or perhaps a woman — something or somebody that made the memory of that night so precious to Hanafan that he could not speak of it openly.

"Was this long ago?" probed the small man inquisitively.

"We walked up and down," said Hanafan, "looking at the snow under the moon and the clouds tumbling. Then Boyhan came out and he took us across the line. He had a fire and we sat around it. The smell of the peat, thick and slab, was stuck into everything in the room."

"Was it only two of you?" prodded the small man, eager to know if it was a woman.

"He showed us photographs of his daughter, the nun, and of his son, Timsy, with, as he said, a lawn tennis in his hand. He had no wife. She was dead. And there he was living alone, in the station, three miles from the village and his only two children in the world away in exile. I quoted Sir Thomas Browne for him, the passage in *The Quincunx*. We all looked out the little window at the stars of the Plow. 'Think!' said I. '*The quincunx of heaven runs low and 'tis time to close the five ports of knowledge. . . . The huntsmen are up in America and they are already past their first sleep in Persia. But who can be drowsy at that hour which freed us from everlasting sleep, or have slumbering thoughts at that time, when sleep itself must end. . . .*'

"Then, by way of no harm, he began to talk about music and singing and he gave us one song after another. He sang us 'Oft in the Stilly Night' — and, you know, he sang it well. He sang 'The Moon Hath Raised Her Lamp Above.' I heard the signal bell ring as he was in the middle of it and far away the train began to purr.

He was singing it so heartily we didn't like to interrupt him, and as the train became a roar across the bog and the lights went flashing across the window, he rose and went out to the platform. By heavens, that man saw the trainload as a vast audience whirled before him. He stood out on the platform singing to them.

"We rushed for the bridge, we had no tickets, he gave us no tickets, and as I ran I shouted back to him, 'Hold the train!' He paid no heed, and when we were up on the middle of the bridge he got to the grand burst, the last crescendo, of 'I come! . . . My heart's delight . . .' and waved the train on. We were left looking at it vanishing up the line. I roared at him for a fool, and a vain fool, but he only bowed to us, and he bowed to the porter, and he bowed his way backward to the office like a Caruso. The train purred into the distance and there we two were with the wind in the wires and the white moon on mountains.

"I went back to abuse him — it was the last train — but he only looked at me like a child you'd strike and said he couldn't hold back a train for anyone. The porter paid no heed to us. He outed the lamps and locked the place up. We left the old fellow alone in the station. We had to walk home. It was a grand, bright night. A lovely, thick night. . . ."

Hanafan's voice broke. Just then a signal bell rang. It was dark over the bog where far away the train murmured and it could easily be heard because the birds had stopped singing. There was nothing but the deep scent of the night air, and below them in a marsh, still deep from the March rains, a prattling as of a thousand tiny frogs.

"This is a lonely place he lived in," whispered Hanafan. "A lonely life. No children. No wife."

The priest rose up and knocked out the ashes of his pipe as the train roared nearer.

"Yes," he agreed.

"But," cried Governey, "what has all that got to do with admiring the scenery?"

"He sang to the night," cried Hanafan passionately. "He sang to the whole night. The moon was up."

His voice fell and they barely heard him over the rumbling train at the end of the platform.

"We saw the moon in the flags of the Liffey as we left the station. In the flags of the river, through the trees."

"Still and all," cried the small man, "he didn't form any intellectual concept. . . ."

The train drowned his voice and its lights flitted across their faces. When they climbed into a carriage the windows were speckled with rain and the three men inside, who leaned back to let them pass, had a cold, damp look. They had been talking when the train stopped, but when they saw the priest they fell silent; looked at him under their brows; and shyly tipped their hats.

"Raining up the line?" asked the priest in a friendly voice.

"Oh, pouring in Dublin, Father," said one of the three men — an elderly, soldierly-looking man, probably a warder in the jail at Maryborough.

The three teachers fell silent, sensing that they had interrupted a conversation. Then they were rolling through the night, looking at the lights racing along the little hedges beside the line. Suddenly the rain that had hit Dublin half an hour before swept down on them across the mountains, slapping the windows like a bucket of water. It kept trickling and shining on the windows.

"He died there last year," said Hanafan suddenly, looking at the trickle outside the pane.

"I once asked him," the priest leaned forward to say to the small man, "what his favorite song was. Do you know what he said? 'Scenes That Are Brightest.' "

The priest leaned back and gave a merry little laugh.

"Still," cried the small man, thumping his knee, "I can't see what this has to do with the question we were discussing!"

The priest looked at him, and kept looking at him as he swayed with the carriage, but he said nothing. Angrily the small man looked back, and then he looked angrily at Hanafan, whose eyes had become cranky and tormented once more. He began to wonder why Hanafan was always so sour, and why he remained on in Newtown if he didn't like the place, and why he had never married. His eye lit up a bit at that and he determined to get it all out of the priest when they were next alone. He tapped Hanafan on the knee and he began to ask him some question, but when he saw that Hanafan's eyes were closed he leaned back again. The priest was still looking at him, so he nodded towards Hanafan and winked. The priest's lidded eyes were as immovable as an owl's.

As they rolled on through the bog the small man kept looking around him restlessly, and at last he shifted over to the three countrymen, determined to find out if the common people really do admire the scenery. He started a conversation about turf cutting, but before he could lead up to the question the train halted at a small station and the strangers got out. Then the three friends were left alone in the cold, damp carriage, listening to the battering rain. Tired and sleepy, nobody noticed that, in his corner, Hanafan was weeping to himself, the drops creeping through his tightly closed eyes.

A Born Genius

PROUT LANE (better known as Little Hell) was wrapped in a softly waving veil of mist and Pat Lenihan, leaning against his doorpost, was staring into it; even as earlier in the afternoon when he had been caught by old Phillips, at the office window of the vinegar factory, staring down into the darkening marshes.

"Lenihan," he had raged, "if I came into this office twenty times a day I'd find you eating your pen with your gob to that window. What the blazes do you be looking at, anyway?"

And shoving up his glasses, he had peered out at the brown evening fog rising through the pollarded willows, mingling as it rose with the barely descending rain. Then he had looked back at Lenihan, and as if slightly in doubt of his clerk's sanity, he had left the room with a low, minatory "Get on with it."

Lenihan smiled to himself as he recalled the question. What had he been looking at, indeed, but at his boat — when it would be finished — chugging out between the forts at the harbor mouth, cutting through the waves and the mists over the open sea.

He was clerk to the old vinegar factory — an easy, even a pleasant job. There was not a great deal of work to be done; the factory was on the outskirts of the city, one might almost say in the country, and Phillips, the manager and owner, was easy to get on with. Besides, Lenihan knew he was not a very satisfactory clerk and not every employer would have put up with him. That afternoon incident at the window was typical. There were other times when Phillips had been known to roar up from the yard to the office window:

"Lenihan, will you stop that blasted singing?"

And the sweet tenor voice, that like a thrush in full music had been trilling up and down the scales with swollen throat for the last half hour, would fall silent in the middle of a run. Then old Phillips would sniff through his great red beak of a nose and with a sigh the workmen would take up their shovels or their hods again, and up in his office Lenihan would raise his shoulders as if to bear a sudden weight before he returned with a sigh to his ledgers.

Even the workmen knew he was not a satisfactory clerk. When they came to the office window on Saturday for the week's pay they might find him sweating with excitement and nervousness over a pile of notes and silver, counting the amounts over and over again, forgetting to which envelope each little pile belonged, making wrong calculations, and finally getting so utterly confused that the men themselves would have to come to his aid before he got it all correct.

In return he occasionally sang for them. If he passed by as they lay resting after the midday meal they would grasp his hands and sleeves and legs and beseech him for a song. They did not care what song he sang — anything so long as they heard him. Not that he always agreed: he would explain that a singer must be very careful of his voice, *so* careful. If he did sing, he would draw himself up, take the key from a tuning fork, puff out his voice in a little cough, face the marsh, the sluggish stream, and the leaning poplars, as if they were an audience, and, with as much care as if he were in the greatest theater in the world, sing for the four or five old workers lying about him, all stained white with magnesia. He would give them

"Flow On Thou Silent River," or "The Gypsy's Warning," which is, he explained, really a song for a contralto, or their favorite, the tenor's part from "The Moon Hath Raised Her Lamp Above," out of Benedict's *Lily of Killarney*. Gently he would sing:

> "Do not trust him, gentle maiden,
>   Gentle maiden, trust him not . . ."

while the men swung their heads in time and winked at one another in delight and admiration.

> "Over in the green grave yonder,
>   Lies the gypsy's only child . . .
>   Soon she perished, now she's sleeping,
>   In that cold and silent grave. . . ."

When he finished he would go away at once with a little bow and a military salute, blushing faintly if he overheard their praise as he went.

"Ah! God!" one would say. "He have a massive voice."

"A marvel!" they would reply in unison.

"But, of course," the first would lean forward to whisper confidentially, "he's a born genius!"

Only Flyer, his brother, would lean back very stiffly, silent as a waxwork image. Presently, he knew, they would turn to him for the latest news of Pat's doings, and then he would tell them — what matter if they had heard it all fifty times before. Meanwhile he would sit silent, his two hands holding his paunch, his two swivel eyes gazing sadly into one another.

"Well, Flyer!" they ask at last. "What is he up to now?"

Before he begins Flyer shakes his head mightily by way of emphasis, as if he were trying to shake his eyes straight or fix his head down properly into his shoulders.

"Pat," he whispers very solemnly and oracularly, "is a marvel!"

Then with a sudden roar he leans forward to them — "He's after painting two swans," he bellows dramatically, "on deh kitchen windas. Wan is facing wan way and d'oder is facing d'oder way. And I swear to God," Flyer continues with the gestures of an orator speaking to thousands, "I swear to God dis day" — here he looks both ways to the sky — "ye'd tink dey'd fly away while ye'd be looking at 'em. And what's more, he's after making a sunnyhouse outside o' deh winda, and he have geraniums, and lilies, and posies, and nasturtiums, and I dunno what else put growin' dere. So dat, so help me God dis day" — again Flyer implores the sky — "ye'd tink deh swans was floatin' in a garden! And deh garden was floating in through deh winda! And dere was no winda! But you all flowers" — here he swims through the air with his outflung hands — "and all swans and all garden . . ."

He never finished his account of anything, his head taken by a kind of gigantic Vitus's dance and his eyes starting from his head. He was subnormal, the factory liar. Pat scarcely ever spoke to him, he was ashamed of him.

The men firmly believed Flyer's tales; wasn't there, at the back of the drying shed where the white chunks of magnesia were stacked on shelves to cake, and had been, for years now, the monument he carved for his sister's grave? It was a huge block of gray vermicular stone which the rains of winter had begun to peel and crumble as if it were plaster. For almost a year he had toiled at it, day and night, in every spare moment, lying on his stomach on the cold stone, kneeling beside it on the clay, getting into all sorts of postures as he hacked away. For that year he never went to a concert or exercised his voice. He worked so hard that old Phillips, seeing him tapping away at the stone during the spare moments of the lunch hour, used to sniff and say, "If you worked as hard as that for me, Lenihan, by George, you'd nearly be worth your hire!"

But when it was all ready except the inscription he had spoiled it. He went at his sister's name in a fury of impatience to be finished, working into the night by candlelight, with the bullfrogs croaking below him in the moon-blanched marsh. Then he stared in horror at the results: all the S's and N's were upside down — it read like Russian script. A month later he began at the name again, carving out a horizontal piece to obliterate what he had done. This time, he got all the S's and N's right, but by some accursed fate he forgot everything else, and the name now read *SUSANNANAN LENI-NAN*. He never completed his task and the monument now lay — as he said bitterly, like a huge letter box to Heaven for "Susannanan Leninan" — covered with a sack, forgotten, unfinished behind the drying sheds. And now, wasn't he making a motorboat!

The veils of mist continued to float in from the sea, as solid as a fog. With a sigh he closed the door and returned to the fire. Summer was ending. He took up a piece of wood carving that he had begun last winter and with a small gouge he scraped at the vein in a leaf. He had the house to himself — Flyer was boozing in the pub at the end of the lane and his mother was gone to the chapel to her confraternity. He laid the piece of wood aside and lit a cigarette and hummed a bar or two from a song — Schubert's "Serenade." Then he turned to the grand piano, and when he had searched for and found the key and shaken out the music, he dusted the worn keys with his silk handkerchief.

Directly opposite the narrow mouth of Little Hell, or so it appears to the eye, are the slopes of Montenotte — tonight no more than a crowd of winking lights hanging, like the stars, but in a lower darkness. From where she had stepped on a mound of ruins somewhere behind Prout Lane, Mrs. John Delaney looked across at those hundred faint lights of which at least a couple might be the windows of her home and the lamps at her lodge gates. She could even distinguish the lay of her own road where the lamps curved in a steady series. Far down to the right, too, she could see through the mists another faint line of lights where the river swung out to meet the harbor, and she halted for an extra second to stare into the impenetrable darkness beyond all, from where the wind blew chill about her legs and blew the mist into her eyes and penetrated her furs. It would be hard for her to say which view of the harbor was more familiar to her — from this side of the city, a narrow ribbon of river threading between factory chimneys and the roofs of houses; from her garden, there across the valley, widening and narrowing to river lochs, the great country houses scattered deep in trees into which she could almost fling a pebble. For it was not really so long ago since, from a laneway door not a mile from this lane, she had stood as a young girl looking at this selfsame night view, taking a breath of air after hours of practice at the piano, and at the "Jewel Song" from *Faust,* and "Absent," and "Flow On Thou Silent River," and "The Gypsy's Warning," and all the rest of them, to be allowed to sing one of which was her reward for an hour Oh'ing and Ah'ing at the scales. Leaning against a crumbling wall she hummed to herself:

> "Do not trust him, gentle maiden,
> Gentle maiden, trust him not . . .
> Soon she perished —"

She pulled herself up suddenly — at this rate she would not get her calls finished by midnight. She saw a solitary lamp ahead of her at the end of a passage and made for it: perhaps Ninety-two B was at that end of the lane, and for the sixth time she smacked her lips in annoyance at not having had the sense to ask for precise directions, or, at least, to bring some kind of torch.

And yet they were always telling her at the society that she was their best woman for dispensing charity. Occasionally she wondered why. There were occasions on which she forgot she had been a lane child herself, or tried to persuade herself that the society and the lane people did not know that it was her voice, and the help of the nuns in her school, that had lifted her out of the rut, that it was

her voice alone that had opened the way for her into amateur theat-
ricals, where she had met her husband. It was her one vanity, her
one hopeless self-deception. For even if they had not remembered
her, the lanes would have seen the mark of their kind in her deep
chest, and her strong arms, and her frosty complexion, and her hard
lips — her only inheritance from her mother, a woman who had
carried a basket of fish on her back around Cork, day after day, for
thirty years. That was the real reason why the society always sent
her to the worst lanes; they knew well that the lane people knew,
and would not try to impose on her with a sorrowful tale and a
whining voice; that the only weapon left to the poor people was
flattery, and that would not succeed with such as her. It was because
of that lane cunning, as strong in her as in them, that she would not
knock now at a door to ask the way. It was old wisdom to her —
"What they didn't know didn't trouble them."

But when she reached the lamp and its light fell on the number to
her left, she knew she was utterly lost in this forest of slummery.
She was about to walk back the way she had come when suddenly
from behind the lighted cabin window by her shoulder a piano flung
out in great strong drops of sound the prelude to an old familiar
arrangement of Schubert's "Serenade" and immediately a fine tenor
voice opened the duet, though where the contralto or baritone
should reply there was silence except for the gently throbbing beat
of the accompaniment. Her heart beat faster than the time of the
music as in one of these half silences she knocked at that door. The
music halted and the door opened. Because the light was strong
behind him she could not see Lenihan's face.

"Can you tell me," she said, "where I can find number Ninety-two
B?"

At the first word she recognized the voice.

"Yes, of course. But I'm afraid you won't find it yourself. Wait one
minute," he said, diving back into the kitchen, "and I'll get my hat
and show you."

She lowered her head to step down into the earthen-floored cabin. She saw the grand piano, almost as long as the whole room; it was gray with a layer of dust and coal ash. A smoke-darkened plaster cast of an angel hung over the wide, low grate. Pieces of wood shaped like monstrous bones leaned in a corner — the ribs of his boat. When he turned she gave him one quick look, and he, caught by the full shock of surprise, cried out:

"Trixie Flynn!"

"Pat Lenihan!" she reproached. "Why did you never come to see me and welcome me home?"

Her voice was deep, rich, pouting.

"I couldn't, Trixie. I couldn't somehow. What brings you here at this hour of the night?"

"The Saint Vincent de Pauls sent me. Mrs Cahill in Ninety-two B is sick."

She had recovered completely from her surprise and she arranged her hair as she looked at him from under her eyebrows.

"Sit down!" he said.

His voice was shaking and he shut the door and leaned against it.

"The old favorite," she said, looking at the score on the piano.

"I haven't sung for nearly a year and a half," he said.

"Why?"

"I'm making a boat," he murmured, almost as if he were a child caught wrongdoing.

"A boat!"

She was shocked.

"Pat Lenihan! A boat! And you with your voice!"

"Ah!" he cried miserably. "It's all very well for you, Trixie. You caught the tide. You've been to Paris and Milan. I read about your concert last March, below in the opera house."

She grimaced with lips and eyebrows and shrugged her shoulders in disdain.

"*Un rien*. A bagatelle."

"And you got married, too," he whispered.

"Aha!" she trilled. "I often thought we'd get together, Pat. But, *chi lo sa?*"

His lips twitched and his eyes strayed to a photograph on the piano. She went over to it, and he followed. There she, as a buxom Marguerite, knelt and looked up at Lenihan in the tights and doublet of Faust.

"And you've been singing in Manchester and Liverpool," he said, looking at her as she looked at the photograph.

"It's my wonderful year," she laughed. "Back from Milan! Married! Several recitals! But" — she pouted again in a deep, sad voice — "you never came to see *ta petite* Marguerite!"

"See what?" asked Lenihan.

"Me!" she pouted, swaying before him.

"Oh! You don't want me now," cried Lenihan.

He slammed down the lid of the piano. The wires vibrated.

"I'll never sing another song!" he declared.

She was about to argue with him, but he interrupted her savagely.

"What's the use?" he cried. "Who hears me? And if they did, what difference would it make? Who could tell in this hole of a city whether I was good or bad? I suppose if the truth were known I wouldn't be taken in the chorus of a traveling Moody-Manners."

"I heard you outside the window," she said. "You were in good voice."

"I'm not. I couldn't be. I haven't practiced for eighteen months. It's all a lot of damned tomfoolery. Look at all the hours I've wasted — the nights. And what good did it do me? I know I have a voice. But it isn't a great voice. I never even got as much as a penny out of it. Not that I want it. Of course the opera house is a bagatelle to you, as you call it. What are we here but a lot of country boys playing at amateur operatics?"

"Why don't you sing in a choir, Pat?" she asked. "You'd make some money that way."

"A choir!"

His voice was like the sour beer that stank in the vinegar factory.

"And what would I sing in a choir?"

Through his nose he began to intone horribly:

> *"Tantum ergo*
> *Sacramentum*
> *Novo cedat*
> *Ritui . . ."*

"Stop, Pat!"

They were silent for a minute or two.

"I want to sing my old part in that serenade, Pat," she said gently.

"No."

"Please, Pat!"

"No! No! No!"

She went to the piano and, leaving a wave of scent in the air as she swished by him, began to turn the music with the ample gestures of a prima donna. As she sat, and with her white fingers plucked out the modulated sounds, the music seemed to mingle sweetly with the scent. She saw, looking over her shoulder at him, that he was wavering.

"Have you never been to any of my concerts, Pat?"

He shook his head. She flung out a few notes like a blackbird full of pride in its song.

"Come on, Pat!" She smiled at him again.

He flung his mood aside and stood by her, his hands clasped tremblingly across his chest, his eyes lost in the dark corner of the room. They began:

> *"Leise flehen meine Lieder*
> *Durch die Nacht zu dir,*
> *In die stillen Hain hernieder,*
> *Liebchen, komm zu mir . . ."*

Her rich, finely trained voice poured into the room and out of it through the lanes. Responding to it his body swayed to and fro as he drew up from his chest the most powerful volume of song he could command. Once where she had a bar or two to sing alone he glanced down at her. Her great bosom, too, rose to the notes, and it was white and suède-smooth in the lamplight. Looking at her, he almost missed a note. He sang with an almost uncontrolled passion the remainder of the song.

When it was finished he fell into a chair by the piano and covered his eyes with his hands.

"My God!" he said. "What a voice! What a marvelous voice!"

He thought he caught the vibration of triumph and pity in her throat as she said:

"Pat! You really have a very nice voice."

Outside the window, in spite of the rain, they suddenly heard a chattering group of men, women, and children, trying to peep through the window slits and the keyhole. He was glad of the interruption and, jerking his head, he led her to the back door and across the yard to another lane.

"Come and see me, Pat!" she said. He did not reply. From time to time she said, "Isn't it wet?" Or, "Mind this hole!" But still he did not reply. At the door of Ninety-two B, she said again:

"Won't you come to see me? Ah! *S'il vous plaît? Mon cher* Pat? *Mon petit* Pat?"

"Yes, yes, yes," he said shortly. "I'll come. Maybe. Good night, Trixie."

"Au revoir, *mon petit* Pat."

The light of the cabin windows fell on him at intervals, as he went. Then the mist and the dark covered him from her sight.

To her surprise, when she heard from him, three months later just before the Christmas holidays, he was in New York. It was a picture postcard of the New York Philharmonic Orchestra with his address and two sentences:

Having a grand time. Richard Trübner has taken me in hand and has great hopes of me. Pat.

With the cunning of the born guttersnipe she went at once to Little Hell on two or three entirely superfluous calls and at each house she said when leaving, "I hear you've lost Mr. Lenihan from the lane."

Before she left the slum she had heard more about him than he would ever have written to her in a hundred letters, and as she was driven back to Montenotte she smiled to think how neatly everything she had heard fitted in with all her previous knowledge of Pat Lenihan — his silence about himself, his poverty, the strain of bitterness and irreligion in him. He had never told her, for example, that he lived in Prout Lane or that he had for years supported his mother and sister. And she recalled, suddenly, how when five years before they were meeting frequently for some amateur operetta he had told her of the monument he was going to carve for his sister's grave. She had said, probing inquisitively:

"And you'll put your father's name on it, too, of course?"

"No! I will not," he had snapped back, and, flushing, walked away.

Well! Here was the secret out at last.

"Ah, sure, Mrs. Delaney," they had said to her in Prout Lane, "that boy could do any mortal thing he liked. D'ye see his house? 'Twould take the sight of your eyes, Mrs. Delaney. It's massive. Oh, sure, his father will make a C'ruso out of him. The two of ye will charm Cork."

She had to halt their flattery several times. She wanted to hear about Pat Lenihan.

"His father? 'N't ye know? Fifteen years ago — no! I'm tellin' a lie — twelve years ago his father ran away from his mother to America. He left her with five children, the blackguard. Three of 'em died since. Susie was the last to go. An' all this time the father is sending for the boy. His mother says, an' Flyer says — but you wouldn't mind Flyer — his mother says the father is rotten with money. But the blackguard never sent a penny since the day he left. Oh, Pat's future is cut out for him. Sure he's a genius. He'd charm the married women. And" — with a burst of hypocritical and delighted laughter — "sure you'd charm the married men, Mrs. Delaney!"

She envied him. She was to have her first child in the spring and her singing days, she felt, were nearly done. For all her promise of triumphant nights and audiences applauding in the gloom across the footlights, she was falling into the routine of a little tawdry provincial city. From this on, the most she could hope for would be an occasional recital in Cork, with more frequent gratis appearances at charity concerts to help her husband to get contracts for churches or convent buildings or for hospitals or schools managed by religious. She did not reply to the postcard. She felt too envious.

New York was wine to Pat Lenihan, and because it was under snow the silence of it filled into his heart. All he could hear above the perpetual whistling of the chains on the automobiles, and the muffled honk of their horns, was the long sad squawk of a train siren cleaving the frozen air, and the low tolling of a bell where an engine drew its load through Manhattan, somewhere to the north. The air was cold, exhilarating, and pure. A few last gentle flakes were added to those clotting the trees in the park, and the low sun, a burning moon, blazed on every twig. The tall, tapering buildings, dim and pale, glittered with their own thousand lights as they rose through the sky.

He was driving in a taxi, back from his singing lesson, to his room in a little downtown theological seminary on Ninth Avenue and Twenty-first Street. He had laughed to think what they would say in Cork if they heard he was living in such a place. But two weeks after his arrival in New York his father had got him a letter to the dean, and because it was cheaper and less frigid than a hotel he had stayed there ever since. Not that he saw his father; the introduction was sent to him, and though that was nearly four months ago he was about to meet his father tonight for the first time.

Ever since the tender disappeared into the early-morning mist at Queenstown four months or so ago, leaving him on the liner, he had been filled by that miracle of elation that comes only once in a life to every man, that fills him when chance at last opens for him some long-desired road. He had never in all his life been so excited as when he stepped off the boat and looked expectantly around the wharf; for half his dreams had been of the day when his father would return with him, successful and wealthy, to live, reconciled to his mother, in Ireland. But he saw nobody and nobody came to meet him. He was planning to go to his father's business address, the only one he knew, when at the customs desk they handed him a letter in which his father explained that he had been called away suddenly to Cleveland on business and they would see one another in a few weeks' time.

"There is, to be sure," his father wrote, "a good deal of money in singing and my Pat must have the best teachers money can buy. Meanwhile you must have a good time."

The letter mentioned several shows; one called *Earl Carroll's Vanities* was a "real bully show." Lenihan smiled at the Americanese, and because he could not meet his father, went that evening to see something that his father had liked. He came out, unhappy and troubled, his eyes and mind soiled by gaudy images of red and purple curtains and sham marble pillars and naked women. Had he not come by chance on a symphony concert and snatched an hour filled with the thunder and whisper of a Beethoven concerto (it was the Emperor) he would have had nothing but an unpleasant memory for his first night in New York, a memory that might have shattered his miracle forever.

After that he lived his own life and the miraculous elation of hope blossomed once more. After another three weeks his father wrote again. He was now in Chicago and in a few weeks they would meet.

Meanwhile Pat must begin to study; "for my Pat must make a name for himself and I'll help my boy to it while I have a dollar left." Things went on like that for another three months, some of the letters containing large checks, and still Lenihan had not met his father. By now, too, his mother was writing long letters from Cork, charging him in an agony of fear with hiding somehing from her, and Lenihan spent a good part of his leisure time writing long letters to both of them. But his master was by now much more hopeful, and even enthusiastic, and Lenihan could already see, a year away, perhaps, the night of his debut — the little concert hall, for it would be a very modest beginning, the accompanist looking to him for the signal, the scattered audience of connoisseurs and critics, and then the notices the following morning in the press giving him his first taste of fame.

It was characteristic of his elation that he found even Ninth Avenue beautiful. And yet, at any rate around Twenty-first Street, it is merely a dirty, paper-strewn cobbled street, darkened and made raucous by an overhead railway. There is the usual Greek fruit store, the usual wide-windowed restaurant and lunch counter, white-tiled like a public lavatory at home in Ireland, and with such names as Charlie's Lunch or The Coffee Pot; an old-clothes shop, a cheap Sicilian haberdasher strayed up from Macdougal Street; there is a Palmist and Phrenologist, with big-breasted Polish gypsies always offering themselves in the doorway. The tramcars raced along the avenue under the thunder of the overhead railway. Only when the snow covers the dirt and the smells and dulls the noise is the place really tolerable. Yet, to Lenihan, it had the charm of a foreign city, the one place that remained indelible in all its details on his memory when he returned to Ireland, that filthy avenue banked in snow, made doubly white by the black girders of the overhead; and side by side for all its length all those vital, struggling, immigrant homes. That long noisy street remained with him as a poignantly lovely memory, a thing more vital and brutal than he could ever explain.

And it was all the more poignant and bitter when he discovered that for all the four months he was in New York his father had watched him coming out of the archway of the seminary in the morning and going in, often very late at night, getting no more in return for his patient vigil than the briefest glance at his son's face raised questioningly to the sky, or, after dark, the outline of his son's back under the lamplight.

In the hall, now, by the telephone booth he stood waiting, and though it was twelve years since they had met, and the old man had grown scant-haired and yellow-skinned and hard-mouthed, they recognized each other at once. But they could say nothing but, "How are you, my son?" and, "How are you, Father?" — looking shyly at each other, smiling and saying nothing, because they had nothing in common they dared talk about.

"Let's go and have a cup of cawfee," said the father at last, and he took his son by the arm and led him across to the white counter of Charlie's Lunch.

In the bright light of the restaurant Lenihan noticed that his father's hands were trembling, and that they were rough with work, and that his suit was odorous of the steam press.

"You've come from Detroit, Father?"

"What?" said the father, taken by surprise.

"You wrote me from Detroit last time, Father," said Lenihan. "Yeah!"

As the white-hatted curate brought them the coffee the father spoke about Detroit to his son, inventing the names of the streets and the squares and the parks.

" 'N't you like New Yawrk?" he asked then, and in spite of the succession of nasals his intonation was pure Cork.

"I do, indeed," said Lenihan.

The old man began at once in a very fast voice to make his confession to his son, but he went round and round it and he could not approach the actual point. He talked instead in a confused way about America and its customs, about democracy and the liberties of

America, about freedom of thought and tolerance and cosmopolitanism, and though Lenihan tried very hard to follow him he could not, and finally he gave it up and, barely listening, merely said, "Yes," or "No," or "Indeed?" or "Do you say so?" He was trying to think how he could get to the point of suggesting to his father that he ought to return to his home and wife in Cork. Suddenly he observed how excited and nervous the old man was, and how his eyes were shifting here and there as his talk grew slower and more deliberate. He felt his father was coming to the point, and he waited for his opportunity, almost trembling himself with hope and expectation.

"Of course," his father was saying, "you are a young maan still, Pat. A very young maan. And in Ireland a maan has little chance of meeting with experience. But you are a clever young maan and I hope you have understanding."

"I hope so, sir," said Lenihan.

The old man looked at him from eye to eye, and said solemnly and deliberately:

"A maan's married life is sacred to him."

"Father!" said Lenihan, grasping his father's hand. How rough it was and how it shook as he held it!

"Yes, Pat?"

"Father, come home to my mother."

With a shock he realized that he had often and often said those words before to his father when he used to meet him as a child, wandering drunk in the streets. His father looked at him. There was silence for a moment and then an overhead train thundered by.

"Pat!" said his father.

"Yes."

"Pat, I want you to stay here."

"But you can go home without me," he was beginning to argue, when the old man interrupted him.

"Pat, boy, I'll make a success of you. I'm very fond of you, and I always was. Aren't you my first son, and why shouldn't I? I have a father's love for you, Pat. My boy! I've done a lot of rotten things, Pat, but you don't hold them against me? You wouldn't hold things out against your old dad?"

A group of men came in and sat at the counter near them.

"Come upstairs, Pat," said the father, taking his hand.

"Upstairs?" said Lenihan.

"Yes," said the father, leading him through the shop. "I know the man here," he explained.

He was like a hare doubling before the dog. He lied at every hand's turn. Upstairs in the room over the shop the first thing Lenihan saw was a panorama of Queenstown and in surprise he turned to his father.

"Yes, Pat?" faltered the old man.

"Queenstown!" said Lenihan in delight.

"Aye," smiled his father, still unable to confess.

"How did it get here?"

"Yes, Pat."

And he laughed with foolish delight, in spite of his nervousness, because at last someone else besides himself was enjoying the old familiar scene.

"Look at the old Deepwater Quay!" said Lenihan. "And look at Spike! And Haulbowline! Isn't it grand!"

Then he stopped, his eyes wandering to the fireplace, over which hung an Irish flag, the old green with the yellow harp, and crossing it an Italian flag, the quartered shield in the white center. Beneath it on the mantelpiece was a photograph. He went towards it. It was himself and Trixie Flynn as Faust and Marguerite. When he wheeled on his father the old man was looking up at him like a dog about to be kicked or a schoolboy waiting for punishment. But before the confession could come the door was flung open and in raced two lovely little black-haired boys, and after them strode a dark-eyed, big-chested Italian woman.

"Whoo! Pop!" cried the children, leaping up joyously at old Lenihan. "We been shoppin'!"

And they began to show him their New Year toys until, seeing the stranger, they fell suddenly quiet.

"Anita!" said old Lenihan. "This is Pat."

It was plain that he had told her at least some of the truth — how much Lenihan never knew; probably that he was a widower and this was his son. Afterwards it tore Lenihan's heart to think the old man had not been able to keep it secret that he had a son whom he loved. Now, however, as the woman looked at him, searching his face for the face of his mother, Lenihan began to think of Prout Lane, wrapped in its veils of mist, and of his mother, hurrying to the chapel to her confraternity at night, and he let his eyes fall, and taking his hat he went slowly out of the room. His father raced down the stairs to stop him, persuading and entreating him, step by step, as he insisted on descending to the street.

That night when he had at last got rid of his father Lenihan packed his bag and took the Shore Line midnight to Boston, his taxi racing with whistling chains through the snow-covered avenues, past the great floodlit towers of the city's buildings, closed for the night, past the theaters he had begun to know so well, dark now and silent, and empty, the shops at rest, the sidewalks deserted, into the great station where the foyer was full of light and life, and the waiting line of Pullmans beyond stood silent and dark, ready for its journey, under the sad whistle of the siren and the low tolling of its bell.

He stayed in Boston for the better part of a year, abandoning all his ambitions and hopes. There was no looking out of the office window here, no singing at the lunch hour for the workmen, no intervals in which he might at his ease exercise his voice. Having saved his fare, and a little more, he returned to Ireland for Christmas.

Not until he was seated in the train from Queenstown to Cork did it occur to him that in those four months in New York his father must have spent on him the best part of his life's savings, that his father was a poor man — that his father probably was quite fond of him. A light snow, rare event in southern Ireland, was blowing past the carriage windows, and in it he saw Ninth Avenue and the black girders of the overhead and, for the first time, his father's face at the window of Charlie's Lunch peering out anxiously to see him leave the seminary in the morning, peering out at night in the hope of seeing him return, and doing that day after day, week after week, afraid to meet his son, and yet aching to talk with him and maybe persuade him to stay with him for the rest of his life. The old fellow, thought Lenihan, must have gone to a great deal of trouble and humiliation persuading the dean to allow me to stay at the seminary; and then he thought of all the devices, all the lies, all the subterfuges his father had employed, and all to no greater result than five minutes' painful argument as they stepped down the stairs of the restaurant-*cum*-haberdasher's shop in Ninth Avenue; and, afterwards, still more painful because bitter and insulting, the pleading and the quarreling in the little room of the theological seminary over the way. Through the whirling snowflakes, curling about the bare beech boughs, and melting on the dark drooping laurels and the tattered hedges, he saw only, and now with a sudden but tardy pity, that his father's sin had borne bitter fruit.

The train rolled into the city, over the red bridge into the railway station, and as he stepped from it and saw his mother coming forward in search of him through the crowd, full of joy at the thought that she was about to see her son again — the sorrow of her husband's early desertion long since forgotten — Lenihan realized that he was divided in pity between these two, and that, for being divided, he could never as long as he lived be at ease again with either.

In the old covered car, as they drove into the city, and up the hills again to Prout Lane, Lenihan told his mother the truth about her husband. But when she began to weep for herself and curse her husband with sudden blasphemy, Lenihan found that he had no longer any hate or resentment left in him. After that, when the news spread through the lane, he refused to talk of it with anybody, and if they insisted on upbraiding his father he would merely say, "Little good it did him," or, "The poor old sod, I pity him sometimes."

All that day a stream of lane people kept trickling in to welcome the genius home. They had expected a night of jollification, but they were just as pleased with the drama of the weeping mother, Flyer drunken and fractious on the porter intended for the feast, and Pat sitting glum and silent by the fire. His piano he had sold before he went to America, never thinking to need it again; his window flowers were withered stumps; the fire had taken his wood carvings one by one, as well as the unfinished portions of his boat that used to lean in the corners of the kitchen.

"Didn't I have a clean kitchen for you, Pat?" his mother wailed. "And what news you brought me! Look at that lovely red marbled wallpaper we got for you, fourpence a dozen, and Flyer to put it up for you with his own two hands. Oh! What a homecoming!" she wailed at each new comforting gossip, until at last he drove out of the house and down to the river's edge to look at the skeleton of his boat, and to look, in the dusk, at the marshes of the vinegar factory. Then the only shelter from the night and his loneliness was the dark lights of Montenotte and Trixie Flynn.

It was no pleasure to him to visit her. Earlier in the afternoon he had observed from an old poster that they were now calling her "Madame Flynn-Delaney, Cork's Own Nightingale," and as he read it he had groaned aloud, like a man in pain. This rat-eaten place still had, he thought bitterly, as he walked through its tawdry front streets whose finery was only the thickness of a brick, and into its warehouse back streets that looked as if they had been rusting and crumbling for centuries, all the mannerisms and unconscious humor ascribed to it by the sniggering Levers and Prouts and Thackerays of a hundred years ago. With a kind of sour joy he began to roam about the city, trying to keep from visiting Montenotte — O romantic Mount of Night! — associating his own misery with the shades of the Spensers and the Warbecks and the Walters — for he refused to ally even his thoughts with the people themselves — the dukes and earls and lords-lieutenant and secretaries whose petty glories were the only ones the place had ever seen. Everywhere he went he sought with deliberate malice for the signs of decayed grandeur — streets of Georgian houses full of cheap shops, a puny bridge called after Wellington, a wide street dubbed a square and given to Nelson, a horse trough presented to a Berwick, a wretched slum street to the whole House of Hanover, and every sooty, mud-deep quay partitioned off here to a Grenville, or a Wandesford, or a Camden, or a Lancaster, a George, a Charlotte, an Albert. Every exiled down-at-heel sighing for St. James's and Pall Mall, with their flea-bitten servants and tarnished finery, had been offered the immortality of their names on the walls of a jakes in this city of exile. But all the time, as if in spite of himself, he approached nearer and nearer to Montenotte. The bored souls of provincial towns are all like that — feeding on one another without pleasure, like leeches.

He had been afraid that she would ask him too many questions about his father and his own plans. She seemed far more interested in showing him her baby and in telling him about the contract for the new cathedral that all the architects in Cork were trying to wheedle out of the bishop. Then her husband came in for dinner and with him her sister-in-law and her brother, and they prevailed on Lenihan to stay. It was a good dinner but noisy with cross-talk, and Delaney bored them with talk about the cathedral — the people who were maneuvering for the contracts, distant relations of the bishop that were being approached by this person and that, the best sites for the cathedral, the soil, the stone, the style, explaining the advantages of Romanesque with his knife and his napkin and a loaf of bread, deriding Pugin because he had filled Ireland with plaster Gothic.

"My God! I'd rather concrete," he would declare. "Though concrete wasn't as popular once as it is now. That's what your Americans" — to Lenihan — "did for us. I remember a competition twelve years ago and I was the first student to suggest a concrete church. 'How in the name of God,' said the adjudicator — it was Sir Edward Luytens — 'how in the name of Almighty God,' says he, 'could that roof stand?' 'Oh, it's concrete, Sir Edward,' says I. 'Indeed,' says Sir Edward, 'an' I suppose the spire is made of cast iron?' But, you know," Delaney went on in spite of the laughter, "you could have a concrete roof in a Romanesque church. And it wouldn't be a smaller church. You'd make in the height what you'd lose in the width; you could have galleries . . ."

And so on and on while Lenihan kept thinking, "I'm back; back in garrulous, windbag Cork." And his mind filled with images of New York and Boston and he ceased to hear Delaney's talk except as the babble of a stream.

After dinner, whiskey and port and coffee were handed around and there was much sniggering in a corner over a *risqué* French pictorial. But Lenihan put such a good face on things that he managed to lift out of his mood into a good humor, and while the rain blown up from the harbor lashed the streaming panes and the fire crackled with drops falling in the chimney he and Trixie sang a comical duet from the *Yeomen of the Guard* while Delaney pranced around the room holding his glass to the ceiling, coming in on the refrain very flat and out of tune. Then he went off to drive his guests home and Lenihan and Trixie were left alone, talking over the fire in a darkened room, of the great singers they had heard, she of Melba, and Patti, and Tonnalerre, and Clara Butt, he of Kennerley Rumford and Caruso and his master Trübner. She began to complain sadly of her life in Cork and he said he could well believe her.

"I have my child, of course," she said, "and I'd die for her. I'd lay down the last drop of my blood for that child," she declared with flashing eyes, and her bosom panted and her voice rose.

The wine was going to both their heads, and Lenihan found himself telling her that her sentiments did her great honor. But then, there was her husband, she said, and her voice fell. There was John gone off to the club now and he wouldn't be back until morning; and she allowed Lenihan to pat her on the hand. He felt he had never liked her so much as tonight, and as she leaned forward and encouraged him to speak he told her readily all about his father. As he left they halted in the door to hum a bar from the "Serenade," and he kissed her hand in good-by.

Then, as he tramped in a midnight downpour back up to the little sleeping cabins of Prout Lane, he felt that he had no right to betray the old man's shame, and late as it was he wrote and posted a letter to Trixie warning her that she had his confidence and imploring her to tell nobody what she had heard. She wrote a long and warm letter in reply saying that she was honored by his confidence and would respect it. She wrote:

> Don't I understand, Pat, only too well that such things are best kept quiet in a city like this. There are always people trying to dig out your past in Cork. As for your father, have nothing to do with the old devil. You never know what he'd try to make out of this. Leave him severely alone, neither writing to him nor communicating with him in any way . . .

Again Lenihan saw his father peering out of Charlie's Lunch for that morning and evening glimpse of himself leaving the seminary, and thinking of it he decided he would never again visit this coarse woman, wandering instead at night, in and out of the back streets, searching always for old names and old memories, sometimes for snatches of accidental beauty where the shadows of a lamp in an archway made a design of glooms, or lights that were more like shadows, or where an empty blank gable end towered dark over a lane, or a whitewashed cottage shone like snow under its purple roof. What was he, after all, but another like those Sydneys and Coburgs and Adelaides and the rest of them, whoever they were, another exile tortured by the empty days and the companionless nights?

In the end he went back to her. After all, they were the only two people in Cork who really knew what singing meant. And when he did go, late one evening, she was so childishly glad to see him, and so unhappy about her husband, that he felt he had been harsh and unkind and readily agreed to sing with her at a forthcoming concert. But it happened that just that night a priest called to bless the house. ("Father Shanahan," she whispered to Lenihan as he came in, "the bishop's secretary"; and, as he went upstairs to pray over the house, "God forgive me, I have my house blessed by half the priests in Cork.") He was a pale-haired saturnine man, with a voice as high-pitched as a girl's, and his eyes were soft with innocence or humility, and immediately he entered the room Trixie began to be charming to him and flirt with him in a loud voice and with much winking. His answers, however, were so awkward that Trixie's talk seemed improper and gross to Lenihan, who pretended to be playing with the baby, leaning over the pram and glaring down at it as if he were about to choke it. Presently he found himself being intrigued into giving a half promise to sing the *Adeste* with Trixie at the parish choir next Sunday, though it enraged him to see his half promise passed on at once as if it were a personal gift of Trixie's to the parish. But she was so charming about it that the little priest grew more and more awkward and finally took his leave, and Lenihan, who had disliked priests at all times, preferred to go with him. Yet the following night he was back at her house again, and again she was delighted to see him, and after that he took to visiting her regularly. There was no other house open to him.

In April he was taken back in the vinegar factory, and little by little the marshes under the office window began to sprout in green patches, and at the lunch hour he could walk abroad in the fields more and more often under dry skies and broken clouds and work longer and longer in the evenings at his boat. He began to feel less resentful of Cork. The loveliness of the country encroaching on and compensating for the empty town, the promise of long Sundays in summer among the inlets within and without the harbor, where the bright green hills dipped down to the blue sea, and the white line of waves seemed never to move — all this weaned him gradually back to his old self, and the memory of the heavy winter passed from him.

He was in that happy mood one Sunday as he went to sing at a charity matinee with Trixie. She was waiting for him in the corridor and at once she called him aside to her dressing room. In the artificial light her hair shone — so much bronze wire piled on her head — and her rich bosom displayed generously in her low-cut evening gown of pink and silver looked as if a touch would reveal that it had a nap on it like a peach or snow-white suède. He took her by her bare, braceleted arm.

"Is it the contract?" he asked eagerly.

"No."

She was awkward. He felt there was something wrong.

"Pat! They are beginning to talk about us. You mustn't come so often."

The music of the orchestra rolled up to them as the stage door was opened and shut.

"Who is talking about us?" he asked, flushing with shame.

"Well! Father Shanahan is dropping hints."

"Oh!"

"My husband says it's unwise."

"It's the contract you're thinking of, Trixie."

"I'm not, Pat. But you know Cork."

With a sudden impulse of defiance of the mean, tattling city he put his arms around her and kissed her, and she did not resist him, returning his kiss even more warmly than he gave it. It seemed natural to her to kiss him, to hold him in her great maternal arms. A knock on the door called them to their duet and they went down the corridor to the stage whispering to each other to be calm, to be calm. But as on that first night when she came to his house in Prout Lane, they sang the duet in a rivalry of almost wild passion, accelerating the tempo of the melancholy serenade until the accompanist found himself never nearer than a quarter of a bar behind. The audience sensed their emotion in Lenihan's flushed cheeks and in the woman by her high-flung chin and flashing eyes, and sharing in that emotion, several seconds before the song ended, they sent their clamorous, thundering applause up from the gloom beyond the bright encircling footlights. In the wings, Delaney, trembling for his contract, waited for his wife: he implored her to be careful — the bishop was in the house and Shanahan was somewhere on the stage. But beyond the billowing curtain the applause rose and fell in wave on wave until they came forward to sing again, choosing with an almost incredible lack of discretion the love duet from *The Lily of Killarney*. By the prompter's box Father Shanahan looked on with tightened lips and disapproving eyes as Lenihan rose breathlessly to:

> "I come, I come, my heart's delight!
> My heart's delight!
> My heart's delight . . ."

sung so feelingly that when it was over and he reached the side of the stage he collapsed in a chair. They brought him a glass of water, and as he sipped it mechanically he saw Delaney come in from the auditorium, in a fury, and lead his wife to her room, and little Father Shanahan looking at them with a cold look in his innocent eyes.

After that painful scene he dared not visit her again, and indeed she wrote to warn him not to come to her. Fortunately it was summer and he could now work for long hours in the evenings at his boat. As he saw it, as it were, come to life under his hands he became as happy as a woman with child. July came and the trestles under his boat were deep in buttercups, and as he worked, the salmon leaped up the falls, splashing, bow-bent silver. During those days he seemed to be tireless, and when the darkness drove him home to his cabin kitchen he worked late into the night making cabinets to exchange with a local firm of furnishers for the timber and the brass and iron and glass fittings he needed. It was August and a woodbine trailed its tendrils from the hedges over the flank of his boat. As with his sister's tombstone he worked in a fever of impatience to be finished. It was so hot that he had to put a tarpaulin over the keel and it burned his hand to lean on it. September came and under his boat were foxgloves, and the wild arum in its tight wrapping. October followed and the denuded trees showed the red berry of the dog rose, burning like the holly berry on its branch. It seemed as if he would not have his boat launched that autumn, but before the month died he had painted the name on her prow — *The Trickster;* and dared write to Delaney asking if he and his wife would come to launch his boat.

That Sunday, after singing in the choir, she came, and the boat was lowered down the slip and it breasted the water and floated there in broken ripples of color. Lenihan rushed forward to thank her, but her husband was impatient to be gone and she would not delay.

All he could say was:

"Thanks. Is he still angry?"

"Yes. He says you lost him that contract."

"Didn't you get it after all?" he cried.

"No," she said. "We heard last night that Cassidy got it."

But Delaney sounded his horn impatiently and she turned to go.

For a week Lenihan was delighted with his boat. He almost slept in it. He visited it before his work every morning. He raced down at the lunch hour to see and fondle it. Then the engineers from whom he had ordered the engine told him it would never be of any use to him. He argued with them for hours, but they only shrugged their shoulders at him. The timbers were too far apart and flimsy to bed the engine on them; the stern post would not bear piercing for the propeller shaft; the sheer of the quarter made it impossible to lead the shaft through at the proper angle.

As in the case of his sister's tombstone he never went near it again. It lay moored under the alders until marauding boys knocked a hole in it, and sinking halfway in the shallow mud, it grew slimy and green and hulklike. You can see it there today — for it has outlived poor Lenihan — but only if you peer closely enough into the fibrous shadows of the bank, where it is almost indistinguishable from the air-searching roots of the trees.

The evening Lenihan discovered that it would never take him out to the misty sea, never nuzzle the swaying flowers that glisten in the carmined inlets of the harbor, it was gray with the first cold rains of November. He stood by his door in Prout Lane, biting his nails, and staring across the dark valley of the Lee at the hanging lights of Montenotte, while the slowly waving mist veiled the moon — a warm haze floated up from the sea, persistent as a fog. Winter had begun again, and again the boredom of the empty days and nights. He could hear the people talking beyond the dividing wall. His mother was gone to the chapel to her confraternity. Flyer was boozing in the pub at the end of the lane.

Searching for the key of his piano — a secondhand, cheap affair — he wiped the dust from the yellow keys and sat to play the Schubert "Serenade." As the worn keys plucked out the drops of sound his voice rose gently to the words. Suddenly he stopped and listened. He rushed to the door and flung it wide. He saw the mist curling about the gas lamp overhead and the lighted cabin windows as they vanished down the winding lane. Slowly he closed the door and returned to his song. The voices in the next house had fallen silent: his fingers drew the notes in slow procession.

"Lass auch dir die Brust bewegen,
Liebchen, höre mich,
Bebend harr' ich dir entgegen,
Komm, beglücke mich . . ."

He could not finish. He began it, several times, and each time he paused, and sat listening for a noise at the door.

Discord

AT the square and low-pitched window of the priest's room high under the eaves and overlooking the city, the two lovers — they had been married only yesterday and were in Dublin for the honeymoon — clutched the window-frame level with their chins and saw the field of roofs. The moving panorama of the sky had blown with it all but the final dusk of smoke. Down in the street a tin can rolled on the flags with a bright clanking. Behind them Father Peter, his black arm pointing between their heads, led their eyes over the aerial plain.

"That's Saint Michan's with the spire. There's the Protestant Saint Michan's with the square tower."

Always awkward with the newly wedded, he had led them straight to the window immediately they entered his room. He now said Pro*test*ant for a joke, hiding his own shyness.

"That?"

To a query of the girl's.

"The Dominican Church. But there now is a very interesting old place, Saint Mary's Abbey. Its real name is Saint Mary's Ostmanby — the East Men, do you see, the Danes. It was a Benedictine church

158

to begin and then the Cistercians took it over. It's all the old Dublin, as you know, there in front of us across the river."

"Girt around by prayer," said the young man, whose eye picked out the spires and towers all around the horizon.

"And girt around by pubs," said Father Peter cynically. "It's wonderful there at night, though, with all the lights. It's like Paris from Montmartre. Those old roofs of that slum house there between us and the river . . ."

One could have spat down across the narrow street at the humped and twisted dents and downs of the rooftop.

". . . they're ugly enough with their lumps of plaster between the slates, but you have no idea how lovely they are if there's a fall of snow. Oh, it's very lovely. Last winter there was a heavy fall and those little crevices of roofs were . . . Ah!"

They could almost see the whirling gentle fall darkening over Dublin as they heard him gurgle behind them with delight. He was forgetting his shyness. Through the windows of the slum house they could see three floors and on each floor iron bed legs. Seeing the poor drabness of it Angela turned away.

"Well, well," teased the girl as she looked over the cozy room with its big mannish furniture and its low roof, "who wouldn't be a priest?"

They sat down in the deep armchairs, their minds brought back by her to the present.

"This is the best of it ye're seeing now," laughed Peter. "Not that I have such a bad time, mind you."

"Are you kept very busy, Father?" she asked kindly.

"No," he said, a bit doubtfully; and then, more positively, "No!" He poked the fire, and leaned back in the capacious settee, and supported his paunch, for it was a cold autumn and he liked his comfort. He lit a cigar and gave them cigarettes, to celebrate the occasion, as he said. "I have two confraternities, the women's every Monday night, and then the first Sunday of each month I have the

Bona Mors. That," he explained, "is for the old people. For a happy death. It's mainly the old weak people who come to that, as you might understand."

The young lovers nodded as if they did understand.

"Then we have a week on and a week off on duty, sick calls and the like. We share that between us. Day and night. I'm unlucky at that. I seem to get more sick calls than any other priest."

"That's because you're so popular, Father," laughed the girl.

"Faith, 'tis not. 'Tis just the way things come. I have one old lad there now in Watling Street and he gets uremic fits. Even if he had me in twice that day and it was three in the morning he'd have me in again."

"And you have to go?" asked the youth.

"Oh," said the priest solemnly, "you couldn't refuse."

"Some of them are divils," commiserated the youth.

"Aha," teased his girl, "wait till you're on your bed of death and you'll be howling for a priest like the worst of them."

"Bedad," laughed Father Peter, "a uremic fit is a pretty bad thing."

"I suppose," she said, "you'd wish sometimes for a little parish down the country?"

"I do," he agreed eagerly. "I do. It's good here. And I meet all sorts of people. And it's interesting work. But — ah, you know . . ."

"Still," said Frank, "I envy you. You meet people, you're in contact with life. There's that fear always over me — being isolated — getting away from life — getting wrapped into myself. Everyone living in the country has that feeling sometimes. It's a bit terrifying."

His eyes wandered to the sea of roofs. His girl looked at him, as if surprised by some cavern in him that she had not seen before and must, maybe, yet explore. She did not guess that in his mind that image of a vast Dublin, growing and decaying, was still dilating like a smoke in wind.

"There's that indeed," said the priest. "You must keep on meeting people. But, then, you know, too, here it's always a certain kind of people. Sad stories. Rotten stories. Down-and-out stories. Always the same. Drunks, paupers, prostitutes — ach!"

"You have a lot of books?" said the girl, again drawing their minds back with hers.

"I'm bankrupt from them. But they're a great refuge for me. As you see, I have no room for any more."

He jumped out of his settee and picked out a volume.

"This *Life of Mangan* reminds me. This room is full of associations. Mangan wrote most of his poetry here: he and Davis and the rest of the writers of the *Nation* used to come here and talk and argue into the dawn. John Mitchel was in this room. That was when the famous Father Meehan — C.P., you remember — lived here. He kept open house for the lot of them. It was called The Attics. They had Attic Nights!"

"Is that a fact?" cried the youth. "James Clarence Mangan in this room?"

He rose and walked about it excitedly. It would have been just the same then — the low ceiling, the windows crushed under it, the green baize door, the cozy fire, the books from floor to roof, and all that poor, decayed city full of life and fashion and movement and color. His mind flooded with vague associations of eighteenth- and nineteenth-century Dublin.

"Surely Wolfe Tone was born somewhere hereabouts?" He pointed. "And Lord Edward Fitzgerald, where did he live?"

His hands seemed to grope with his memory.

"Why, man," cried Father Peter, "Thomas Street is just behind us. Emmet had his depot for making bombs a stone's throw away. They hanged him in the street — you can see Saint Catherine's spire just over the spot from my bedroom window. The street between us and the castle is Lord Edward Street."

"Mangan!" said the young man, and he recited, moodily but finely, while his wife looked at him, troubled, and at the priest almost with distrust:

> "I saw her once, one little while, and then no more.
> 'Twas paradise on earth awhile, and then no more.
> Ah, what avails my vigil pale, my magic lore?
> She shone before mine eyes awhile and then no more.
> The shallop of my peace is wrecked on Beauty's shore.
> Near Hope's fair isle it rode awhile, and then no more . . ."

"He was a fine poet," said Father Peter, and then, thinking this too melancholy for honeymoon days, he said, "They had one great night here, I believe, when they had an argument on Shakespeare. Davis was reciting Antony's speech to the mob: 'Lend me your ears . . .' 'What nonsense,' cries Mangan. 'That's a misreading. He said, "Lend me your cars." Sure, they were going to a funeral.' "

They laughed lightly at that, but the fume of memory was still in the young man's brain.

> "I saw her once, one little while, and then no more.
> The earth was Peri-land awhile, and then no more.
> Oh, might I see but once again as once before,
> Through chance or wile, that shape awhile, and then no more!
> Death soon would heal my griefs! This heart now sad and sore
> Would beat anew a little while, and then no more . . ."

"Aye," said Father Peter, "and the O'Hussey's 'Ode to the Ma-guire' is magnificent.

> "An awful, a tremendous night is this meseems,
> The floodgates of the rivers of heaven, I think, have been burst
>   wide . . ."

The girl had fallen silent. The priest noticed it.
"Come and see the chapel," he said. "Or the crypt."
"What's there to be seen?" asked the girl distrustfully.

"Why," cried the priest, "it's most historic. There's maybe a hundred people buried there. Great huge vaults there like wine cellars. Do you know who's there? Leonard MacNally."

MacNally the spy. The scrubby lawyer who was the friend of the Earl of Clare, the traitor who used to eat his nails and was so dirty the bar mess would not admit him. The friend of Tone. The friend of Emmet. He had defended him and betrayed him. Not until he was dead did the people discover it. The priest laughed.

"Yes, he's down there. And his coffin falling to pieces. Every time I go down I give it another kick. When he was being brought there I believe the poor of the city crowded the vaults to be sure he wasn't laid near or nigh to one of their own. Come on and let's have a look at the church."

After descending the long dark stairs and entering the chapel by a side door they were surprised to find the high altar so marble-white and glittering. As they looked reverently at it a young man with his hands joined and his eyes cast down approached the priest. The lovers moved away, but they heard the man's request; his wife was outside and she wanted her baby to be baptized. Father Peter gruffly told him the name of the priest on duty. In one place an old woman was muttering prayers under her shawl. An old man told his beads under the light of the candles by the Virgin's altar. They were all poor and ragged. Suddenly they saw a wild-bearded, hollow-faced man standing away back in the nave, praying devoutly. His beard was soft but tangled; his hair was to his shoulders; he held his two arms aloft as he prayed; his eyes shone. Curiously they watched him, a little frightened.

"Who is he?" asked the girl of the priest.

"He's daft," whispered the priest. "An ex-soldier. He sometimes preaches to the empty church. Come this way."

"He'd terrify me," said the girl.

Peter laughed again as he led them down another flight of stairs through an old trap door.

"You'd go off your nut here if you took too much notice of things. Wait till I light this candle."

Down they went and the air was close and it was pitch dark beyond the candle gleam. In that little light they saw the vaults open right and left of the great supporting arches. She took her man's hand as the shapes of the coffins emerged out of the dark. A hanging bit of rusted wire caught in her hair and she gave a little scream.

"That's a bit of wire," said the priest cheerfully.

Two eyes of light from the street level stared at them.

"Do you see those holes?" he said, and they were all stooping. "The cats come in there from the street."

Before them the wall under the high altar was pierced by two tiny arches. Behind was a tiny enclosure in which they barely fitted. "Here we are." He held the candle sideways to show the lettering on a coffin plate. With his spittle he tried to rub the name clear.

"Philip Betagh," he read out. "That was the first man to be buried here. He was a hedge schoolmaster who bought the property and set up a school here. This" — he was speaking like a guide — "I forgot to say, is the site of the old Smock Alley Theatre where Peg Woffington used to foot it one time. Betagh bought the site and afterwards the church was built on it. The land belongs to the Protestants, so we still pay them a hundred and sixty pounds a year for ground rent. Think of it — nearly two hundred thousand pounds they have from us by now. Isn't it a shame!"

They felt hot and clammy. The candle smelled of its own grease. They clambered out of the place, and he showed them another and another coffin.

"I smell putrefaction," said Frank.

The priest showed them a pile of tiny coffins.

"There's something the gas people never put in their front window. An explosion that wiped out a whole slum tenement."

The girl clung, horrified, to her lover. She thought of the young wife whose baby had to be baptized, as she looked at the tiny little boxes, now falling apart and immovable.

"Oh!" she cried. "Come out, come out."

"I want to see MacNally," said Frank obstinately.

"There you are."

It lay all alone in a great vault. It was unusually large because of the lead casing. The wood was a fine red dust. A finger on it left a hole. To show them that it was of lead the priest kicked it, and for bravado the young man kicked it.

"Come, come," said the girl. "I'm baking."

They went back as they had come. The wild eyes of the mad soldier had not deflected from the high altar. The youth who had intercepted them still stood by the side door, his fingers peaked, his eyes downcast.

"Why didn't you come at the right time?" said the priest to him as he passed out to the windy, sunny September air: outside the young girl waited with her baby in an old battered pram.

The priest spoke to her more gently. "You should have come at twelve o'clock," he said.

"We were late, Father," said the girl humbly. "I was workin'."

They re-entered the presbytery and Father Peter challenged them to race him up the stairs. He took it three steps at a time. He left them in the room while he went for his hat and overcoat. He was going to take them out for a "bit of fun to celebrate."

They did not speak while he was away. She sat looking into the fire and he stood by the window, looking over the city. A light or two had begun to twinkle. The roofs were melting into one another. Somehow, since they had met the priest, several years had been added to both of them. They had come upon one of those moments of life when, like the winter butterflies in the high corners, they felt the hurt of cold. Breezily the priest returned, coated, buttoned, slapping his hands.

"Well, now, boys and girls, we'll see what Dublin has to offer in the way of life."

Meekly and slowly they followed him and on the stairs they groped for one another's fingers, and when they met they held and clutched. Outside the dusk was fallen and the night air was blue and the water of the river held an autumn mist.

While they were with him they tried hard to be gay, and they delayed him when he wanted to go, and Frank even made him promise to meet them in the morning; but, once he was gone, they hurried to their hotel along the quays, faster and faster, their hands clasped like children lost in a wood. Not until they were quite alone, and he had drawn down the window blinds, and closed the windows, shutting out the faint cry of a barking dog, did they begin to laugh; and they laughed and laughed over Peter, with his penny candle, until they had him turned into a fat Punch like the Devil in the play. Then he closed the old-fashioned plush curtains so as to shut out the least glow from the arc lamp. They undressed hastily. They lay beside one another in the dark and their passion was wild in its unrestraint.

The Confessional

IN the wide nave the wintry evening light was faint as gloom and in the shadows of the aisle it was like early night. There was no sound in the chapel but the wind blowing up from the river valley, or an occasional tiny noise when a brass socket creaked under the great heat of a dying flame. To the three small boys crouched together on a bench in the farther aisle, holding each other's hands, listening timidly to the crying wind, staring wide-eyed at the candles, it seemed odd that in such a storm the bright flames never moved.

Suddenly the eldest of the three, a redheaded little ruffian, whispered loudly; but the other two, staring at the distant face of the statue, silenced him with a great hiss like a breaking wave. In another moment the lad in the center, crouching down in fear and gripping the hand on each side of him, whispered so quietly that they barely heard, "She's moving."

For a second or two they did not even breathe. Then all three expelled a deep sigh of disappointment.

It was Monday afternoon, and every Monday, as they had each heard tell over and over again in their homes, Father Hanafin spoke with the Blessed Virgin in the grotto. Some said she came late at night; some said in the early morning before the chapel was opened; some said it was at the time when the sun goes down; but until now nobody had dared to watch. To be sure, Father Hanafin was not in the chapel now, but for all that the three little spies had come filled with high hope. The eldest spoke their bitter disappointment aloud.

"It's all my eye," he said angrily. The other two felt that what he said was true, but they pretended to be deeply shocked.

"That's an awful thing you said, Foxer," whispered the boy in the middle.

"Go away, you, Philpot!" said Foxer.

"Gor! I think it's a cause for confession, Foxer!" whispered Philpot again.

"It's a mortal sin, Foxer!" said the third, leaning over to say it.

"Don't you try to cod me, Cooney, or I'll burst yer jaw!" cried Foxer angrily.

Philpot hushed them sternly and swiftly, but the spell was broken. They all leaned back in the bench.

Beside them was Father Hanafin's confession box, its worn purple curtain partly drawn back, his worn purple stole hanging on a crook on the wall inside, and as Foxer gazed into the box with curiosity the Adversary tempted him in his heart.

"Come on, Cooney!" he invited at last. "Come on, and I'll hear yer confession."

"Gor! Come on," said Cooney, rising.

"That's a sin," said Philpot, though secretly eager to sit in the priest's chair.

"You're an awful ould Aunt Mary!" jeered Foxer, whereupon all Philpot's scruples vanished and the three scrambled for the confessor's seat. But Foxer was there before either of them, and at once he swished the curtains together as he had seen Father Hanafin do, and put the long stole about his neck. It was so nice in there in the dark that he forgot his two penitents waiting beyond the closed grilles on either side, and he was putting imaginary snuff into his nostrils and flicking imaginary specks of snuff from his chest when Cooney's angry face appeared between the curtains.

"Are yeh going to hear me confession, Foxer, or are yeh not?" he cried in a rage, eager for his turn to be priest.

"Go back, my child," said Foxer crossly, and he swished the curtains together again. Then, as if in spite, he leaned over to the opposite grille and slowly and solemnly he drew the slide and peered into the frightened eyes of Philpot.

"Tell me how long since your last confession, my child," he said gravely.

"Twenty years," whispered Philpot in awe.

"What have you done since then?" intoned Foxer sadly.

"I stole sweets, Father. And I forgot my prayers. And I cursed, Father."

"You cursed!" thundered Foxer. "What curse did you say?"

"I said that our master was an ould sod, Father," murmured Philpot timidly.

"So he is, my child. Is there anything else?"

"No, Father."

"For your penance say two hundred and forty-nine Rosaries, and four hundred and seventy Our Fathers, and three hundred and thirty-two Hail Marys. And now be a good, obedient boy. And pray for me, won't you? Gawd bless you, my child."

And with that Foxer drew the slide slowly before the small astonished face.

As he turned to the other side his hand fell on a little box — it was Father Hanafin's consolation during the long hours spent in that stuffy confessional listening to the sins and sorrows of his parishioners. Foxer's awkward fingers lifted the cover and the sweet scent rose powerfully through the darkness as he coaxed the loose snuff down from the cover. Then drawing the slide on Cooney, he gravely inhaled a pinch and leaned his ear to the cool iron of the grille.

Outside a footstep sounded on the marble floor, and peering out Foxer saw the priest walk slowly up the farther aisle, turn and walk slowly down again, his breviary held high to the slanting radiance of the Virgin's altar.

"It's Father Hanafin," whispered Foxer to Cooney; and to Philpot, "Keep quiet or we're all ruined."

Up and down the solemn footsteps went, and high above their heads in the windows of the clerestory and along the lath and plaster of the roof the wind moaned and fingered the loose slates, and now and again they heard the priest murmur aloud the deep, open vowels of his prayer, *Gaudeamus Domine,* or *Domine, Domine meo,* in a long breathing sigh.

"He's talking to the Virgin," breathed Cooney to Foxer.

"He's talking to the Virgin," breathed Foxer in turn to Philpot.

"Amen," sighed the priest, and went on his knees before the candles that shone steadily and were reflected brilliantly in the burnished brass.

The three spies had begun to peep from their hiding place when the snuff fell on Foxer's lap and the grains began to titillate his nose. In agony he held his mouth for a full minute and then burst into a furious sneeze. In astonishment the priest gazed about him and once again Foxer held his breath and once again he sneezed. At the third sneeze the priest gazed straight at the box.

"Come out!" he said in a loud voice. "Come out of that box!"

And as the three guilty forms crept from the three portals he commanded again, "Come here!"

Awkwardly they stumbled forward through the seats, trying to hide behind one another, pushing and upbraiding one another until they stood before him.

"What were you doing in there?" he asked Foxer.

"I was hearing their confession, Father," trembled Foxer, and half raised his arm as if to ward off a blow.

For a moment the priest glared at him and then he asked, "And what penance did you give?"

"I — I gave three hundred and thirty-two Hail Marys, Father, and I think it was four hundred Our Fathers, Father, and two hundred and forty-nine Rosaries, Father."

"Well!" pronounced the priest in a solemn voice. "Go home and let each one of ye say that penance three times over before nine o'clock tomorrow morning."

Stumbling over one another's heels the three crept down the dark aisle and crushed out through the green baize door and into the falling night that was torn by the storm. The street lamps were lit and under one of these they halted and looked at each other, angry and crestfallen.

"Nine hundred and ninety Hail Marys!" wailed Philpot, and Cooney squared up to Foxer with clenched fists.

"Yerrah!" said Foxer. "It's all a cod!"

And he raced suddenly away to his supper, followed by the shouts and feet of the other two.

Mother Matilda's Book

IN their starched and pointed coifs, beaklike, their winged blue sleeves, their skirts pouched about them like balloons, the sisters of Saint John of the Cross look for all the world like geese. As they talk, their cowls slew about in the air. They move as if on casters.

But, in her heyday, Mother Matilda simply was a goose. She was shapeless as a ball of fur; she clucked and stuttered — her teeth never fitted her — and as the smiling novices hopped about her, she was forever waving her hands up and down in the air as if she were winging water through the air, from the tips of her little fat hands. And as in her youth she had been a goose, in her years she was a wretched little gosling. Her clothes hung from her, she had developed a dropped eyelid, her cowl fell over her blind eye, her voice was a pip cough. When she slept in the sun, with her breath coming in gusts through her mouth, her face red with sun and sleep, her bibulous coif, and her teeth sinking slowly down to her lower lip, she was a picture nobody in the convent, least of all the novices over whom she once held power, cared to look at. She was become one of those pensioners of religion that you find in every convent, and whose doings are a constant worry to their house. She was come to

that stage when the new reverend mother — the third since her day
— began to conspire with the sisters against her; as she had in her
time conspired against the pensioners above in the graveyard.

Daily they gossiped about her, looking over their shoulders lest she
should come on them unawares; they said, nodding many times over
it, that she was a dear old soul, everyone in the convent knew that.
But after all (we get old, and she can't help it, poor dear), this
latest habit of losing her teeth was too much. Why, you might walk
on them! And Sister Eunice said that if she straightened Mother
Matilda's coif once a day, she straightened it twenty times. And
Sister Agnes whispered behind their backs that it was a pity she
dropped tea on her gimp. And Sister Ignatius thrust in her red,
country face with the two buckteeth, and cried that yesterday as
she was walking by the oratory with Father Kennedy they almost
fell over her legs, where she had them stretched out right in front
of her like a man, and she sitting on the grassbank snoring like a
trooper. They all laughed at that, but Mother John sighed impatiently and hushed them away to their tasks. They were no help to
her.

Then as she stood in the green distempered hall and looked up at
the portrait of their foundress, her eye fell on the list of *Mothers of
This House* framed beneath it. There was Matilda's name, and two
other names after it, and then, last of all, her own name, Mother
John O'Connell. Poor old Matilda had inscribed that list herself, in
a firm uncial hand with grotesque Celtic capitals — she had been
drawing mistress in her day; and, as the name *Mother John O'Connell* showed — clear and soft and flowing — inscribed only a few
months ago, she had not yet lost her skill. Mother John noted all
that; but she noted, too, with a little start of fright, the date beside
the first name of all. In five years' time that house of the North
Abbey would be seventy-five years in existence. At once she turned
and went smiling in search of Matilda.

She found her telling her beads in a shady corner, sheltering from

the summer sun and wind. She straightened her coif and, holding
her hand, led the talk to the history of the order. From their nook
the city roofs fell into the valley, hung there in a swaying hammock
of smoke. From the near back yards, with the shirts and shifts drying in the wind, and the cries of the lane children and the mothers
calling them at the top of their voices, that aerial plain narrowed out
and up to the farthest smoke rim beyond. There they could barely
see another piece of churchyard calm, the second house of Saint John
of the Cross — the South Abbey.

"Do you realize, Mother," said Mother John, "that in five years'
time it will be the jubilee of this house?"

"I do," said Mother Matilda.

"We must begin to prepare for it," said Mother John.

At the word *we* Matilda looked up with a faint hope; then she
said humbly:

"Indeed, you must, Mother."

Quickly John began to talk about their foundress, the wealthy and
charitable spinster Georgina Tinsely, whose people had made their
money out of sweet Kerry butter and lived, through the last century,
in the North Abbey. That was her portrait in the hall, a sharp,
long-jawed face, shadowed by its frilled coif. Mother John began
to complain that in spite of the interdictions of generations of reverend mothers, the frame beneath was worn shapeless by "the lanes"
about.

"Year after year," she wailed, "they rub their dirty fingers on the
wood. I even saw a woman scraping off a piece of gilt the other day
and blessing herself with it. As if it were Holy Water or a bit of
the True Cross!"

"Ah, wisha, sure," soothed Matilda, "it's no wonder. She did great
work for them."

"They don't do it in the South Abbey," said John, looking across
at it.

"She didn't live in the South Abbey," said Matilda.

"She founded it," said John.

"Well, in a way she did," said Matilda, "but it was her sister gave her wealth to it."

Gabbling away, while John listened cutely, she began to trace the spread of the order all over Ireland, recalling how a third house had been founded by a convert, how a parish priest in Kinsale had asked for a fourth, because he wanted free schools for the soldiers' children, how a bishop gave land for a fifth near Cashel, and how the order had prayed night and day when a lawsuit was being fought to get money for a sixth.

"I often heard Mother Mary, God rest her," said Matilda, "tell about the novenas they said that time. If we lost that case we'd be beggared for the next fifty years, aye, and longer!"

John looked at her — she was a bright old woman yet, she thought. Yes, she could do it all right. And if she didn't, what harm was done.

"Mother Matilda," she ordered, and she straightened the dropped coif once more, "you shall write the history of the North Abbey and the order. The book will be like the Book of Kells. It must be ready for the jubilee, and every house in the country will see it and pride in it."

She rose and looked down smilingly at the old pensioner. Matilda, like an old cat rejoicing in a sudden wave of sunshine, had stuck out her tongue between her teeth and was gazing over the city and the hills beyond. She clapped her little hands and waved the tiny sausages of fingers up and down in the air. Then her hands fell and she sighed.

"I'll begin it, Mother. But I'll never live to see the jubilee, mind you."

"You'll live to see the centenary," laughed Mother John, as she raced away, delighted with her plan.

For the first couple of years Matilda did quite well at the history. She got a huge vellum book, bound in tooled leather, a book so huge and heavy that she always had a novice beside her to lift and move it. (This was part of Mother John's cunning — it gave her an excellent excuse for putting a warder over the old nun.) With the most perdurable inks, of scarlet and violet and gall black, with Chinese white and tiny drops of gold, Matilda framed each small block of handwriting. She would spend a month tracing out the convolutions of the patterns in which she bedded her capitals, peering at them for hours through a magnifying glass held out by the trembling hand of the novice. She copied these designs from Irish manuscripts of the tenth and eleventh centuries, the great period of manuscript illumination, and she expended so much patience in making her plantlike animals brilliant and glittering, after their long voyage through their own deformities, that by the time she had spent three years on the book and covered twenty years of history, there was not a convent of the order that had not borrowed the unfinished manuscript, to show it to their sisters and patrons. Nobody cared now if she snored over her work, or if her coif fell on her neck, or if she mislaid her teeth. For she did all these things in the privacy of her cell, and if she escaped to do them elsewhere they could chide the novice to their hearts' content.

Alas! She then grew ill and her eyes began to fail her, and she grew weary of her work. She had copied all the more interesting pieces of illumination and she grew perverse and headstrong and began to invent designs for herself. But they were always the same kind of thing — vines twined about a trellis with bunches of purple grapes and great vine leaves wandering into the body of the text. A little later on she ceased to make capitals, and her round uncial declined into a ragged minuscule, from that into an angular running hand, and lastly into a childish typescript of her own. Because she was too lazy to rule her page it sloped out of the horizontal. There were several errors in spelling and the leaves were often smudged.

It grew so bad that by the time Mother Philomena succeeded Mother John the book could no longer be sent out of the North Abbey. They tried to suggest to her that she was tired and should allow

somebody else to finish the book, for by now it had become, in their
minds, a prized possession of the house. They would cluster over
her as she worked, sighing at one another behind her back, while
the novice stared at them all with a stony face, or looked at the
old nun as one might look at a strange animal. Or they would hint
that she needed more light; or one of them would lend her a ruler
that was "nicer than her own"; or the more daring ones brought
new pieces of illuminated work that they "thought she might like
to get ideas from." She would just raise her fat face with the graying mustaches and smile her thanks and go on ruining the book.

With the approach of the jubilee the last step was reached. She
hurried and scurried over the page like a rabbit, scarcely seeing
what she wrote. Her vines became leafless; their staffs sagged;
the grape bunches were either pills or big as onions. She did not
even notice if her sleeve suddenly swept a whole page into a mist.
But that was not the worst of it. She talked of nothing but the jubilee day. Clacking her teeth like an enraged monkey, she would peer
up suddenly at the novice through the thick lenses of her spectacles
and cry:

"I think we ought to exhibit it in the chapel!"

Then she would turn the half-filled page, with a stuttering, tremu-
lous:

"Where did I leave off? What last? What last?"

Or she would jump up and, wrapping her glasses in her sleeve,
hobble off to search out the new reverend mother — Philomena.

"The hall, Mother," she would grin. "That's the best place. I just
thought of it. In the hall! Can I show it in the hall?"

Whereupon Philomena, who was a shrewish city woman with a
cocked nose and a lisp, would see his Lordship stooping in amazement over the childish efforts of the old nun, or the visiting mothers
smiling sweetly at her and telling her what a great work the mother
house had done for the order, and how well they could understand
now why the book was kept from them during the last three years.

"No, dear," snapped Philomena — red to the summit of her nose — "it is a very bad place. Do straighten your cowl, Mother dear. What? In the hall? In everybody's way! Sister Agnes!" she calls out to a nun flitting by. "You know, dear, you have no right to be . . ."

So she leaves the old pensioner drooping like a broken plant, and that afternoon three separate sisters come privately to her to tell her that "poor Mother Matilda is weeping all alone in the oratory and will not leave it for anybody."

"Why," she implores Mother John (already sinking to the stage of pensioner herself), "why did you ever suggest to that poor soul to write a history of the order?"

"Oh!" cries John. "How can you be so hard on the old dear? Why, the whole convent knows she is a born saint. Please, Mother, let me tell her you will exhibit the book somewhere."

"Tell her anything you like," cried Philomena. "This jubilee will be the death of me."

And before she could retract her promise, off goes John to fetch the scribe, and off goes Philomena to conspire against the pair of them. From her office window she could see them, a few minutes later, coming hand in hand down the rosary, Matilda shining like a moon, as she unwrapped her glasses to add a few more smudges and a few more monstrous grapes to her manuscript.

It was the reverend mother, as usual, that settled the problem. She took Matilda aside and told her she had made special arrangements for the book. They would have a lectern sent up from the North Cathedral. They would drape it in purple velvet. She could have candles about it and flowers. They would give her the best room in the school, where everybody could see it in comfort.

The result was that the novice watched in terror while Matilda madly filled page after page, composing now as she went, making the most loving personal remarks about everybody in the convent, down to the new washerwoman, whose steam was even then rising from the basement.

"A most praiseworthy and Christian woman," read the novice over her shoulder. "She is married, we are informed on the best authority, to the most disgraceful . . ."

"Disgraceful?" popped Matilda back at the novice, while her hand made impatient circles over the page. "What else is he?"

"Mother, I don't know him!" wailed the novice.

"Oh! What else? What else? Disgraceful? What else could he be?" Her hand raced on.

". . . and disreputable drunkard of a man. She has ten children, she tells us, all by different husbands. But the hand of God has watched over her and lighted her a way out of the . . ."

"The what?" she cries. "The what?"

"I don't know, Mother!"

"What do you get lit out of? What? What?"

". . . pit!" writes the hand.

"Pit of what?" she cries again. "Of what?"

". . . iniquity," writes the hand, while the novice groans and tells her beads.

They finished the book so late on the eve of the jubilee day that Matilda was too exhausted to question if anybody would ever come to the geography room to see her masterpiece. It was three stories up, and all that evening they tramped up and down stairs, carrying flowers and candles, and bickering with other nuns who wanted the same flowers and candles for something else.

They barely had the room and the book prepared as the first guests arrived the following morning. The lawns were green after a providential night of showers and a morning of burning sun. The Chinese lanterns barely swayed on their strings and the tablecloths barely flapped a lazy wing under the jellies and the wines and the teacups and the cones of sweet cake. The gentle wind had cleared the city roofs of smoke and the clouds were building castles in the air. The two nuns, the old nun and the young novice, remained for hours watching the green grow black with priests as if a flock of crows had alighted there and were pecking on the lawn. They all had shiny tall hats; a neat circle of white cuff on every wrist; here and there a warm ribbon of scarlet marked out a canon or a dean.

Then his Lordship came with Mother Philomena on his right and her second-in-charge on his left, and the Mistress of Novices accompanied his secretary behind. As he passed through the crowd of clergy and lay people, he was like some giant walking through a field of rushes; at every step they sank before him on a half knee. Then he went indoors and the two nuns fluttered about their book and lit the candles and tipped the flowers.

But he did not come to their room — and no priest came to their room, and through the livelong day nobody came. Until, several hours after lunch, Mother John managed to round up two giggling schoolgirls who looked and blushed at one another, and were heard giggling louder than ever as soon as they got outside the door. John had tried hard (so she whispered to the novice), but Philomena had her cohorts so well deployed that it was impossible to get anybody even as far as the door of the school.

Then, from their window perch, the novice suddenly saw a friend of still earlier novitiate days entering with the reverend mother of the Kilcrea house. After being cooped up in that room all day, far from the fun and excitement below, her flesh weakened and she ran to seek her. ("Just for one minute, Mother dear, you won't go away, will you, his Lordship might come?") It was ten minutes, however, before she did find her, and then, hand in hand, the two young nuns went wandering under the lilacs by the gardener's shed, pressing one another's fingers under cover of their long sleeves, and smiling foolishly, as if they were both a little tipsy, and sometimes pausing to kiss when they recalled some particularly happy morning in Kilcrea. They were so full of joy that they lost all sense of time.

Left to herself, Matilda blew out the candles and wandered down, painfully, step by step, to the main parlor, and from that to the guests' parlor, and so from room to room. One or two nuns, sitting there with friends, smiled at her coldly and she retired at once. Then she heard voices in the common room, and peeping in, she saw that it was filled with priests, standing or sitting about comfortably, sipping tea or wine or smoking cigarettes. There were two or three nuns there, but though they stared at her, she did not retire. With a little croak of joy she had spied old Father Mulligan in a far corner, a parish priest she had known years ago, and she was beckoning to him and making noises like a bird to attract his attention.

At last somebody pointed her out to him and with delight he came forward and drew her in. He was a hearty, rude-faced man who had been given a small parish twenty years before in a village by the sea and he had never left it. Whiskers stood out of his ears and a kind of invading wilderness of white hair was stopped on each cheek by the razor. He was the only priest there smoking a pipe. He bowed over her and flattered her, and they talked for a while over everybody they knew — though it was one long litany of God-rest-them! — until his curate came by and he was led forward to meet the old nun.

"The oldest sister in the house," boomed Father Mulligan.

"Interesting!" murmured the curate humbly. "It should be commemorated. The *doyenne* of the house."

The next thing Matilda knew was a sudden fall in the clamor of talk about her and they were all listening to old Father Mulligan calling on them to drink "in wine, whiskey, or good strong tay" the health of the *doyenne* of the North Abbey.

"And she's still at work, I may say. She has completed the history of the order of Saint John of the Cross."

"History?" one or two murmured with interest.

"Illuminated like the Book of Kells," palpitated Matilda. "It's on exhibition in the geography room and I wish you'd all come and see it."

"Let's all go and see it," said Father Mulligan, while the three nuns looked at one another in horror.

"This way," piped Matilda, turning round and round like a peg top, unable, in her excitement, to find the door.

But then she clapped her hands to her mouth and stared around at them in fright.

"What's wrong, Mother?" asked the curate in his miserable, whining, too-humble voice.

"My teeth," wailed Matilda. "I've lost my teeth. I think I had them in my hand when I came into the common room."

"Let's find them," cried a merry little man with a bush of curly hair.

He had drunk just a shade too much Beaune in the wine tent.

"A search! A search!" he cried.

Whereupon they all began to wave their hands in the air and lift cushions and flowerpots, and, stooping, they raised their behinds before armchairs and peeped under settees, and they opened cupboards that they should not have opened, while the three nuns fled for Philomena and her cohorts, and above all for the wretched novice who had allowed Matilda to escape.

"Lost! A row of delft!" cried Curly Mop.

"Aurora's pearls," said the classical scholar.

"Upper or lower?" teased Father Mulligan, while Matilda in a corner searched herself all over.

The fun and scurry was at its height when his Lordship entered, ushered in by Philomena's second-in-charge.

"Oh, my!" he said in his gentle country brogue that broke every word into an iambic sigh. "O-oh, m-my!"

"It's Mother Matilda," explained Father Mulligan's curate in a sad voice, dropping his cigarette behind him where a friend deftly crushed it under his toe. "She has mislaid her denture," he went on, and he said it like a naughty schoolboy, looking up at the bishop under his fair eyebrows.

"Oh, my!" groaned his Lordship sympathetically.

"And who," he croaked in his graveyard voice, that with time had become gentle and slow, because nobody had ever dared to interrupt him, "who may Mother Matilda be?"

"She is Father Mulligan's friend," said the curate wickedly, as if he were saying, "It's poor old Mulligan at it again, milord."

But Father Mulligan did not mind. He led her forward.

"The oldest sister of the order," he said. "The *doyenne* of the abbey."

Matilda dropped on her two knees and kissed the extended ruby, once, twice, three times.

"Once for a man," murmured the curate under his breath, "twice for a woman, three times for a fool."

"Well, well!" smiled his Lordship, and the first "well" was up in a tree, and the second "well" was as deep as a well. "Well, well!"

"Give me your blessing, your Lordship," pleaded Matilda.

His hand wavered it over her crooked coif. The priests gathered near, away from the wineglasses, and watched with interest.

"I hope, my child," smiled the bishop, "that you will have many more long and happy years."

The face of Philomena appeared in the door, behind it a bunch of dismayed faces peeping over her shoulder.

"Dear Mother Matilda," greeted Philomena, coming forward. "I hear Sister Kieran left you. It was naughty of her."

She smiled at the bishop and led Kieran forward.

"Sister Kieran wants to show you a pigeon's egg," she went on to Matilda.

The round face of the little novice was pale as a mushroom.

"A lovely little pigeon's blue and white spotted egg," she babbled, "such a lovely little egg, come and see it."

Matilda looked blankly at her.

"Go," croaked his Lordship, and he smilingly patted Matilda's arm, "go and see the pigeon's egg!"

"It's green with blue spots on it," said the novice eagerly. "It's marvelous! It's lovely!"

She led her charge out and away down the corridor. She almost dragged her in her haste.

"But my teeth," wailed Matilda, stumbling after her. "And the book."

"In the geography room," said Kieran. "You left them there, maybe."

"And the book?" wailed Matilda. "They are coming to see the book."

"You left that in the geography room, too. We must light the candles. Hurry. Hurry."

Matilda was panting before she reached the room. While Kieran lit the candles she drew her breath at the window. From there she saw the bishop go out into the garden and then down the alley to the main gate. The priests, like cockchafers, flowed in his wake. Matilda said nothing, but her coif slewed after them as they passed out of sight.

The rumble of the evening of the city came to her, and near at hand a mother calling loudly to her child. A gentle mist was beginning to fall and Matilda lost herself in gazing out through that shimmer of haze. The novice was looking at the flame of a candle, and her eyes were soft and her mouth trembling. She sniveled.

"He's a lovely priest," said Matilda suddenly. "And he gave me his blessing. But," she gulped, "he never saw the book."

Suddenly she noticed the tears in the novice's eyes.

"Never mind, dear. We'll show the book another day," encouraged the old nun.

"It isn't that," wept the novice, who was thinking of her little friend in Kilcrea. "But Sister Mary Michael is — is — is as thin as a latch."

And she wept openly at the thought that her friend might die.

For a moment Matilda tried to understand, but then she began to pick at her back tooth and look over the misted roof and her eyes, once more enlarged with her own little grief, went gray with the light of the falling rain.

"Ja-a-a-anie!" screamed the mother below in the lane. "Come ho-o-a-ame! I'll give you lamb-and-sally when I ca-a-a-atch yeh! Ja-a-a-anie!"

Faintly in the distance a child's voice replied. Then they heard, far away, the rumble of the town. One by one the novice extinguished the candles and led the old nun down to the babble of the refectory for her supper. As she had not found her teeth, however, she could eat nothing. So she spent the whole hour looking before her and listening vacantly to the nuns talking of the excitement of the day.

One True Friend

THE lonely woman was as big a . . . No! I won't say it. 'Twasn't a very kind thing I was going to say. And I suppose that's the way God made her. And, as the old joker said, we're all as God made us — and some of us worse. But I will say this about her, and her own sons often said it — and 'twas they gave her the name of the lonely woman — she was (if you will pardon my saying so) a damn nuisance. Mind you, she was a good soul — a good, pious, kindly, Christian soul. But she was a nuisance. Her trouble was that she really was lonely, and she was always complaining about how lonely she was, but she would never do anything about it because, so I firmly believe, she liked being lonely.

Where she lived, of course, was no fit place for any Christian to live. She lived in her old rooky-rawky of a house over a tinsmith's shop, where she'd lived since she was first married, and where she'd brought up her family, and where her husband was carried out on the flat of his back, but where now — for she had let her extra rooms, one by one, to the tinsmith downstairs — you heard nothing all day long but the tinny hammering, a *tic-tac-too, tic-tac-*

too that would drive anybody mad. And what kind of a house was it, where you smelled nothing but boiling solder from morning to night?

Her sons were always at her to leave it and she'd say, "I know I ought to leave it. I know it's no place for a lonely woman like me. Nobody to hand me as much as a drop of cold water if I got a stitch in the middle of the night, or maybe an appendicitis. But sure where can I go?"

"But," they'd say then, "Mother, come and live with us!"

"Oh, no!" she'd say then. "Oh, no! Is it go and live with a daughter-in-law? Ha! Cock 'em up with comfort. 'Tisn't mother-in-laws they want. Oh, no! Nobody wants a poor lonely old woman like me."

And then her sons would persuade her, and their wives would persuade her, and perhaps, after a lot of persuading, she would agree, and they would go home and get a room ready for her. She would change her mind during the night. Not that they blamed her. Her little kitchen was her palace, and she was the queen of it. She had her cup and her saucer, and her knife and her fork, and she could come when she liked and go when she liked. And if it was a bit silent there at night, when there wasn't a sound from the city, and not a sound in the house but the mice scrabbling downstairs in the dustbin, or the tap dripping, well, she had other things. She had company of her own kind. She would sit looking into the fire in the range, her eyes lost in the great distance of her love for her dead husband, her dead sisters, or the saints. Her sons had each, at one time or another, seen her like that, and as they would look about them at their childhood home picked to the bone, they would find that even in the middle of the day the busy, hammering house would cease to exist, and the little city streets would drop away. Looking at her, and hearing her gentle sigh, how could anyone say to her then, as they so often said on other occasions, "Mother, why the blazes don't you try to make some friends?" — not seeing her glance up with a smile at Saint Francis, and Saint Francis smiling back.

Then one day, one August second, to be precise, out of the blue, lo and behold, she wrote to one of her sons that she had just met a very nice woman. It had apparently happened when she was doing the Ins and Outs. The Ins and Outs is a devotion where you pay as many visits as possible to a church on the feast called Portiuncula. You go in one door, and say a prayer, and come out another, and that counts as a visit. Then you go back, say another prayer, come out, and that is a second visit, and so on until weariness defeats the pious heart. Mrs. Moore was doing this, very contentedly, when she suddenly noticed a young girl in a red beret passing quietly from one Station of the Cross to another. She smiled happily, and went on with her prayers. The church was warm with imprisoned sunlight and the candles on the altar drank in the air. The hot gladioli consumed themselves among the consuming lights. Peace and comfort fell on the old lady, and when the girl slipped in beside her on the bench she was about to put out her hand to stroke the child's head when she saw the girl's fingers creep along the bench, take her purse, and disappear. The next thing was the girl running up the aisle. Mrs. Moore ran after her. The girl ran faster. The old woman called on her to stop. The worshipers stood up and looked at them. The girl dropped the purse in the hall and ran across the street — where she was nearly killed by a bus — and the lonely woman fainted. When she woke up she was in the sacristy, and a lady whom she had often seen before was giving her a glass of water.

"You're all right now, Mrs. Moore," said the lady.

"How well you know my name," she whispered.

"Oh, sure, we all know Mrs. Moore," said the lady. "Is there a church in the city that doesn't know you? Sure, you live in the churches."

"It's my only company," she sighed.

"A holy woman," said the lady. "We know you as well as we know the priests. My name is Mrs. Calvert."

"What a shocking thing to happen!"

"Frightful," said Mrs. Calvert. "Especially when you think the girl was so young. Think of the condition of her soul!"

"We must do something about it," said the lonely woman.

At once the two old ladies became as friendly in that common cause as if they had been friends all their lives. They toddled across the street to the dairy where Mrs. Calvert lived, and each had a glass of milk. If anybody had looked in through the open door and seen them or if anybody had heard them, he would have said that they were sisters. It turned out that they were alike in everything except what didn't matter. They were both widows. Their families were scattered. They both lived alone. Each was the kind of woman who tells the time by the tolling of the church bells. Mrs. Moore hated the noise of the tinsmith. Mrs. Calvert was waked every morning by the clank of churns. And if the smell of boiling solder is not nice, neither is the smell of sour milk and cow manure. Nothing distinguished them except that, as they laughingly said, one of them swore by Saint Francis and the other swore by Saint Peter in Chains. After a while, when they were getting up to go, it was a case of:

"And now, Mrs. Moore, that we know each other, won't you pray for me?"

"Oh, Mrs. Calvert, how can you say that? It is you who must pray for me."

"Now, now, Mrs. Moore, you know you're a saint anointed."

"Ah, Mrs. Calvert, that's all you know. I'm a sinner. A wicked sinner. But when I look at you, I say to myself, 'If there was ever a soul with the mark of salvation on her, it's Mrs. Calvert.' "

"Now, Mrs. Moore, it's not kind of you to flatter a wicked person. You must pray for me every day. I need it badly."

"Mrs. Calvert, we'll pray for one another."

When she had come home from this happy adventure the lonely woman met a strange man on her doorstep.

"Am I speaking to Mrs. Moore?" he said politely.

"How well you know my name," she said.

"Oh," he smiled, "sure, we all know Mrs. Moore."

"Really?" she said, very pleased, very grand, but very humble. "A poor lonely woman like me that I thought nobody knew!"

He laughed at that.

"Now," he said, "I believe you had a purse snatched from you this morning?"

"Oh? And who told you that?"

"A friend of yours."

"A friend of mine? Who on earth can that be?"

"She gave her name as Mrs. Calvert. She rang up the police station a quarter of an hour ago. I'm a police detective, and I must investigate the matter. We've had a lot of these complaints recently. Mrs. Calvert said you'd recognize this girl. Is that right?"

"You mean would I know her again? I'd know her painted."

"Fine! Now, I'll tell you what I'll do. If I have a motor car here at your very door, tomorrow morning, will you come down to the Bridewell, and if we have that girl there will you recognize her?"

"O-o-oh, n-o-o-o!" said Mrs. Moore. "I couldn't do *that!*"

And she began a long, long rigmarole that went on for half an hour about how she never went out except to go to the church, and how she could never go down there, behind the old-clothes' market, to the Bridewell, where all the drunks are put every night, and how she really never did go anywhere, and how her sons were always at her to go out more and make friends, and what a lonely life she had, and how it would be far better if she did go out, and all about how she used to go out long ago with her husband, and all about her sisters, and her daughters-in-law, and he listened with the endless curiosity of the born detective, and the endless patience of a man whose spirit is broken from dealing with women, and he kept on talking about that motor car, and how she would drive across the city, and be driven back again, until, gradually, his tempting began to win out. She began to see herself in the car. She thought how she would tell her sons about it. She yielded. Off he went, wiping his brow, exhausted but victorious.

But she did not yield in her mind. At the back of her head, there was a feeling that everything was not quite right. However, her sons had always told her that she was much too suspicious, and that she would make many more friends if she were less suspicious, so she shoved it down and tried to forget all about it.

The following morning she went to the Bridewell in the car, and though her old heart began thumping at the sight of the room the detective took her to, and the handcuffs hanging up, and all the police with their collars open, she did exactly as she was told. She went in and looked at the line-up and came out and said, "Yes. She was there. The fifth girl from the end, in the red beret." She was so happy at having done this that she did not pay a great deal of attention to what else they told her, and she was home, after a ride again in the car, before it dawned on her what exactly they had told her. Then she realized that she would have to go to the district court, and get up, before everybody, in the witness box and swear that this was the girl. At that she sat down and shook all over. The girl's relatives would see her. Rough lane people. Her father, her brother, her mother would accost her in the street and abuse her.

"Oh!" she gasped. "The clever woman! She knew that she might be called on to identify the girl. That was why she sent the detective to me. Oh, the guile! The guile and cleverness of some people! And me, a poor, lonely old woman! What a thing to do to a poor, simple old woman the like of me!"

Whereupon she clapped her hat on her head, and with her white hair flying in the wind she went back to the Bridewell, and sought out the detective and said to him:

"I made a mistake. It was the wrong girl. I remember now. My head is getting addled. I'm so old I don't know what I do be saying. You must forget all about it."

And even though that man was a patient man, and knew how to handle women, he could not budge her; not with pleading, begging, imploring, even threatening, not even when he sat down on one of the iron-legged stools and growled at her like a tiger.

"Oh, no!" said the lonely woman. "I'm not able for the world at all. I'm all alone by myself, and I can't be up to the clever and calculating people that are in it. Let the wise and clever Mrs. Calvert do it this time — the brave and gallant Mrs. Calvert, with her Saint Peter in Chains, and her 'Pray for me, Mrs. Moore!' "

And she told him about her lonely life, and her sisters, and her dead husband, and her sons, and her daughters-in-law, and he listened, and then he said:

"You know! Mrs. Calvert *is* going to identify the girl for us. She promised me today that she would. You're wronging her. It's just that she wants you to keep her company. As she says herself, she is of a very nervous disposition and a melancholy turn of mind."

"Nervous?" cried Mrs. Moore. "I'm five and forty times as nervous as her! What right has she to be nervous and she living over a dairy? Not like a poor, wretched, abandoned creature like me, living with a hammering in my ears all day long — a boozing and a woozing would addle a saint."

And off she went again about her sons and her sisters and her husband and her daughters-in-law, but it was all to blind herself against the fact that she *had* been wronging Mrs. Calvert, and that her suspicious mind — against which her sons so often warned her — had led her astray. At the same time, the detective, in his ingratiating country brogue, kept talking about the car and the drive, and once more, before she rightly knew what she was doing, she yielded, and before she could change her mind, he fled from her and took two double whiskeys at his own expense.

Next morning there was Mrs. Calvert smiling sweetly down at

her, as if it was *her* bag that was snatched, and as if it was *she* owned the car, and as if the detective was *her* chauffeur, and as if it was *she* who had planned it all. They started off, and the two old ladies chatted the whole way. They enjoyed the sun, and the crowds, and the traffic, and whenever they saw anybody they knew walking along the streets they waved whether the people saw them or not. They said they were doing the right thing, and the girl would be thankful in the end, and the church would be thankful, and the city ought to be thankful, and by the time they had said all that, they were being ushered together into the room with the handcuffs hanging on the wall and the bare stools and the policemen with their collars open as always.

They went in together. Side by side, very pale, Mrs. Moore and Mrs. Calvert walked up and down before the row of suspects, and sure enough, they saw the bag snatcher staring up at them as bold as brass. They said nothing; they were not supposed to until they came out; but when they came out they said nothing either. At this, the detective, very much surprised, challenged them:

"Well? Ye *did* recognize her! I saw ye did!"

The two pious old ladies gave one another short glances, and the lonely woman whispered:

"What would you say, Mrs. Calvert?"

"Did *you* recognize her, Mrs. Moore?" murmured the other, shaking from head to foot, and with her mouth in a twisty smile like a woman with palsy.

"I was wondering, Mrs. Calvert, what *you* would say," the lonely woman replied, her two little fists tightly clutched.

"Look here!" put in the detective. "After all my trouble, don't tell me ye're going to let me down again?"

"Oho! You can't be up to the cleverness of the world nowadays!" said the lonely woman.

"*You* have been very nice about everything," Mrs. Calvert said, turning to him. "It was a lovely motor drive. I enjoyed it very much."

The detective gazed at them, first the one shut mouth, and then the other. He saw them looking at him pityingly.

"I understand," he growled. "If *you* went in first you'd say 'No,' and leave it to the other. And if *you* went in first, you'd say 'No,' and leave it to her. Oh, ye're a lovely pair, by the holies! That she may rob yeer mangy sowls from ye at the Day of Judgment!"

He let them walk home. It was a hot day, and the two ladies were soon tired. They did not speak to each other as they walked across the city. They were so exhausted that they passed two churches without stopping to go in. At last, they came to their own parish church, and at the entrance they separated, bowing to each other without a look or a word. They went into the cool dimness of the church, each to her separate corner, and presently the two gray heads were drooping piously and the familiar beads of prayer dropped from their lips. The lonely woman looked up at Saint Francis, and the other looked up at Saint Peter in Chains. Cautiously, now and again, each looked across the nave when the other was not looking, and then she would turn back, with a sigh of trust and happiness, to look up again at her one true friend.

The Man Who Invented Sin

IN OUR youth when we used to pour into the mountains to learn Irish, places that were lonely and silent for the rest of the year became full of gaiety during the summer months. Every day there were picnics and expeditions; every night there were dances, moonlight boating parties, singsongs in the cottages. The village street became a crowded promenade; its windows never went black before one in the morning; the pub was never empty. Where once you could have been utterly alone half a mile off the road, in the bog or up the mountain, you could not now be sure of privacy anywhere. If you went up the mountain to bathe naked in some tiny loch you might suddenly see a file of young students like Alpineers coming laughing down on you over the next scarp; you might turn the corner of a lonely mountain pass courting your girl and burst upon a bevy of nuns sedately singing choruses among the rocks — for every kind of teacher, laymen and women, nuns, priests, and monks were encouraged in those years to come out into the hills.

How we all got accommodation I do not know. The priests took lodgings in the villages. The monks and nuns purchased derelict houses which had been abandoned by the landlords after the Revolution. The people gave up their best rooms to the rest of us, turned lofts into dormitories, one or two even set up secondhand bell tents. One July, so stifling was the house where I stayed — six at least to every room — that I used to take a rug every night and climb into the high hay in the barn; and there were always four or five like me who preferred to be bitten by the ticks and waked early by the birds and the mountain air than to be half suffocated in featherbeds under the baking slates. By the end of the month, however, I got so tired of digging the little crablike ticks from under my skin that I moved two miles out the road to a place called Ryder's, a small house on the lower lake, which usually took nobody at all. Indeed, only by great cajoling did I persuade Mrs. Ryder to take me in. My only fear, then, was that I might be lonely. But before she knew what had happened Mrs. Ryder had not merely one lodger but five; for with the beginning of August the monks' hostel overflowed, and the nuns' hostel overflowed, and she had to take in two of the monks and two of the nuns.

There was nothing remarkable about my fellow students, except, perhaps, that little Sister Magdalen was so dainty and gay and spirited that it seemed a shame to lock her away from the world in a convent. Sister Chrysostom was tall, delicate, with big hands and a blotchy skin, and she walked with her toes turned in. She was a bit of a Miss Prim, and I think she had been chosen as companion for Sister Magdalen because she was so prim. Brother Virgilius was a countryman with a powerful frame and a powerful voice, round red cheeks, and no nerves, and why he had chosen to be a monk was hard to understand. It seemed to me that he would have made a better farmer than a teacher. However, I found that he was a fine hurler and I am sure the boys loved him for his natural ways. Brother Majellan was very different, a gentle, apple-cheeked man with big glasses, a complexion like a girl's, teeth as white as a hound's, and soft, beaming eyes. He was an intelligent, sensitive man. I took to him immediately.

At first we saw very little of one another. They had their principal meal at their own hostels, were studying most of the day, and the only time we all met was in the evenings, when we sat in the little garden and passed discreet remarks across the path about politics or the weather; or, if there was rain, we would meet in the drawing room, where there was a turf fire, and talk of the day's lessons. They kept convent hours, were off to their rooms by nine at the latest, and long before I rose were gone down to the village to morning Mass. That year, however, the weather broke suddenly in the middle of August so that we found ourselves in the drawing room almost every evening, over our notebooks and dictionaries and grammars. We had, by then, become like travelers on a long railway journey who have broken the silence and are beginning to chat companionably. We might still sit silent for, say, a quarter of an hour, but then somebody would say something and we would all get going. One night, for instance, Majellan lifted his eager, earnest, doggy eyes, and said:

"Sister Magdalen, how do you pronounce the word which I call *cearrbhach?*"

"Oh, Brother Majellan," she laughed, shocked at herself, entertained by her own folly, "I am afraid I do not even know what the word means!"

Virgilius clapped his two big countryman's paws together and roared out laughing.

"Sister Magdalen, I'm surprised at you! I'm surprised at you! Not know the word *cearrbhach?* It means a card player or a gambler."

"And is that what it means? *Cearrbhach.*" And she pronounced the guttural word as daintily as if it rhymed with *peruke.*

She was a city girl and had never before heard Irish spoken by anybody but city people.

"No! You're not saying it right at all. You're too ladylike about it. Say it the way the people say it. *This* way."

"I see." And again the dainty pronunciation like *peruke.* "Like that?"

"Listen, Sister. I'll show you the way to talk Irish. If you'll pardon the expression, make a great big shpit inside in your mouth and gurgle it. Like this: *carrrwoochhhk.*"

Chrysostom immediately protested.

"Please, Brother Virgilius! If we cannot speak our own language like ladies let us not speak it at all."

"But," from Majellan, "that really is the way the people speak. It is a guttural language. Like German."

"Not Bavarian German. It is true that the Prussians . . ."

And off they went into a heated argument — the sort of argument we were always having in those days, about whether Ireland must always be a peasant country, and what other countries had achieved, and Virgilius, who hated arguments, blew out his lips and looked gloomily at his two big feet stretched out before him, and Majellan and Magdalen got so excited that Chrysostom had to stop it with her usual:

"Sister, I really think it is our hour to retire."

One day at the college, as we called the sun-baked tin building where we studied from ten to one, we were asked to write an essay on a proverb to which the nearest Saxon equivalent is "The child is father to the man." I remember, that evening, how the mists lifted from the hills, and the sun began to raise gentle wisps of steam from the rocks, and the trout were leaping from a lake as blue as the patches of sky between the dissolving clouds. We spread newspapers on the two damp garden seats, and as we discussed the proper Irish terms to be used, the four of them began, without noticing it, to speak of their own childhood; where they had been born, where they went to school, and so on. Sister Magdalen sucked the end of her silver pencil and said:

"I know the Gaelic for 'I was born.' That is *Do rugadh mé.* And the place — Templemore. Of course, that is *An Teampall Mór.* The Great Temple. Or The Big Church. Though the Lord knows there's no big temple in Templemore." She sighed. Then she

cocked her head suddenly. "I suppose you were never in Templemore, Brother Majellan? But, sure, why would you! It's an out-of-
the-way little place."

Chrysostom tapped my fingers irritably with her pencil. I was idly
pulling a fuchsia flower to pieces.

"How would you say that, Sister?"

"Which? What? What was it you said, Sister Chrysostom?"

" 'It's an out-of-the-way little place.' You see, I want to say that,
too. I was born in a small little place like Templemore."

"Where was that?" asked Virgilius idly. He had been staring
solemnly at the fuchsia that I threw into his lap.

"Kilfinnane," said Chrysostom, "in County Limerick."

At once Virgilius whirled and slapped her thigh.

"Yerrah, Chrysostom, do you mean to tell me that you come from
Kilfinnane!"

"Brother!" And she held his arm excitedly. "Do you know Kilfinnane?"

"Do I know my own father? Wasn't I born just below in Kilmallock? Oh, wisha, then, 'tis many the fine Sunday I took the old
bicycle out to Kilfinnane hunting hares behind the rath. If you come
from Kilfinnane you must surely know the rath?"

"The rath is on our land!"

"Ah, no?"—in a huge childish delight.

"Often and often I stood on the rath and looked down at the
smoke of the train coming into Kilmallock—in and out of the
woods—the little white smoke. And I could watch it again for another half an hour after it left Kilmallock, puffing away down towards Cork."

"I well believe you! It's a wonderful view. They say you can see
six counties!"

"For a whole hour," she remembered. "The little white smoke. I
used to wonder who might be in it, and would I ever travel away
in it myself."

"Didn't I go every night to meet it at the station and gather the Dublin papers, for my uncle kept a paper shop in the Main Street? The Cork train we called it. Majellan, you're a Corkman, aren't you?"

Majellan was not listening to us. He was gazing across the darkening lake whose headlands were faint as smoke.

"My father," said Sister Magdalen thoughtfully, "was a doctor. I know how to say that, too. My mother died when I was fourteen. . . . I was a lone child. . . . My father married a second time."

Majellan kept staring over the lake. She said something about a notebook and flitted indoors. I got tired of listening to Virgilius and Chrysostom and got up to go to the dance. It was only then I noticed that Majellan and Magdalen were in the hall. She was dabbing her eyes with his big red handkerchief.

When I came back from the dance the half-moon had vaporized the moist land with a melancholy, filmy light. The house was black and silent.

I think it was Virgilius who first began to play pitch-and-toss along the garden path, and it was that evening that Magdalen called Majellan "Jelly." I came on them laughing over the game, which Brother Virgilius was trying to teach to the other three. Brother Majellan was, by then, calling Sister Magdalen "Maggie," Chrysostom naturally became "Chrissy," and Virgilius, of course, joined Jelly as "Jilly." How they laughed over that! I crowned the night for them by taking them up to the drawing-room piano and teaching them all a song with a chorus: *"Bab Eró'gus O mo mhíle grá."*

And Chrissy so surprised us by the strength and sweetness of her voice that at the end Virgilius clapped his hands and shouted, "I wouldn't doubt you, Chrissy. I knew you had it in you," and made her sing the song again alone. As she sang we heard a clear echo: it was a boating party out on the lake. They took up the chorus and gave it back to her until they faded around a headland still singing.

"But you know," gurgled Magdalen, "I really don't know what it all means. Can you translate it for me, Jelly?"

"No trouble at all," said Majellan. "It is a young fellow singing a song to his lady and this is what he says."

As he translated he gradually blushed redder and redder, and Virgilius winked at the big, rolling eyes of Magdalen, and her rounded little mouth, just ready to burst into laughter. When Majellan stuck his head right out through the window to look at the lake Magdalen burst. Chrysostom said, "I really think, Sister, it is our hour to retire."

"Jelly," said Virgilius, when they were gone, "you big gom! You have as much sense as a child of two."

When monks and nuns quarrel, I found, they seem to be astonished and shocked rather than angry: like children who have bumped against a door or a calf who has tried his first nettle. Grown men would have ended it with a curse or a clout. I escaped down to the kitchen to practice my Irish on Mrs. Ryder. She was baking a cake, and humming *"Bab Eró . . ."* Her cousin, who was the clerk in the post office, was sitting on the settle. She asked me which had the lovely voice. Mrs. Ryder said her house was blessed.

"The creatures! Isn't it grand to hear them enjoying themselves? Four saints I have in the house."

"Only four?" I protested.

"What time did *you* come in last night?" she asked, and the conversation became exuberantly coarse.

The next evening, too, was exquisitely silent. The tiny trout splashes could be heard clearly, and the cattle lying on the dry strand across the water chewing the cud. We were all upstairs, I playing the piano, Virgilius seated in the open window singing and beating time with a silver tankard that young Ryder won in a tug of war, Jelly and Maggie trying to waltz, and when Chrissy was not laughing at poor Jelly's efforts to learn the steps she, too, was singing, at *"Bab Eró,"* like a blackbird. The music must have carried a long way over the water.

The door was slashed open with a bang that made the piano hum, and there was our local curate's black barrel of a body blocking the opening: for though he was not more than twenty-five — I believe it was his first parish — he was very fat. He was also pompous and cocksure. In the college we called him Lispeen, which is the Irish for a frog. For that second it was as if a cinema reel stopped dead — the tankard held in the air, the two dancers like a waxworks, and Chrissy with her mouth open.

"Glory be to God," he moaned. "So I have been informed correctly." (It was only after that I thought of the postmistress on the settle the night before; you might as well talk to a microphone as to a postmistress.) "To think that this kind of thing has been going on under my nose for weeks." He let his voice fall solemnly, even secretively. "Unknown to anybody!" He roared then. "To think I cannot go for a summer walk to read my office without hearing this kind of caterwauling!" His voice fell again. "If Martin Luther could only see this! What's your name?" he stabbed at Chrissy. She had turned as pale as her coif.

"Sissster Chryssossostom, Father."

"And your name, Sister?"

"My name is Sister Mary Magdalen," said Maggie, very dignified and entirely self-possessed, and looking very angry.

"Well named," he growled. I saw Jelly grow red with fury. "Go to your rooms, please. I'll talk to these gentlemen." With a scornful emphasis on the last word.

They fluttered out obediently, Magdalen with her head in the air, Chrysostom with terror in her eyes. Majellan turned on him. I held his arm. He was only a monk, and no match for a curate in his own parish.

"You had no right, Father, to talk to the sisters like that."

The curate swelled.

"Are you daring to answer me back, young man?"

Majellan's voice shook, but he held his ground.

"We were doing no harm."

Even Virgilius spoke up, though more respectfully — he knew the power before him.

"Sure we were only having a bit of singsong, Father?"

The curate gasped, melodramatically — I swear he had taken a prize for elocution at his seminary — then dropped into a wonderful tone of sarcasm.

"Only having a bit of a singsong? *Only* having a bit of a singsong? Well, well!" He put his stick behind him like a shooting stick and teetered back and fro on it. He was very sure of himself. "Perhaps, gentlemen, we think that we are back in the days of the Reformation?" Then he did his roar again. "Singing? Dancing? Drinking?" He whirled his stick and cracked the tankard.

Virgilius stared into the tankard, and sighed. "Shweepstake tickets."

That sent the blood to Lispeen's forehead.

"I'll talk to you young bucks in the morning when I've had a word with your superior. Good evening to you."

The door slammed. We heard him go downstairs. His voice boomed in the kitchen at the Ryders. Then we saw his shadow passing across the paling sheen of the lake.

"The bosthoon," hissed Majellan.

"Jelly," moaned Virgilius, who had seized the situation at once, "we're for the long drop!"

With that we stole down the corridor and tapped at the sisters' doors and conferred in a huddle, and Virgilius and Chrysostom blamed Majellan for speaking back, but Magdalen said, "You were quite right, Brother. He is no gentleman." But Chrysostom kept pulling her fingers and looking at each of us in turn. She knew, too, how all this would appear back in the city, where the bishop and their superiors would say, "What is this! Nuns and monks living in the same house? Dancing together? Singing choruses? Playing pitch-and-toss out in the garden? And what's all this about *a tankard?*"

Magdalen said next morning that she heard Chrysostom crying late into the night.

Actually nothing at all happened. Old Ryder and the parish priest between them must have put a stop to the curate's gallop. After all, curates come and curates go but parish priests, like the brook, go on forever. But the story spread, and the students gathered around the four to comfort and encourage them, and of evenings people started to walk out to Ryder's and, in spite of Sister Chrysostom's warnings and tremors, we began to have regular concerts in the garden. The four even began to go out on surreptitious boating parties, and the bed-at-nine rule gradually became bed at ten, and even bed at eleven, until they were soon having as happy a time as anybody. Or should have, if their consciences were at ease. But were they? For, looking back at it now, I think I understand what had occurred. The Serpent had come into the garden with the most wily of temptations. He had said, "How dare you eat this apple?" And straightaway they began to eat it. They swallowed the last morsel of their apple the night before they were due to return to the city, perhaps for a lifetime, among the smelly slums about their schools.

We were moody that evening in the garden.

"I suppose this will be the last time we'll see the moon on the lake," said Sister Magdalen.

But the moon would not be up until after eleven, and a fairy wind in the reeds, ruffling the stars in the water into a fuzz, meant that even then there might be a clouded night.

"Our bus goes at seven," said Sister Chrysostom. "When does yours go, Brother Virgilius?"

By anticipation they were already becoming formal with one another.

"Half past seven," said Brother Virgilius.

"Who'll walk as far as the lake?" suggested Brother Majellan.

They went down the white road. Autumn was coming already. A white mist hung low over the river. The lake was breathed upon. They stood at the edge of it and looked at the low hills beyond.

"Sure, we can be looking forward to next year," said Brother Virgilius cheerfully.

"If there are any summer courses next year," murmured Sister Magdalen.

The soft sound of oars was heard and a boat appeared out on the water. The people in it were singing quietly; a last boating party. It was one of those big bargelike boats built for excursion parties, and there must have been twenty people in it, crushed shoulder to shoulder. Majellan hailed them and they approached and when they invited the four out for a row even Chrissy hardly demurred. The presence of the two monks and the two nuns seemed to cheer them up, for as they rowed away towards the narrows, making for the upper lake, the songs became louder and more merry. The lights of the village overflowed into the lake. Promenaders there heard them and sang back. Doubtless the curate heard them, too, and thanked God they would all be gone in the morning.

Time ceases to exist on a lake: every fisherman knows that. Somebody said that the moon would be up at eleven and would light them home. Chrissy whispered to Maggie that that would be very late, and what would happen if some message came from the hostel? But Maggie hushed her passionately, and Virgilius cried, "Let the last night be the longest."

It was much later than eleven before they got through the narrows — the old barge stuck there as it always did. Then the gray mountain slowly swelled up like a ghost against the spreading moon, and the whole land became black and white. On the bright side of the land the white cottages shone under their tarry roofs, and on the dark hills their scattered yellow lights invited us home. It became cold on the water. Rowing back against the current was a slow business. Heavy drops of phosphorescence fell from the blades. Presently a voice said, "It is near twelve, lads, put your backs into it." Now they were not singing at all; nor did they sing again until they saw the remaining village lights — only one or two left now. And they did not sing Irish songs, which are nearly all melancholy, but old music-hall songs like "Daisy, Daisy," and "The Girls You Can't Forget," and "I'm One of the Knuts of Barcelona." The barge was not much more than twelve feet from the shore when they saw, clear in the moonlight, the black figure standing on the causeway. Majellan yelled, "Backwater!" The barge slewed around.

"I suppose, my dear ladies and gentlemen, that it does not matter to you that you are keeping the whole village awake?"

Nobody replied. The rowers set off for the opposite shore. The two brothers turned up their coat collars to hide their Roman collars. The two nuns hid their gimps and coifs with borrowed coats. Everybody was feeling cross and tired. As they neared the far shore the same black figure awaited them. He had raced round by the bridge, and gone leaping over heather and bog pool.

"You won't land here tonight until I have the name of every person on that boat!"

The midnight mountain cried back, "On — that — boat."

The boat pushed off again and in mid-lake they held a conference: for even lay teachers do not like falling out with a priest. And the four religious? There was only one thing to do. It was easy to disguise Majellan and Virgilius: caps for black hats, and the Roman collars ripped off. The nuns had to remove gimps, and cowls, put on kerchiefs and pin up their skirts. Then the boat again rowed to the landing place, the men crushed around the priest arguing loudly, and the rest ran. In five minutes he was alone on the causeway. At his feet he saw a white object on the stones: a nun's starched gimp. As he looked at it he trembled like a dog.

He was no longer alone by the moon-flooded lake. He was roaring in the pulpit, holding up the gimp: he was in the bishop's palace quietly unfolding a pale linen object out of brown paper: he was in the parish priest's sitting room and the white thing lay between them on the table: he was knocking at Ryder's door — yes, even if it was nearly one o'clock in the morning. He might have done all these things if, when he got back to his cottage, there had not been a sick call before him, and he had to get out his car and drive at once three and a half miles into the heart of the hills. Half an hour later he was tearing back. He had been hoaxed. The window of his cottage was open. The gimp was gone. It was the one good deed I did for my four friends.

I was awakened by the supernaturally bright light: it was not the sunrise: it was the sinking moon. My watch showed me that it was barely turned five o'clock. Dew and mist were all around the silent house: the lake was frosty; the sky pallid. The trees were weighted with sleep. Only the ceaseless mountain stream and the deceived birds made a sweet noise. Below in the garden, by the wooden gate, stood Majellan and Magdalen, talking. . . .

I never saw Magdalen again; I never saw Virgilius again; I never saw Chrysostom again.

That was 1920, and not for twenty-three years did I meet Majellan. He was, of course, still a monk, and will always be: he was graying, and a little stooped, and much thinner. His eager, doggy eyes lit up for me: until I began to joke about those days, and then the light faded. I asked him about the others, and he told me that Virgilius was now a principal somewhere. He had not heard of the two nuns since that night on the lake.

"Ah!" I sighed. "Great days! But nobody wants to learn the language now. The mountains are empty."

"Yes. The mountains are empty."

"What a shame!"

"Mind you," he said, after a moment, "I'm not sure that I altogether approve of young people going out to these places. I hope I'm not being puritanical or anything like that, but . . . well, you know the sort of thing that goes on here."

I was so shocked that I could not reply for a moment.

"But, surely, it's all very harmless?"

He shook his head seriously.

"Maybe. You *never* know."

I said something idle. Then I asked him did he go out there at all nowadays.

"That was our last year."

"I hope it wasn't any trouble with your superiors?" I asked anxiously.

"Oh, nothing like that. No. It was just . . ." He looked away. Then he said over his shoulder, "I didn't much want to, really." Then he looked at me, and in a little gush of confidence he said, "You mightn't understand it, now! But it's not good to take people out of their rut. I didn't enjoy that summer."

I said I understood that. After a few more words, we parted. He smiled, said he was delighted to see I was looking so well, and went off, stooping his way back to his monastery in the slum.

By coincidence, two hours later, I found myself side by side with Lispeen, looking into a bookshop window. He was scarcely changed, except for a faint brush of gray at each ear; he wore a tall silk hat and carried a silver-headed umbrella. When I spoke to him and he turned, the sunset struck his rosy face and lit the sides of his hat so that they glowed and shone. With difficulty I brought his mind back to those years, but when I did he greeted me as heartily as if I was his best friend, and laughed so merrily at the memory of those old days that I almost expected him to clap me on the back.

"Of course, you know," he confided, with wide eyes, "they were only children. Such innocents!" He laughed at the thought of the innocents. "Of course, I *had* to frighten them!" And he laughed again, and then threw up his head and said "Heigh-ho" in a big sigh. Then he shook my hand, and beamed at me, told me I was looking grand, and went his cheerful way. He bowed benevolently to every respectful salute along the glowing street, and, when he did, his elongated shadow waved behind him like a tail.

Teresa

O N THE platform at Dieppe, at a corner so near the sea and the boat as to be part of the quay, there stood a small nun, flanked by three shapeless bags of that old-fashioned kind known as portmanteaus. Lovely as a black wallflower, large-eyed by nature, her eyes were now enormous: for she was looking across the quays with delight at the sun-blazing confections of houses on the other side. Now and again an old nun came hobbling up to her from the busier end of the platform, muttering something that drew a shadow across the lovely face, and then hobbling away again, head down, to this official and that official, wavering around like a top as each one hurriedly threw a few words at her and rushed past. At last the old nun came back to the novice, with her two hands out in appeal. The novice, followed by the old nun, at once walked straight down to the first official she saw and said in clear English:

"Where is the train for Rouen?"

The official glanced at her, then smiled, then bowed, and said politely, indeed with deference:

"There it is, *mademoiselle*," and pointed to it.

"Mais non, non," babbled the old nun. *"Pas aller à Rouen! Aller à Leesoo!"*

"That's all right, Sister Patrick," said the other. "We change at Rouen." And taking charge of the situation, she led the still-protesting nun up to the waiting train, put in the bags, helped — almost pushed — the old woman before her, and settled herself for the journey. The old woman clambered out again, red with fluster. Once more she ambushed official after official, all of whom said a word so like "Wrong" that she insisted on hauling out her companion.

"Listen, Sister Patrick," begged the novice, with saintly patience, "I know the route backwards. It's Dieppe, Rouen, Elbeuf St. Aubin, Serquigny, and then Lisieux. This is the train."

The guard confirmed this, as far as concerned Rouen, and they clambered in at the last moment; but the old woman was still saying that they would never get to "Leesoo," that they would find themselves landed in Paris in the middle of the night, that she had told Mother Mary Mell not to send her, that thirty-one years is too long out of a country for anyone to remember the language, and so on and so on, while the younger nun gazed wide-eyed out of the window at the passing fields.

"Our pilgrimage has begun," she said in a dreamy voice, almost to herself.

"And what's going to be the end of it at this rate?" snapped the old woman. But then she gave a frightened look at the little face before her. The big eyes had lowered. A tremble was flitting across the red lips. The old woman immediately calmed down, laid a rough hand on the novice's knee, and said, gently, "Sure, don't mind me, Sister Teresa. I'm all of a flusther. We're on the road now. Just as you say. When we get to Leesoo, 'twill be all right, a gilly. Saint Teresa will look after you and . . . Look't, I have no sense. We should be eating our lunch."

"I'd love a cup of tea!" said the girl. "I have a raging headache."

"Tut tut," clucked the old woman, and then she grabbed the girl's flank. "Are ye wearing your double petticoat, Sister Teresa?"

"Yes, Sister," said Teresa, with a blush and a warning look into the corner of the carriage, where an old Frenchman was devouring a roll and slugging red wine.

"Have ye the red flannel drawers on ye?" demanded the old nun.

"Yes, Sister. Sssh!"

"There's nothing like red flannel next the skin," said the nun, fiddling with the lunch parcel. " 'Tis a touch of cold you've got."

" 'Twas the heat down under that deck," said Teresa, and big floods of water entered her eyes. Her chaperone did not notice. "I never saw Dieppe from the sea," she whimpered. "And Mother Mary Mell says that it's lovely from the sea."

"Will ye have egg and cress, or tomato?" asked the old woman, too intent on her own appetite to take notice of anything else. "We earned it," she laughed, with a happy look about her and a countrywoman's smile and nod to the old Clemenceau in the corner. He just dug a chunk of his roll off with his penknife, wiped the back of his hand right and left across his mustaches, and, with an idle glance at her, opened both mouth and eyes simultaneously to devour the chunk.

The nuns began to nibble their food. Two hens could not have pecked more nimbly or neatly. Their traveling companion finished his lunch almost before they had well begun. He carefully stowed away his bottle, produced a long cheroot, and began to fill the carriage with smoke. Then, to the dismay of the novice, he leaned across and closed the window tightly. By the time she had finished eating, she had already begun to lean her aching head on her palm. In minute imitation of the Frenchman, the old woman rubbed her mustaches and her beard clean of crumbs, leaned back, closed her eyes, began to eat chocolates and to breathe through her nose. She woke with a start to hear Teresa say to the Frenchman:

"*C'est assez chaud, monsieur. Veuillez bien ouvrir la fenêtre.*"

The old tiger-face glared, growled, tapped his chest fiercely, poured out a flood of uncompromising French, and leaned back. His sideward glare thereafter was like a cat ready to pounce.

"What's that?" asked the old nun apprehensively.

"My head," groaned Teresa.

"Offer it up, girl," advised the old woman. "Offer it up to Saint Teresa for the success of your intention."

"I've offered it up on the boat the whole way over," retorted the novice.

" 'Tis a cross," said the old woman easily. " 'Tis put on you by Saint Teresa to try you. Suffer it for her sake."

The girl looked at her coldly. Then she observed that they had a second traveling companion. He was a cavalry officer who, with more consideration than their "Clemenceau," was walking up and down in the corridor to smoke his pipe. Each time he passed the door he glanced up at his luggage on the rack. She raised her eyes appealingly the next time he passed. He paused, glanced at her, was about to pass on, paused again to look. A tiny gesture of her hand, a widening of her eyes held him. He came in, sat down, looked around him, and stared at her.

"*Monsieur,*" she begged, "*j'ai mal à la tête. La fenêtre. Est-ce que nous pouvons l'ouvrir?*"

"With pleasure," he said, in English, stalked over to it and slapped it down.

A raucous argument started up at once between the officer and his fellow countryman. Sister Patrick sat up, glared at her charge, and drew herself in from the combatants. The argument ended with the abrupt flight of the old man, cursing as he went, a laugh from the officer, and a frightened smile from the novice, accompanied by a glance at her chaperone, who, in the greatest suspicion of the officer, had lowered her head to look crookedly at him, like a duck, out under her coif. He was stroking his little line of mustache and smiling at Teresa. When Patrick slewed full around to survey her charge, Teresa had cast her eyes down demurely on her clasped hands.

Presently the officer got up, and went out to smoke another pipe. Every time he passed, he bowed in to the two nuns. Teresa never looked higher than his knees. When he had passed for about the sixth time, Patrick said:

"Sister, do you realize that officer is bowing to us every two minutes?"

"He is very kind," said the little nun. "Everybody is very kind," she sighed, and began to pray on her beads.

But when he passed again, and bowed, the old nun said crossly: "I believe you're looking at him, Sister Teresa!"

Teresa shook her head sadly and looked out of her big eyes at her chaperone.

"It is sad," she said. "He will be killed in the wars." And her eyes swam with tears.

"And what's that to you?" whispered the old nun angrily.

"He reminds me of my brother, Jim, in the army," said Teresa. "He will be killed on the battlefield too. Oh, let us pray for the pair of them."

The old nun could not refuse to do this, so they prayed together, and when the officer passed, and bowed, and smiled, the two nuns bowed and smiled back, and went on with their prayers for the repose of his soul when he would be killed in the wars. But he was useful at Rouen. He bought them two lovely cartons of *café au lait,* with buttered rolls, and showed them where the autorail would start. Then for the last time he bowed, and smiled, and went away, and they never saw him again.

It was the fading hour of day before their little autorail came and took the two travelers (and about eight others) trotting out of Rouen. A light haze of rain began to float down through the air. They passed a village deep in trees. There the first lights were beginning to contest the supremacy of the day. Soon the rain shone in rivulets on the lighted windows of the auto. The other travelers leaned closer together in a kind of animal companionship and chattered in loud voices, as if to keep the night at bay.

"I wonder," murmured Teresa, "what are they doing now back in Saint Anthony's?"

"Ah, yes!" sighed the old nun wearily. "It makes England seem very far away to think of Saint Anthony's now."

"And Dublin?" smiled the novice sadly.

"Ha!" said the old nun, with a yawn that dropped the subject into vacancy. Her youth and her friends were too remote for serious reflection.

"I know what my sisters are doing now in Dublin," whispered Teresa. "Having tea and making plans for the night." And she looked out at the evening shower and the thickening night. "I wish I never came," she said suddenly. "I feel terribly lonely."

"Sssh! Tut tut!" chided the old nun; she had begun to eat more chocolates, and did not want to talk.

"It's all right for you," complained the novice. "You're going to meet your aunt. I'll know nobody in Lisieux. And if I find out there that I have no vocation, what'll I do?"

"Now, now, now," grumbled the old woman, "you know you'll get peace and calm in Leesoo. The saint will reveal your heart to you. You'll quieten down. You'll know that all these scruples of yours mean nothing at all. Sure, we all had them!" In spite of herself she became impatient. Her soothing voice gradually took on an edge. "And anyway, goodness knows, you were eager enough to come! And let me tell you it isn't every reverend mother would let you. And it's not a holiday you're on, miss. It's thinking of the holy saint you should be, and not of gillygooseys in Dublin."

The novice withdrew into herself. She was too tired to pray; from sheer repetition the words were becoming meaningless.

Presently the old nun said, as if she were thinking aloud:

"And even if I have an aunt . . . ha! . . . I suppose she won't know me."

She stopped again and folded her hands deep into her sleeves. "Thirty-one years," she mused to the window.

The autorail rattled along for several miles. Then Patrick leaned over and said comfortably:

"A terror for the hot milk at night. She'd drink two pints of it. Sure, 'twas enough to kill a plowhorse."

From that on she kept on letting occasional little gasps of laughter escape her. It was as if somebody tickled her every three minutes. Then, after a protracted giggle out of each side of her mouth, she went off into a beatific sleep and the broad smile never left her face until they stopped abruptly in Lisieux.

As they left the station and emerged on the great square, Teresa cried in delight:

"But it's really a big place!"

Through the rain the little town shone into the station like a prismatic waterfall. She saw a green neon light flitting through the wetness over a hotel door. She saw a vis-à-vis crawling shiningly across the *place,* and it made the town seem both cozy and intimate, and at the same time enormous and important. But Patrick had flown into a hurry and scurry, fumbling with her umbrella, and clutching her bags, and gazing all around her in a new rush of timidity; the two, in this conflict of absorption, nearly lost one another in the crush. The novice said:

"Oh, Sister Patrick! Couldn't we have one cup of tea in a restaurant before we go to the hostel?"

"Wh-a-t?" cried Patrick, hunching up her shoulders, and laying her hand on her gimp like a stage Frenchwoman. *"Mon pethite, que dites-vous? Du thé? Vous savez bien . . . vous savez bien que nous . . . Il faut . . . Il faut . . ."* She groaned furiously. "I can't talk French. I told Mother Mary Mell . . . Are you talking about tea? Do you realize, miss, that you're on a pilgrimage? Gosthering in the middle of the street! Hurry! Hurry!"

They did hurry, under their two black umbrellas, like two ants with top-heavy loads. Suddenly Teresa stopped and sneezed resolutely; once . . . twice . . . four times. Patrick towered over her. She started to gibber at her like a baboon.

"You're after getting a cold on me! That's yourself, and your window, and your fine officer!" Teresa sneezed a fifth time. "Are you sure," demanded Patrick, "that you have the double petticoat?"

The novice's big eyes were directed miserably into a confectioner's window. It was bright with the brightest cakes.

"Dear Sister Patrick!" she wheedled. "Don't you think we could have one small, tiny little cup of tea?"

The nun opened her mouth to say "No," looked at the window, looked at Teresa, and after a struggle said:

"Well! Since you have a cold coming on you, I'll let you have just one hot cup of coffee. Just one, mind you!"

It was warm in the café. Patrick had an éclair. Over their heads a radio kept weaving waltzes that made the novice sway gently on her chair. Patrick had two éclairs. The novice made her coffee last as long as possible. Patrick had a third éclair. Then, in spite of a fleck of cream on her jaw, Patrick's face was unusually forbidding as she looked up and said:

"Well, miss, I hope you're feeling better now?"

"Thank you very much, Sister," said Teresa, and rose with an air of firm resignation. "We must go to the hostel."

A bell rang eight o'clock as they emerged. They wasted ten minutes searching for the hostel, a bald-faced house rising plumb from the pavement. Its brass-tipped, reed-woven half screens were damply inhospitable. Its closed door and iron grille were shining with the rain. The lay sister who drew the slide of the grille spoke in unintelligible, provincial French, of which they understood only one word, *impossible!*

"*Quoi?*" squawked Patrick, clawing the grille, as the slide shot to in her face. "What did that wan say?"

The bell jangled down the hall again. This time the lay sister was even more emphatic, and therefore even less intelligible, and she became still less intelligible as Patrick hung to the grille and blustered in Franco-English. Teresa firmly pushed her aside, with a calm sanity:

"*Vous ne comprenez pas. Tout est bien arrangé. Notre mère a écrit une lettre à votre mère. . . .*"

The lay sister interrupted. She said, "*Trop tard.*" She said, "*Huit heures.*" She said these words several times. She closed the grille with the slowness of curiosity that commented on the folly of the two foolish virgins who had come too late. Teresa turned to Patrick, and burst into peals of laughter at the look of horror on her face.

"We're too late!" she cried, joyously. "Now we must go to a hotel!"

Patrick rent her.

"You and your tea! You did it deliberately! Wait until we get back to Mother Mary Mell! I'll tell her you're not fit to be a nun! You're a little flitthermouse! You're a gillygoosey! What a pilgrim we have in you! There's your answer for you! You're not fit to be a nun! You're a slip! You're a miss! What're we going to do? What'll my aunt say to me? What'll Mother Mary Mell say to me? What's going to happen to us?"

Teresa began to cry. Patrick at once hushed her tirade, unfurled her umbrella (it was as big as a bookmaker's), dragged up two of the bags, and set off, in a mouth-buttoned fury, to find a hotel. The rain was now a downpour. Their bags weighted them down. She halted. She gave the girl a look that was worse than a blow, shoved her into a doorway, and said, "Don't stir from there till I come back." She left the bags in her care, and butted out into the rain.

Men kept approaching the door, and seeing the nun, they would stop dead, and push away. At first this merely frightened her for she did not realize her predicament: but suddenly a cistern flushed noisily behind her and she recognized that she was standing in the doorway of a *cabinet*. Clutching her bags, she fled down the street, down a side street, another side street, and halted panting under a café awning.

The old proprietor came out and looked at her, cocked his head to one side, bowed, considered her, smiled, said that it was a bad night, and wiped his indifference onto the tabletop. Then he gazed around him, looked at her again, shrugged, and went indoors. More men passed her, on their way in or out, always pausing, after the first glance, to smile and bow. Twice she got up to fly, wondered whether Patrick would ever find her, sat again on the damp iron chair. A drunken old man with a beard finally put her to flight by taking off his hat, leaning on the tabletop, and starting a flowery speech. She ran into a gendarme who was accompanying Sister Patrick down the street. Patrick threw her two hands up to the sky preparatory to a tornado of abuse. She was soaked; her gimp was a rag; her coif hung around her face like lace. Before she could speak, Teresa hurled herself on the old woman's breast and sobbed out all her awful adventures, so that the gendarme and the nun calmed her with difficulty. They took her bag, then, and led her, whimpering, to the little pension-pub that Patrick had chosen for their night's lodging. There Patrick put her into bed, in a cozy little room all to herself, with red stuff curtains and a dusty-looking carpet — it was nearly threadbare — and with her own two hands Patrick lit a fire, brought an omelet, rolls, and coffee, and tucked her in for the night; and all the time Patrick kept begging her pardon for that outburst at the hostel. What with the comfort, the kindness, and the vestigial excitement, the little novice was melted to tears of happiness.

"Our pilgrimage is beginning," she whispered happily to Patrick. "Isn't it, dear Sister Patrick?"

" 'Twill begin in the morning," temporized Patrick. "And then the saint will smoothen everything out."

Right cheek touched right cheek, and left cheek touched left cheek, in the way of all nuns kissing. Old fingers laid out her glossy black hair on the pillow. The light went out. A rough palm smoothed her forehead. The door clicked. The flames flickered on the ceiling.

In Kent, at Saint Anthony's, the only sound around the convent at night had been the crackle of twigs in the damp wood, the hoo-hoo of an owl. Here she heard footsteps in the street below, an occasional motor car swishing over the cobbles, the soft, whispering downfall of April rain. Looking up at the wavering ceiling, she attended to those sounds, whose tumult, and whose unfamiliarity, and whose suggestiveness made England and her convent, Dublin and her home utterly remote — less part of another country than part of another life. More than anything else they said, "The pilgrimage has begun!" They said, "O dear Saint Thérèse, I will leave all things in thy hands." They said, "O most omnipotent God, I yield all the world to Thee."

"I want to be a saint!" she cried out, and beat the coverlet with her palm. And at that she fell asleep, curled up in bed as softly as a cat.

Only the hens were awake as they walked to first Mass at Saint Pierre. The sun was glittering in the water between the cobblestones. Teresa felt that she alone possessed the town. She felt that all things converged on the forthcoming visit to the shrine. Even the warm prophecy of the steam rising from the streets and the cloudless whiteness of the sky seemed not something general to everybody in the world, but particular to her life alone. She whispered to Patrick, "Thérèse is calling! I hear her!" Patrick nodded, too excited to speak.

After breakfast they began the ritual of Lisieux. Les Buissonnets, the Martin home (Saint Thérèse Martin), was exactly as they had foreseen it, just like all the photos and descriptions in biographies of the saint. They saw the "trim lawn in front of the house," and "the useful kitchen garden at the back." From the attic windows there was the expected "distant view over the plain." Teresa said to Patrick, with a sigh of happiness:

"It was all made for her. If I had lived here, I, too, would have been a saint!"

Patrick nodded in agreement with the general proposition. For the novice to say that she could have been a saint was merely a way of saying that God had chosen one and could as easily have chosen another.

" 'Tis Heaven!" she murmured, and clasped Teresa's hand.

It was the same in the sacristy of the Carmelite convent, where the saint's hair lies strewn under glass in its reliquary, and the walls are covered by mementos of those who have paid honor to her memory — decorations, orders, swords, letters from all over the world. Here, where Patrick became almost incoherent at the prospect of meeting her aunt, thirty-one years after, now a reverend mother in the Carmelites, Teresa filled with sadness.

"The folly of the world!" she murmured, sighing again and again. "They honor her now. They did not know the sorrow of her heart while she was alive."

The two touched cheek to cheek again.

A Carmelite lay sister next led them to the grave of the saint. From that they would go on to the convent proper to meet Patrick's aunt. They began to palpitate in mutual sympathy. The grave calmed them by its simplicity.

When they rose, the aunt stood beside them. Patrick toddled to her with cries of joy. The aged woman, her head a mere skull, her hands bony and ridged, gave no sign of recognition other than to say, "God bless you, my child." Old Patrick drew back like a frightened child. Timidly she introduced the novice. She explained falteringly why they had come.

"She's not sure if she wants to be a nun, Mother."

The Carmelite looked at the novice. She, too, at once drew back.

But the Carmelite smiled to hear the English name, Teresa, and took her hand gently and led her (Patrick following) across the garden to the convent anteroom. On the way she talked of simple things like the budding shrubs and the blessing of the rain. They sat in the anteroom and the Carmelite rang a bell.

They talked of the price of vegetables, until a faint passage of light in one wall drew their eyes to the grille — the last portal of the inner Carmelite hermitage. Behind the grille was a gauze, and presently Teresa's eyes made out, behind the gauze, a still face from which the gauze had eroded all recognizable character. All she could see was the vaguest outline of a countenance. As if she realized in that second how the discipline of the order must have likewise eroded from the little girl of Les Buissonnets all human emotion, and in a flash of understanding knew what sacrifice really means, she flung herself at the Carmelite's knees and cried out hysterically:

"*Ma mère!* I have no vocation!"

Patrick intervened hurriedly:

"Pay no heed to her. She's upset and sick in herself. The child doesn't know what she wants."

The aged Carmelite waved her aside and lifted the novice to her feet. Looking into her face with a clear eye, she said, after a frightening silence:

"Could you be a Carmelite?"

"No!" panted the novice, and she drew back, as if she were at that moment about to be imprisoned behind the grille.

"If you cannot be a Carmelite, my child, you can be nothing."

"She'd be happy enough," intervened Patrick comfortably, "in an easier order."

"She will be happy — we will all be happy — only in Heaven," said the Carmelite coldly. "Could you not even try to be a Carmelite?" asked the aged woman.

"No!" begged the novice. "I couldn't do it!"

"Why not?"

"To be always shut in?" trembled the girl.

"It is an enclosed order," agreed the superioress calmly.

"I couldn't stand it!"

"How do you know?" catechized the superioress.

For answer the girl burst into such a sobbing wail that Patrick drew her to her broad bosom and turned on her aunt.

"Ye have no heart!" she upbraided. "Badgering the poor child! 'Tisn't that we expected from you! Don't heed her," she comforted Teresa. "My poor little girsha! Don't mind her. Sure we can't all be saints. You'll do your best. You can't do more."

"But," sobbed Teresa, "I want to be a saint. 'Tis to . . . to . . . to be a saint I joined the nuns." Her voice came out through her nose, miserably. "If I can't be a saint, I don't *want* to be a nun!"

The old woman comforted her, and finally restored her to a whimpering silence. Looking up, they saw they were alone. The grille was closed. The veil was hidden. The superioress had gone.

The two pilgrims went back to their pension. That afternoon, without discussion, they went on to Saint-Malo. There the novice was expected to find bodily rest, as at Lisieux she had been expected to find calm of soul.

Saint-Malo faces across a wide estuary the modern watering place of Dinard. At night they saw the lights in the hotels, and cafés, and more colored lights beaded all around the roof of the casino; and sometimes they heard music across the still surface of water. Steamers from Southampton and the Channel Islands floated in the bay at anchor. Patrick was charmed with her room in the convent where they stayed. It looked directly across at Dinard. She wrote to Mother Mary Mell that she had a "grandstand," and that she was thinking of going across in a rowboat some night to gamble in the casino and make the fortune of the order. Becoming serious in a postcript, she said that Teresa had not yet made up her mind, but that she was "behaving with the most edifying devotion."

Not only did the novice attend every service in the convent, but she had become pious beyond description, daily spending long hours alone in adoration in the chapel. But when Patrick noticed that she left her lunch untouched on her table on the third day of her arrival, and went up to the novice's cell to ask if this were wise, she made a frightening discovery. She found that the mattress and bedclothes had been rolled up and put away under the bed, and all the girl's flannel underclothing was hanging in her cupboard. At once she went down to the chapel, and hissed at the solitary worshiper to come out, beckoning madly with her bony finger.

"Sister Teresa," she said severely, "you are refusing your food. Is there any reason for this?"

The novice hung her head and said nothing.

"Answer me, Sister."

Still the novice kept her eyes on the parquet.

"I command you, Sister, to answer me."

"There is no reason," whispered the novice.

"Then eat up your food in future," ordered the nun. "Do you want to make a skeleton out of yourself?" And she added more easily, "Don't you know right well I'm supposed to bring you home as plump as a duck?"

The novice raised two large, sad eyes.

"Sister Patrick," she begged, "I will obey if you command me. But I want to do penance for my sins, and for the sins of the world. I feel I have received a higher command."

"What higher command?" blustered the old woman, taken aback. "What on earth are you talking about, Sister?"

Teresa sighed.

"The sins of the world are all about us," she smiled sadly. "I see them every night from my window, across the water, in the dens and gambling houses. All lit up like the fires of Hell to lure poor souls astray. I dreamed the first night I came here that the Devil lives over there. I saw his red eyes in the air. I saw that this convent was put here specially to atone for the wickedness that surrounds it."

"Holy Mother!" cried the nun. "What are you talking about, girl? Sister Teresa, let me tell you that if you ate a proper supper . . . And by the same token, miss, no wonder you have dreams if you sleep on the laths of the bed. Do you," she threatened, "sleep on the laths of the bed?"

The novice once more hung her head, and once more she had to be bullied into replying.

"I do, Sister," she confessed unhappily.

"Well, then, let there be an end of it! What right have you to be going on with these Andrew Martins off of your own bat? You know right well you must ask permission of your superior before you do the like. And that reminds me," she cried, grabbing the girl's flank, and then standing back from her in horror, with her gummy mouth open. "You haven't a stitch on you! Go upstairs at once, miss, and dress yourself properly. I'll be after you in two minutes. I'm worn out and tormented with your vagaries! Ten times I told Mother Mary Mell . . ."

She pointed upstairs — a figure of justice.

The novice went, tearful, head hanging. In two minutes the old nun followed. She opened the door of the cell. The girl lay on the ground, her arms stretched out like a crucifix, her dilated eyes fixed as on a vision over her head. The old nun entered the room, closed the door, and thundered:

"Get up out o' that!"

The novice did not move.

"Miss!" said the old woman, pale as a sheet. "How dare you disobey me!"

The novice trembled as if a wind had ruffled her spirit. With her heart battering inside in her, Patrick walked over and looked down. The big brown eyes, so strikingly dark in that pale pink-and-white face, stared up past her. Patrick looked up at the electric light bulb. She looked all about her. The thick-moted afternoon sun slanted in across the bed. A hissing suspiration below the window was followed by the little groan of the gravel dragging back under the wave. Then she saw a slimy brown insect, with wavering head, creep to the white ear of the novice, and she screamed:

"An earwig! Climbing into your ear!"

Teresa sat up as if she were stung. The fright passed. The two looked at each other with hate in their eyes. At the door, Patrick said:

"I'll wait in the garden."

In complete silence they walked four miles that afternoon. They did the same the following morning. That was their last full day. On the final afternoon Patrick spoke:

"We will be in Saint Anthony's tomorrow night. Do you know, yet, my dear, if you have a vocation?"

"I have decided to join the Carmelites," said the novice.

They halted. They looked across the sea wall into the blue of Dinard. A few lights were already springing up over there — the first dots in the long golden necklet that already they had come to know so well. A lone sea gull squawked over the glassy water. The sunset behind the blue pinnacles of the resort was russet.

"And what's wrong with our own order, Sister dear?" asked Patrick of the vacancy before her.

"I feel, dear Sister Patrick," judged the novice, staring ahead of her, "that it is too worldly."

"How is it too worldly?" asked Patrick in a whisper.

"Well, dear Sister Patrick," pronounced the novice, "I see, for example, that you all eat too much."

The little wavelets fell almost inaudibly, drunken with the fullness of the tide, exhausted and soothed by their own completion.

"I shall tell Mother Mary Mell that you think so," whispered the old nun.

"There is no need, dear Sister. It will be my duty to tell her myself. I will pray for you all when I am in the Carmelites. I love you all. You are all kind and generous. But, dear Sister, I feel that very few nuns really have the right vocation to be nuns." Patrick closed her eyes tightly. The novice continued: "I will surrender myself to the divine Love. The death I desire is the death of Love. The death of the Cross."

They heard only the baby tongues of the waves. The evening star blazed in the russet sky. The old nun saw it, and she said, in part a statement, in part a prayer, in part a retort:

"Sweet Star of the Sea!"

Teresa raised her dark eyes to the star and she intoned in her girlish voice the poem of Saint Thérèse:

> "Come, Mother, once again,
> Who camest first to chide.
> Come once again, but then
> To smile—at eventide."

The old nun fiddled with her beads. She drew long breaths through her nose. She tried several times to speak. She gestured that they must go back. They turned and walked slowly back to the convent, side by side; the old nun as restless as if she were in bodily agony, the novice as sedate and calm as a statue. After a while Patrick fumbled in her pocket, and found a chocolate, and popped it into her mouth. Then she stopped chewing, and threw an eye at her companion. At the look of intense sorrow in the face beside her, she hunched up her shoulders and as silently as she could, she gulped the fragments whole.

On the journey homeward they did not speak one word to each other: all the way to Rouen in the trotting autorail; in the clanking train to Dieppe; on the boat; in the English train. In silence they arrived at Saint Anthony's, among the dank beech woods, now softly dripping, in time to hear the first *hoo-hoo* of the owl, and to troop in with the rest of the community for evening chapel. Mother Mary Mell barely had time to ask the old nun how she had enjoyed her holiday — that first holiday in thirty-one years. Patrick's eyes fluttered. She recalled the lights of Dinard.

"It was lovely, Mother!"

Mary Mell caught the flicker of hesitation. Just as they crossed the tessellated threshold of the chapel, she whispered quickly, "And Teresa?"

Patrick, who had been waiting for that question ever since the final afternoon in Saint-Malo, and yet had no answer ready, took refuge behind the chapel's interdiction of silence. She smiled reassuringly, nodded, smiled, nodded again, and then, very solemn and pious, she walked in with her head down. She said her prayers badly. She slept hardly at all that night. She heard every crackling branch and fluttering night bird. For what, in the name of the Most High, was she to say to Mary Mell? And what was she to say to the community in the morning? As she tossed and tumbled, she thought of Teresa sleeping peacefully in her cell, and the old woman burst into tears of rage.

In the morning there was no Teresa. She had left the convent, through a ground-floor window, before anybody was awake, and gone on the milk train to London. She had walked across the city at that hour when the sun emphasizes the position of the East End, and the sleepers in the parks that she traversed are unwrapping their newspaper blankets. A sister-in-law coming out to collect the morning post found a nun sitting on the doorstep. She had breakfast, in a tennis frock, along with the family.

She saw the convent only once again — about two years later when she brought her husband to see it. As they got out of the train she looked up into the familiar beeches at the steam of the engine caught in the branches, and she remembered how every train used to make the woods seem infinitely lonely and the convent darker and more melancholy, because that white steam suggested people traveling, and the luxury of the world she had renounced. Her George, who was a Protestant, and who was much excited by this expedition, nodded solemnly, and began to get an uncomfortable feeling that he was married to a nun. They were entertained politely. Old Sister Patrick did not appear. As they left, the starting train again sent its gushes of steam into the branches, and now those branches again seemed to Teresa to clutch not only at the white smoke but at her own heart. She felt that the woods enclosed a refuge from the world of which she had, irrevocably, become a part. As she snuggled down into her fur collar she gazed out of her big eyes at her husband, and said, with a shake of her little head:

"Ah, George! George! You will never know what I gave up to marry you!"

He smiled adoringly at her as, in obedience to a gesture, he leaned over to put a cigarette between her rouged lips.

"My precious Teresa," he murmured softly, and patted her knee.

She shook her head at him again, with a pitying smile.

"Has it upset you, my sweet?" he asked dismally.

Saying never a word, she kept gazing at him fixedly, as if he were a stranger. He huffed, and hawed, and hedged himself behind his newspaper, looking as despondent as he considered proper. For as he explained to his colleagues in the morning, his wife was "a very spiritual woman" and on occasions like this she always made him feel that he had the soul of a hog.

Unholy Living and Half Dying

JACKY CARDEW is one of those club bachelors who are so well
groomed, well preserved, pomaded, medicated, and self-cosseted
that they seem ageless — the sort of fixture about whom his pals
will say when he comes unstuck around the age of eighty, "Well,
well! Didn't poor old Jacky Cardew go off *very* fast in the end?"

For thirty years or so he has lived in what are called private hotels;
last winter he said to his friends, "These bloody kips are neither
private nor hotels, I'm going to take a flat." What he got in the end
was the sort of makeshift thing that goes by the name of a flat in
Irish cities — two rooms (that is, one room cut in two), with the
W.C. on the ground floor and the bathroom on the top floor; and
in the bathroom an unpleasant, greasy-looking gas stove such as
Prince Albert might have unveiled at the Great Crystal Palace
Exhibition of 1851.

But Jacky was delighted. At least he now had privacy. Nobody
lived in the house but himself and his own landlady; for a tinsmith
had the ground floor (rather noisy and smelling of solder), there
were solicitors' offices on the second floor, the old lady lived under
the slates, above Jacky's flat, and he hardly ever saw her except
when he paid his rent.

230

About two o'clock one bad February morning just as Jacky and a
few friends were settling down for the fourth time to their last game
of solo they gradually became aware that a dog was beating his tail
on the floor above. There was no other sound then — for a while —
but the flick of the cards and the rain spitting on the window and
the slight exclamations of the players. Then they heard the rapping
again.

"Better go easy, boys," somebody said, playing a card, "we're keeping the old lady upstairs awake."

They played on intently. Again they heard the rapping, this time
insistent and loud. Jacky glanced around at the lifted eyebrows, at
his wrist watch, at the dying fire, at the drops sparkling on the pane
in the arc light of the square below, and went out with the sort of
frown he would have turned on a junior in the bank who had not
been soapy enough. Striking matches he climbed the stairs. The nail-
heads shone. Hearing him stumble and curse she called his name,
and he made his way towards the voice, stooping under the great
rafters of the attic, elbowing aside the damp washing that she had
hung there to dry, feeling the cold within a few inches of his poll.
He found her room, a bare attic. He was affronted by its poverty,
its cold stuffiness, its sloping attic window that wept in ripples with
the lights of the city.

In the matchlight he saw her pale eyes staring up at him in terror
from the pillow; he saw her hollowed cheeks; the white beard on
her chin; her two pigtails tied with bits of red wool. The match
burned his fingers. Through the dark he heard her whisper:

"Mr. Cardew, I'm dying."

He was so frightened that he immediately lit another match. He
was even more frightened by what she replied when he asked her if
he could call in one of her friends.

"God help us," she panted. "Friends how are ye? I haven't a
friend to wet me lips. Not a friend. In the world."

He raced down the stairs. One of his pals was a doctor; he went
up and examined her, soothed her, came down, said there was noth-

ing much wrong with her except old age and perhaps a touch of indigestion, and ordered two aspirins and a hot-water bottle on her stomach. They made her comfortable for the night and the party went home, heads down to the rain, shouting commiserations all round.

Jacky came back to his disheveled room and sat by the cold fireplace. He heard every quarter hour strike from the city hall, sometimes bold and clear, sometimes faint and sad, according to the mood of the wintry wind. He suddenly remembered that his own mother had gone on a night like this. He wondered who would attend to the old woman if she died, and for the first time he took notice of the family photographs hung around the walls, mainly young men and women and vacant-looking babies with their mouths open. There was a big black enlargement of a man with a gray mustache and a bald head. He reminded him of old Cassidy, his last manager, who now dined regularly every Tuesday of the year with another retired banker called Enright. As Jacky poked the dead cinders it came to him that Cassidy probably had no other friend in the world, and, begod, anyway, once you turn fifty what is it but a gallop down the bloody straight?

At half past three he went up to have another look at her. She was asleep, breathing heavily. He tried to feel her pulse but could not remember what a normal beat is and felt hers was as slow as a hearse. He returned to his cold room. The rain still spat. The square outside shone. He felt a dull pain in his groin and wondered, could it be appendicitis? He thought that he should have called in the priest to her and he counted the years since he last went to confession. At half past four he had another look at her and found her breathing easily and decided she was all right. As he pulled up his pajamas he gave his paunch a dirty look.

He was awakened at his usual hour by the old lady herself, bringing him his usual hot cup of tea and buttered toast. She had a prayer book under one arm and was dressed for the street.

"Good heavens," he gulped, "I thought you were . . ."

Her tall lean body swayed over like a reed with the gusts of laughter.

"Mr. Cardew, 'tis well known you can't kill a bad thing. My little hot seat in Purgatory isn't ready for me yet. Ah, I knew I'd pay for that load of bacon and cabbage I ate yesterday." An inelegant gesture from her stomach to her throat made him hastily lay down the buttered toast. "I was all swelled up with it the day long."

Jacky dressed, blaspheming. On his way out he decided to have a serious word with the woman. She had returned from chapel and was sitting in her kitchen sucking up a big basin of soup.

"Look here, Mrs. Canty," he said severely, "is it an actual fact that you have no friends whatsoever?"

"I have plenty friends, Mr. Cardew," she smiled happily. "The best friends any woman ever had." She laid her bony hands on a pile of prayer books — there must have been about twelve of them, a pile a foot high, all in shiny black cloth coverings. "Haven't I the souls suffering in Purgatory? I have Saint Anthony." Her glance directed his to a big brown-and-cream statue on the dresser. "And haven't I the Sacred Heart?" He eyed the red-and-gold statue over the sink with the withered palms of last Easter crossed before it. "Look at the Little Flower smiling at me. And what about Saint Joseph and Saint Monica?"

Jacky's head was going around like a weathercock.

"And amn't I only after coming in from praying to the Left Shoulder? Friends, Mr. Cardew?"

She smiled pityingly at him. He strode out, to prevent himself from saying, "Then why the hell didn't you call on them last night instead of rapping me up to you?" Instead he took it out of his secretary at the bank.

"Pure damn superstition, that's what I call it. Crawthumpin' by day and bellyachin' by night. The usual Irish Miserere. All based on fear of hell-fire and damnation. It would turn anybody into an atheist!"

The girl talked up to him; they almost quarreled; she told him he should be ashamed of himself; she even told him his "day would come"; she drove him beside himself by telling him she "would pray for him." At lunch he got into a violent argument about religion during which he kept on using the word "Benighted! Benighted!" He was still at it that night in the club, but he had to go easy there as most of the members were Knights of Columbanus and business is business. He took the middle line of:

"Mind you, I have a great regard for what I call *real* religion. And, mind you, I'm no saint. I'm honest about that. Though I suppose I'm no worse than the general run, and maybe a bit better if the truth were told. And I'll say this for it, religion is a great consolation for old age. But if religion doesn't go with *character* — character first and before all — then it crumbles away into formalism and superstition!"

They all considered it safe to agree with that. He surveyed his cards contentedly.

"I think it's your lead, Maguire."

He found himself strolling homewards with Maguire: a gentle night after all the rain, and a delicate spring touch in the air.

"We won't know where we are now," said Maguire, "until Easter is on us." And he gave an uncomfortable little laugh.

"What's the joke?"

"Wisha, I was just thinking there tonight when you were gassing about religion that . . . begod, do you know, 'tis a year since I was at confession. With Easter coming on now I suppose we'll have to get the ould skillet cleaned again. Easter duty, you know. Where do you go? I always pop up to Rathfarnham to the S.J.'s. Men of the world. Nobody like 'em."

"I usually go there, too," lied Jacky. "You can talk to those fellows."

And he began to wonder, would he or would he not make a dash for it this year?

On the Thursday of Holy Week, just after midnight, Jacky and the boys were in the middle of a hot game of nap when a faint knocking percolated through the ceiling.

"No bloody fear," he grunted. "Once bitten, twice shy. More cod acting."

They gathered up their hands and began to play. Through the slap of the cards the rapping came again, this time more faintly.

"That one, now . . ." said Jacky. "You play, Jim. That one . . . God, have you nothing but the ace? That one is a typical example of the modern Irish Crawthumper. Behind all this piety, believe you me . . . Who said I reneged? What are you talking about, didn't I put the seven on Redmond's deuce? Behind all this so-called piety there's nothing but a child's fear of the dark."

Maguire laughed at him.

"Now, Jacky, there's no earthly use your beefing about religion. The stamp of the Church is on you. 'Tis on all of us. 'Tis on you since the day you were born and sooner or later they'll get you and you may as well give in and be done with it. Mark my words, I'll live to see the day you'll have holy pictures all around your bloody bedroom! The stamp is on you! The stamp is on you."

Jacky flared. Here was a fellow who barely confessed once a year and he was talking as if he were a blooming saint.

"Stop wagging your finger at me, please. And, anyway, with all your guff, when were you at confession last, I'd like to know?"

Maguire laughed smugly.

"I don't in the least mind telling you. I was there three days ago. A grand old priest." He clicked his fingers and looked around him at the group. "He let me off like that. I think if I'd told him I'd committed murder all he'd say would be, 'Any other little thing troubling you, my child?' "

They laughed approvingly.

"Ah, there's nothing like an S.J.," Maguire went on. "Listen, did ye ever hear the one about the fellow that went to confession the time of the troubles here and said, 'Father, I shot a Black and Tan'?

Do you know what the priest said? 'My child,' says he, 'you may omit your venial sins.' Honest to God, I believe 'tis a fact."

They all laughed again although they had heard the yarn many times before: it is the sort of story every hardy sinner likes to hear. Through their laughter the knocking came again.

"I'm afraid, Jacky," said another of them, a commercial named Sullivan, "you'll have to have a look at the ould geezer."

With a curse Jacky flung down his cards. He climbed to the attic. He struck a match and gave one look at her and at once he knew that she was bad. Her forehead was beaded. Her chest rose and fell rapidly.

"Mr. Cardew. I'm finished. Get me the priest. For God's sake."

"Certainly. Certainly. Right away. And I'll get the doctor."

He belted down the stairs and burst in on them.

"God, lads, 'tis no joke this time. She's for it. I can tell it. I can see it. Maguire, run out for the priest like a good man. Sullivan, there's a telephone down by the kiosk, call the doctor, get Cantillon, Hanley, Casey, any of 'em. Hurry, hurry!"

He brought her up a stiff whiskey, but she was too weak to sip it. When the priest came, a young man with the sad eyes and bent head of a Saint Francis, the gamblers huddled outside under the rafters, looking through the skylight at the wide Easter moon. They were all middle-aged men, younger than Jacky, but replicas in every other way.

"Oh," whispered Maguire, " 'tis true. Just as the old priest told me. Like a thief in the night. We never know the day or the hour."

" 'Twas a terrible winter," whispered Sullivan. "I never saw so many people popping off. I see where old Sir John Philpott went off yesterday."

"Ah, God, no?" begged Jacky, shocked at the news. "You don't mean Philpott of Potter and Philpott's? I was talking to him in the club only three days ago." (He said it as if he were affronted at Sir John's giving him no previous warning of the event.) "But he was a comparatively young man! Was he sixty-two itself?"

"Heart," whispered Wilson. "He went off very fast in the end."

"Here today," sighed Maguire, "gone tomorrow."

"The best way to go," murmured Sullivan. "No trouble to anybody."

"That is," whispered Maguire, "provided our ticket's been punched for —" And he pointed respectfully upwards. "I heard a preacher say one time that he knew a man who came into his confession box after being twenty years away. He said he had just lifted his fingers and said the *Absolvo te*" — here Maguire lifted his two first fingers — "when the man dropped dead at his feet in the box! There was a close shave for you!"

Jacky moved uneasily; he knew the story was just a preacher's yarn, but he had not the spirit to say it.

"The best death of all," murmured Sullivan, "is the soldier's. I believe, just before a battle, a priest can give a whole regiment a general absolution, and if a man is killed he goes straight up to Heaven. That's what makes Irishmen such good soldiers. Straight up to Heaven!"

"Grand in attack," said Jacky judiciously, "not so good in defense."

"And that's why!" said Sullivan. "And, what's more, I wouldn't be surprised if that isn't why the English are better on the defensive than in the charge. Sure any man would fight like a divil if he knew what was coming after? Death has no terrors for a man in a situation like that."

They fell silent. A cloudlet dimmed the moon. Then all their faces were illumined again. The city's roofs shone. The priest's voice murmured softly.

"He's taking a long time," said Jacky. "And it isn't," he whispered, trying to make a little joke, "as if she had so much to tell. *She's* all right anyway."

"And," said Maguire piously, "on Good Friday. A lovely death!"

"So it is," said Wilson. "Good Friday!"

They all sighed deeply. The priest came out, stooping under the beams, removing his stole and kissing it. Maguire asked him, "Will she last, Father?" The priest sighed, "A saint, a saint," as if he were sighing for all the sinners of the world. Jacky showed him out, and as he walked away the doctor came down. Jacky shut him into his car and shoved in his head anxiously.

"Is she bad, doctor?"

"Anno Domini. We can't live forever. The works give out — just like an old motor car. All we can do at that age is wait for the call," and he beckoned with one finger. Jacky drew back hastily. The headlamps whirled and the car purred away across the empty square as if its red taillight were running away with somebody.

Jacky was left alone in his room. He sank into an armchair by the open window. The spring night was gentle. The blood of life was pulsing through everything. Even the three old London planes in the middle of the square had their little throb and the high Easter moon was delicately transparent as if with youth. He leaped up and began to circle the room. He had never seen anything so lovely, it seemed to him, as those little babies gazing at him out of their big eyes, with their soft little lips parted. He was looking again over the shining roofs and the blank chimney pots, and as if a shutter flicked he felt for one moment the intense vacancy and loneliness of his life and saw it, as the years went by, becoming more lonely and more empty. And when he was gone, that moon out there, the old trees below, would still be there, still throbbing. A little wind scurried furtively in the dust of the square. He looked at the decanter. Low tide. Like his own life. He'd be able to rest tomorrow anyway. He paused before the black enlargement. Good Friday morning. One more day to Easter. A veined red face with a blue nose, thin ruffled hair, bags under the eyes was looking at him out of the mirror. He licked his lips and got a horrible taste in his mouth and felt an uneven thumping in his heart.

He sat down heavily by the open window, before the moon's indifferent beauty, and began to go back over the years. There were a couple of things it wasn't going to be too easy to . . .

"Not, mind you," he assured the empty square, with bravado, "that I'm going to hand myself over to some bogtrot from the County Meath. Pick the right man and . . . 'Well, Father,' he rehearsed, flicking a grain of ash from his pants and pulling his ear, 'I'm afraid, er, I've got more than a few little peccadilloes to tell you. We're only human, Father. Children of Adam, and all to that and so on.' That was the ticket. Frank and open. Two men of the world. 'Of course, there's been a spot of liquor, Father. And, er . . . Well, er . . . I mean, er . . .'" Jacky coughed and ran his finger around inside his collar. This thing was going to take a bit of doing. He closed his eyes and began to think of all those nights that had seemed such grand nights — at the time.

When he opened his eyes again the sun was warm on his face, the square was gay with sunlight, somebody was shaking his shoulder. It was his landlady smilingly handing him his tea and buttered toast.

"Well, Mr. Cardew," she cackled, "since I didn't go last night I'll live to be a hundred!"

As Jacky looked blearily down at the three plane trees the misery of the night flooded on him. He gave her one maddened look, banged down the cup, and started up to tell her just what he thought of her. An unholy gripe pierced a red-hot needle through the small of his back.

"Oh, Mr. Cardew, what on earth made you sit by the open window!"

But now the pain ran across the back of his neck, and with a hand to his back and a hand to his neck all he could do was to crawl away moaning and cursing to his bed.

As he lay there through the holidays he found himself being petted and cosseted as he had never been in his life before. She rubbed his back and she rubbed his chest and she brought him hot punch and fed him with Easter delicacies until, gradually, if sourly, he decided that he would be a fool to change his landlady. At the same time, and especially on Easter Sunday morning as he lay with the sun slanting warmly across his chest, his hands behind his head, smoking his after-breakfast cigarette, his Sunday paper on his lap, listening to the silvery bells of all the churches of the city, he was aware of a certain slight feeling of discomfort — nothing much, just a coiled shadow at the back of his mind, the merest hint of apprehension. Cautiously he turned his stiff shoulders to look at the mantelpiece where she had placed a little spray of palm in a glass vase, and beside it a little glass bowl of holy water. He grunted as he considered them. He'd get rid of those things all right when he got on his feet again! Just then he remembered Maguire, and all that about the stamp being on you. He smiled uncomfortably. Oh, well! He flicked his ash on the carpet. Some day, no doubt. Some day.

How lovely the sun was. It was nice to hear all the footsteps across the square below, going to Mass. Their shadowy reflections passed softly on the ceiling, and the silvery bells went on calling everybody to be happy because Christ was risen.

He took up the paper and began to study form.

Up the Bare Stairs

A pity beyond all telling is hid in the heart of love.

ALL the way from Dublin my traveling companion had not spoken a dozen words. After a casual interest in the countryside as we left Kingsbridge he had wrapped a rug about his legs, settled into his corner, and dozed.

He was a bull-shouldered man, about sixty, with coarse, sallow skin stippled with pores, furrowed by deep lines on either side of his mouth: I could imagine him dragging these little dikes open when shaving. He was dressed so conventionally that he might be a judge, a diplomat, a shopwalker, a shipowner, or an old-time Shakespearian actor: black coat, striped trousers, gray spats, white slip inside his waistcoat, butterfly collar folded deeply, and a black cravat held by a gold clasp with a tiny diamond.

The backs of his fingers were hairy: he wore an amethyst ring almost as big as a bishop's. His temples were graying and brushed up in two sweeping wings — wherefore the suggestion of the actor. On the rack over his head was a leather hat case with the initials F.J.N. in Gothic lettering. He was obviously an Englishman who had crossed the night before. Even when the steam of the train lifted to show the black January clouds sweeping across the Galtees, and a splash of sleet hit the window by his ear, he did not waken. Just then the ticket checker came in from the corridor and tipped his shoulder. As he received back his ticket he asked, "What time do we arrive in Cork?" He said the word *Cork* as only a Corkman can say it, giving the *r* its distinctively delicate palatal trill, not saying "Corrrk," or "Cohk." He was unmistakably a Corkonian.

At Mallow I came back from tea to find him stretching his legs on the platform and taking notice. He had bought the evening paper and was tapping his thigh with it as he watched, with a quizzical smile, two tipsy old countrymen in amiable dispute, nose to nose, outside the bar. A fine man on his feet; at least six foot two. I bought a paper, also, at the bookstall and as we went on our way we both read.

My eye floated from a heading about a licensing case — the usual long verbatim report, two men found hiding under the stairs, six men with bottles in the stable, much laughter in court, and so on — to a headline beside it: CORKMAN IN BIRTHDAY HONORS LIST. The paragraph referred to "Francis James Nugent, Baronet: for War Services." I looked across at him.

"Did you say something?" he asked.

"No, no! Or, rather, I don't think so."

"Pretty cold," he said, in a friendly way. "Though I will say one thing for the G.S.R., they do heat their trains."

"Yes, it's nice and warm today. They're not, of course, the G.S.R. now, you know. They're called Corus Iompair Eireann."

"What's that? Irish for G.S.R.?"

"More or less."

We talked a bit about the revival of the language. Not that he was interested; but he was tolerant, or perhaps the right word is indifferent. After a bit I said:

"I see there's a Corkman in the new honors list."

"Oh?"

I glanced up at the rack and said, with a grin:

"I see the initials on your hatbox."

He chuckled, pleased.

"I suppose I'd better plead guilty."

"Congratulations."

"Thank you."

"What does it feel like?"

He glanced out at the wheeling fields, with their lochs of water and cowering cattle, and then looked back at me with a cynical smile.

"It doesn't feel any different. By the time you get it you've pretty well enjoyed everything it stands for. Still, it helps."

"I see from the paper that you went to the same school as myself."

"Are you the old Red and Green, too?"

"Up the Abbey!"

He laughed, pleased again.

"Does all that go on just the same as before?"

"It goes on. Perhaps not just the same as before."

We talked of West Abbey. I knew none of the men he knew, but he thawed out remembering them.

"Are all the old photographs still in the main hall? Chaps in the Indian Civil, the Canadian Mounted, the Navy, the Indian Police? God, I used to stare at them when I was a kid."

"They're gone. They've been replaced by Confirmation groups all wearing holy medals."

He made a bored face.

"I suppose in those days you little thought you'd be coming back to Cork one day as Sir Francis Nugent."

He peered at me through his cigarette smoke and nodded sagely.

"I knew."

"You did!"

"I shouldn't have said that. I couldn't know. But I had a pretty good idea."

Then he leaned forward and let down all his reserves. As he began my heart sank. He was at the favorite theme of every successful man: "How I Began." But as he went on I felt mean and rebuked. I doubt if he had ever told anyone, and before he finished I could only guess why he chose to tell me now.

"You know, it's extraordinary the things that set a fellow going. I always knew I'd get somewhere. Not merely that, but I can tell you the very day, the very hour, I made up my mind I was going to get there. I don't think I was more than fourteen or fifteen at the time. Certainly not more than fifteen. It was as simple as that" — clicking his fingers. "It was all on account of a little man named Angelo — one of the monks who was teaching us. He's gone to God by now. There was a time when I thought he was the nicest little man in the whole school. Very handsome. Cheeks as red as a girl's, black bristly hair, blue eyes, and the most perfect teeth I've ever seen between a man's lips. He was absolutely full of life, bursting with it. He was really just a big boy and that's probably why we got on so well with him. I've seen him get as much fun out of solving a quadratic equation or a problem in Euclid as a kid with a new toy. He had a marvelous trick of flinging his *cappa* over one shoulder, shoving his two wrists out of his sleeves like a conjurer, snapping up a bit of chalk and saying, "Watch what I'm going to do now," that used to make us sit bolt upright in our desks as if . . . well, as if he was going to do a conjuring trick. And if you could only have seen the way he'd kick ball with us in the yard — you know, the old yard at the back of West Abbey — all we had was a lump of paper tied with twine — shouting and racing like any of us. He really was a good chap. We were very fond of him.

"Too fond of him, I've often thought. He knew it, you see, and it made him put too much of himself into everything we did. And the result was that we were next door to helpless without him. He made us depend on him too much. Perhaps he wasn't the best kind of teacher; perhaps he was too good a teacher — I don't know — have it whichever way you like. If he was tired, or had a headache, or sagged, we sagged. If he was away sick and somebody else had to take charge of us we were a set of duffers. They could be just as cross as he was — he was very severe, he'd take no excuses from anybody — or they could be as merry as he was: it just wasn't the same thing. They had a job to do, and they did the best they could, but with him it wasn't a job, it was his life, it was his joy and his pleasure. You could tell how much the fellows liked him by the way they'd crowd around him at play hour, or at the end of the holidays to say good-by.

"One particularly nice thing about him was that he had no favorites, no pets, as we used to call them. Did you call them that in your time? But he was — what shall I say? — more than a little partial to me. And for a very, if you like to call it, silly reason. In those days, you see, politics were very hot in Cork city; very hot, very passionate. Of course, they were the old Irish Party days, long before your time, when politics were taken much more seriously than I've ever seen them taken anywhere else. John Redmond had one party called the Molly Maguires, and William O'Brien had another party called the All for Irelanders. Mind you, if you asked me now what it was all about I'd find it very hard to tell you, because they were all the one party at Westminster, and they were all agreed about home rule, but once it came to election time they tore one another to pieces. Fights in the street every night, baton charges, clashes between rival bands, instruments smashed on the pavements. One night, with my own eyes, I saw a big six-foot countryman take a running jump down the grand parade and land right on top of a big drum.

"Well, Angelo was a Molly, and I needn't tell you he was just as excited about politics as he was about everything else, and I was also a Molly and a very hot one. Not that I understood anything at all about it, but just that my father was one of the hottest Redmondites in the city of Cork. And, of course, nothing would do Angelo but to bring politics into class. He'd divide the class into Mollies and All Fors and when we'd be doing Euclid or reciting poetry he'd set one team against the other, and he'd work up the excitement until the fellows would be clambering across the desks, and if any fellow let down his side we'd glare at him until he'd want to creep away out of sight, and if he scored a point we'd cheer him as if he'd kicked a goal in an All Ireland Final.

"It was on one of these days that it happened. We were at the Eighth Problem. The Mollies wanted one point to pull even. I was the last man in — and I muffed it. And no wonder, with Angelo shouting at me like a bull, 'Come on, now, Frankie. If A.B. be placed on C.D. . . . Up the Mollies! Go on, Frankie. Go on. If A.B. . . .'

"The All Fors won. Angelo laughed it off with, 'Very good, very good, back to yeer places now. Work is work. This isn't the Old Market Place. Now for tomorrow,' and so on.

"But he kept me in after school. There I sat, alone in the empty classroom upstairs — you know the one, near the ball alley — with the crows outside in the yard picking up the crusts, and the dusk falling over the city, and Angelo, never speaking a word, walking up and down the end of the room reading his office. As a rule we were let out at three. He kept me there until five o'clock rang. Then he told me to go home and went off himself up to the monastery.

"I walked out of the yard behind him, and at that moment if I had had a revolver in my hand I'd have shot him. I wouldn't have cared if he'd beaten me black and blue. I wouldn't have cared if he'd given me extra work to do at home. He deliberately got me into trouble with my father and mother, and what that meant he understood exactly. Perhaps you don't. You don't know my background as he knew it. When I tell you that my father was a tailor and my mother was a seamstress I needn't tell you any more. When a kid's mother has to work as hard as his father to push him through school you can guess the whole picture. I don't seem to remember an hour, except for Sundays, when one or other, or both, of these machines wasn't whirring in that little room where we lived, down by the distillery, sometimes until twelve or one o'clock at night. I remember that day as I walked home I kept saying to myself over and over again, 'If only my mummy wasn't sick.' All the way. Past the distillery. Around by the tannery. You possibly know the little terrace of houses. They've been there since the eighteenth century. Dark. We had only two rooms. In the hall. I can still get that stuffy smell that had been locked up there for a hundred and fifty years — up the bare stairs. On the landing there was a tap dripping into an old leaden trough that had been there since the year dot. I could hear the machine whirring. I remember I stopped at the window and picked a dead leaf from the geraniums. I went up the last few steps and I lifted the latch. My father was bent over the machine; specs on his forehead, black skeins of thread around his neck, bare arms. My mother was wrapped in shawls in the old basket chair before the fire. I could draw that room; the two machines, my bed in one corner, my dinner waiting on the table, the tailor's goose heating on the grate. The machine stopped.

" 'In the name of God what happened to you, boy?' says my father. 'Is there anything wrong? What kept you? Your poor mother there is out of her head worrying about you.'

" 'Ah, I was just kept in, sir,' says I, passing it off as airily as I could. 'How are you, Mummy?'

"The old man caught me by the arm.

" 'Kept in?' says he, and the way he said it you'd think I was after coming out of the lockup. 'Why were you kept in?'

" 'Ah, 'twas just a bit of Euclid I didn't know, that's all.'

"It was only then I noticed that the mother was asleep. I put my hand to my lips begging him not to waken her. He let a roar out of him.

" 'A nice disgrace! Kept in because you didn't know your Euclid!'

" 'What is it, what is it, Frankie?' she says, waking up in a fright. 'What did they do to you, boy?'

" ' 'Twas nothing at all, Mummy, just that I didn't know a bit of Euclid. I had to stay back to learn it.'

" 'A nice how d'ye do! And why didn't you know your Euclid?' — and he had me up against the wall and his fist raised.

" 'It wasn't really Euclid at all, Father. It was all Angelo's fault. It was all politics. He divided the class into All Fors and Mollies and because the All Fors won he kept me in out of spite. Honestly, that's all it was, Mummy, there was nothing else to it.'

" 'Holy God,' whispers the old man. 'So it wasn't only the Euclid, but lettin' down John Redmond in front of the whole class. That's what you did, is it?'

" 'Oh, for God's sake, Billy,' says the mother, 'don't mind John Redmond. 'Tis little John Redmond or any other John Redmond cares about us, but 'tis the work, the work. What are we slaving for, boy, day and night, and all the rest of it? There's your poor father working himself to the bone to send you through school. And so on. Nothing matters, boy, but the work! The work!'

" ' 'Tisn't only the work,' says the old man. ' 'Tisn't only the work,' and he was sobbing over it. 'But to think of poor John Redmond fighting night after night for Ireland, standing up there in the House of Commons, and you — you brat — couldn't even do a sum in Euclid to stand by him! In your own school! Before everybody! Look at him,' he wails, with his arm up to the picture of John Redmond on the wall, with his hooked nose and his jowls like an old countrywoman. 'Look at the dacent gentleman. A man that never let down his side. A gentleman to the tips of his toes if there ever was one. And you couldn't do a simple sum in Euclid to help him! Th'other fellows could do it. The All Fors could do it. But my son couldn't do it!'

"And with that he gave me a crack that nearly sent me into the fire.

"The end of it was that I was on my knees with my head

on the mother's lap, blubbering, and the old man with his two hands up to John Redmond, and the tears flowing down his face like rain, and the mother wailing, 'Won't you promise, Frankie, won't you promise to work, boy?' and I promising and promising anything if she'd only stop crying.

"That was the moment that I swore to myself to get on. But wait! You won't understand why until I've finished.

"The next day Angelo took the same problem, at the same hour, and he asked me to do it again. Now, kids are no fools. I knew by the look on his face why he asked me to do it. He wanted to make friends with me, to have everything the same as if yesterday had never happened. But he didn't know what had happened inside in me the night before. I went through the problem, step by step — I knew it perfectly — down to the Q.E.D.

"'Now, isn't it a pity, Frankie,' he says, smiling at me, 'that you wouldn't do that yesterday?'

"'Oh,' I said, in a very lordly, tired voice, 'I just didn't feel like it.'

"I knew what was coming to me, and I wanted it, and to make sure that I got it I gave him that sort of insolent smile that drives grownups mad with children. I've seen that smile on my own children's faces now and again, and when I see it I have to go outside the door for fear I'd knock them the length of the room. That is what Angelo did to me. I got up off the floor and I sat back in my place and I had the same insolent smile on my face.

"'Now, if you please,' says Angelo, reaching for his cane, and he was as white as his teeth, 'will you kindly do the next problem?'

"I did it, step by step, calm as a breeze, down to the Q.E.D. I'd prepared it the night before.

"'Right,' says Angelo, and his voice was trembling with rage. 'Do the next problem.'

"I had him where I wanted him. He was acting unfairly, and

he knew it, and the class knew it. I had that problem prepared too. Just to tease him I made a couple of slips, but just as he'd be reaching for the cane I'd correct them. I was a beast, but he'd made me a beast. I did it, down to the Q.E.D., and I smiled at him, and he looked at me. We both knew that from that moment it was war to the knife.

"I worked that night until twelve o'clock; and I worked every night until I left school until twelve o'clock. I never gave him a chance. I had to, because until the day I left that place he followed me. He followed me into Middle Grade. And into Senior Grade. He made several efforts to make it up with me, but I wouldn't let him. He was too useful to me the other way. I sat for the Civil Service and I got first place in the British Isles in three subjects out of five, geometry, chemistry, and history, third in mathematics, fifth in German. I did worst in German because I didn't have Angelo for German. I think I can say without arrogance that I was the most brillliant student that ever passed out of West Abbey School."

Sir Francis leaned back.

"You must have worked like a black."

"I did."

"Well, it was worth it!"

He looked out over the fields which were now becoming colorless in the falling dusk and his voice sank to a murmur, as if he were thinking aloud.

"I don't know. For me? Yes, perhaps. I had no youth. For them? I don't know. I didn't work to get on, I worked to get out. I didn't work to please my mother or my father. I hated my mother and I hated my father from the day they made me cry. They did the one thing to me that I couldn't stand up against. They did what that little cur Angelo planned they'd do. They broke my spirit with pity. They made me cry with pity. Oh, I needn't say I didn't go on hating them. A boy doesn't nourish hatred. He has his life before him. I was too sorry for them. But that's where they lost everything. A boy can be sorry for people who are weak and pitiable, but he can't respect them. And you can't love people if you don't respect them. I pitied them and I despised them. That's the truth."

He leaned back again.

"You don't look like a man whose spirit was ever broken," I laughed, a little embarrassed.

"The spirit is always broken by pity. Oh, I patched it up pretty well. I made a man of myself. Or, rather," he said with passion, "with what was left of myself after they'd robbed me of my youth that I spent slaving to get away from them."

"You'd have slaved anyway. You were full of ambition."

"If I did I'd have done it for ambition alone. I tell you I did it for pity and hate and pride and contempt and God knows what other reason. No. They broke my spirit all right. I know it. The thing I've put in its place is a very different thing. I know it. I've met plenty of men who've got along on ambition and they're whole men. I know it. I'm full of what they put into me — pity and hate and rage and pride and contempt for the weak and anger against all bullying, but, above all, pity, chock-a-block with it. I know it. Pity is the most disintegrating of all human emotions. It's the most disgusting of all human emotions. I know it."

"What happened to Angelo?"

"I don't know. Nor care. Died, I suppose."

"And . . . your father?"

"Fifteen years after I left Cork he died. I never saw him. I brought my mother to live with me in London."

"That was good. You were fond of her."

"I was sorry for her. That's what she asked me for when I was a boy. I've been sorry for her all my life. Ah!"

His eyes lit up. I looked sideways to see what had arrested

him. It was the first lights of Cork, and, mingling with the smoke over the roofs, the January night. Behind the violet hills the last cinder of the sun made a saffron horizon. As the train roared into the tunnel we could see children playing in the streets below the steep embankment, and he was staring at them thirstily, and I must have imagined that I heard their happy shouts. Then the tunnel opened and swallowed us.

There were no lights in the carriage. All I could see was the occasional glow of his cigarette. Presently the glow moved and my knee was touched. His voice said:

"She's with me on this train. My mother. I'm bringing her back to Cork."

"Will she like that?"

"She's dead."

The train roared on through the tunnel. As we passed under the first tunnel vent a drip of water fell on the roof. The tiny glow swelled and ebbed softly.

"I'm very sorry."

His voice said, in the darkness:

"I meant to bury her in London. But I couldn't do it. Silly, wasn't it?"

After a while another drip of water splashed on the roof. The windows were gray.

"You did the kind thing."

His voice was so low that I barely heard it.

"Kind!"

In a few more minutes we were drawing up in steam alongside the lighted platform. He was standing up, leaning over his hatbox. From it he lifted a silk topper and a dark scarf. He put on his black frock coat. "Good-by," he said politely, and beckoned for a porter.

From the platform I watched him walk down towards the luggage van where a tiny group already stood waiting. They were all poor people. There was a bent old woman there in a black shawl, and three or four humble-looking men in bowler hats and caps. As I watched him bow to them and doff his hat to the old woman and introduce himself, the yellow pine-and-brass of the coffin was already emerging from the van and the undertaker's men in their brass-buttoned coats were taking it from the porters. Among his poor relations he walked reverently, bare-headed, out into the dark stationyard.

They slid the coffin into the motor hearse; he showed his relatives into the carriages, and, stooping, he went in after them. Then the little procession moved slowly out into the streets on its way to whatever chapel would take her for the night into its mortuary.

The Judas Touch

"MUMMY!" he screamed from the doorstep as she raced up the path for the bus.

"What is it?" she shouted back, halting, fumbling in her handbag to see if she had her compact. She heard the hum of the starting bus and raced again for the gate.

"Mummy!" he shouted again, and went racing up the path after her.

"Well?" she yelled, looking out the gate, and then looking back, and then looking out again and putting up her hand to stop the bus.

"Can't I go to *The Bandits of Sherwood Forest?*"

"No!" and she was out through the gate and the gate went *bang!*

He raced madly up the path and out after her, and clutched her skirt as the brakes whined and the driver glared at her.

"Mummy, you promised!"

She swept his hand away, furious at the public scene, and climbed on the bus. Then, remembering that she had promised and that she must make some excuse, she added from the step of the bus:

254

"It's Lent. Nobody goes to movies in Lent!"

And the bus went on its way. He raced, bawling, after it until her promise and his hopes were swept around the corner. The road was empty. He collapsed sobbing on the footpath. With the sobs his tummy went in and out like an engine. He tore penny-leaves from the wall. He said all the bad words he knew, which are the same bad words we all know only that he did not know what they meant. Lent was *foutu!* He had already given up sweets for Lent. Sweets were *foutus!* He had given them up to be a good little boy. Good little boys were all *foutus!* He dragged himself up and with one hand he played harp strings of misery along the wall back to the gate. He dragged his feet through the gravel of the path to make tram lines. He scraped with a rusty nail on the new paint of the door. Then he went slowly into the break-fast room, where the morning paper stood up like a tent. Upstairs the vacuum cleaner moaned. A sputter of March rain hit the windows briefly. He saw an aged fly make a smooth landing on the marmalade. His five fingers stole up over it and squashed it into the marmalade. He wiped his fingers all across the tablecloth. Then he surveyed the table in search of something else to do that he ought not to do. The maid stood at the door.

"Did she let you go?"

"No."

"Did you do what I told you and ask God in your prayers last night to make her let you go?"

"No."

"You couldn't have luck." And she went off for the dustpan.

He waited until she had gone upstairs and he heard her *swish-swish.* Then he said, "God is no blooming good!" with a quick look at the door to be sure that nobody heard that one. His eye caught the shine of the ould jug on the sideboard. His daddy always called it an ould jug; he would say to Mummy, "I might as well be talking to that ould jug." He surveyed the jug for a bit out of the corners of his eyes. Then he looked at the door again, up at the ceiling, back to the door, back to the ould jug. His heart thumped fiercely. He took down the jug — it was pink lustre outside, gold inside — and he put it on the chair. He flopped down on his knees before it, joined his two sweaty palms, and said, staring earnestly at the pink belly of the jug:

"O Jug, I adore thee and bless thee. Please, O my good Jug, send me to *The Bandits of Sherwood Forest* at the Plaza."

He looked up at the ceiling and stuck out his tongue. He looked at the jug. He wagged his palms at it swiftly, a dozen times.

"Jug, gimme half a dollar."

Not a sound but the upstairs *swish-swish.* He sat back on his heels and considered the jug. He put his nose up to the jug to see himself round and fat; and he blew out a big face to see himself twice as round and fat. Then he bethought himself and kneeled up reverently. He cocked his head on one side and said:

"Jug?"

Nothing happened. He grabbed it and shook it and shouted furiously:

"JUG!"

The next moment he had his fist in the jug, grubbing excitedly. He pulled out two raffle tickets, a bottle of red pills, a foreign coin, a champagne cork, and a half-crown piece. In two shakes of a lamb's tail he was in the hall, dragging on his blue gaberdine, and out the gate with his skullcap down over one eye, pelting up to the village. Billy Busher was there, floating a tin motorboat in a puddle of water. He yelled, "Busher, I got half a dollar." And he hunched up to him, swaggering the silver half crown forward guardedly in his palm. Busher's eyes became as big as half crowns and at once he shouted:

"Bandits of Sherwood Forest?"

"No!"

The tin motorboat meant sea, and sand, and roundabouts, and ice cream, and swimming, and holidays.

"Busher, come on and we'll go down to the seaside."

They marched off down the hill to the station. A cab driver's erect whip floated over his shoulder like a single strand of hair. The station was empty; there would not be a train for an hour and five minutes. They were content wandering about the platforms, watching a goods train shunting, its steam blowing about them, or they jumped up and down on the weighing machine, and they played with an idle truck. Their tickets cost tenpence each, which left tenpence for grub. They worked it out that they could spend fourpence on ice cream and sixpence on lemonade, cakes, and sweets. They tried to buy ice cream at the bookstall, but the woman gave them a sour look, pulled her scarf more tightly around her chest, and sold them a packet of cough lozenges for twopence: coffee-colored things, hexagonal, flat, stamped *Mother Markey's Marvels*. They had a rotten taste, like bad licorice. They stuck them with a quick suck to the windows of the carriage.

Long before they came within sight of the sea they said they could smell it — cool, damp, deep, salty, spumy, windy, roaring; the big green animal of the sea that opens up long white jaws to swallow you up with a swoosh and a roar, but you always run away from it just in time, jumping on the wet sand, shrieking and laughing, and then you run in after it until another long white mouth curls up its jaws to eat you up and spit you out and you run away shrieking again. In their joy and terror of the millions of long white mouths they climbed on the dusty seats of the carriage, and clawed the glass, and hunched their shoulders and hissed at one another like geese. They clung their cheeks sideways to the windows in order to be, each, the first one to shout, "I see it!"

When the train stopped they were jolted onto the floor. They scrambled up and out, and galloped ahead of the only two other travelers, who drove off into the town on a sidecar, collars up. When they reached the embankment above the station they were blown back on their heels by the wind. They held on to their caps, coats flapping, bodies bumping, looking at the waves thundering on the groaning gravel, and the dust of the waves in the wind, and every cement-fronted villa boarded up and shiny in the spume and the sun.

"Come on away up to the merry-go-rounds," he screamed, and they ran for the end of the prom and the hillock beyond it where the roundabouts always stood. All they found was a circle of cinders and big pools of water snaked with petrol. When his cap blew into one of those greasy pools he laughed loudly, and Busher laughed loudly, and for fun threw his own cap into another pool. At that they both laughed like mad.

"Come on away up to the ould Crystal Café," Busher shouted into his ear, "and we'll buy the ould lemonade."

They raced one another around the broken wall and up the steps to the upper road, shoving, falling over one another. In the window of the café was a big yellow-and-black notice: TO LET. A rain squall blasted down on them out of the purple sky. For a while they hugged back into the shelter of the café porch. Then Busher said in a flat voice:

"It's all a blooming suck-in."

When the rain stopped they went slowly to the big tin shelter beside the railway restaurant; it was wide open to the front so that halfway in across its concrete was wet with the rain. They bought one bottle of lemonade in the restaurant and took it out to the long bench of the shelter, and had every second slug out of the bottle. They got one laugh out of that, when the fizz choked Busher's nose. Every few seconds the tin roofs squeaked above the kettledrums of another downpour. At last Busher said:

"You and your shaggin' ould cough lozenges!"

Calvert did not say anything.

"If we had that tuppence now we could buy a cake."

Calvert did not reply.

"You and your swimming!" Busher snarled. "You and your merry-go-rounds! Why didn't you come to *The Bandits of Sherwood Forest* when I asked you?"

Calvert said nothing to that either.

"I'm going home," said Busher and walked off to the station.

Calvert watched him go away. After a few minutes his heart rose — Busher was coming back.

"There's no train," Busher started to wail, "until nine o'clock. There's only two trains a day in the winter." His wail broke into a shameless bawling. "You're after getting me into a nice fix. My da will leather hell out of me when he catches me home."

Calvert looked at him in silence.

"And where did you get that half dollar anyway?" Busher charged. "I bet you stole it from your ma."

Calvert told him. Busher stopped sniveling.

"Gawd! Calvert! You're after praying to the divil. You'll be damned for a-a-all E-eturnity!"

And he tore out his railway ticket and flung it in terror on the concrete and ran bawling out into the rain. He ran and ran, down into the streets of the town, where, taking thought in his desperation, he made his way to the bus stop, told a sad yarn to the driver and the conductor, and got carried home, gratis and in good time.

The rain hammered the convex roof; the wind rattled its bones; bits of paper went whispering around the corners like mice; the gutters spilled; the light faded. He heard the drums of the high tide pounding the beach. Twice he went out looking for Busher. He returned each time with his hair plastered down his forehead. At six o'clock the woman in charge of the restaurant came out, locked up, and saw him in the dim corner of the shelter. She came over to him, found him shivering, and told him to take shelter in the waiting room of the station.

Nobody had bothered to light the room. There was nothing

there but a pine table, two benches, an empty grate, and a poster showing the Bay of Naples. It was so dark that he saw only the table and the poster whenever the eye of the lighthouse beam from Pitch Point looked in through the misted window. He sat there until nearly nine o'clock, not daring to stir, watching and watching for that peering eye.

When he got home his father rushed at him and shouted at him to know where the blazes he had been, and his mother was crying, but when they saw the cut of him they stopped. His mummy and the maid got a hot bath ready for him before the fire, and his da called him "old man" and undressed him on the warm hearthrug, and his mummy brought him in hot chocolate, and for the first time that day he suddenly began to cry. As he sat in the hot bath and his mummy soaped him they asked him again what had happened to him, and they were so nice about it that he began to bawl and he told them all about the ould jug. His daddy, first, and then his mummy and the maid burst into peal upon peal of laughter, while he sat there in the hot water, holding his mug of chocolate, bawling at the cruelty of everything and everybody who ever had anything to do with him since the day he was born.

The Trout

ONE of the first places Julia always ran to when they arrived in G—— was The Dark Walk. It is a laurel walk, very old; almost gone wild; a lofty midnight tunnel of smooth, sinewy branches. Underfoot the tough brown leaves are never dry enough to crackle: there is always a suggestion of damp and cool trickle.

She raced right into it. For the first few yards she always had the memory of the sun behind her, then she felt the dusk closing swiftly down on her so that she screamed with pleasure and raced on to reach the light at the far end; and it was always just a little too long in coming so that she emerged gasping, clasping her hands, laughing, drinking in the sun. When she was filled with the heat and glare she would turn and consider the ordeal again.

This year she had the extra joy of showing it to her small brother, and of terrifying him as well as herself. And for him the fear lasted longer because his legs were so short and she had gone out at the far end while he was still screaming and racing.

When they had done this many times they came back to the house to tell everybody that they had done it. He boasted. She mocked. They squabbled.

"Cry babby!"

"You were afraid yourself, so there!"

"I won't take you any more."

"You're a big pig."

"I hate you."

Tears were threatening, so somebody said, "Did you see the well?" She opened her eyes at that and held up her long lovely neck suspiciously and decided to be incredulous. She was twelve and at that age little girls are beginning to suspect most stories: they have already found out too many, from Santa Claus to the stork. How could there be a well! In The Dark Walk? That she had visited year after year? Haughtily she said, "Nonsense."

But she went back, pretending to be going somewhere else, and she found a hole scooped in the rock at the side of the walk, choked with damp leaves, so shrouded by ferns that she uncovered it only after much searching. At the back of this little cavern there was about a quart of water. In the water she suddenly perceived a panting trout. She rushed for Stephen and dragged him to see, and they were both so excited that they were no longer afraid of the darkness as they hunched down and peered in at the fish panting in his tiny prison, his silver stomach going up and down like an engine.

Nobody knew how the trout got there. Even old Martin in the kitchen garden laughed and refused to believe that it was there, or pretended not to believe, until she forced him to come down and see. Kneeling and pushing back his tattered old cap he peered in.

"Be cripes, you're right. How the divil in hell did that fella get there?"

She stared at him suspiciously.

"You knew?" she accused; but he said, "The divil a' know," and reached down to lift it out. Convinced she hauled him back. If she had found it, then it was her trout.

Her mother suggested that a bird had carried the spawn. Her father thought that in the winter a small streamlet might have carried it down there as a baby, and it had been safe until the summer came and the water began to dry up. She said, "I see," and went back to look again and consider the matter in private. Her brother remained behind, wanting to hear the whole story of the trout, not really interested in the actual trout but much interested in the story which his mummy began to make up for him on the lines of, "So one day Daddy Trout and Mammy Trout . . ." When he retailed it to her she said, "Pooh."

It troubled her that the trout was always in the same position; he had no room to turn; all the time the silver belly went up and down; otherwise he was motionless. She wondered what he ate, and in between visits to Joey Pony and the boat, and a bathe to get cool, she thought of his hunger. She brought him down bits of dough; once she brought him a worm. He ignored the food. He just went on panting. Hunched over him she thought how all the winter, while she was at school, he had been in there. All the winter, in The Dark Walk, all day, all night, floating around alone. She drew the leaf of her hat down around her ears and chin and stared. She was still thinking of it as she lay in bed.

It was late June, the longest days of the year. The sun had sat still for a week, burning up the world. Although it was after ten o'clock it was still bright and still hot. She lay on her back under a single sheet, with her long legs spread, trying to keep cool. She could see the D of the moon through the fir tree — they slept on the ground floor. Before they went to bed her mummy had told Stephen the story of the trout again, and she, in her bed, had resolutely presented her back to them and read her book. But she had kept one ear cocked.

"And so, in the end, this naughty fish who would not stay at home got bigger and bigger and bigger, and the water got smaller and smaller. . . ."

Passionately she had whirled and cried, "Mummy, don't make it a horrible old moral story!" Her mummy had brought in a fairy godmother then, who sent lots of rain, and filled the well, and a stream poured out and the trout floated away down to the river below. Staring at the moon she knew that there are no such things as fairy godmothers and that the trout, down in The Dark Walk, was panting like an engine. She heard somebody unwind a fishing reel. Would the *beasts* fish him out!

She sat up. Stephen was a hot lump of sleep, lazy thing. The Dark Walk would be full of little scraps of moon. She leaped up and looked out the window, and somehow it was not so lightsome now that she saw the dim mountains far away and the black firs against the breathing land and heard a dog say *bark-bark*. Quietly she lifted the ewer of water and climbed out the window and scuttled along the cool but cruel gravel down to the maw of the tunnel. Her pajamas were very short so that when she splashed water it wet her ankles. She peered into the tunnel. Something alive rustled inside there. She raced in, and up and down she raced, and flurried, and cried aloud, "Oh, gosh, I can't find it," and then at last she did. Kneeling down in the damp she put her hand into the slimy hole. When the body lashed they were both mad with fright. But she gripped him and shoved him into the ewer and raced, with her teeth ground, out to the other end of the tunnel and down the steep paths to the river's edge.

All the time she could feel him lashing his tail against the side of the ewer. She was afraid he would jump right out. The gravel cut into her soles until she came to the cool ooze of the river's bank where the moon mice on the water crept into her feet. She poured out, watching until he plopped. For a second he was visible in the water. She hoped he was not dizzy. Then all she saw was the glimmer of the moon in the silent-flowing river, the dark firs, the dim mountains, and the radiant pointed face laughing down at her out of the empty sky.

She scuttled up the hill, in the window, plonked down the ewer, and flew through the air like a bird into bed. The dog said *bark-*

bark. She heard the fishing reel whirring. She hugged herself and giggled. Like a river of joy her holiday spread before her.

In the morning Stephen rushed to her, shouting that "he" was gone, and asking "where" and "how." Lifting her nose in the air she said superciliously, "Fairy godmother, I suppose?" and strolled away patting the palms of her hands.

The Fur Coat

WHEN Maguire became Parliamentary Secretary to the Minister for Roads and Railways his wife wound her arms around his neck, lifted herself on her toes, gazed into his eyes and said, adoringly:

"Now, Paddy, I must have a fur coat."

"Of course, of course, me dear," Maguire cried, holding her out from him admiringly; for she was a handsome little woman still, in spite of the graying hair and the first hint of a stoop. "Get two fur coats! Switzer's will give us any amount of tick from now on."

Molly sat back into her chair with her fingers clasped between her knees and said, chidingly:

"You think I'm extravagant!"

"Indeed, then, I do not. We've had some thin times together and it's about time we had a bit of comfort in our old age. I'd like to see my wife in a fur coat. I'd love to see my wife take a shine out of some of those straps in Grafton Street — painted jades that never lifted a finger for God or man, not to as much as mention the word *Ireland*. By all means get a fur coat. Go down to Switzer's tomorrow morning," he cried with all the innocence of a warm-

266

hearted, inexperienced man, "and order the best fur coat that money can buy."

Molly Maguire looked at him with affection and irritation. The years had polished her hard — politics, revolution, husband in and out of prison, children reared with the help of relatives and Prisoners' Dependents' funds. You could see the years on her finger tips, too pink, too coarse, and in her diamond-bright eyes.

"Paddy, you big fool, do you know what you'd pay for a mink coat? Not to mention a sable? And not as much as to whisper the word broadtail?"

"Say a hundred quid," said Paddy, manfully. "What's a hundred quid? I'll be handling millions of public money from now on. I have to think big."

She replied in her warm Limerick singsong; sedately and proudly as befitted a woman who had often, in her father's country store, handled thousands of pound notes.

"Do you know, Paddy Maguire, what a really bang-up fur coat could cost you? It could cost you a thousand guineas, and more."

"One thousand guineas? For a coat? Sure, that's a whole year's salary."

"It is."

Paddy drew into himself. "And," he said, in a cautious voice, "is that the kind of coat you had in mind?"

She laughed, satisfied at having taken him off his perch.

"Yerrah, not at all. I thought I might pick up a nice little coat for, maybe, thirty or forty or, at the outside, fifty quid. Would that be too much?"

"Go down to Switzer's in the morning and bring it home on your back."

But, even there, she thought she detected a touch of the bravo, as if he was still feeling himself a great fellow. She let it pass. She said she might have a look around. There was no hurry. She did not bring up the matter again for quite fifteen minutes.

"Paddy! About that fur coat. I sincerely hope you don't think I'm being *vulgar?*"

"How could you be vulgar?"

"Oh, sort of *nouveau riche*. I don't want a fur coat for show-off." She leaned forward eagerly. "Do you know the reason why I want a fur coat?"

"To keep you warm. What else?"

"Oh, well, that too, I suppose, yes," she agreed shortly. "But you must realize that from this on we'll be getting asked out to parties and receptions and so forth. And — well — I haven't a rag to wear!"

"I see," Paddy agreed; but she knew that he did not see.

"Look," she explained, "what I want is something I can wear any old time. I don't want a fur coat for grandeur." (This very scornfully.) "I want to be able to throw it on and go off and be as well dressed as anybody. You see, you can wear any old thing under a fur coat."

"That sounds a good idea." He considered the matter as judiciously as if he were considering a memorandum for a projected bypass. She leaned back, contented, with the air of a woman who has successfully laid her conscience to rest.

Then he spoiled it all by asking, "But, tell me, what do all the women do who haven't fur coats?"

"They dress."

"Dress? Don't ye all dress?"

"Paddy, don't be silly. They think of nothing else but dress. I have no time for dressing. I'm a busy housewife and, anyway, dressing costs a lot of money." (Here she caught a flicker in his eye which obviously meant that forty quid isn't to be sniffed at either.) "I mean they have costumes that cost twenty-five pounds. Half a dozen of 'em. They spend a lot of time and thought over it. They live for it. If you were married to one of 'em you'd soon know what it means to dress. The beauty of a fur coat is that you can just throw it on and you're as good as the best of them."

"Well, that's fine! Get the ould coat."

He was evidently no longer enthusiastic. A fur coat, he had learned, is not a grand thing — it is just a useful thing. He drew his brief case towards him. There was that pier down in Kerry to be looked at. "Mind you," he added, "it'd be nice and warm, too. Keep you from getting a cold."

"Oh, grand, yes, naturally, cozy, yes, all that, yes, yes!"

And she crashed out and banged the door after her and put the children to bed as if she were throwing sacks of turf into a cellar. When she came back he was poring over maps and specifications. She began to patch one of the boy's pajamas. After a while she held it up and looked at it in despair. She let it sink into her lap and looked at the pile of mending beside her.

"I suppose when I'm dead and gone they'll invent plastic pajamas that you can wash with a dishcloth and mend with a lump of glue."

She looked into the heart of the turf fire. A dozen pajamas . . . underwear for the whole house . . .

"Paddy!"

"Huh?"

"The last thing that I want anybody to start thinking is that I, by any possible chance, could be getting grand notions."

She watched him hopefully. He was lost in his plans.

"I can assure you, Paddy, that I loathe — I simply loathe all this modern show-off."

"That's right."

"Those wives that think they haven't climbed the social ladder until they've got a fur coat!"

He grunted at the map of the pier.

"Because I don't care what you or anybody else says, Paddy, there *is* something vulgar about a fur coat. There's no shape to them. Especially musquash. What I was thinking of was black Indian lamb. Of course, the real thing would be ocelot. But they're much too dear. The real ones. And I wouldn't be seen dead in an imitation ocelot."

He glanced sideways from the table. "You seem to know a lot about fur." He leaned back and smiled benevolently. "I never knew you were hankering all this time after a fur coat."

"Who said I'm hankering! I am *not*. What do you mean? Don't be silly. I just want something decent to wear when we go out to a show, or to wear over a dance frock, that's all. What do you mean — hankering?"

"Well, what's wrong with that thing you have with the fur on the sleeves? The shiny thing with the what-do-you-call-'ems — sequins, is it?"

"*That!* Do you mean *that*? For heaven's sake, don't be talking about what you don't know anything about. I've had *that* for fourteen years. It's like something me grandmother wore at her own funeral."

He laughed. "You used to like it."

"Of course, I liked it when I got it. Honestly, Paddy Maguire, there are times when . . ."

"Sorry, sorry, sorry. I was only trying to be helpful. How much is an ocelot?"

"Eighty-five or ninety — at the least."

"Well, why not?"

"Paddy, tell me honestly. Honestly, now! Do you seriously think that I could put eighty-five pounds on my back?"

With his pencil Maguire frugally drew a line on the map, reducing the pier by five yards, and wondered would the county surveyor let him get away with it.

"Well, the question is: will you be satisfied with the Indian lamb? What color did you say it is? Black? That's a very queer lamb."

Irritably he rubbed out the line. The wretched thing would be too shallow at low water if he cut five yards off it.

"It's dyed. You could get it brown, too," she cried. "You could get all sorts of lamb. Broadtail is the fur of unborn Persian lambs."

That woke him up: the good farmer stock in him was shocked.

"Unborn lambs!" he cried. "Do you mean to say that they . . ."

"Yes, isn't it awful? Honest to Heaven, Paddy, anyone that'd wear broadtail ought to be put in prison. Paddy, I've made up my mind. I just couldn't buy a fur coat. I just won't buy it. That's the end of it."

She picked up the pajamas again and looked at them with moist eyes. He turned to devote his full attention to her problem.

"Molly, darling, I'm afraid I don't understand what you're after. I mean, do you or do you not want a fur coat? I mean, supposing you didn't buy a fur coat, what else could you do?"

"Just exactly what do you mean?" — very coldly.

"I mean, it isn't apparently necessary that you should buy a fur coat. I mean, not if you don't really want to. There must be some other way of dressing besides fur coats? If you have a scunner against fur coats, why not buy something else just as good? There's hundreds of millions of other women in the world and they all haven't fur coats."

"I've told you before that they dress! And I've no time to dress. I've explained all that to you."

Maguire got up. He put his back to the fire, his hands behind him, a judicial look on him. He addressed the room.

"All the other women in the world can't all have time to dress. There must be some way out of it. For example, next month there'll be a garden party up at the President's house. How many of all these women will be wearing fur coats?" He addressed the armchair. "Has Mrs. de Valera time to dress?" He turned and leaned over the turf basket. "Has Mrs. General Mulcahy time to dress? There's ways and means of doing everything." (He shot a quick glance at the map of the pier; you could always knock a couple of feet off the width of it.) "After all, you've told me yourself that you could purchase a black costume for twenty-five guineas. Is that or is that not a fact? Very well then," triumphantly, "why not buy a black costume for twenty-five guineas?"

"Because, you big fathead, I'd have to have shoes and a blouse and hat and gloves and a fur and a purse and everything to match it, and I'd spend far more in the heel of the hunt, and I haven't time for that sort of thing and I'd have to have two or three costumes — Heaven above, I can't appear day after day in the same old rig, can I?"

"Good! Good! That's settled. Now, the question is: shall we or shall we not purchase a fur coat? Now! What is to be said for a fur coat?" He marked off the points on his fingers. "Number one: it is warm. Number two: it will keep you from getting cold. Number three . . ."

Molly jumped up, let a scream out of her, and hurled the basket of mending at him.

"Stop it! I told you I don't want a fur coat! And you don't want me to get a fur coat! You're too mean, that's what it is! And, like all the Irish, you have the peasant streak in you. You're all alike, every bloody wan of ye. Keep your rotten fur coat. I never wanted it . . ."

And she ran from the room sobbing with fury and disappointment.

"Mean?" gasped Maguire to himself. "To think that anybody could say that I . . . Mean!"

She burst open the door to sob:

"I'll go to the garden party in a mackintosh. And I hope that'll satisfy you!" and ran out again.

He sat miserably at his table, cold with anger. He murmured the hateful word over and over, and wondered could there be any truth in it. He added ten yards to the pier. He reduced the ten to five, and then, seeing what he had done, swept the whole thing off the table.

It took them three days to make it up. She had hit him below the belt and they both knew it. On the fourth morning she found a check for a hundred and fifty pounds on her dressing table. For a moment her heart leaped. The next moment it died in her. She went down and put her arms about his neck and laid the check, torn in four, into his hand.

"I'm sorry, Paddy," she begged, crying like a kid. "You're not mean. You never were. It's me that's mean."

"You! Mean?" he said, fondly holding her in his arms.

"No, I'm not mean. It's not that. I just haven't the heart, Paddy. It was knocked out of me donkeys' years ago." He looked at her sadly. "You know what I'm trying to say?"

He nodded. But she saw that he didn't. She was not sure that she knew herself. He took a deep, resolving breath, held her out from him by the shoulders, and looked her straight in the eyes. "Molly, tell me the truth. You want this coat?"

"I do. O God, I do!"

"Then go out and buy it."

"I couldn't, Paddy. I just couldn't."

He looked at her for a long time. Then he asked:

"Why?"

She looked straight at him and, shaking her head sadly, she said in a little sobbing voice:

"I don't know."

The End of a Good Man

MEN who go into competition with the world are broken into fragments by the world, and it is such men we love to analyze. But men who do not go into competition with the world remain intact, and these men we cannot analyze. They are always contented men, with modest ambitions. Larry Dunne was that kind of man. All that there is to say about him, therefore, is that he bred pigeons and was happy.

And yet, this unconditional lump of reality, this unrefracted thought in the mind of God, suddenly did fall into fragments. He fell for the same reason as Adam. For when God was saying, "Orchards for Adam," and "Finance for J. P. Morgan," and "Politics for Teddy Roosevelt," and "Pigeons for Larry Dunne," He must have added (*sotto voce*), "But one pigeon he must never control." And it was to that one pigeon, that one ambition, that Larry Dunne gave his heart. The pigeon's name was Brian Boru. Larry got him on his thirty-fifth birthday from his father.

Any evening that summer you could have met Larry at the pigeon club — it sat every night under the canal bridge on the towpath — and you might have guessed in what direction his heart was already moving by the way he talked endlessly without ever mentioning the fatal bird. You might have heard him, towering over the rest of the club, talking of his runts, tumblers, pouters, homers, racers, without ever mentioning Brian Boru; you might have heard how he had a jacobin, and nearly had a scandaroon; how "pigeons, mind you, must never be washed, only sprayed with rain water. And what's more, pigeons should be sprayed from the shoulders down — never the head, unless you want them to die of meningitis." What a scoundrel the man in Saint Rita's Terrace was, a low fellow who kept budgerigars and had once actually said that pigeons were mere riffraff. How his father had stolen a sacred pigeon out of an Indian temple, when he was in Rangoon with the Royal Irish, and how the rajah chased him into the jungle for two miles trying to catch him. "And what's more, you should never dry a pigeon, unless, to be sure, you wrapped him up in warm flannel — which isn't the same thing." And anyway, what were budgerigars, only pups off parrots? "They are not even called budgerigars! They call them budgies — as if anyone would ever dare to call a pigeon a pidgy! Doesn't it show yeh?"

But whatever he spoke of, or whomever he spoke to, you might notice that he never spoke to one little runt of a man who always listened to him with a sly, sneering smile on his face. That was the club member whose Michael Collins the Second had beaten Larry's Brian Boru in every race since the season began — beaten the bird that had laid its beak on Larry's heart.

Nobody knew the history of this Brian Boru. Larry's father swore he was the great-grandson of the Indian rajah's sacred pigeon, but that, of course, was a tall yarn. Whatever its pedigree, the bird was a marvel. Such speed! Such direction! Such a homer! A bird that had only one flaw! Time and again, when there was a race, Larry had seen that faint speck of joy come into the sky over the flat counties and the checkered market gardens where he lived, each time half an hour, at the very least, ahead of every other bird in the team; and on one occasion as much as fifty-eight minutes ahead of them, and that in the teeth of a thirty-mile gale.

For while other birds had to follow the guiding shore line, or the railway line that dodged the hills, Brian came sailing over mountain-top and moor like an arrow from the bow. Time and again, after greeting him with an adoring shout, Larry had gone tearing back down the lane to his tumble-down cottage, roaring to his da to get out the decoys, and to light the primus stove for some new concoction whose smell was to tempt Brian Boru down to his loft. Back then to the bridge, waving to the sky, calling the bird by name as it came nearer and nearer to the parapet on which stood the club's timepiece — a clock with a glass front on which there was a blue-and-green painting of a waterfall. (A bird was not officially home until its owner had tipped the waterfall with its beak.)

But . . . time and again the one flaw told. Brian Boru would circle, and Brian Boru would sink, and inevitably Brian Boru would rise again. After about thirty minutes of this he would come down to the telegraph pole over Larry's back yard, and stay there until some slow coach like Michael Collins the Second had walked off with the race. The bird so loved the air that it could not settle down.

"Oh!" Larry had been heard to moan, as he looked up at the telegraph pole. "Isn't it a sign? Isn't it a symbol? Isn't that poor Ireland all over again? First in the race. Fast as the lightning. But she won't settle down! That bird has too much spirit — he's a highflier — and aren't we the same? Always up in the bloody air. Can't come down to earth." And then he would beseech the bird, as it looked down at him over its prima-donna chest with a bleary eye, rather like an old damp-nosed judge falling asleep on his bench: "O Brian Boru! Yeh sweet limb o' the divil, will you come down? Look! I've custards for yeh. I have sowanies for yeh. I have yer loft lined with the sweetest straw." And he would start clucking and chortling at it. "Coordle-coordle-coordle, Brian Boru-u-u-yu." Or: "Tchook, tchuc, thc, thc, thc, thc. Ychook, thc, thc . . . oh, but I'll tchook you if I lay me hands on you, you criminal type from British India! Brian, my *darling,* aren't you *going* to come *down* to me?"

Brian would snuggle his beak on his chest, or make a contemptuous noise like a snore.

Then, that night at the bridge — for on race nights Larry simply had to talk about Brian Boru:

"It's not fair," Larry would protest. "The rules should be altered. That bird is not being given his due. That bird is suffering an injustice. Sure, it's only plain, honest reason. The bird is first home in every race — will any member of the club deny it?"

"No, Larry!" they would reply, appeasingly. "No! He's a grand bird, we all admit it, but a bird who won't settle is no good. And, for another thing, as we're sick and tired of telling you, supposing two birds come into sight at one and the same time, who the blazes is going to tell which one of them is first past the winning post — if there's going to be no winning post?"

"Ah!" Larry would roar. "But sure this bird is home hours before any of your so-called pigeons — cripples, I call them." And then, true to his happy, lighthearted nature, he could not help laughing and making a joke of it. Six feet two, and as innocent as a child. "Did I call them cripples? Cripples is too good for them. The one half of ye must be breeding yeer birds from a cross between penguins and pelicans!"

At which he would recover something of his natural good humor again, and go off chortling — a chortle that would die as he remembered what began it.

As the season approached its end the bird got fat, and Larry got thin; but the bird retained its speed, and Larry became slow-moving and sullen. Those who had always known him for a gay fellow shook their heads sadly over it. He still entered Brian for the races; but each Saturday, now, he would barely stroll to the bridge when the regular two hours were passed since the birds had been released down the country. And when he saw the familiar speck in the sky he would actually turn his back on it.

It was the Easter Monday race that brought things to a head.

That day a passing stranger said to him, as Brian Boru came into sight, "Whose bird is that?"

Larry, leaning with his back and two elbows on the parapet, gave an idle glance over his shoulder at the sky.

"Him? He's my bird. But — eh — he's not in the race, you know. He's what you might call a gentleman pigeon. He's doing it for fun. That bird, sir, could win any race he wanted to. But the way it is with him, he couldn't be bothered. Pride is what's wrong with that bird, sir. Pride! Pride, they say, made the angels fall. Maybe it did. I wish something would make that fellow fall."

Whereupon, Larry, as if a new understanding of the nature of pigeons had suddenly been vouchsafed to him, turned and gave the circling speck a terrible look. It was the look of a man struck by rejected love. Just at that moment it was that the man who owned Michael Collins the Second said the fatal word, as they all remembered and often recounted long after. He was a shrimp of a creature, a Tom Thumb of a man, who worked as a boots in a hotel and bred his pigeons out of his tips. Seeing that look of misery in Larry's face he laughed and said, "Why don't you breed budgerigars, Larry? At least you could take them out of their cage and kiss 'em." The row of pigeon fanciers, staring up at the sky, chuckled. They did not see the look of hate in Larry's face, or notice the way he slouched away home to his cabin.

There, as he was at his tea, he suddenly heard the clatter of wings like tearing silk and, looking up through his cabin window, he saw his bird in its loft among the custards and dainties, and now and again it glanced indifferently towards the cabin door. Pushing aside his cup, Larry said to his father — the old man recorded it when there was no use in recording it — "I wish to God, Da, you never gave me that pigeon. That bird isn't human. He despises me." And he put his head between his hands.

Later in the night, while the drizzle of rain fell on him, and the red reflections of the city illuminated the sky, he stood outside until his hair was pricked with the dew of the drizzle, talking now to himself, now to Brian; and though his father kept coming to the door, telling him not to be behaving like a child of two, Larry would not stir. He was like a boy hanging about under the window of his beloved.

"Is it the way you're faulting me?" he whispered. "Is there something you think I ought to do? But what is there I can do? I can't alter the rules, and you won't come down! I know it's a dishonor. It's a dishonor for both of us. I know that, Brian my darling, just as well as you know it. But honest to God, I don't think it's my fault. I brought you up well. I did my best for you. I swear to God above this night I'd lay down my life for you. But, bar flying up in the air myself and bringing you down, what *can* I do?"

From the loft no reply, except the deep breathing of sleep.

Once more he entered the bird. Once more the pigeon scorned the earth. Once more the boots mentioned budgerigars, and this time he added that canaries can at least sing. Once more, Michael Collins won the race. That finished it. Larry went home, and on the following Monday he sold every bird, box, loft, packet of food, and medicine bottle that he possessed. With the money he bought an old Smith and Wesson, thirty-two bore, and five rounds of ammunition from a former pal of the I.R.A. Then, for the last time, he entered the bird, saw it come, as always, first of the team up against the clouds that floated like bridesmaids over the hedgerows; saw through the veils of the sun how Brian swerved, and circled, and sank . . . and rose again; and did so his usual number of times before making for the inaccessible perch on the telegraph pole. While the dozen heads along the bridge shook their commiseration, Larry gripped his revolver in his pocket, and waited for the boots to laugh. The boots laughed. At that Larry's body took on the old fighting slouch; he pulled his hat savagely down over one eye; he buttoned his coat across his chest; he became the old down-looking

gunman he had been fifteen years ago when he was in the I.R.A.
Then with a roll of his shoulders like a militiaman, a trick learned
from his soldier da, he looked at the boots between the shoulder
blades, put on the final bit of the gunman's manner — the omi-
nously casual strolling gait — and walked quietly down the lane.
There he found Brian on the pole.

"Brian," he whispered, but without hope, "will you come down to
me now?"

The bird rose and flew away, circled and came back again.

"So yeh won't come down?" whispered Larry out of the corner of
his mouth. The bird looked haughtily over the lane roofs, as if con-
templating another circle of flight. Before it could stir the shot
cracked. With one head-sinking tumble it fell with a plop to the
ground. Larry stooped, lifted the hot, twitching body in his palms,
gave it one agonized look, and pelted back to the bridge, roaring
like a maniac.

"By the Lord Almighty!" they said, when they saw him coming,
screeching, with the bird in his palms. "Brian Boru is after winning at last!"

Shouldering their cluster right and left, Larry snapped the beak
to the glass of the clock, displayed the celluloid ring on the stiff
ankle, and shouted, pale as the clouds, "Has he won?"

It was only then that they saw the blood oozing down between his
trembling fingers; but before they could tell him what they thought
of him they saw the mad look in his eyes, and the way his hand
stole to his pocket.

"Well?" yelled Larry at the boots. "Has he won? Or has he not
won? Or maybe you'll say there's a rule that a dead bird can't win
a race?"

"He's w-w-won, all right," trembled the boots.

"Gimme his prize!" said Larry.

In fear they gave it to him. It was a new dovecot, painted a lovely
green. (*Eau de canal,* the boots called it afterwards, being the sar-

castic brute he was.) Larry took the dovecot, and with the reddening beak hanging from his fist he slouched away. On Monday he
sold the dovecot, had the bird stuffed and put in the window of his
lane cabin for the world to see.

You never see Larry Dunne at the canal bridge now. He walks
moodily by himself along the towpaths, idly flickering a little twig
against the hedges: or he sits with his father at the other side of
the fire, learning off bits from his favorite book, *Who's Who,* or he
sits gazing into the dancing devils of flame. The sky outside is
lurid with the lights of Dublin. And in the little curtained window, the pigeon looks with two glassy eyes out over the damp
market gardens and the heavy, odorous night fields at the bloody
sky.

The Silence of the Valley

O NLY in the one or two farmhouses about the lake, or in the fishing hotel at its edge — preoccupations of work and pleasure — does one ever forget the silence of the valley. Even in the winter, when the great cataracts slide down the mountain face, the echoes of falling water are fitful: the winds fetch and carry them. In the summer a fisherman will hear the tinkle of the ghost of one of those falls only if he steals among the mirrored reeds under the pent of the cliffs, and withholds the plash of his oars. These tiny muted sounds will awe and delight him by the vacancy out of which they creep, intermittently.

One May evening a relaxed group of early visitors were helping themselves to drink in the hotel bar, throwing the coins into a pint glass. There were five of them, all looking out the door at the lake, the rhododendrons on the hermit's island, the mountain towering beyond it, and the wall of blue air above the mountain line. Behind the counter was an American soldier, blond, blankly handsome, his wide-vision glasses convexing the sky against his face. Leaning against the counter was a priest, jovial, fat, ruddy, his Roman collar off and his trousers stuck into his socks — he had been up the mountain all day rough-shooting. Leaning against the pink-washed wall was a dark young man with pince-nez; he had the smoldering ill-disposed eyes of the incorrigible Celt — "always eager to take offense," as the fourth of the party had privately cracked. She was a sturdy, red-mopped young woman in blue slacks now sitting on the counter drinking whiskey. She sometimes seemed not at all beautiful, and sometimes her heavy features seemed to have a strong beauty of their own, for she was on a hair trigger between a glowering Beethoven and *The Laughing Cavalier*. Sometimes her mouth was broody; suddenly it would expand into a half-batty gaiety. Her deep-set eyes ran from gloom to irony, to challenge, to wild humor. She had severe eyebrows that floated as gently as a veil in the wind. She was a Scot. The fifth of the group was a sack of a man, a big fat school inspector, also with his collar off. He had cute, ingratiating eyes. He leaned against the opposite pink-washed wall.

In the middle of the tiled floor was a very small man, a tramp with a fluent black beard, long black curls, a billycock hat, a mackintosh to his toes, and a gnarled stick with a hairy paw. The tramp (a whisper from the priest had informed them all that he had once been a waiter on the Holyhead–Euston Express) held a pint of porter in his free hand and was singing to them in a fine tenor voice a ballad called "Lonely I Wandered from the Scenes of My Childhood." They heard him in quizzical boredom. He had been singing ballads to them on and off for nearly two hours now.

Outside, the sun was seeping away behind the far end of the valley. From the bar they could see it touching the tips of the tallest rowans on the island. Across the lake the tip of a green cornfield on a hillock blazed and went out. Then vast beams, cutting through lesser defiles, flowed like a yellow searchlight for miles to the open land to the east, picking out great escarpments and odd projections of the mountains. The wavelets were by now blowing in sullenly on the shore, edging it with froth.

The tramp ended. They applauded perfunctorily. He knew they

were sated and when the redheaded young woman cried, "Tommy, give us 'The Inchigeela Puck Goat,' " he demurred politely.

"I think, miss, ye have enough of me now, and sure I'm as dry as a lime kiln."

"More porter for the singer," cried the priest with lazy authority, and the lieutenant willingly poured out another bottle of stout and rattled a coin into the pint glass.

"I suppose," asked the Celtic-looking young man, in a slightly critical voice, "you have no songs in Irish?"

"Now," soothed the school inspector, "haven't you the Irish the whole bloody year round? Leave us take a holiday from it while we can."

"I had been under the impression," yielded the Celt, with a — for him — amicable smile, "that we came out here to learn the language of our forefathers? Far be it from me to insist pedantically on the point." And he smiled again like a stage curate.

"Tell me, brother," asked the American, as he filled up the tramp's glass, "do you remain on the road the whole year round?"

"Summer and winter, for fifteen years come next September, and no roof over my head but the field of stars. And would you believe it, sur, never wance did I get as much as a shiver of a cold in my head."

"That is certainly a remarkable record."

The proprietor of the hotel entered the bar from the kitchen behind it and planked a saucepan full of fowls' guts on the counter. He was accompanied by a small boy, long-lashed, almost pretty, obviously a city child, who kept dodging excitedly about him.

"Have any of ye a match?" he asked. He was a powerful man, with the shoulders of a horse. He wore neither coat nor vest. His cap was on his poll. His face was round and weather-beaten as a mangold. He had a mouthful of false teeth.

"What do you want a match for, Dinny?" asked the priest with a wink at the others.

The American produced a match. Dinny deftly pinched a fold of his trousers between the eye of his suspenders and inserted the match through the fold: there it effectively did the work of a button. The priest twisted him around familiarly. A nail had performed the same service behind. They all laughed, but Dinny was too preoccupied to heed.

"What's this mess for?" The American pointed to the stinking saucepan.

Dinny paid no attention. He stretched up over the top of the shelves and after much fumbling brought down a fishing rod.

"Give it to me, Dinny, give it to me," shouted the child.

Dinny ignored him also as he fiddled with the line. He glanced out the door, turned to the kitchen and roared:

"Kitty cows coming home tell Patsy James have ye the buckets scalded blosht it boys the day is gone."

Or he said something like that, for he mouthed all his words in his gullet and his teeth clacked and he spoke too fast. They all turned back to watch the frieze of small black cows passing slowly before the scalloped water, the fawny froth, the wall of mountain.

"The cobbler won't lasht the night," said Dinny, pulling with his teeth at the tangled pike line. The priest whirled.

"Is he bad? Did you see him? Should I go down?"

"Still unconscious, Father. No use for you. Timeen was up. He was buying the drink."

"Drink?" asked the Scots girl grinning hopefully.

"For the wake," explained the Celt.

"Well, do you know what it is, by Harry?" cried the inspector earnestly to them all. "He's making a great fight for it."

"He may as well go now and be done with it," said Dinny. "Gimme the guts. We're fishing for eels."

"Gimme the rod, Dinny, gimme the rod," screamed the child and taking it he dashed off like a lancer, shouting with joy. Dinny lumbered after him with the saucepan.

"I reckon these people are pretty heartless?" suggested the soldier.

"We Irish," explained the Celt, "are indifferent to the affairs of the body. We are a spiritual people."

"What enchanting nonsense!" laughed the young woman and threw back her whiskey delightedly.

"It is nonetheless true," reprimanded the Celt.

"You make me feel so old," sighed the young woman, "so old and so wise."

"Are you a Catholic?" asked the Celt suspiciously.

"Yes, but what on earth has that to do with anything?"

"Well, I reckon I don't know much about the spirit, but you may be right about the body. Did you see those hens' guts?"

The priest intervened diplomatically.

"Did you ever see them fishing for eels? It's great fun. Come and watch them."

All but the tramp walked idly to the edge of the lake. The waves were beating in among the stones, pushing a little wrack of straw and broken reeds before them. Dinny had stuck a long string of windpipe to the hook and the boy had slung it out about twelve feet from the shore. To lure the eels a few random bits of guts had been thrown into the brown shallows at their feet and there swayed like seaweed. The group peered. Nothing happened. Suddenly Dinny shouted as fast as a machine gun's burst.

"Look at 'em look at 'em look at the divils blosht it look at 'em look at 'em."

A string of intestines was streaking away out into the lake. Dark serpentine shapes whirled snakily in and out of the brown water. The eels had smelled the rank bait and were converging on it.

"By golly," cried the American, "they must smell that bait a mile away."

The reel whirred, the line flew, the rod bent, they all began to shout, the child trembled with excitement.

"You have him pull him you divil," roared Dinny and seized the rod and whirled a long white belly in over their dodging heads. The girl gave a cry of disgust as the five men leaped on the eel, now lashing in the dust, and hammered savagely at it with heels, stones, a stick, screaming, laughing, shoving. The eel seemed immortal. Though filthy and bleeding it squirmed galvanically. The child circled dancing around the struggling group, half delighted, half terrified.

"Well, Jo," said the young woman as she looked disdainfully at the last wriggles of the corpse, "it seems that boys will be boys. Dinny, do you really eat eels?"

"Christ gurl I wouldn't touch one of 'em for a hundred pounds."

"Then why catch them?"

"For fun."

Her face gathered, ceased to be *The Laughing Cavalier* and became *Beethoven in Labor*. She saw that the men had now become absorbed entirely in the sport. The American had thrown out the line again and they were all peering excitedly into the water. The sun left the last tips of the mountains. The lake grew sullen. Its waves still hissed. They did not weary of the game until eight eels lay writhing in the dust.

Just as they were becoming bored they observed a silent countryman at the edge of the ring looking down at the eels. The priest spoke to him, saying, "Well, Timeen, how is he?" He was a lithe, lean, hollow-cheeked young man with his cap pulled over his eyes. He lifted his face and they saw that he was weeping.

"He's gone, Father," he said in a low voice.

"The Lord have mercy on him," said the priest and his own eyes filled and the others murmured the prayer after him. "The poor old cobbler. I must go and see herself."

He hastened away and presently, tidy and brushed and in his Roman collar, they saw him cycle down the road. The child called after him, "Will you roast the eels for me tonight?" and over his shoulder the priest called, "I will, Jo, after supper," and disappeared wobblingly over the first hill.

"By Harry," cried the inspector, "there'll be a powerful gathering of the clans tonight."

"How's that?" from the American.

"For the wake," explained the Celt.

"I'd certainly like to see a wake."

"You'll be very welcome, sur," said Timeen.

"Did he go easy?" asked the inspector.

Dinny threw the guts into the lake and took Timeen by the arm.

"He went out like a candle," said Timeen, and let Dinny lead him away gently to some private part of the house.

The group dissolved.

"I do wish," said the American, "they wouldn't throw guts into the lake. After all, we swim in it."

"It's very unsanitary, all right," the inspector agreed.

"What are we all," said the Celt philosophically, "but a perambulating parcel of guts?"

The girl sighed heavily and said, "The lamp is lighting."

In the hotel window the round globe of the lamp was like a full moon. A blue haze had gathered over everything. They strolled back to the bar for a last drink, the child staggering after them with the heavy saucepan of dead eels.

The cobbler's cottage was on the brow of a hill about a mile down the road. It was naked, slated, whitewashed, two-storied. It had a sunken haggard in front and a few fuchsias and hollies behind it, blown almost horizontal by the storms. On three sides lay an expanse of moor, now softened by the haze of evening. From his front door the dead cobbler used to look across this barren moor at the jagged mountain range, but he could also see where the valley opened out and faded into the tentative and varying horizons of forty miles away.

When the priest entered the kitchen the wife was alone — the

news had not yet traveled. She was a tiny, aged woman who looked
as if her whole body from scalp to soles was wrinkled and yellow;
her face, her bare arms, her bare chest were as golden as a dried apple; even her eyeballs seemed wrinkled. But her white hair flowed
upward all about her like a Fury in magnificent wild snakes from
under an old fisherman's tweed hat, and her mobile mouth and her
loud — too loud — voice gave out a tremendous vitality. When she
was a young girl she must have been as lively as a minnow in a
mountain stream. The priest had known her for most of his adult
life as a woman whose ribald tongue had made the neighbors delight
in her and fear her: he was stirred to tears to find her looking up at
him now like a child who has been beaten. She was seated on the
long settle underneath the red lamp before the picture of the Sacred
Heart.

He sat beside her and took her hand.

"Can I go up and pray for him?"

"Katey Dan is readying him," she whispered, and the priest became aware of footsteps moving in the room over their heads.

She lumbered up the ladderlike stairs to see if everything was
ready. While he waited he looked at the cobbler's tools by the window — the last, and the worn hammer, and the old butter box by
the fire where the cobbler used to sit. Everything in the kitchen had
the same worn look of time and use, and everything was dusted
with the gray dust of turf — the kettle over the peat fire, the varied
pothooks on the crane, the bright metal of the tongs, the dresser
with its pieces of depth, a scalded churn lid leaning in the window
to dry. There was nothing there that was not necessary; unless, perhaps, the red lamp and the oleograph of the Sacred Heart, and even
that had the stiff and frozen prescription of an icon. The only un-
usual thing was two plates on the table under the window, one of
snuff and one of shredded tobacco for the visitors who would soon
be coming down from every corner of the glens. The only light in
the cottage came from the turf fire.

As he sat and looked at the blue smoke curling up against the brown soot of the chimney's maw he became aware, for the first time in his life, of the silence of this moor. He heard the hollow feet above the rafters. A cricket chirruped somewhere behind the fire. Always up to now he had thought of this cottage as a place full of the cobbler's satirical talk, his wife's echoes and contradictions. Somebody had once told the old man that he was not only the valley's storyteller but its "gossip columnist": the old chap had cocked a suspicious eye, too vain to admit that he did not know the phrase, and skated off into one of his yarns about the days when he had cobbled for the Irish workers laying rails out of Glasgow along the Clyde. The priest smiled at the incident. Then he frowned as he looked at the fire, a quiet disintegration: a turf fire never emits even the slightest whisper. He realized that this cottage would be completely silent from now on. Although it was May he had a sudden poignant sensation of autumn; why, he could not tell.

The old woman called him up. After the dusk of the kitchen this upper room was brilliant. She had lighted five wax candles about her husband's head. Snowy sheets made a canopy about his face. The neighbor woman had just finished the last delicately fluted fold on the lacy counterpane that lay ridged over the stomach and toes. Silently the three knelt and prayed.

When they rose, the old woman said, looking down at the calm countenance on the pillow:

"He's a fine corse and a heavy corse."

"He was a great man. I loved him."

"He had a fierce veneration for you, Father."

They lumbered down the steep stairs. She was as quiet as if the business in hand was something that had happened outside the course of nature. She thanked God for the fine weather. She asked him were there many staying at the hotel. When he told her, she muttered, "We must be satisfied," as if she were talking about the hotel and not about her man. When two more neighbor women came and stood looking at them from the doorway, he took leave of her, saying that he would return later in the night.

The hollies at the door were rubbing squeakingly against each other. The moon was rising serenely over the pass to the east. He felt the cold wind as he rode back to the lake.

They were at supper when he entered the hotel. He joined them about the round table in the bay window through which he could barely discern the stars above the mountains. The rest of the long room, beyond the globe of the lamp, was in shadow. He mentioned that he had seen the cobbler, that they must go down later to the wake, and then set about his food. He paid small heed to the conversation although he gathered that they were loud in discussion over the delay in serving supper.

"Just the same," the American was saying, "I cannot see why it would not be perfectly simple to hang up a card on the wall announcing meal times. Breakfast, eight to ten. Luncheon, one to three. And so on. It's quite simple."

"Just as they do," suggested the young Scotswoman, "in the Regent Palace Hotel?"

"Exactly," he agreed, and then looked in puzzlement at her because she was giggling happily to herself.

"You must admit," the inspector assured her, following his usual role of trying to agree with everybody, "that they have a wonderful opportunity here if they only availed of it. Why don't they cater more for the wealthy clientele? I mean, now, suppose they advertised Special Duck Dinners, think of the crowds that would come motoring out of Cork for them on summer afternoons. It's only about forty miles, a nice run."

"Gee, how often have I driven forty miles and more for a barbecue supper down the coast? I can see those lobster suppers at Cohasset now, two dollars fifty, and the rows and rows of automobile lines outside on the concrete."

"What does our Celt say to this perfectly hideous picture?" asked the red mop.

"I can see no objection — provided the language spoken is Gaelic." She broke into peals of laughter.

"We," the Celt went on, dark with anger, "envisage an Ireland both modern and progressive. Christianity," he went on, proud both of the rightness and intellectual tolerance of his argument, "is not opposed to modernity, or to comfort, or to culture. I should not mind" — his voice was savage, for she was chuckling like a zany — "if seaplanes landed on that lake outside. Why should I? All this admiration for backwardness and inefficiency is merely so much romantic nonsense. Ireland has had enough of it."

She groaned comically.

"Fascist type. Definitely schizoid. Slight sadistic tendency. Would probably be Socialist in Britain, if not" — she wagged her flaming head warningly and made eyes of mock horror — "dare I say it, C.P.?"

"You," cried the Celt scornfully, "merely like the primitive so long as it is not in your own country. Let's go to Nigeria and love the simple ways of the niggers. Let's holiday in Ireland among the beautiful peasants. Imperialist!"

"I beg your pardon," she cried, quite offended. "I am just as happy in the Shetlands or the Hebrides as I am here. Britain's pockets of primitiveness are her salvation. If she ever loses them she's doomed. I very much fear she's doomed already with all these moth-eaten church wardens in Parliament trying to tidy us up!"

And she drew out her cigar case and pulling her coffee towards her lit a long Panatella. As she puffed she was sullen and unbeautiful again as if his hate had quenched her loveliness as well as her humor.

"Well, now, now, after all," soothed the inspector, "it's all very well for you. Your country is a great country with all the most modern conveniences . . ."

"Heaven help it!"

". . . whereas we have a long leeway to make up. Now, to take even a small thing. Those guts in the lake."

"O God!" she groaned. "What a fuss you make over one poor little chicken's guts! Damn it, it's all phosphates. The Chinese use human phosphates for manure."

The priest shook in his fat with laughter — it was a joke exactly to his liking — but the other three took the discussion from her and she smoked in dudgeon until the priest too was pulling his pipe and telling her about the dead cobbler, and how every night in winter his cottage used to be full of men coming to hear his views on Hitler and Mussolini and the prophecies of Saint Columcille, which foretold that the last battle of the last world war would be fought at Ballylickey Bridge. The others began to listen as he retold some of the cobbler's more earthy stories that were as innocent and sweaty as any Norse or Celtic yarn of the Golden Age: such as the dilemma of the sow eating the eel which slipped out of her as fast as it went into her until, at last, the sow shouted in a fury, "I'll settle you, you slippery divil!" and at one and the same moment snapped up the eel and clapped her backside to the wall.

Laughing they rose and wandered, as usual, into the kitchen for the night. They expected to find it empty, thinking that everybody would be going down to the wakehouse; instead it was more crowded than ever; it had become a sort of clearinghouse where the people called on their way to and from the cobbler's cottage, either too shy to go there directly or unwilling to go home after visiting their old friend.

The small boy was eagerly awaiting them with the saucepan of eels. The priest set to. He took off his clerical jacket and put on a green windbreaker, whose brevity put an equator around his enormous paunch, so that when he stooped over the fire he looked like one of those global toys that one cannot knock over. When the resinous fir stumps on the great flat hearth flamed up — the only light in the kitchen — he swelled up, shadows and all, like a necromancer. He put an eel down on the stone floor and with his penknife slit it to its tail and gutted it. The offal glistened oilily. While he was cutting the eel its tail had slowly wound about his wrist, and when he tied its nose to a pothook and dangled it over a leaning flame and its oil began to drip and sizzle in the blaze, the eel again slowly curved as if in agony. The visitors amused themselves by making sarcastic comments on the priest as cook, but four countrymen who lined the settle in the darkness with their caps on and their hands in their pockets watched him, perfectly immobile, not speaking, apparently not interested.

"Aha, you divil, you," taunted the priest, "now will you squirm? If the cobbler's sow was here now she would make short work of you!"

That was the only time any of the countrymen spoke: from the darkness of a far corner an old man said:

"I wondher is the cobbler telling that story to Hitler now?"

"I sincerely hope," said the Scots girl, "that they're not in the same place."

The old man said:

"God is good. I heard a priesht say wan time that even Judas might be saved."

"Jo," said the inspector, steering as usual into pleasant channels, "do you think that eel is alive?"

The small boy was too absorbed to heed, lost in his own delight.

Now and again a handsome, dark serving-girl came to the fire to tend the pots or renew the sods, for meals were eaten in this house at all hours: she seemed fascinated by the eel and every time she came she made disgusted noises. The men loved these expressions of disgust and tried in various ways to provoke more of them, offering her a bite or holding up the entangled saucepan to her nose. Once the American chased her laughingly with an eel in his fist and from the dark back kitchen they could hear them scuffling playfully. By this time many more neighbors had come into the kitchen and into the bar and into the second back kitchen, and two more serving-girls became busy as drinks and teas and dishes of ham passed to and fro, so that the shadows of the men about the fire, the scurrying girls, the wandering neighbors fluttered continually on the white walls and the babble of voices clucked through the house like ducks clacking at a night pond.

Above this murmuring and clattering they heard the tramp singing in the bar a merry dancing tune, partly in Gaelic and partly in English:

> So, little soldier of my heart,
> Will you marry, marry me now,
> With a heigh and a ho
> And a sound of drum now?

"So the little bastard does know Irish," cried the Celt much affronted as the song broke into Gaelic:

> *A chailin óg mo chroidhe*
> *Conus a phósfainn-se thú*
> *Agus gan pioc de'n bhróg do chur orm . . .*

"Perhaps he suits his language to his company?" the red-haired girl suggested.

> I went to the cobbler,
> The besht in the town,
> For a fine pair of shoes
> For my soldiereen brown,
>   So-o-o . . .
> Little soldier of my heart,
> Will you marry, marry me now . . .

The girl peered around the jamb of the door into the bar and then scurried back dismayed. The tramp had spotted her and at once came dancing fantastically into the kitchen on her heels. His long mackintosh tails leaped, and their shadows with them. His black beard flowed left and right as his head swayed to the tune and his black locks swung with it. His hands expressively flicked left and right as he capered about the girl. His billycock hat hopped.

> But, O girl of my heart,
> How could I marry you
> And I without a shirt
> Either white or blue?

"Would you ate an eel?" asked the green-jacketed porpoise by the fire holding up the shriveled carcass to the dancer, who at once gaily doffed his hat (into which the priest dropped the eel) and went on his way back to the bar dancing and singing, followed in delight by the boy:

> So *chuadhas dti an tailliúr,*
> The besht to be found,
> And I bought a silken shirt
> For my *saighdiúrin donn* . . .

"Come, lads," cried the priest, suddenly serious, "it's time for us to visit the poor cobbler."

It was full moonlight. The lake crawled livingly under it. The mountains were like the mouth of hell. It seemed to the priest as if the dark would come down and claw at them. He said so to the Celt, who had become wildly excited at the sight of the dark and the light and the creeping lake and strode down to the beach and threw up his arms crying, "O Love! O Terror! O Death!" — and he broke into Balfe's song to the moon from *The Lily of Killarney:* "The Moon Hath Raised Her Lamp Above."

"If you don't stop that emotional ass," growled the girl as she wheeled out her bicycle, "he'll start singing the 'Barcarole,'" and showed her own emotion by cycling madly away by herself.

"Grim! Grim!" said the American and the inspector agreed with, "In the winter! Ah! In the winter!"

They were cycling now in single file, switch-backing up and down over the little hills until the glow of the cobbler's window eyed them from the dark. Near the cottage dark shapes of men and boys huddled under the hedges and near the walls and as they alighted drew aside to let them pass, fingers to caps for the priest. The causeway to the kitchen door was crowded, unexpectedly noisy with talk, smelling of turf smoke and pipe smoke and bog water and sweat and hens.

In her corner by the enormous peat fire, the little old woman seemed almost to be holding pleasant court, her spirits roused by the friendliness and excitement of the crowds of neighbors.

The babble fell as the strangers entered. It rose again as they disappeared up the ladder stairs to pay their respects to the cobbler. It sank again when they clambered down. Then gradually it rose and steadied as they settled into the company.

They were handed whiskey or stout or tea by Timeen and the priest began to chat pleasantly and unconcernedly with the nearest men to him. To the three Irishmen all this was so familiar that they made no wonder of it, and they left the American and the girl to the cobbler's wife, who at once talked to them about America and Scotland with such a fantastic mixture of ignorance and personal knowledge — gleaned from years upon years of visitors — that all their embarrassment vanished in their pleasure at her wise and foolish talk.

Only twice did her thoughts stray upstairs. A neighbor lifted a red coal in the tongs to kindle his pipe: she glanced sharply and drew a sharp breath.

"Light away, Dan Frank," she encouraged him. "Lasht week my ould divil used to be ever reddening his pipe, God rest him, although I used to be scolding him for burning his poor ould belly with all the shmoking."

Once when the babble suddenly fell into a trough of silence they heard a dog across the moor baying at the moon. She said:

"Times now I do be thinking that with the cobbler gone from me I'll be afraid to be by meself in the house with all the idle shtallions going the road."

It was her commonest word for men, shtalls or shtallions, and all the neighbors who heard her must have pictured a lone tramp or a tinker walking the mountain road, and she inside listening through the barred door to the passing feet.

Elsewise she talked of things like hens and of prices and several times seemed to forget the nature of the occasion entirely. Then, in her most ribald vein, she became scabrous in her comments on her visitors, to the delight of everybody except the victims, who could only scuttle red-faced out the door without, in respect for her, as much as the satisfaction of a curse. It was after one of these sallies that the priest decided to close his visit with a laughing command to them all to kneel for the Rosary. With a lot of scuffling they huddled over chairs or sank on one knee, hiding their faces reverently in their caps.

Only the soldier did not join them. He went out and found more men, all along the causeway and under the hedges, kneeling likewise, so that the mumbling litany of prayer mingled with the tireless baying of the dog. All about them the encircling jags of mountains were bright and jet, brilliant craters, quarries of blackness, gleaming rocks, gray undergrowth.

The journey back was even more eerie than the journey out, the moon now behind them, their shadows before, and as they climbed the hills the mountains climbed before them as if to bar their way and when they rushed downward to the leaden bowl that was the lake, and into the closed gully of the coom, it was as if they were cycling not through space but through a maw of time that would never move.

The kitchen was empty. The eels lay in the pot. Two old boots lay on their sides drying before the fading fire. The crickets whistled loudly in the crannies. They took their candles and went in their stockinged feet up the stairs to bed, whispering.

The morning was a blaze of heat. The island was a floating red flower. The rhododendrons around the edges of the island were replicated in the smooth lee water which they barely touched. As the American, the girl, and the Celt set off for their prebreakfast swim from the island they heard the sounds of spades striking against gravel. They saw the tall thin figure of an aged man, with gray side chops, in a roundy black hat and a swallow-tailed coat, standing against the sky. He held a piece of twig in his hand like a water diviner. He was measuring, taking bearings, solicitously encouraging the gravediggers below him to be accurate in their lines. He greeted the strangers politely, but they could see that they were distracting him and that he was weighed down by the importance of his task.

"For do you see, gentlemen, the cobbler was most particular about where he would be buried. I had a long talk with him about it lasht week and the one thing he laid down was for him to be buried in the one line with all the Cronins from Baurlinn."

"But," demurred the American, "would a foot or two make all that difference?"

"It is an old graveyard," the old man admonished him solemnly, "and there are many laid here before him, and there will be many another after him."

They left him to his task. The water was icy and they could bear only to dive in and clamber out. To get warm again they had to race up and down the brief sward before they dressed, hooting with pleasure in the comfort of the sun, the blue sky, the smells of the island, and the prospect of trout and bacon and eggs for breakfast. As they stepped back on the mainland they met a mountainy lad coming from the depths of the coom, carrying a weighted sack. His gray

tweed trousers were as dark with wetness to the hips as if he had
jumped into a bog hole. He walked with them to the hotel and
explained that he was wet from the dew on the mountain heather
and the young plantations. He had just crossed from the next valley, about two hours away. He halted and opened the mouth of the
sack to show them, with a grin of satisfaction, the curved silver and
blue of a salmon. He said he would be content to sell it to the hotel
for five shillings and they agreed heartily with him when he said,
"Sure what is it only a night's sport and a walk over the mountain?"
Over breakfast they upbraided one another for their lie-abed laziness
on such a glorious day.

The day continued summer hot, burning itself away past high
noon. The inspector got his car and drove away to visit some distant
school. The American took his rod and rowed out of sight to the
head of the lake. The girl walked away alone. The Celt went fishing from the far shore. The priest sat on the garden seat before
the hotel and read his office and put a handkerchief over his head
and dozed, and when the postman came took the morning paper
from him. Once a farm cart made a crockerty-crock down the eastern road and he wondered if it was bringing the coffin. In the farmyard behind the hotel the milk separator whirred. For most of the
time everything was still — the sparkling lake, the idle shore, the
tiny fields, the sleeping hermit's island, the towering mountains,
the flawless sky. "It is as still," thought the priest, "as the world before life began." All the hours that the priest sat there, or walked
slowly up and down reading his breviary, or opened a lazy eye under his handkerchief, he saw only one sign of life — a woman came
on top of a hillock across the lake, looked about her for man or animal, and went back to her chores.

Towards two o'clock the redheaded girl returned from her walk
and sat near him. She was too tired or lazy to talk: but she did ask
after a time:

"Do you think they really believe that the cobbler is talking to
Hitler?"

"They know no more about Hitler than they do about Cromwell. But I'm sure they believe that the cobbler is having nice little chats with his old pals Jerry Coakley and Shamus Cronin — that's Dinny's father that he will be lying next to — up there in the graveyard — in a half an hour's time."

She smiled happily.

"I wish I had their faith."

"If you were born here you would."

"I'd also have ten children," she laughed. "Will you join me in a drink?"

He could not because he must await the funeral and the local curate at the chapel on the island, and, rising, he went off there. She went alone into the bar and helped herself to a whiskey, and leaned over the morning paper. She was joined presently by the Celt, radiant at having caught nothing. To pass the time she started a discussion about large families and the ethics of birth control. He said that he believed that everybody "practiced it in secret," a remark which put her into such good humor that, in gratitude, she made him happy by assuring him that in ten years' time the birth rate in England would be the lowest in the world; and for the innocent joy he showed at this she glowed with so much good feeling towards him that she told him also how hateful birth control is to the poor in the East End of London.

"I always knew it," he cried joyfully. "Religion has nothing to do with these things. All that counts is the natural law. For, as I hope you do realize, there is a law of nature!"

And he filled out two more whiskeys and settled down to the unburthening of his soul.

"You see, I'm not really an orthodox Catholic at all. To me religion is valid only because and in so far as it is based on nature. That is why Ireland has a great message for the world. Everywhere else but here civilization has taken the wrong turning. Here nature still rules man, and man still obeys nature. . . ."

"As in the East End?" she said.

He hurried on, frowning crossly.

"I worship these mountains and these lakes and these simple Gaelic people because they alone still possess . . ."

"But you were angry last night when I defended primitive life. You wanted seaplanes on the lake and tourists from Manchester in Austin Sevens parked in front of . . ."

"I have already explained to you," he reproved her, "that to be natural doesn't mean that we must be primitive! That's the romantic illusion. What I mean to say is — that is, in very simple words, of course . . ."

And his dark face buttoned up and he became ill disposed again as he labored to resolve his own contradictions.

She was about to fly from him when, through the wide-open door, she saw a dark group top the hillock to the east. As the sky stirred between their limbs she saw that they were a silhouette of six men lumbering under a coffin. Its brass plate caught the sun. They were followed by a darker huddle of women. After these came more men, and then a double file of horsemen descended out of the blue sky. On the hermit's island some watcher began to toll a bell.

"I'm going to the island," she said. He followed her, nattering about Darwin and Lamarck.

The priest stood under the barrel arch of the little Romanesque chapel, distent in his white surplice, impressive, a magician. The two went shyly among the trees and watched the procession dissolving by the lakeside. The priest went out to meet the local curate.

Presently the coffin lumbered forward towards the chapel on the six shoulders and was laid rockingly on four chairs. The crowd seeped in among the trees. The widow sat in the center of the chapel steps, flanked on each side by three women. She was the only one who spoke and it was plain from the way her attendants covered their faces with their hands that she was being ribald about each new arrival; the men knew it too, for as each one came forward on the sward, to meet the judgment of her dancing, wicked eyes, he skipped hastily into the undergrowth, with a wink or a grin at his neighbors. There was now a prolonged delay. The men looked around at the weather, or across the lake at the crops. Some turned their heads where, far up the lake, the American in his boat was rhythmically casting his invisible line. Then the two priests returned and entered the chapel. Their voices mumbling the *De Profundis* was like the buzzing of bees. The men bowed their heads, as usual holding their caps before their faces. Silence fell again as the procession reformed.

In the graveyard the familiar voices of the men lowering the dead into the earth outraged the silence. Nobody else made a sound until the first shovel of earth struck the brass plate on the lid and then the widow, defeated at last, cried out without restraint. As the earth began to fall more softly her wailing became more quiet. The last act of the burial was when the tall man, the cobbler's friend, smoothened the last dust of earth with his palms as if he were smoothening a blanket over a child. The priest said three Aves. They all responded hollowly.

They dispersed slowly, as if loath to admit that something final had happened to them all. As each one went down the path he could see the fisherman far away, steadily flogging the water. But they did not go home. They hung around the hotel all the afternoon, the men in the crowded bar, drinking; the women clucking in the back kitchens. Outside the hotel the heads of the patient horses, growing fewer as the hours went by, drooped lower and lower with the going down of the sun, until only one cart was left and that, at last, ambled slowly away.

It was twilight before the visitors, tired and not in a good temper — they had been given only tea and boiled eggs for lunch — could take possession of the littered bar. They helped themselves to drinks and threw the coins into the pint glass. Drinking they looked out at the amber light touching the mountain line.

"It's queer," murmured the priest. "Why is it, all today and yesterday, I keep on thinking it's the autumn?"

" 'Tis a bit like it all right," the inspector agreed pleasantly.

"Nonsense," said the red-haired girl. "It's a beautiful May day."

"Thanks be to God," agreed the inspector.

A frieze of small black cows passed, one by one, along the beach. They watched them go. Then Dinny put his head in from the kitchen.

"Supper, gentlemen."

"I hope we'll have that salmon that came over the mountains," smiled the Celt.

Nobody stirred.

"In America, you know, we call it the Fall."

"The Fall?" said the priest.

"The fall of the leaves," explained the soldier, thinking he did not understand.

The priest looked out over the dark lake — a stranger would hardly have known there was a lake if it had not been for the dun edge of froth — and, jutting out his lower lip, nodded to himself, very slowly, three times.

"Yes, indeed," the inspector sighed, watching his face sympathetically.

"Aye," murmured the priest, and looked at him, and nodded again, knowing that this was a man who understood.

Then he whirled, gave the Celt a mighty slap on the back, and cried, "Come on and we'll polish off that salmon. Quick march!"

They finished their drinks and strolled into the lamplit dining room. As they sat around the table and shook out their napkins the soldier said, "I reckon tomorrow will be another fine day."

The red-haired girl leaned to the window and shaded her eyes against the pane. She could see how the moon touched the trees on the island with a ghostly tenderness. One clear star above the mountain wall gleamed. Seeing it her eyebrows floated upward softly for sheer joy.

"Yes," she said quietly, "it will be another grand day — tomorrow."

And her eyebrows sank, very slowly, like a falling curtain.

The End of the Record

THE news went around the poorhouse that there was a man with a recording van in the grounds. He was picking up old stories and songs.

"And they say that he would give you a five-shilling piece into your hand for two verses of an old song," said Thomas Hunter, an old man from Coomacoppal, in West Kerry, forgetting that five-shilling pieces were no longer in fashion. "Or for a story, if you have a good one."

"What sort of stories would them be?" Michael Kivlehan asked skeptically. He was from the barony of Forth and Bargy, in County Wexford, and had been in the poorhouse for eleven years.

"Any story at all only it is to be an old story and a good story. A story about the fairies, or about ghosts, or about the way people lived long ago."

"And what do he do with 'um when he have 'um?"

"Hasn't he a phonograph? And doesn't he give them out over the wireless? And doesn't everyone in Ireland be listening to them?"

"I wonder now," said Michael Kivlehan, "would he give me five shillings for the 'Headless Horseman and the Coacha Bowr'?"

Thomas Hunter sighed.

"One time I had a grand story about Finn MacCool and the Scotch giant. But it is gone from me. And I'd be getting my fine five-shilling piece into my fist this minute if I could only announce it to him."

The two old men sat on the sides of their beds and tried to remember stories. But it was other things they remembered and they forgot all about the man outside who had set them thinking of their childhood.

The doctor had taken the collector into the women's ward to meet Mary Creegan. She was sitting up in bed, alone in the long room; all the other women were out in the warm sun. As the two men walked up the bare floor the collector was trailing a long black cable from a microphone in his hand, and the doctor was telling him that she came from a place called Faill-a-ghleanna in West Cork.

"She should have lots of stories because her husband was famous for them. After he died she went a bit airy so they had to bring her to us. 'Twas a bit tough on her at first. Sixty years in the one cottage — and then to finish up here." They stood beside her bed. "I brought a visitor to see you, Mary," he said in a loud voice.

She did not appear to see them. She was humming happily to herself. Her bony fingers were wound about an ancient rosary beads. Her white hair floated up above a face as tiny and as wrinkled as a forgotten crab apple. All her teeth were gone so that her face was as broad as it was long: it was as if the midwife had pressed the baby's chin and forehead between thumb and forefinger. The doctor gently laid his hand under the tiny chin and turned her face towards him. She smiled.

"Put down the kettle and wet the tay," she ordered.

The doctor sat on the bed; so did the collector.

" 'Tis down, Mary, and two eggs in the pot. This poor man here is after coming a long way to talk to you. He's tired out."

She turned and looked at the stranger. Encouraged by a brightening spark in the depths of her eyes he turned aside and murmured quietly into the microphone, "Reggy? Recording ten seconds from . . . now."

"It's a bad road," she said. "Ask Jamesy is he keeping that divil of a cow out of the cabbage."

"She's all right," the doctor cried into her ear. "Jamesy is watching her. Be talking to us while we're waiting for the tay. You told me one time you saw a ghost. Is that true?"

She looked out of the window and her eyes opened and narrowed like a fish's gills as if they were sucking something in from the blue sky outside. The collector stealthily approached her chin with the microphone.

"Ghosts? Ayeh! Ha! My ould divil of a tailor is forever and always talkin' about 'um. But, sure, I wouldn't heed him. Bummin' and boashtin' he is from morning to night and never a needle to be shtuck in the shtuff. Where is he? Why don't you ask him to be talking to you about ghoshts?"

The doctor looked across the bed at the collector and raised his eyebrows.

"Maybe you don't believe in them yourself?" he mocked.

"I do *not* believe in 'um. But they're there. Didn't I hear tell of 'um from them that saw 'um? Aye, and often. And often! Aye" — still collecting her thoughts from the sky above the bakehouse chimney — "wasn't it that way the night Father Regan died? Huh! They called him Father Regan, but he was not a right priest. He was silenced for some wrong thing he did when he was a young priest, and they sent him to Faill-a-ghleanna to be doing penance for it. When his time came to die it was a bad, shtormy night. And when he sent for the parish priest to hear his confession the priest said he could not come. And that was a hard thing to do, for no man should refuse the dying. And they sent another messenger for the priest, and still the priest could not come. 'Oh,' said Father Regan, 'I'm lost now.' So they sent a third messenger. And for the third time the priest could not come. And on his way back wasn't the messenger shtopped on the road by a woman? It was Father Regan's own mother. 'Go back,' says she, 'and if the candles by his bed light up,' says she, 'of their own accord,' says she, 'he is saved.' And the messenger went back, and Father Regan gave wan look at him and he closed his eyes for the last time. With that all the people went on their knees. And they began to pray. If they did, there were three candles at the head of the dead priest. And didn't the one beside the window light up? And after a little while the candle beside the fire clevy lit up. And they went on praying. And the wind and the shtorm screaming about the house, and they watching the wick of the last candle. And, bit by bit, the way you'd blow up a fire with a bellows, didn't the candle over the priest's head light up until the whole room was like broad daylight."

The old woman's voice suddenly became bright and hard.

"Isn't that tay ready a-yet? Domn and blosht it, ye'll have them eggs like bullets." She looked alertly at the two men. "Where am I? Where's Jamesy? What are ye doing to me?"

The doctor held her wrist. Her eyes faded. She sank back heavily.

"I thought," she wailed, "that it was how I saw a great brightness."

The collector spoke one word into the microphone. The old woman had fainted. Overcome with regrets he began to apologize, but the doctor waved his hand at him.

"Excited. I'll send up the sister to give her an injection. Sometimes she loves to talk about old times. It does her good."

They went out of the empty ward, the cable trailing softly. They passed the male ward. Michael Kivlehan and Thomas Hunter were sitting on their beds. As the doctor led the way downstairs, he said, "When that generation goes it will be all over. Wait for me outside. There are a couple more. You might get bits and scraps from them."

The engineer put his head out of the van and said, in the gloomy voice of all engineers, "That might come through all right."

When the doctor came out again they sat with a middle-aged man from Wicklow, named Fenelon. He had been on the roads until arthritis crippled him. When he counted the years he spoke in Urdu. He had scraps of the tinker's language which is called Shelta. He said:

"I often walked from Dublin to Puck, and that's a hundred miles, without ever disturbing anything but a hare or a snipe. I'd make for Ross, and then cross to Callan, and by Slievenamon west to the Galtees."

He did not see the microphone; he did not see his visitors; as the needle softly cut the disc he was seeing only the mountainy sheep that looked at him with slitted eyes, a thing as shaggy as themselves.

They moved on to an old woman who sang a love song for them in a cracked voice. She said she had learned it in Chicago. She gave them a poem of twelve verses about a voyage to the South Seas. They were finishing a disc with a very old man from Carlow when the sister came out and hastily beckoned to the doctor. As they folded up the cable he came back. He said, with a slow shake of the head:

"It's old Mary. I must leave ye. But ye have the best of them. The rest is only the shakings of the bag."

When they had thanked him and were driving away, the collector said, eagerly:

"Pull up when we're out of the town. I want to play back those discs."

They circled up and out of the town until its murmur was so faint that they could hear only the loudest cries of the playing children. There they played back the discs, and as they leaned towards the loud-speaker and the black record circled smoothly they could see, sideways through the window, the smoke of the hollow town. The last voice was Mary Creegan's.

"... and after a little while the candle beside the fire clevy lit *up. And they went on praying. And the wind and the shtorm screaming about the house, and they watching the wick of the last candle. And, bit by bit, the way you'd blow up a fire with a bellows, didn't the candle over the priest's head light up until the whole room was like broad daylight. . . . Isn't that tay ready a-yet? Domn and blosht it, ye'll have them eggs like bullets. . . . Where am I? Where's Jamesy? What are ye doing to me? . . . I thought that it was how I saw a great brightness."*

The listeners relaxed. Then from the record came a low, lonely cry. It was the fluting of a bittern over moorland. It fluted sadly once again, farther away; and for a third time, almost too faint to be heard. Many times the two men played back those last few inches of disc. Every time they heard the bittern wailing over the mountains.

It was dusk. They laid the voices in a black box and drove away. Then they topped the hill, and the antennae of their headlamps began to probe the winding descent to the next valley.

Lord and Master

EVERY time Master Kennedy and his wife passed the gates of Carewscourt House, and the round little gate lodge and smooth pond, he said that when he retired he would rent that cottage. The summer he retired he did rent it. He was sad that his wife had not lived to share it with him, but he was as happy, otherwise, as a Chinese philosopher, with his books, and his cat, and his tiny garden with its four standard roses, its six gooseberry bushes and its single pear tree.

Around Christmas he fell ill with a cold that nearly finished him, and it was as he lay in bed that he first noticed the patches of damp on the walls. He did not pay much attention until February, when his foot went through the floor of the front room and his boot sole came up green with mildew. He took his stick, put on his hat, and sought out Paddy Markham, the mason, whom he found plastering the base of the wall of Neville's pub in the Main Street.

"Paddy," he said, "I have a little job for you."

Paddy had a hump and a squint and was half the height of the teacher. He had the trowel in one hand and the hawk in the other, and as he listened he kept mixing the bit of mortar on the hawk with the point of the trowel. In the end he chucked the trowel into the mortar and looked up at his old teacher.

"Masther! I'll tell you no lie. I've been tinkerin' with that ould cottage for the last thirty-five years. I made people spend hundreds of pounds on that cottage trying to get the damp out of it. And," he said triumphantly, "it's as soppin' as if they never spent a penny on it. I put a damp course under it. I waterproofed it. I plastered it with Pluvex and Supex and Pudlo and Cudlo and Dudlo and the divil knows whato. And you might as well be tryin' to plaster up th' Atlantic Ocean. Oh, mind you," Paddy went on comfortingly as the master stared down gloomily at his enthusiastic, stupid face, "It's a nate little house. The house is all right. 'Tis well built, 'tis solid as the Rock o' Gibraltar. But there's wan thing wrong with it."

"And what the devil is that, pray?"

" 'Tis the pond that you have in front of you that's seeping onderneath your foundations. There'll be days, Masther, and if you were to take up a floor board in the front room you'd find a lake of wather onderneath it!"

"Oh, well, in that case," cried the master happily, "all I have to do is get rid of the pond!"

Paddy cocked his quizzical crooked eye up at him.

"How?" he asked.

"Where does the water in the pond come from?"

Paddy drew back and looked sideways at him.

"It comes in a stream from the big lake in front of Carewscourt House, where else? Or are you coddin' me? As if you didn't know! Do you mean to say you don't know the ould gully with the wooden dam beside Beechmount crossroads? Sure all the water in the town comes down there. Down through the channel from the River Villy that the Carews cut hundreds and hundreds of years ago."

The master touched his beard.

"And flows into their lake? And out of the lake into my pond? And from my pond in front of all the cottages? And from . . ."

He stopped. He saw a small boy throwing stones into the stream that runs down the middle of the main street of Rathvilly between two low walls and two lines of lime trees. The child stood on the far pavement, which is three steps above the street on that side. The master looked down at the base of the wall that Paddy had been plastering.

"Then that stream must be seeping under every shop along this side of the street? And under every cottage back along the road? As well as under my cottage?"

"To be sure it does," the mason agreed placidly.

"Then I have no job at all for you, Paddy. The County Council must wall up the dam at Beechmount crossroads."

And off with the Master back down the street, past the last line of cabins, each with its own little wooden bridge, to his cottage by the pond. There he sat down and wrote a long letter to the secretary of the County Council requesting that the dam at Beechmount be permanently closed.

"But sure, my dear Michael," laughed the county engineer, Corny Cosgrave, when he called on the master (who had taught him his first pothooks in the national school), "if we did what you want us to do we'd dry up the bloody lake in Carewscourt."

"And why not, Cornelius?" the master asked calmly.

"But, it's *their* lake!"

"Is that a fact, Cornelius?" The master smiled patiently. "And who gave them the right, Cornelius, to deflect the water to make the lake? Did they ask permission of the town of Rathvilly to make the lake? Did they get permission from the County Council to make the lake?"

"You know damn well," cried Corny testily, "that there was no such a thing as asking permission in those days. Are ye daft? Sure, if there was even such a thing as a County Council in those days they *were* the County Council. And as for asking permission from the town, sure they made, owned, and ran the bloody town."

"And do they still own the town, Cornelius?" asked the master, glaring at his pupil like Moses at a backsliding Israelite. "Is this all our much-vaunted liberty has brought us? You," persisted the master, in his slow Biblical voice, "were one of the first young men in this county to take up arms for the independence of your country. You fought . . ."

Corny held the master's arm.

"Look, Master! For God's sake, leave politics out of this. You'd drag politics into the sale of a wheelbarrow. This question is not a political question. It is a legal question."

"And is the law of Ireland," asked the master fiercely, "for the Saxon or is it for the Gael?"

"The law," said Cornelius, throwing his arms as wide as possible as if to throw the whole matter as far away from himself as possible, "is for everybody. Rich and poor. Gentle and simple. Christian and Jew. Young and old. Male and female. Without the slightest distinction of class *or* creed."

The master smiled at his pupil. Then, as if he had a cane behind his back and was saying, "Kindly tell me what is the capital of Arakan," he said:

"Kindly tell me, Cornelius, what is the law in this matter?"

"That will be for the courts to decide."

At that the master let such a roar out of him that Corny, from old habit, half raised a protective arm.

"So!" the master cried. "Your decision is that I must go behind the County Council to the courts?"

Corny saw that he had fallen into a trap.

"Now! Now! Don't take me up on a word! How do I know what the council will decide to do?"

"You know damn well that you've decided already what you're going to tell them to do!"

Corny took the master by the arm again. He spoke like a fluting pigeon to him.

"Listen to me, Mr. Kennedy." (The old man did not fail to notice the change from "My dear Michael" to "Master" and from "Master" to "Mister," together with the increasing amiability.) "You and I were old campaigners together. You were a Fenian, and the son of a Fenian. You were the first man to open my eyes to the true facts of the national question. Sure, the way you taught Irish history was a marvel! A positive marvel! And you know that I'm as sound an Irishman as you'll get in the four quarters of Ireland. You know me. I know you. And the two of us understand one another's lingo. But what you forget, and a lot of other people forget, and I say this, now, with the greatest respect for you and in the highest possible regard, is that the people of Ireland can't be going back over old sores forever and ever. There are such things, you know, as what they call *fate accomplee*." He slapped the master on the shoulder as if it were he who was the ex-teacher and the master the ex-pupil. "I often heard of people wanting to turn back the clock, but this is the first time I heard of a man wanting to turn back a blooming river!"

The master listened sourly to his peals of laughter.

"Are you telling me, Mr. Cosgrave, that you're not able to dam a little stream no bigger than a dog's piddle for the sake of the health of your own town?"

"My dear sir, give me one man with a shovel and I'll do it for you in five minutes."

"Then why don't you do it in five minutes?"

"Because, dammit, certain people have certain rights, and that's why."

"It's not by any chance because certain people are afraid of certain people, and that's why?"

Corny went pink. He seized his hat.

"I will make my report directly to the County Council," he said coldly. He paused at the door. "You were always a cantankerous ould divil."

"And," the master shouted after him, "I never gave you enough of the stick on your backside when I had you!"

The clang of the motor-car door and the bang of the cottage door were simultaneous.

Within a week the master's pond had the whole town turned upside down. If a child's cap blew into the stream in the middle of the street, or if he got his feet wet beside the cottages, or if a woman as much as sneezed, or if some old fellow who had never done a day's work in his life got a twinge of rheumatism, somebody would start cursing the stream. He might even strike an attitude and say, "Is it for this we bled and died?" There was nothing that couldn't be and wasn't connected with the stream. When the price of coal went up, somebody was heard to say:

"And timber galore in the demesne! How fair they wouldn't give it out to the poor? Oho no! All they ever gave us to warm us was their dirty ould wather!"

It wasn't only the Carews. Their relations all over the county came in for it, the Eustaces, the Brodricks, the Connollys, and the Suttons, until, as one of the opposition said, you'd think the stream had as many tributaries as the Ganges. And then there was an ex-soldier who told a whole pub how he once met an Englishman in Burma who said, "Rathvilly? Isn't that the place where the river runs down the middle of the street?" Hammering the counter this traveler shouted, "Are we to deshtroy a shtrame that have us made famous the world over?"

"I agree," the doctor said in the lounge of the Royal Hibernian Hotel, "that, ideally, the stream ought to be closed. But you know very well that if you close up the stream they'll simply throw their rubbish into the street. And if you block up the stream the cottages will have no running water to wash their clothes in."

Nobody said anything to that. But the vet winked at the ceiling. They all knew that the doctor attended the Carews.

"Aesthetically speaking," said the bank clerk, "it would be a pity to dry up the stream. It's a very pleasant feature in the town. I grant you there's a bit of a niff off it in the summer, but . . ."

"Am I wrong," the town's cryptosocialist said, "in thinking that your bank handles the Carews' account?"

"Aha!" from the bank clerk. "There's Russia talking! You don't mind having your own sister working as a parlormaid in Carewscourt?"

"A perfect example," the cryptosocialist cried, "of the evil network of feudalism."

"Why the hell's blazes," said John Jo Sullivan, who owned the garage, and used to be a commandant of the I.R.A. thirty-two years ago, before he got paunchy and balding, "don't we go out some night and settle the whole bloody thing with one good stick o' dynamite under the ould dam?"

"Well, why don't you, John Jo?" smiled the inspector of the guards, who used to be John Jo's adjutant in those good old days when every question was "settled with one good stick of dynamite."

"Because I don't trust you, you bastard," said John Jo bitterly.

"There was a time when you'd have taken a chance, John Jo," said the inspector easily. And he added, by way of no harm, from the depths of his armchair, "By the way, did Carew order that new Humber Hawk from you yet?"

The master thus found support on all sides.

He was all the more dumfounded when he got a letter a week later from Corny Cosgrave saying that "in view of the enclosed document no action can be taken in the matter until the next meeting of the County Council." The document was "A Grand Petition," pleading for the preservation of the stream, signed by 279 out of Rathvilly's total of 395 inhabitants. When he had read down the list of names he hurled the paper on the floor and cursed Rathvilly, man, woman, and child, lock, stock, and barrel, back to their seventy-seven generations, for a pack of cowards, liars, and cringing slaves.

Not that he did not know perfectly well the pressure that lay be-

hind every signature on the list. The first name on it was Paddy
Markham's. Paddy's brother worked in the Carewscourt sawmills.
Every shopkeeper in the town was there: which meant that the
Carews owed hundreds of pounds all over the place, and everybody knows there is only one way to treat creditors and that is to
make them hop or they'll walk on you. As he examined the list he
could find only two names that had not been extracted by force:
they were two old women who, to his knowledge, were dead and
buried for at least three years. When he saw the two names the
master cursed Rathvilly more bitterly than ever.

"My God!" he ground out. "All we've taught the Carews is
how to beat us at our own game!"

It was three weeks to the next meeting of the council. He spent
every day of it canvassing the members. Not one man of them refused him support, none promised it. What maddened him above all
was the way somebody who had signed the "Grand Petition" would
accost him and congratulate him on the fight he was making.

"But," he would say coldly, "your own name is on the petition,
signed there in black and white!"

The man would say something like:

"Yerrah, Master, what signify that? Sure all I told them was to
throw me name on the ould paper if it gave them any satisfaction. I
can assure you, Master, that I'm *one hundred per cent* with you for
getting rid of that old stream. 'Tis destroying the health of the town.
Fight them, Master! We're behind you to the last ditch."

At the next meeting of the council he sat at the rear of the room.
To his delight one man stood up to support him. He was the Labor
member.

"I maintain, Mr. Chairman," the Labor member declared, "that it
would be a most progressive action, which, as well as giving much-
needed employment to the town and borough, would benefit the
health and sanitation of the working classes, if it was a thing
that the stream at present pursuing its noxious course through the

main street was to be filled up. It would, for one thing, widen the street."

"That's right," put in the Ratepayers' member. "The unemployed could park their motor cars there."

"That," shouted the Labor member, "is an unworthy remark, but no more than I would expect from the low quarter from whence it came."

"Your own brother," shouted the Ratepayers' member, "signed the petition for to keep it."

"The brother," roared the Labor member, "is as good an Irishman as anybody in this room. And he was never before the courts for keeping his pub open after hours!"

"No, nor for poaching salmon either, I suppose?" taunted the Ratepayers' member.

The chairman banged the table for three solid minutes, during which the two speakers investigated the history of their respective families between the years 1810 and 1952.

"May I ask," he said, when he had restored order, "where the sewage would go if we were to fill up the stream?"

"That, Mr. Chairman," declared the Labor member, "is the whole point. It is high time that the sewage system of this town was put into a proper condition."

"Aha!" the Farmers' member shouted. "Now we're getting at it! And your own uncle a contractor!"

This time it took the chairman five minutes to restore order. He gave the floor to John Jo Sullivan, who, they all knew, was going to stand at the next general election for the Dail.

"Mr. Chairman," John Jo said, "I do not think that I need to make any excuses for what I am going to say here today. I do not think I need to blow my own trumpet. I have no wish nor desire to boast of my national record, nor of those far-off days when Ireland lit a torch that shone around the world. Be that as it may, today, thanks be to God, we have a free country (all but the six northern counties, I hasten to say) in which every man is guaranteed his rights under a free constitution, equally approved by church and state. We have a country, moreover, where any man who may have any doubts as to his rights can have free recourse to the courts of law, where all such little disputes can be amicably settled in honesty and in friendship. Our people," he intoned, "have made themselves — and our dear little island — famous all over the world for their long fight down the ages for liberty, and for Christianity. In these dark and troubled days, Mr. Chairman, that surround us, with the specters of war . . ."

At the rear of the room the master rose and walked out so quietly that nobody noticed his going. On his way home he almost admired Carew. Outnumbered four hundred to one he could still keep the rabble under his heels.

On the next morning he went into Limerick city to a solicitor. The solicitor listened to him patiently. Then he said, in the sad, tired voice of a man who is sick to death of all litigation:

"I'm afraid, Mr. Kennedy, you have a case. I'm sorry to say I think you have a case."

"Afraid? Sorry? What do you mean?"

"I mean that you'll go ahead with it. And you won't win it. I know Carew, Mr. Kennedy. He is a determined man. If you beat him in the lower courts he'll take you up to the Four Courts, and he won't stop until he ruins you. And if you should, by some miracle, beat him in law he won't stop until he runs you out of the town. He'll fight you to the last ditch, and beyond it. And I must confess, Mr. Kennedy, I don't blame him."

The master rose in his chair.

"That's queer kind of talk to be going on with to your own client. Are you on his side or are you on mine?"

"Sit down there and listen to me! I'm not on his side. But I can put myself in his position. And if you could do the same you'd see that if you were Lord Carew you'd do to him exactly what he is doing to you. Tell the truth, Mr. Kennedy. If somebody tried to take away from you something that you and your people had owned for going on two hundred and fifty years, something that you'd looked at every day of your life, ever since you were a boy, something that all your memories were wrapped up in, and your father's and your mother's before you, and back behind them for the seven generations — something you were very, very fond of, Mr. Kennedy — wouldn't you fight that man down to the last brass farthing you possessed?"

The master scattered the air with his hands.

"There's no sense nor meaning to this kind of talk! I'm not interested in hypotheses. I'm not Lord Carew, and I don't want to be Lord Carew, and I know nothing about Lord Carew, but I know this, that if I *was* Lord Carew and I wanted to make a lake in front of my house I hope I'd do it some other way than by draining my dirty water past every cottage between my front gate and the gable wall of the chapel." The old man leaned halfway over the desk. His voice rose. "If I wanted to make a lake this minute in front of *my* house would I be allowed to run away with half the river to do it? They stole the river!" he shouted. "They stole the river, and if there's justice in the country they should be made to give it back to the people that owns it. Lord Carew? How could I be . . ." He laughed derisively. "Do you know," he ground out hatefully, "what the Carews did to Rathvilly during the Rebellion of 1798? Do you know that . . ."

The solicitor listened wearily. When the old man sank back, panting and trembling, he said:

"Very well. You evidently feel strongly about it. And if your mind is made up, your mind is made up. But I warn you that it's going to leave a blister on you to the end of your days. It would be far cheaper for you to leave the cottage altogether."

"I will *not* leave the cottage. Ever since my wife, God rest her, saw that cottage twenty-five years ago she wanted me to have it. I put the best part of my life's savings into furnishing that cottage. I love the cottage."

"So be it."

The master calmed down.

"Why have I a case?"

"If the water is damaging your property somebody must be liable."

"Good."

"Mind you, it may not be Carew. It may be the County Council."

"It *is* Carew. And I'll get him."

"But Carew will get at the council, you know."

"How?"

The solicitor parted the air gently with his hands.

All the way back in the train the old teacher kept remembering that gesture. It reminded him of the priest at Mass turning to the people to say *Dominus vobiscum*. He kept murmuring the words to the wet, wheeling fields. They recurred to him many times during the following days, which he spent, often late into the night, writing appealing letters to everybody of position whom he had ever even slightly known. During those nights when he would hear nothing but the swish of the willow outside, or an occasional car driving fast through the town, it seemed to him that, in some way, his desire to go on living in his cottage was linked with his wife's desire to possess it, and that those words, *Dominus vobiscum,* were words of encouragement from her to him. He would seize a new sheet then, and write another long angry letter, to a member of the Dail, to a priest, or to the bishop. He even wrote to the President of Eire. To not one of these letters did he ever receive a reply.

The lawyers were writing more letters. His solicitor quoted against the council a statute from the reign of King John about public waterways. The council's solicitor countered that the lake and its tributaries were Lord Carew's private property. The master's solicitor quoted this against Carew's solicitors. Carew's solicitors replied that they acknowledged responsibility as for the lake, but that once the stream left the demesne it became the public property of the people of Rathvilly. They were sparring all the winter.

Then one afternoon, in late April, the words *Dominus vobiscum* suddenly came to the master with a new meaning. As he murmured the words he looked out of his window. He saw a rainbow that seemed to leap directly from his pond across the sky to the spire on Chapel Hill, and he heard his wife's voice saying, as she had so often said, "Ah, wisha, Patrick, why do you be always growling against the Church? 'Tis our only friend." He took his hat and stick and stumped down into the town, and up Chapel Hill to the presbytery. Painfully he climbed the long steps. Puffed, he pulled the china handle of the bell and asked the housekeeper for the monsignor. She put him to wait in the small side parlor.

As he stood and looked over the woven reed of the half screen across the smoky thatch of the little town he saw something he had not noticed before: a big motor car below at the presbytery gate. It was the Carewscourt car.

At the same moment, across the hall, he became aware of a murmur of voices and the sound of somebody laughing. He opened his door a crack. It was the delicate laugh of the monsignor, and he could imagine the dainty little figure, the white hair, the rosy cheeks, the jigging hand, and the touches of red on his vest and his biretta. He felt his heart thrusting against his breastbones. The blood pumped up under his eyes. He crossed the hall and flung open the parlor door. There was Lord Carew, as sallow as an old spoon, long-faced, smiling; and the monsignor seated opposite him, with his pale-pink hand on the big ordnance map spread on the plush-covered table between them. The master lashed the table with his stick so that the papers flew.

"I knew it," the old man whispered, glaring from one astonished face to the other. "For forty-five years," he gasped, "I've taught in this town, and my poor wife with me. I served you" — he pointed his trembling stick at the monsignor — "since I was a boy serving Mass at the altar, and now I find you conspiring against me with the gentry!" The monsignor had risen, fluttering his two palms. "I hoped," the master sobbed, "I hoped to find the Church on my side and on the side of my poor wife. But the Church is against us! As the Church was always against us. Against the Fenians. The men of forty-eight. Parnell. Sinn Fein. In the fight for the Republic. . . ."

At that he collapsed. After they had partly revived him, they helped him out between them, down the long steps, and into Carew's car. The cries of the children at play did not pause.

On the way, Carew remembered that the old chap lived alone and instead of pausing at the lodge gates he went on into the avenue to his own front steps. There the butler, hearing him come, was already waiting to open the door of the car. By this time the master had recovered. He looked out at the butler, an old pupil of his, one Timsy Twomey, realized where he was, and scrambled out in angry disdain.

"You'd better have a brandy, Mr. Kennedy," Carew suggested and nodded to Twomey.

"I want nothing from you but the one thing," the master began haughtily, "and that . . ."

He stopped. Behind the haze of fishing flies on Carew's tweed hat he saw an oblong sheet of water burning below its low granite coping, fiery in the sun that was sinking between a rosy scallop of clouds and the flowing hills of Villy, now as hard as jewels in the cold April air. Its long smooth glow was broken only by a row of cypresses at its far end, the reflection of whose black plumes plunged into the burning pool to spear the light again. Beneath them were two wrestling Tritons from whose mouths two fountains rose, and crossed and fell with a soft splash. Carew watched the old man's eyes for a moment or two. They were a play of astonishment, delight, and hate.

"Well, Mr. Kennedy, there's the cause of it all. And you're looking at it, I think, for the first time? And, probably, for the last time."

The master looked quickly at him, arrested by his tone.

"I mean," Carew said, with a little crooked smile on his long sallow face, "the lake is going to be drained."

"You're closing the dam?" the master asked, unbelievingly, and looked back at the water which, already, was growing dark and cold.

"You may as well know, if it gives you any pleasure, I'm selling Carewscourt. I've sold it to a teaching order of nuns. Good teachers, I believe. Or so the monsignor tells me. One of the first things they're going to do is to drain the lake. And I'm not much surprised, for it has damn near drained me."

And he began to explain how badly it had been constructed, with somebody always having to empty it and mend the bottom, or grout the sides, or repair the plumbing of the fountain, or dredge the channels down through the town.

"The sisters are going to plant a sunken garden in it. I'm sorry, but . . . Oh, well! They haven't sat here of summer evenings as I have, watching the sun go down."

The splash of the fountains had become more distinct. The hills were dark when Twomey opened the glass doors behind them, and stood waiting for his old teacher.

"It'll be a hard frost tonight," said Carew. "Do come in. We use the hall now for a dining room," he said, and he and the master went up the three shallow steps into the house. Twomey held out the glasses on a salver. Each took one. "I've emptied nearly every room in the house," Carew said. "I'll sell everything except those books."

They walked across the hall to the big bookcase. The master looked into them with interest.

"Mostly Irish books," Carew said. "Family history. I'll keep these."

"And where," asked the master, speaking for the first time since he asked who would dam the lake, "where are you going to live, Lord Carew?"

Carew tapped his chest.

"I haven't long to run." He drained his brandy. "Can I drive you as far as the gates?"

It took the master a long time to reply. Then he said:

"Thank you. I'd be obliged to you."

They drove circuitously, around the far end of the lake. There Carew halted the car for a few seconds to look. One star shone greenly in the water. At the far end the hallway made a brief dagger of light. The house rose square, and straight and clear-cut in the last of the sun.

"It is a fine house," said the master grudgingly.

"It was," said Carew.

They drove on over the gravel to the gates, the cottage, and the pool.

"Good night, Mr. Kennedy. Take care of yourself."

"Good night, Lord Carew. I suppose the sisters will want this cottage?"

Carew lifted an uncertain hand, meshed his gears, drove away.

When the car lights vanished down the road the master walked towards his cottage. In his willow pool he saw the evening star. He stood looking at it for a long time, serene in the water. As he looked it began to fade. Clouds were coming across the sky. It gleamed again, more brilliantly than before. Then it went out.

He went into his cottage and closed the door. From where he sat inside he could hear the willow whispering to the water and the wall. He would miss his little pool.

Persecution Mania

THERE are two types of Irishman I cannot stand. The first is always trying to behave the way he thinks the English behave. The second is always trying to behave the way he thinks the Irish behave. That sort is a roaring bore. Ike Dignam is like that. He believes that the Irish are witty, so he is forever making laborious jokes. He has a notion that the Irish have a gift for fantasy, so he is constantly talking fey. He also has a notion that the Irish have a magnificent gift for malice, mixed up with another idea of the Irish as great realists, so he loves to abuse everybody for not having more common sense. But as he also believes that the Irish are the most kind and charitable people in the world he ends up every tirade with, "Ah, sure, God help us, maybe the poor fellow is good at heart." The result is that you do not know, from one moment to the next, whom you are talking to — Ike the fey or Ike the realist, Ike the malicious or Ike the kind.

I am sure he has no clear idea of himself. He is a political journalist. I have seen him tear the vitals out of a man, and then, over a beer, say, with a shocked guffaw:

"I'm after doin' a terrible thing. Do you know what I said in my column this morning about Harry Lombard? I said, 'There is no subject under the sun on which the eloquence does not pour from his lips with the thin fluidity of ass's milk.' Honest to God, we're a terrible race. Of course, the man will never talk to me again."

All as if right hand had no responsibility for left hand. But the exasperating thing is that his victims do talk to him again, and in the most friendly way, though why they do it I do not know considering some of the things he says and writes about them. He is the man who said of a certain woman who is in the habit of writing letters to the press in defense of the Department of Roads and Railways, "Ah, sure, she wrote that with the minister's tongue in her cheek." Yet the Minister for Roads and Railways is one of his best friends, and he says, "Ike Dignam? Ah, sure! He's all right. The poor divil is good at heart." And the cursed thing is that Ike *is* good at heart. I have long since given up trying to understand what this means. Something vaguely connected with hope, and consolation, and despair, and the endless mercy of God.

Ike naturally has as many enemies as friends, and this is something that *he* cannot understand. Somebody may say:

"But you're forgetting, Ike, what you said about him last year. You said every time he sings 'Galway Bay' he turns it into a street puddle."

Ike will laugh delightedly.

"That was only a bit o' fun. Who'd mind that?"

"How would you like to have things like that said about yourself?"

He will reply, valiantly:

"I wouldn't mind one bit. Not one bit in the world. I'd know 'twas all part of the game. I'd know the poor fellow was really good at heart."

A few weeks ago he got a taste of his own medicine. He committed the folly of granting to his rivals the ancient wish of all rivals, "That mine enemy would write a book." The subject of his book — it was a pamphlet rather than a book — was *The Irish Horse in Irish History,* and it was savagely disemboweled in an anonymous review in one of the popular weeklies. The sentence that wounded him, as it was intended to do, said, "Mr. Dignam's knowledge of hunters is weak, of hacks most profound."

That very afternoon I met him in Mooney's pub, on the quay. He was staring into the bog-hole deeps of a pint of porter. Seeing me he turned such a morose eye on me that I could tell he had been badly hit.

"You saw what the *Sun* said about my book?" he asked, and when I nodded: "That's a low paper. A low rag. A vicious-minded rag. That's what it is. Full of venom and hate and the lust for power. And," he added, slapping the counter, "destruction!"

"Somebody getting his own back, I suppose?"

"What did I ever do to anybody? Only a bit of give and take. What's done every day of the week in journalism. Surely to Gawd, nobody takes me as seriously as all that!"

"Well, that's more or less all your reviewer did with your book."

Again the indignant palm slapped the mahogany.

"That's exactly what I dislike about that review. The mean implication. The dirty innuendo. Why couldn't he come out and say it in the open like a man? It's the anonymity of the thing that's so despicable." Here he fixed me with a cunning eye. "Who do ye think wrote it?"

I spread my hands.

"I think," he said sourly, "that it was Mulvaney wrote it. I made a hare of him one time in my column. But I'm not sure. That's the curse of it. He hasn't enough brains to write it." He gazed at me for a moment through his eyelashes. "You didn't write it yourself by any chance?"

I laughed and told him I hadn't read his book. I'd bought it, of course (which I had not), and had every intention of reading it (which was also untrue).

"Or it could be that drunk Cassidy," he said. "That fellow has it in for me ever since I said that he spoke in the Dail with the greatest sobriety." He laughed feebly. "Everyone knew what I meant. Do you think it might be Cassidy?"

"Ikey, it might be a dozen people."

"It could be anybody," he snarled. "Anybody! Damn it all, if I ever say a thing I say it straight out from the shoulder. Why can't they come into the open?" He leaned nearer and dropped to a whisper. "I was thinking it might be that redheaded bastard from the All Souls Club. That fellow thinks I'm anticlerical. And," he guffawed, "I'm not! That's the joke of it, I'm not!"

"What in the name of all that's holy," I asked crossly, "has anti-clericalism got to do with horses?"

He scratched his head fiercely and moaned and shook it.

"Ye never know. The people in this country have as much sense when it comes to religion . . . Tell me, did ye ever hear of a thing called Discovery of Documents?"

It was only then I fully realized how badly he had been hit.

"You're not being such an idiot as to be thinking of taking this thing to law?"

"Look't! I don't give one tinker's curse about what anybody says against me, but the one thing I *must* know is who wrote it! If I don't find out who wrote it I'll be suspecting my best friends for the rest of my born days."

"Well," I said, finishing my drink and leaving him, "happy hunting to you."

A couple of days later I saw him cruising towards me along O'Connell Street glowing like a sunrise.

"I'm on the track of that," he shouted at me from fifteen yards off. "I'm on the right scent," he babbled, and I had time to remember what he was talking about while he explained how he had worked up a friendship with a girl in the office of the *Sun*. "'Tis none of the people I suspected at all. Do you know who I think wrote it now?"

"God knows, maybe you wrote it yourself."

He shook with laughter.

" 'Twould be great publicity if I could say I did." Then he glowered. "They're entirely capable of saying I did. If they thought anybody would believe 'em. No!" He gripped my arm. " 'Twas a woman did it. I should have guessed it from the word 'Go.' "

"Who is she?"

"I don't know," he said, sadly.

"Then why did you say . . . ?"

"I had a dhream about it. Didn't I see the long, lean, bony hand holding the pen, coming out like a snake from behind a red curtain? Didn't I see the gold bangle on the wrist and all?"

"Did you pull the curtain to see who it was?"

"I pulled and I pulled," Ikey assured me enthusiastically. "Dear Gawd, I was all the night pullin'!"

"And," I suggested bitterly, "I suppose the curtain was made of iron? You know, Ikey, you'll go crackers if you go on like this."

With his two hands he dragged his hat down on his head as if he wanted to extinguish himself.

"I will!" he cried, so loudly that passers-by turned to look at the pair of us. "I'll go stark, staring, roaring mad if I don't find out who wrote that dirty thing about me."

"Look," I pleaded. "What does it all matter? The whole thing is gone completely out of everybody's head but your own. It's all over and done with. And even supposing you did find out who wrote it, what could you do then?"

He folded his arms and gazed down O'Connell Street like Napoleon looking over the Atlantic from St. Helena.

"I'd write a Limerick on him. I'd *shrivel* him. I wouldn't leave a peck on his bones. As a matter of fact" — cocking an eye on me — "I've done it already. I wrote ten Limericks the other night on ten different people who might have written that review. I'm thinking of publishing the whole lot of 'em, and if the cap fits they can share it and wear it."

And before I could stop him he recited to the sky four blistering quatrains on "Irish Bards and Botch Reviewers." I took his arm.

"Ikey, that'll be ten enemies you'll make instead of one! Come in here, Ikey, and let me talk to you like a father."

We went across to Mooney's and I talked for half an hour. I told him we had all been through this sort of thing. I told him that no man who cannot grow an epidermis against malice should try to live in small countries like ours. I said that all that matters is a man's work. I assured him, Heaven forgive me, that he had written a masterly record of *The Irish Horse in Irish History* and that that was the main thing. I developed this soundly into the theory that everything is grist to the mill, and that instead of worrying about this silly review he should go home and write a comic piece about it for *Dublin Opinion,* which, indeed, he could do very well. I built him up as Dignam *solus contra mundum.* He agreed to every word of it. We parted cordially. He was in the happiest temper.

Three days later he came striding towards me, beaming. From afar he hailed my passing ship, roaring like a bosun:

"I found out that bastard! Mulvaney! A friend of mine charged him with it and he didn't deny it."

"Good. You're satisfied now."

"I am. I don't give a damn about it now. Sure that fellow's brains are all in his behind. Who'd mind anything he'd say?"

"The whole thing is of no importance."

"None whatsoever."

"Splendid. It's all over now."

"Finished. And done with!"

"Grand!"

"I sent him a hell of a postcard!"

"No?"

"I did," he chortled, "I did. All I wrote on it was what I said to yourself: 'Your second front is your behind.' An open postcard. It was a terrible thing to do," he beamed. "Oh, shocking!"

His laughter gusted.

"And you put your name to that?"

"I did not. What a fool I'd be! That'll keep him guessing for a while. 'Twill do him no harm in the world. He's not a bad poor gom. Ah! Sure! The poor divil is good at heart."

Off he went, striding along, as happy as a child. I went into Mooney's. There at the counter was Mulvaney, sucking his empty pipe, staring in front of him, his bushy eyebrows as black as night. I wheeled quickly, but he caught the movement and called me. His hand strayed to his breast pocket.

"I'm after receiving a very myst-e-e-rious communication," he said somberly.

I did not hear what else he said. I realized that you could do nothing with these people. I realized that the only sensible thing to do was to write a satire on the whole lot of them. I began to wonder could I get any editor anywhere to publish it anonymously.

An Enduring Friendship

WHEN Georgie Canty saw Louis Golden at the customs counter of the airport he muttered "Bastard!" under his breath: which was what he hoped most people in Ireland thought of Mr. Louis Bloody Well Golden, editor of the *Daily Crucifix,* "Ireland's One and Only Catholic Daily" — and one too many at that!

Georgie's eyes closed, his mouth zipped tight. His duodenum walked slowly all round his waist with spiked boots. It stuck a red-hot sword in through his navel. It pulled his liver out through his ribs. His eyes closed in agony. . . .

He lifted his lids and his eyes swiveled down the counter length at Golden — at his long neck like a heron, his little rabbit's puss with the two white teeth like a nutria, the hunched shoulders of a constipated stork, and the same soapy grin for the customs officer that he probably switched on whenever he'd be talking to a bishop. As he looked at him Georgie wondered if there ever had been a plane crash in which everybody was saved, except one man.

That night at the United Bankers! With himself and Golden, two of a platform of four, debating the motion *That the Irish Are the Most Tolerant Race in the World.* Three sentences. Three not

334

too lengthy sentences about how silly it is for Irishmen to be chasing Freemasons as if they had four horns and two tails; and there he was, the next morning, crucified in the *Crucifix* under a three-column headline — BANKERS DEFEND MASONS — and, on page four, a leading article entitled, "So This Is Holy Ireland?" signed *Louis Paul Golden*. Naturally he was barely inside the door of the bank before he was called into the parlor.

"I understand, Mr. Canty," old Plummer smiled at him across the carpet with teeth that would clip a hedge, "I understand that you saw fit to defend Freemasonry in public last night? Is that correct?"

Now, of course every man in the bank knows perfectly well that there isn't a month that old Plumtree Gum doesn't toddle off to the Masonic Hall with his little apron and all the rest of his regalia; and, for all anybody knows, he might be the great Mah Jong of Molesworth Street, he might be the Prince Mason of the Western World. So, what could Georgie do but rub his palms, smile a man-of-the-world smile, and utter these famous last words:

"Irishmen are in many ways absurd . . ."

They heard Plummer's roar outside in the Foreign Exchange Department. After that it was ding-dong bell for five minutes. . . . Who — would somebody please, *please,* tell him — who ever asked anybody to defend anybody in private or in public? And if, by any possible chance, however remote, anybody ever did happen to require the kind services of anybody why should anybody think that *his* brilliant services were what was specifically demanded by the occasion? And, furthermore, there were people in this city who were very well equipped to defend themselves for themselves. And, furthermore, he himself had lived in this city for fifty-odd years and he had never made any secret of the fact that he was a member of the Worshipful Grand Order, and if he was ever required to defend himself he could do it very well indeed thank you without anybody's assistance! And, furthermore, and especially, he would be greatly obliged if people would have the goodness to remember that their job, first, foremost, and before all, was to consider the interests of the institution that paid them and made them, which would be a jolly sight better thing for all concerned than to be going out and opening their bloody gobs to make roaring asses of themselves in the bloody press, and he would be infinitely obliged to Mr. Canty if he would remember *that*. And, furthermore . . .

Not a peep out of Georgie. He sat dumb as a goldfish until he heard the voice of God Almighty bidding him good morning in a voice like a hangman's chaplain, followed by the words: "I will consider later, Mr. Canty, what disciplinary action may be most appropriate to the occasion." As Georgie walked back over the two and a half miles of marble floor to his cubbyhole not a sound was heard, not a funeral note, except for some scut softly whistling "Will Ye No' Come Back Again?" He had not done much work in his cubbyhole that day, waiting to be packed off to some back-of-beyond like Killorglin or Cahirciveen. After six weeks without one good night's sleep, he had applied for a week's leave of absence, on a doctor's certificate.

The loud-speaker retailed a female voice in Irish, of which he understood only the word *Gurrabbulluballoo*, which means, "Thanks." He opened his eyes to see the queue trailing out. He was the last man on the plane. He took the last seat. He found himself sitting beside the last man in the world he had wanted to see again. Their safety belts got entangled. Golden looked up and at once shot out his paw.

"Georgie Canty, for all the world! Well, isn't this the real McCoy! This is great luck."

Georgie shook his hand warmly.

"Louis Golden. Well, I'm delighted, simply delighted to see you. Traveling far?"

"Let me help you with that belt," said Golden, and he tucked Canty in like a baby in its pram. Then he patted his thigh. "How's tricks? I heard you weren't too well."

"Not bad, not bad. And yourself? And the missus? All the care doing well?"

As they roared down the runway for the take-off Golden blessed himself piously. Canty thought it just as well to do a fiddle, also, around his third vest button.

"I suppose," he said presently, trying to suggest (but only suggest) a faint sneer, "you're off to some ecclesiastical conference?"

Golden leaned over with a confidential, crooked grin and nudged Canty.

"Mattherofact, d'ye know what I was doing the last time I was in Paris? I was touring an Australian Jesuit around the night clubs. He was very agreeably surprised."

"In which sense?" asked Georgie, modulating between innocence and insinuation. Golden only laughed and waved a tolerant claw.

"Harmless. A bit of leg. Nothing more. The usual routine. We did about five or six of them. Folies Bergère. Bal Tabarin. Chin-Chin. Eve. The Blue Angel. Nothing at all to it."

Georgie squinted sideways at him, thinking of the moths in the Bal Tabarin coming out in the altogether.

"Did *you* approve?" he inquired.

"It's not a question of approving." When he said "question" his two white teeth went bare. "It's all a matter of atmosphere. When in Rome, and so on."

He grabbed the hostess by the hip and ordered two double brandies. This, mind you, at nine-thirty in the morning!

"Morals," he explained to Georgie, "morals in the sense of *mores* are always affected by time and place. For example, would you walk down O'Connell Street in the middle of the noonday with nothing on but a Lastex slip?"

"The Guards'd have me in the Bridewell in two ticks."

"There was a fella walked down the Rue Royale last year with nothin' at all on. He was only fined five francs. Betty Grable could walk down the beach at Biarritz in a G-string and a smile and nobody would look twice at her."

The brandy was going to Georgie's head. He leaned over and laughed.

"I believe Lady Godiva rode down Broadway wan time in her skin and everybody ran out in wild excitement to see the white horse. But if that be so what's this I hear about the bishops not wanting to see girls wearing cycling shorts?"

"Who would?" cackled Golden, and they went hard at it.

They were still arguing the toss over the Channel, and whether it was the six double brandies, or the elevating sensation of being up in the air, Georgie began, in spite of himself, to find the little runt almost bearable. It was not until the Eiffel Tower appeared out of the smoke that he brought down the question of Freemasons.

"You knew blooming well that night that I wasn't defending Freemasonry. But in spite of that, you bastard, you came out in your rotten rag and tore the guts out of me."

"Editorial policy." Blandly.

"Do you realize that you nearly cost me my job?" And he told him all about it.

"Ah! No!" cried Louis, genuinely distressed. "For God's sake! Is that true? Well, now, doesn't that show ye what Freemasons are!"

All the same he stuck to his guns. Georgie had to grant him that he stuck to his guns.

They were still at it as they whirled around the Undying Flame in the bus; and as Georgie had not booked a hotel he went off with Louis; and by the time they were finishing lunch, and two bottles of Nuits Saint George, they had arrived at the Arian heresy — about which they both knew sweet damn-all — and were still at Homoiousian and Homoousian at half past four in front of two Otards and the Café de Paris in the blazing sun.

"Now, look, Louis, you flaming scoundrel," Georgie was saying, "your trouble is you're a moralist. All you want is an autocratic, oligarchic church laying down the law about everything from cremation to contraceptives. You're a Puritan! That's what you are!"

Louis leaned a gentle hand on Georgie's arm and breathed on him like a father confessor.

"Georgie! I'll tell you something. Here in Paris. As bloke to bloke. I have exactly the same pashuns as you have. But I *know* me pashuns! I *know* them — and they're dynamite! And what's more, the pashuns of every Irishman are dynamite! And double dynamite! And triple dynamite! And if the priests of Ireland are hard on their own people, it's because they know that if they once took the lid off the pashuns of Irish men and Irish women, aye and of Irish children, the country would *blow up!* Look at Saint Paul!"

Georgie looked and saw a smashing blonde. Louis dragged him ashore, and the pair of them took Saint Paul down to the Rue Donau where Golden knew a little bar called, of all things, *Le Crucifix;* and then they took Saint Augustine, who was a bloke Georgie said he never liked — and he didn't care *who* knew it! — across to a bar on the Quatre Septembre where they had four flat Guinnesses for ould Ireland's sake; and then they took the Manichees, and the Jansenists, and Pascal, up to the bar at the Gare du Nord; and then they went up to Sacré Coeur to say a prayer, and lean on the balustrade, and Louis explained all about Modernism to Georgie, and Georgie said it was his cup of tea, and to hell with the Council of Trent anyway for jiggering up everything; and then they had dinner near the old Pigalle, with two more bottles of Nuits Saint George; and then nothing would do Louis but to prove he wasn't a Puritan by going off to the Bal Tabarin, where they had two bottles of *champagne obligatoire* at three thousand francs a nose.

All Georgie could remember after that was seeing twelve girls coming out on the platform, with about as much on them, if it was all sewn together, as would make a fair-sized loincloth for one Zulu, and telling Louis, with his arm out to the twelve girls:

"There y'are! Janshenist'd shay thatsh shinful! And you — and you're a fellow I never liked, and I don't care what you think! — *you* agree with them!"

"No! Exhplain to ye! Nothing that God made is shinful. Couldn't be. Shin is in us. Those girls aren't even an occashun of shin. And why? 'Cos they don't bother us."

"Bother me," said Georgie. "Bother me a helluva lot. That little wan with the green hair would bother Saint Augustine!"

"God's truth?" asked Louis.

"'Struth," said Georgie.

"Come on out," said Louis, getting up.

"Sit down," shouted Georgie, dragging him back.

"C'mout," said Louis, getting up again.

"Down!" shouts Georgie, hauling him down again.

"Out!" shouts Louis.

"Be quiet!" shouts everybody, and your two men began to shout at everybody else, and to fight one another, and a table gets knocked over, and champagne gets spilled on a girl's dress, and the twelve girls pay no attention at all, only kicking away up in the air like galvanized geese, and the two of them get hauled out and slung out on their backs on the pavement. Like one man they rush back. Like one man they get slung out again. At that they get up and they look into one another's faces, their noses one inch apart.

"You dirty little Freemason!" says Golden, baring his two teeth, and his lips glistening in the moonlight.

"You rotten little Puritan!" says Georgie with the hate of hell in his voice.

At that the two of them stopped dead as if they were a pair of waxworks out of the Musée Grevin, horrified by the sight of the hate in one another's faces. They were so horrified that they burst into a wild fit of laughing. They rocked there in one another's arms, falling over one another with the bitterness of the laughing and the hatred and the shame.

A taxi drew up beside them. They tumbled into it. And the next place they were was in the square in front of Nôtre Dame because Georgie said he wanted to see if the moon could laugh at them as much as it laughed at the gargoyles. The square was empty — it was after one in the morning. The two of them linked arms and began to stroll along the river singing the saddest Irish dirges they knew. Georgie used to say afterwards that he often thought of the poor women inside in the Hôtel Dieu enduring the pangs of childbirth while the two of them were bawling away about their Wild Irish Rose, and wouldn't she come home again, Kathl-e-e-en!

For the rest of the week they were inseparable.

When Georgie and Louis meet nowadays in the street, they always greet one another warmly. They ask after one another's health. They send their regards to one another's wives. If a companion asks either of them, "Who was that?" he will say the name, add, "Not a bad sort of chap," and feel the shame of that night burning in him all over again. For, of course, the truth of the whole matter is that once you go on a drunk with a fellow you're stuck with him for life; and in Ireland every bitter word we say has to be paid for sooner or later in shame, in pity, in kindness, and perhaps even in some queer sort of perverted love.

Childybawn

WHEN Benjy Spillane's mother got a letter signed "A True Friend" informing her that Benjy had been "carrying on" for years with a young lady in the bank she at once sank beneath all the appropriate maternal emotions. She saw her treasure looted, her future imperiled, her love deceived. She saw her poor, foolish child beguiled, his innocence undermined, his sanity destroyed. At this time Benjy was just turned forty-one, a cheerful man-about-town with a winy face like a Halloween turnip with a candle inside it, a pair of merry bull's eyes, a hint of gray at his temples, and his overcoat hung down straight from his paunch as if he was going to have a baby. He was an accountant at the bank, his rank and his cubicle next to the manager's.

For two weeks Benjy could not go out for a walk or open a letter at the breakfast table without evoking long, anxious, secretive looks from his mother. At last she could stand it no longer, and put the question point-blank to him.

"Benjy, lovey, is it true what I heard? That you're thinking of getting married? Not, of course, childybawn, that anything would give me more joy than to see you settled down. But, of course, you have time enough, too, and I'd like to see you happy. It isn't a thing you'd rush into, you know."

Benjy's eyes were normally *à fleur de tête*. At this they protruded as if he had goiter. His little mouth was open like a toy fish. Then he hooted loudly.

"Me? Married? In the name of God where did you get that yarn?"

"I dunno now what put it into my head," she said, her heart beginning to glow with relief and joy. "I wonder could it be something that ould jade Ma Looney said to me the other night at the chapel? About how I'd soon be losing you, or something like that. She was always a bad-minded ould rip."

"Well, you can tell her from me she's talking through her left leg. I know, Mammy, when I'm well off," and he slapped her knee. "Aren't you better to me than any wife? And amn't I as good as a second husband to you?"

Which, natural functions apart, was quite true; for, like all Irish mothers, she had him fastened to her with hoops of comfort, and he was so devoted to her that his young lady at the bank once told her that it made her sick to see the pair of them together. So she thought no more about it, beyond petting and spoiling him worse than ever, until she got another letter, this time signed "A Well Wisher," a few days after he came home from his Easter holidays, informing her that the young lady at the bank had gone with him to Paris and Cannes. At this she began to steam open his correspondence. Since Benjy and his ladylove were at the same bank it was over a month before she was rewarded. She was scarlet before she finished the first sentence: "Darling Benjy Wenjy, Your poor little Angela is in bed with the flu, and isn't it a shame, a show and a scandal that 'tis only the flu I'm in bed with. . . ." As she watched Benjy reading the letter that evening over dinner, with a foolish smile on his fat face, she wished that his Angela would get double pneumonia and never rise from her bed again.

The first thing she did was to toddle off to her father confessor.

He annoyed her exceedingly by advising her to pray for her son's early marriage. She thanked him. She said she would. But she had no intention of doing anything of the kind; firstly because it was the last thing she wanted herself, and secondly because she had to face the fact that it was the last thing Benjy wanted either. She thought up a much more satisfying plan. She had always had an intense devotion to Saint Monica, the mother of Saint Augustine, and she now started to make a novena to the pair of them. She hung up their pictures in Benjy's bedroom. One day she went so far as to borrow a copy of *The Confessions of Saint Augustine* from the free library, and laid it casually under the *Sporting Chronicle* on Benjy's armchair. It was the night he usually took her to the pictures, so when she said she was a bit tired and would rather stay at home he naturally sat down on the book.

"Hello!" he said, lugging it out. "Where did you get this?"

"That?" she said, peering at it over her specs. "Wisha, I dunno now where did I get that? Ah, yes, I remember now I got it in the free library. I suppose 'tis edifying, but . . . Anyway, the old print is too small for my poor eyes."

"Would you like me to read a bit of it for you?" said Benjy, who used sometimes to read aloud to her on their nights at home.

"If you like," she said without enthusiasm.

He humored her, but after a few minutes he began to ruffle the pages.

"Why doesn't he come to the point?" he asked impatiently. "This is all Crawthumping stuff. There's not as much as a bottle of stout in it yet. I mean, what did he do anyway after all his old guff?"

"Not much, then," she said, and gazed sadly into the fire. "God help the poor creature!" she sighed. "That's all I have to say — God help her!"

"God help who?" said Benjy. "Oh, but you're right, didn't he go off with a woman or something?" — and he began to turn the pages more hopefully.

"I'm referring to Monica," said his mother severely. "He broke his poor mother's heart. But," she said cheerfully, "he mended it again, God bless him and protect him. When he turned from his bad ways! Ah, that was a lovely scene, the two of them sitting in the window, and the sun going down over the sea. Hand in hand. Mother and son. Lovely! Ah! Lovely! Lovely!"

"You seem to have the book off by heart. We didn't come to that at all yet."

"Yerrah, what book, childybawn? I don't need any book. Amn't I going to the special anniversary sermon on him every year for the last forty years down in Saint Augustine's? And that was another lovely scene, the day in the orchard. When the poor boy was feeling down in the dumps. His conscience at him, I suppose. And the voice said, *Tolle lege, tolle lege.* And there and then he took up the book, and what did he read in the first line?" She fixed her eye on Benjy, who was looking at her in astonishment out of his cheerful, ruddy, turnip face, and she let him have it full blast: *"Not in rioting nor in wantonness, not in chambering nor in drunkenness, but put ye on the garment of the Lord Jesus Christ."* She said it so dramatically that Benjy thought she was going to begin the next sentence with "Dearly beloved brethren." "Aha!" she went on. "That was when the arrow struck him. As it strikes each and every one of us sooner or later. Even the hardest hearted amongst us. *I come,* says the Lord, *like a thief in the night, seeking whom I may devour!"*

Benjy looked at her sourly.

"There was a great preacher lost in you," he said, and went on looking for the spicy bit.

She was silent for a while. He had succeeded in finding a not-too-bad description of what he took to be a bullfight, so he did not see the sharp looks she was giving him. Then he heard her say, lightly, to nobody in particular:

"I was at confession today."

Benjy grunted. That was nothing new.

"Father Benignus I went to. Over at the Capuchins."

Benjy was now deeply interested in the bullfight, so he said nothing to this either.

"He says he knows you."

At this Benjy looked up.

"Me? I never laid eyes on him." And he looked down again.

"He laid eyes on you, then. He says he knows you as well as a bad ha'penny."

Benjy laid down the book. The Crawthumping stuff had begun again.

"Oho? So ye were talking about me?" with an ominous note in his voice which she nervously observed and dared to ignore.

"No, no! Sure, amn't I telling you it was inside in confession? 'Twas only just how we were talking about poor Saint Augustine."

"Is that so?" says Benjy, giving her a long look. "Tell me! Is there, by any chance, any other priest who knows me like that?"

"Father Semple at the South Chapel told me he often saw you at the bank. And Father Milvey up in the Lough Chapel says you have a great future if you'll only mind your p's and q's."

At that Benjy flared:

"I see you have me well bell-a-ragged around the town! I suppose you're telling them all that I'm a trial and a torment to you?"

"Oh! Benjy! What a dreadful thing you're after saying! All I ever said to anyone, and I'd say it to the Pope himself, is that you're the best son ever trod shoe leather. As you are! So far as I know!" A hurt came into her voice as she added, "What do I know about your affairs? Only what you tell me." A long pause. "Your life is your own." A still longer pause. "To make or to mar."

There was a long silence between them after that.

"I think," said Benjy, "I'll take the ould dog out for a walk."

He got no farther than the local, where he had a couple of brooding drinks. He needed them. So did she, and had them. For it was one of her little habits — which she never mentioned to Benjy; it would be only troubling the poor boy — to have a nip of brandy every night, or if the poor heart was weak, or overexcited, maybe two. She felt so much better after them that she was able to put on her specs again and have a look in the *Sporting Chronicle* for tomorrow's starters at Leopardstown; an old County Kildare woman, she had never lost her interest in the nags.

The Monica regimen went on for about three months. During all that time she never said a single word of reproach to him. Every morning she said good-by to him with a sad smile. She welcomed him home every evening with a fond, pathetic kiss, going down then on her knees, in spite of all his protests, to remove his galoshes. He was never so well looked after. She used to heat the seat of his trousers by the fire every morning before letting him put them on. But she stopped going to the pictures. She said she had no heart for them. Instead she would sit opposite him saying the Rosary. If he said anything cheerful she would let out a deep sigh. He found it hard to concentrate on the *Sporting Chronicle.*

After about three months of this both their nerves were so shaken that when he was going to Biarritz for his summer holidays he gave himself away to her by assuring her three times that he was going alone. She decided to call in the help of the bank manager.

"But, my dear Mrs. Spillane," he said to her, when she had finished her extraordinary story, "what on earth can I do? The private lives of my staff are no concern of mine — provided, of course, that there isn't any public scandal, and that it doesn't interfere with the affairs of the bank. I can assure you that your son is an exemplary official. In fact, what you tell me astonishes me. Have you any proof of it?"

She couldn't mention that she had been opening his letters, so she side-stepped that one. What she did say was:

"Amn't I his mother? And let me tell you that if you're astonished I'm more astonished to think you'd allow lassies like that one to be working in a respectable bank like this. 'Tis against nature to have women in banks. 'Tis against God! Banks, indeed! I know another name some people would give them with straps like that one waiting to put their claws into the first poor innocent boy they can capture!"

This rattled him. He had married a lady bank clerk himself and had lived to regret it.

"Mrs. Spillane, your son is not a boy. He's a grown man. And you're doing him no good at all with this kind of talk. Your son will probably become a manager himself one day, but it's unlikely unless he gets married. Now, wouldn't the very best solution to all this be if your *boy* were to marry this young lady?"

She rose up before him to her full height, a small, humpty-dumpty old woman, and with misery in her pale-blue eyes and hatred in her voice she said:

"I'd rather see him in his pools of blood at my feet than see him married to that Jezebel!"

The day after he came back from Biarritz he fell down at her feet spouting blood from a burst ulcer, and was rushed off to hospital. Before they started to operate they brought in the priest to him, and by then Benjy was in no state — moral, physical, or strategical — to resist his administrations. It was a close shave; they barely pulled him through; and by the time he was recuperating he was a changed man. The day Mrs. Spillane passed a bold-looking strap on the stairs of the nursing home, her eyes as red as her painted lips from crying, and walked in to find Benjy reading *The Life of the Curé d'Ars* of his own free will, she knew that mother love had triumphed at last.

After that Benjy developed a great regard for Saint Augustine. Every evening, now, side by side, he and his mother sat in the bay window of their little villa watching the sun slowly draw its light away from the bay. He never went out of evenings except on works of charity with the Saint Vincent de Pauls. He gave up the liquor.

He banned the *Sporting Chronicle*. The only visitors were other fellows from the S. V. de P.'s, or Father Benignus from the Capuchin priory, or Father Semple from the South Chapel, or the curate who had salvaged him in the nursing home. One night when he saw his mother reading a novel called *Her Scarlet Lover* he got up, went to his shelves, and with a sad little smile he handed her a new biography of a Peruvian Jesuit who used to flagellate himself with whips made of old safety-razor blades. There was an embarrassing moment another night when he came home a bit early from his charitable rounds, moved a cushion, found a half-empty bottle of Hennessy's Three Star, and got a definite smell of brandy in the air. Not that he said anything. Nor did he a few evenings later when, with a wry memory of his past follies, he took up that morning's paper to have a look at the racing page and found that day's starters at Hurst Park all checked off pro and con in pencil, with the odds written in beside them. But he began to remember things; he even began to brood—the steak that night had been a bit tough and she had brought him Bordeaux instead of Burgundy. He remembered how, about a year back, he had come one morning on a little heap of colored betting slips behind D'Alton's six-volume *History of Ireland* on his bookshelves, and hastily and fearfully burned them as his own. He became aware that she was backbiting Ma Looney:

"God forgive me," she was saying, "I ran into that ould jade Ma Looney this morning after Mass, and it didn't do me a hap'orth of good. That one is always detracting and backbiting. Oh, an envious jade! Do you remember the time she wanted to persuade me, right or wrong, that you were getting married? Pure jealousy, that's what it was! She's eaten up with it. Do you know now what that one is . . ."

In his years of wickedness Benjy would have listened to her with an indulgent smile. She saw him looking at her now as coldly as if she were a strange woman in a bus. She faltered, shuffled, petered out, and suggested humbly to him that he might like to take the dog for a walk. He did. She profited by his absence: two quick ones. The next night he profited by hers when she toddled off to confession: he rooted the house upside down. He found two empty brandy bottles, eight more betting tickets, her grocer's bills with several incriminating items, and the three anonymous letters. With a sad heart he put them all back where he found them.

"The poor old divil," he was saying to himself. "What a lousy, lonely, empty life I've driven her to! God! I've been a bastard to her!"

That night when she came home he had a new bottle of Three Star ready for her. She took a great deal of persuading before she would accept a teeny, little nightcap. She took less and less persuading every night after, but always she took the nip from him humbly, cringingly. He began to collect racing tips for her at the bank.

"You should put a bob on, now and again," he would say, with his cheery hoot of laughter. "There's no harm in it, Mammy! 'Twill only amuse you."

After that it was a joy to him to see her handing out her shilling to him every morning with a cackle of laughter at her own folly — until the day she won at ten to one on an outsider. In her excitement she let out a wail:

"Oh, what misfortune I had that I didn't put ten bob on him!"

With a shock he thought that maybe she always used to put half a crown on her fancy before. He cursed his meanness.

"Never mind," he comforted her. "Sure, 'tis only fun. I mean, what do you want the money for?"

"Oho, then, and oho, then," she said fretfully, "we could all do with the money. 'Tis all right for you; you don't have to worry about it. Housekeeping isn't what it was when you were a boy."

"Mammy, are the accounts a worry to you? Would you prefer me to take them off your chest?"

"No, no, no!" she cried at once. "No worry at all! What would the worry be? Chuchuchu! For goodness' sake, what worry?"

All the same he dropped in to the grocer the next morning on his way to the bank. He came out trembling. Not a bill paid for six months. The butcher had the same story for him. All that morning at the bank he was distracted by misery at the thought of the poor old creature crimping for money while he had been gallivanting with her ladyship in Paris and Biarritz and Cannes. At his lunch hour he went sadly into Joe Rosenberg's betting office to put her shilling on a horse called Silver Lining. It was Joe who took the bob. He looked at it, looked at Benjy, and said:

"Mr. Spillane, could I have a word with you for a minute?"

Much surprised at being addressed by name, Benjy passed the lifted lid of the counter to where Joe's big fat hand was already slowly turning the pages of a ledger. Benjy's stomach was slowly turning over with it. Sure enough, when Joe had smoothened out a page with his big fingers that looked as if they had been worn flat by delving in his money satchel, Benjy saw her name at the top of the page. His eye raced down to the foot of the page. A total, in the red, of £125. 17. 6.

"I thought you didn't know," said Joe, seeing the look in his face. Then, slowly tapping out "The Dead March" with his fingers across the total: "I suppose my money is safe with you?"

"You'll get it," said Benjy, knowing well that Joe knew well that it was as much as his job was worth to plead the Gaming Act and disown it. He saw that there was no bet under two pounds, several for a fiver, and there was one wild splurge of a tenner.

"What did she back that day?" he asked. Joe had to laugh.

"Do you remember that old four-year-old mare of Billy Morgan's at Punchestown last year?"

"Jasus!" Benjy moaned. "Sure they're looking for her yet. You'll have to take it in installments, Joe. Give her no more credit."

When he got back to the bank he had to sit down. When he saw Angela's legs as she sailed down the aisle, the seam of her black nylons as straight and swelling as the line of a yacht, he thought his ulcer was going to burst all over again. Twice during that afternoon he caught her flirting gaily with the teller in the next cubicle and he got so dizzy that he had to hold on to the desk.

That night as he ate his dinner opposite his mother the silence lay heavy between them like a gramophone record that has not been started. He waited until they were by the fire to let it go.

"Mammy," he said, leading with his left and ready with the right for her answer, "would it upset you very much if I got married?"

She turned joyfully to him.

"Oh, Benjy! Isn't that great news? Who is the lucky girl?"

"A young lady I know at the bank," said Benjy, giving her the right, and waiting with the left for the knockout. "Her name is Angela."

He found his two hands being grasped and kissed.

"Childybawn, I'm simply delighted. How soon will it be?"

"You seem," he said, taken aback, "to be bloody anxious to get rid of me?"

"No! No, Benjy love! No!" And she began to sniffle. "Only you've been so cross with me this last six months. There's no pleasing you."

"Cross?" he roared. "Cross? Am I hearing things? Was I cross about the brandy? Was I cross about the grocer's bills? Or about the butcher? And what about your hundred and twenty-five pounds, seventeen shillings and sixpence that you owe Joe Rosenberg?"

She crouched down in her chair, her two withered hands clasped before her, and stared at him in horror.

"Oh, Benjy!" she fluttered. "Is that all you found out?"

You could have counted out one hundred and twenty-five pounds, seventeen shillings, and six pennies before Benjy could close his mouth and control his wandering paws.

"Sacred Heart!" he whispered at last. "What else is there?"

Her snuffle rose into a wail:

"There's the bloody old money lenders!"

As Benjy sank back into his armchair and gazed at the ceiling, as helpless as a man in a barber's chair, her wail sirened up into a bawl.

"I only wish to God. You got married years and years ago. Ever since you took to. That old piety of yours. You've made my life a misery. Giving me thimblefuls of brandy like a baby. Making me bet in measly ould bobs. Picking and prying at me. From morning to night. Watching every penny I spend. Go on!" she bawled. "Go on, and get married! And torment some other misfortunate woman. The way you're tormenting *me!*"

Benjy's eyes roved patiently all over the ceiling as if he were in search of the answer to the mystery of life. Not finding it in any part of the ceiling he looked out at the sky. He sought for it in the grass of the garden. At last he sought for it in her face, at the sight of which, all puckered up comically like a baby with the gripes, he burst into laughter. He laughed and he laughed.

"Honest to God, Mammy," he howled, "you ought to be put in the budget. You bloody ould rip of hell you!"

She clutched his two hands and drew him towards her.

"Oh, childybawn, they're the first natural words you've said to me in six months!"

He detached himself from her, got up, and looked down at her, flooding with pity at the thought of what the two of them had been through since the Easter before. He patted her hand and said:

"I'm going for a walk."

He was back in ten minutes with a new bottle of Hennessy. He got out the tumblers and slapped out two hard ones. He put one in her fist, sat on the arm of her chair, put his arm around her shoulder, and made her clink classes. She was beginning to protest when his look stopped her. The two of them were soon laughing like children or lovers, and discussing his wedding like any natural mother and son the world over.

An hour later, well fortified, he put on his hat and coat and went down to Angela's digs. She was in slacks, and shapely in them, and only that he was not too sure of his ground he would have loved to squeeze the life out of her. Instead she led him into the back parlor, closed the door, walked over to him, and slapped his face. She called him a creeping rat, a cringing worm, a bloody mammy's darling. She asked him did he think she could be picked up and dropped again at his own sweet will. She told him she wouldn't marry him if he was the last man on earth. She asked him did he think she was a common trollop. She asked him why didn't he go and marry his mother since he was so bloody fond of her. To none of this was Benjy in a position to give a truthful, or indeed any, answer. She slapped his face once more. Then she burst into floods of tears on his shoulder. At a quarter to two in the morning the landlady came down in her dressing gown and threw him out, battered, exhausted, but affianced.

When his old mother died, about five years later, he did marry Angela. As he said when a bachelor pal teased him at the wedding for marrying so young:

"That's all very fine, but, damn it all, I mean to say, a fellow has to have *some* regard for his mother!"

Lovers of the Lake

"THEY might wear whites," she had said, as she stood sipping her tea and looking down at the suburban tennis players in the square. And then, turning her head in that swift movement that always reminded him of a jackdaw: "By the way, Bobby, will you drive me up to Lough Derg next week?"

He replied amiably from the lazy deeps of her armchair.

"Certainly! What part? Killaloe? But is there a good hotel there?"

"I mean the other Lough Derg. I want to do the pilgrimage."

For a second he looked at her in surprise and then burst into laughter; then he looked at her peeringly.

"Jenny! Are you serious?"

"Of course."

"Do you mean that place with the island where they go around on their bare feet on sharp stones, and starve for days, and sit up all night ologroaning and ologoaning?" He got out of the chair, went over to the cigarette box on the bookshelves, and, with his back to her, said coldly, "Are you going religious on me?"

She walked over to him swiftly, turned him about, smiled her smile that was whiter than the whites of her eyes, and lowered her

355

head appealingly on one side. When this produced no effect she said:

"Bobby! I'm always praising you to my friends as a man who takes things as they come. So few men do. Never looking beyond the day. Doing things on the spur of the moment. It's why I like you so much. Other men are always weighing up, and considering and arguing. I've built you up as a sort of magnificent, wild, brainless tomcat. Are you going to let me down now?"

After a while he had looked at his watch and said:

"All right, then. I'll try and fix up a few days free next week. I must drop into the hospital now. But I warn you, Jenny, I've noticed this Holy Joe streak in you before. You'll do it once too often."

She patted his cheek, kissed him sedately, said, "You are a good boy," and saw him out with a loving smile.

They enjoyed that swift morning drive to the Shannon's shore. He suspected nothing when she refused to join him in a drink at Carrick. Leaning on the counter they had joked with the barmaid like any husband and wife off on a motoring holiday. As they rolled smoothly around the northern shore of Lough Gill he had suddenly felt so happy that he had stroked her purple glove and winked at her. The lough was vacant under the midday sun, its vast expanse of stillness broken only by a jumping fish or by its eyelash fringe of reeds. He did not suspect anything when she sent him off to lunch by himself in Sligo, saying that she had to visit an old nun she knew in the convent. So far the journey had been to him no more than one of her caprices; until a yellow signpost marked TO BUNDORAN made them aware that her destination and their parting was near, for she said:

"What are you proposing to do until Wednesday?"

"I hadn't given it a thought."

"Don't go off and forget all about me, darling. You know you're to pick me up on Wednesday about midday?"

After a silence he grumbled:

"You're making me feel a hell of a bastard, Jenny."

"Why on earth?"

"All this penitential stuff is because of me, isn't it?"

"Don't be silly. It's just something I thought up all by myself out of my own clever little head."

He drove on for several miles without speaking. She looked sideways, with amusement, at his ruddy, healthy, hockey-player face glimmering under the peak of his checked cap. The brushes at his temples were getting white. Everything about him bespoke the distinguished Dublin surgeon on holiday: his pale-green shirt, his darker-green tie, his double-breasted waistcoat, his driving gloves with the palms made of woven cord. She looked pensively towards the sea. He growled:

"I may as well tell you this much, Jenny, if you were my wife I wouldn't stand for any of this nonsense."

So their minds had traveled to the same thought? But if she were his wife the question would never have arisen. She knew by the sudden rise of speed that he was in one of his tempers, so that when he pulled into the grass verge, switched off, and turned towards her she was not taken by surprise. A sea gull moaned high overhead. She lifted her gray eyes to his, and smiled, waiting for the attack.

"Jenny, would you mind telling me exactly what all this is about? I mean, why are you doing this fal-lal at this particular time?"

"I always wanted to do this pilgrimage. So it naturally follows that I would do it sometime, doesn't it?"

"Perhaps. But why, for instance, this month and not last month?"

"The island wasn't open to pilgrims last month."

"Why didn't you go last year instead of this year?"

"You know we went to Austria last year."

"Why not the year before last?"

"I don't know. And stop bullying me. It is just a thing that everybody wants to do sometime. It is a special sort of Irish thing, like Lourdes, or Fatima, or Lisieux. Everybody who knows about it feels drawn to it. If you were a practicing Catholic you'd understand."

"I understand quite well," he snapped. "I know perfectly well that people go on pilgrimages all over the world. Spain. France. Mexico. I shouldn't be surprised if they go on them in Russia. What I am asking you is what has cropped up to produce this extra-special performance just *now?*"

"And I tell you I don't know. The impulse came over me suddenly last Sunday looking at those boys and girls playing tennis. For no reason. It just came. I said to myself, 'All right, go now!' I felt that if I didn't do it on the impulse I'd never do it at all. Are you asking me for a rational explanation? I haven't got one. I'm not clever and intelligent like you, darling."

"You're as clever as a bag of cats."

She laughed at him.

"I do love you, Bobby, when you are cross. Like a small boy."

"Why didn't you ask George to drive you?"

She sat up straight.

"I don't want my husband to know anything whatever about this. Please don't mention a word of it to him."

He grinned at his small victory, considered the scythe of her jawbone, looked at the shining darkness of her hair, and restarted the car.

"All the same," he said after a mile, "there must be some reason. Or call it a cause if you don't like the word reason. And I'd give a lot to know what it is."

After another mile:

"Of course, I might as well be talking to that old dolmen over there as be asking a woman why she does anything. And if she knew she wouldn't tell you."

After another mile:

"Mind you, I believe all this is just a symptom of something else.

Never forget, my girl, that I'm a doctor. I'm trained to interpret symptoms. If a woman comes to me with a pain . . ."

"Oh, yes, if a woman comes to Surgeon Robert James Flannery with a pain he says to her, 'Never mind, that's only a pain.' My God! If a woman has a pain she has a bloody pain!"

He said quietly:

"Have you a pain?"

"Oh, do shut up! The only pain I have is in my tummy. I'm ravenous."

"I'm sorry. Didn't they give you a good lunch at the convent?"

"I took no lunch; you have to arrive at the island fasting. That's the rule."

"Do you mean to say you've had nothing at all to eat since breakfast?"

"I had no breakfast."

"What will you get to eat when you arrive on the island?"

"Nothing. Or next to nothing. Everybody has to fast on the island the whole time. Sometime before night I might get a cup of black tea, or hot water with pepper and salt in it. I believe it's one of their lighthearted jokes to call it soup."

Their speed shot up at once to sixty-five. He drove through Bundoran's siesta hour like the chariot of the Apocalypse. Nearing Ballyshannon they slowed down to a pleasant, humming fifty.

"Jenny!"

"Yes?"

"Are you tired of me?"

"Is this more of you and your symptoms?"

He stopped the car again.

"Please answer my question."

She laid her purple-gloved hand on his clenched fist.

"Look, darling! We've known one another for six years. You know that like any good little Catholic girl I go to my duties every Easter and every Christmas. Once or twice I've told you so. You've growled and grumbled a bit, but you never made any fuss about it. What are you suddenly worrying about now?"

"Because all that was just routine. Like the French or the Italians. Good Lord, I'm not bigoted. There's no harm in going to church now and again. I do it myself on state occasions, or if I'm staying in some house where they'd be upset if I didn't. But this sort of lunacy isn't routine!"

She slewed her head swiftly away from his angry eyes. A child in a pink pinafore with shoulder frills was driving two black cows through a gap.

"It was never routine. It's the one thing I have to hang on to in an otherwise meaningless existence. No children. A husband I'm not in love with. And I can't marry you."

She slewed back to him. He slewed away to look up the long empty road before them. He slewed back; he made as if to speak; he slewed away impatiently again.

"No?" she interpreted. "It isn't any use, is it? It's my problem, not yours. Or if it is yours you've solved it long ago by saying it's all a lot of damned nonsense."

"And how have you solved it?" he asked sardonically.

"Have you any cause to complain of how I've solved it? Oh, I'm not defending myself. I'm a fraud, I'm a crook, I admit it. You are more honest than I am. You don't believe in anything. But it's the truth that all I have is you and . . ."

"And what?"

"It sounds so blasphemous I can't say it."

"Say it!"

"All I have is you, and God."

He took out his cigarette case and took one. She took one. When he lit hers their eyes met. He said, very softly, looking up the empty road:

"Poor Jenny! I wish you'd talked like this to me before. It is, after all, as you say, your own affair. But what I can't get over is that this thing you're doing is so utterly extravagant. To go off to an island, in the middle of a lake, in the mountains, with a lot of Crawthumpers of every age and sex, and no sex, and peel off your stockings and your shoes, and go limping about on your bare feet on a lot of sharp stones, and kneel in the mud, psalming and beating your breast like a criminal, and drink nothing for three days but salt water . . . it's not like you. It's a side of you I've never known before. The only possible explanation for it must be that something is happening inside in you that I've never seen happen before!"

She spread her hands in despair. He chucked away his cigarette and restarted the car. They drove on in silence. A mist began to speckle the windscreen. They turned off the main road into sunless hills, all brown as hay. The next time he glanced at her she was making up her face; her mouth rolling the lipstick into her lips; her eyes rolling around the mirror. He said:

"You're going to have a nice picnic if the weather breaks."

She glanced out apprehensively.

"It won't be fun."

A sudden flog of rain lashed into the windscreen. The sky had turned its bucket upside down. He said:

"Even if it's raining do you still have to keep walking around on those damn stones?"

"Yes."

"You'll get double pneumonia."

"Don't worry, darling. It's called Saint Patrick's Purgatory. He will look after me."

That remark started a squabble that lasted until they drew up beside the lake. Other cars stood about like stranded boats. Other pilgrims stood by the boat slip, waiting for the ferry, their backs hunched to the wind, their clothes ruffled like the fur of cattle. She looked out across the lough at the creeping worms of foam.

He looked about him sullenly at the waiting pilgrims, a green bus, two taxiloads of people waiting for the rain to stop. They were not his kind of people at all, and he said so.

"That," she smiled, "is what comes of being a surgeon. You

don't meet people, you meet organs. Didn't you once tell me that when you are operating you never look at the patient's face?"

He grunted. Confused and hairy-looking clouds combed themselves on the ridges of the hills. The lake was crumpled and gray, except for those yellow worms of foam blown across it in parallel lines. To the south a cold patch of light made it all look far more dreary. She stared out towards the island and said:

"It's not at all like what I expected."

"And what the hell did you expect? Capri?"

"I thought of an old island, with old gray ruins, and old holly trees and rhododendrons down to the water, a place where old monks would live."

They saw tall buildings like modern hotels rising by the island's shore, an octagonal basilica big enough for a city, four or five bare, slated houses, a long shed like a ballroom. There was one tree. Another bus drew up beside them and people peered out through the wiped glass.

"Oh, God!" she groaned. "I hope this isn't going to be like Lourdes."

"And what, pray, is wrong with Lourdes when it's at home?"

"Commercialized. I simply can't believe that this island was the most famous pilgrimage of the Middle Ages. On the rim of the known world. It must have been like going off to Jerusalem or coming home brown from the sun with a cockle in your hat from Galilee."

He put on a vulgar Yukon voice:

"Thar's gold somewhere in them thar hills. It looks to me like a damn good financial proposition for somebody."

She glared at him. The downpour had slackened. Soon it almost ceased. Gurgles of streams. A sound of pervasive drip. From the back seat she took a small red canvas bag marked T.W.A.

"You will collect me on Wednesday about noon, won't you?"

He looked at her grimly. She looked every one of her forty-one years. The skin of her neck was corrugated. In five years' time she would begin to have jowls.

"Have a good time," he said, and slammed in the gears, and drove away.

The big, lumbering ferryboat was approaching, its prow slapping the corrugated waves. There were three men to each oar. It began to spit rain again. With about a hundred and fifty men and women, of every age and, so far as she could see, of every class, she clambered aboard. They pushed out and slowly they made the crossing, huddling together from the wind and rain. The boat nosed into its cleft and unloaded. She had a sensation of dark water, wet cement, houses, and a great number of people; and that she would have given gold for a cup of hot tea. Beyond the four or five white-washed houses — she guessed that they had been the only buildings on the island before trains and buses made the pilgrimage popular — and beyond the cement paths, she came on the remains of the natural island: a knoll, some warm grass, the tree, and the roots of the old hermits' cells across whose teeth of stone barefooted pilgrims were already treading on one another's heels. Most of these bare-footed people wore mackintoshes. They not only stumbled on one another's heels; they kneeled on one another's toes and tails; for the island was crowded — she thought there must be nearly two thousand people on it. They were packed between the two modern hostels and the big church. She saw a priest in sou'wester and gum boots. A nun waiting for the new arrivals at the door of the women's hostel took her name and address, and gave her the number of her cubicle. She went upstairs to it, laid her red bag on the cot, sat beside it, unfastened her garters, took off her shoes, unpeeled her nylons, and without transition became yet another anonymous pilgrim. As she went out among the pilgrims already praying in the rain she felt only a sense of shame as if she were specially singled out under the microscope of the sky. The wet ground was cold.

A fat old woman in black, rich-breasted, gray-haired, took her kindly by the arm and said in a warm, Kerry voice: "You're shivering, you poor creature! Hould hard now. Sure, when we have the first station done they'll be giving us the ould cup of black tay."

And laughed at the folly of this longing for the tea. She winced when she stepped on the gritty concrete of the terrace surrounding the basilica, built out on piles over the lake. A young man smiled sympathetically, seeing that she was a delicate subject for the rigors before her: he was dressed like a clerk, with three pens in his breast pocket, and he wore a Total Abstinence badge.

"Saint's Island they call it," he smiled. "Some people think it should be called Divil's Island."

She disliked his kindness — she had never in her life asked for pity from anybody, but she soon found that the island floated on kindness. Everything and everybody about her seemed to say, "We are all sinners here, wretched creatures barely worthy of mercy." She felt the abasement of the doomed. She was among people who had surrendered all personal identity, all pride. It was like being in a concentration camp.

The fat old Kerrywoman was explaining to her what the routine was, and as she listened she realized how long her stay would really be. In prospect it had seemed so short: come on Monday afternoon, leave on Wednesday at noon; it had seemed no more than one complete day and two bits of nights. She had not forseen that immediately after arriving she must remain out of doors until the darkness fell, walking the rounds of the stones, praying, kneeling, for about five hours. And even then she would get no respite, for she must stay awake all night praying in the basilica. It was then that she would begin the second long day, as long and slow as the night; and on the third day she would still be walking those rounds until midday. She would be without food, even when she would have left the island, until the midnight of that third day.

"Yerrah, but sure," the old woman cackled happily, "they say that fasting is good for the stomach."

She began to think of "they." They had thought all this up. They had seen how much could be done with simple prayers. For when she began to tot up the number of paternosters and Aves that she must say she had to stop at the two thousandth. And these reiterated prayers must be said while walking on the stones, or kneeling in the mud, or standing upright with her two arms extended. This was the posture she disliked most. Every time she came to do it, her face to the lake, her arms spread, the queue listening to her renouncing her sins, she had to force herself to the posture and the words. The first time she did it, with the mist blowing into her eyes, her arms out like a crucifix, her lips said the words but her heart cursed herself for coming so unprepared, for coming at all. Before she had completed her first circuit — four times around each one of six cells — one ankle and one toe was bleeding. She was then permitted to ask for the cup of black tea. She received it sullenly, as a prisoner might receive his bread and water.

She wished after that first circuit to start again and complete a second — the six cells, and the seven other ordeals at other points of the island — and so be done for the day. But she found that "they" had invented something else: she must merge with the whole anonymous mass of pilgrims for mass prayer in the church.

A slur of wet feet; patter of rain on leaded windows; smells of bog water and damp clothing; the thousand voices responding to the incantations. At her right a young girl of about seventeen was uttering heartfelt responses. On her left an old man in his sixties gave them out loudly. On all sides, before her, behind her, the same passionate exchange of energy, while all she felt was a crust hardening about her heart, and she thought, in despair, "I have no more feeling than a stone!" And she thought, looking about her, that tonight this vigil would go on for hour after hour until the dark, leaded windows colored again in the morning light. She leaned her face in her palms and whispered, "O God, please let me out of myself!" The waves of voices beat and rumbled in her ears as in an empty shell.

She was carried out on the general sliding whispering of the bare feet into the last gleanings of the daylight to begin her second circuit. In the porch she cowered back from the rain. It was settling into a filthy night. She was thrust forward by the crowd, flowed with its force to the iron cross by the shingle's edge. She took her place in the queue and then with the night wind pasting her hair across her face she raised her arms and once again renounced the world, the flesh, and the Devil. She did four circles of the church on the gritty concrete. She circled the first cell's stones. She completed the second circle. Her prayers were become numb by now. She stumbled, muttering them, up and down the third steeply sloped cell, or bed. She was a drowned cat and one knee was bleeding. At the fourth cell she saw him.

He was standing about six yards away looking at her. He wore a white raincoat buttoned tight about his throat. His feet were bare. His hair was streaked down his forehead as if he had been swimming. She stumbled towards him and dragged him by the arm down to the edge of the boat slip.

"What are you doing here?" she cried furiously. "Why did you follow me?"

He looked down at her calmly:

"Why shouldn't I be here?"

"Because you don't believe in it! You've just followed me to sneer at me, to mock at me! Or from sheer vulgar curiosity!"

"No," he said, without raising his voice. "I've come to see just what it is that you believe in. I want to know all about you. I want to know why you came here. I don't want you to do anything or have anything that I can't do or can't know. And as for believing — we all believe in something."

Dusk was closing in on the island and the lake. She had to peer into his face to catch his expression.

"But I've known you for years and you've never shown any sign of believing in anything but microscopes and microbes and symptoms.

It's absurd, you couldn't be serious about anything like this. I'm beginning to hate you!"

"Are you?" he said, so softly that she had to lean near him to hear him over the slapping of the waves against the boat slip. A slow rift in the clouds let down a star; by its light she saw his smile.

"Yes!" she cried, so loudly that he swept out a hand and gripped her by the arm. Then he took her other arm and said gently:

"I don't think you should have come here, Jenny. You're only tearing yourself to bits. There are some places where some people should never go, things some people should never try to do — however good they may be for others. I know why you came here. You feel you ought to get rid of me, but you haven't the guts to do it, so you come up here into the mountains to get your druids to work it by magic. All right! I'm going to ask them to help you."

He laughed and let her go, giving her a slight impulse away from him.

"Ask? You will *ask*? Do you mean to tell me that you have said as much as one single, solitary prayer on this island?"

"Yes," he said casually, "I have."

She scorned him.

"Are you trying to tell me, Bobby, that you are doing this pilgrimage?"

"I haven't fasted. I didn't know about that. And, anyway, I probably won't. I've got my pockets stuffed with two pounds of the best chocolates I could buy in Bundoran. I don't suppose I'll even stay up all night like the rest of you. The place is so crowded that I don't suppose anybody will notice me if I curl up in some corner of the boathouse. I heard somebody saying that people had to sleep there last night. But you never know — I might — I just might stay awake. If I do, it will remind me of going to midnight Mass with my father when I was a kid. Or going to retreats, when we used all hold up a lighted candle and renounce the Devil.

"It was a queer sensation standing up there by the lake and saying those words all over again. Do you know, I thought I'd completely forgotten them!"

"The next thing you're going to say is that you believe in the Devil! You fraud!"

"Oh, there's no trouble about believing in that old gentleman. There isn't a doctor in the world who doesn't, though he will give him another name. And on a wet night, in a place like this, you could believe in a lot of things. No, my girl, what I find it hard to believe in is the flesh and the world. They are good things. Do you think I'm ever going to believe that your body and my body are evil? And you don't either! And you are certainly never going to renounce the world, because you are tied to it hand and foot!"

"That's not true!"

His voice cut her like a whip:

"Then why do you go on living with your husband?"

She stammered feebly. He cut at her again:

"You do it because he's rich, and you like comfort, and you like being a 'somebody.'"

With a switch of her head she brushed past him. She did not see him again that night.

The night world turned imperceptibly. In the church, for hour after hour, the voices obstinately beat back the responses. She sank under the hum of the prayer wheel, the lust for sleep, her own despairs. Was he among the crowd? Or asleep in a corner of the boatshed? She saw his flatly domed fingers, a surgeon's hand, so strong, so sensitive. She gasped at the sensual image she had evoked.

The moon touched a black window with color. After an age it had stolen to another. Heads drooped. Neighbors poked one another awake with a smile. Many of them had risen from the benches in order to keep themselves awake and were circling the aisles in a loose procession of slurring feet, responding as they moved. Exhaustion began to work on her mind. Objects began to disconnect, become isolated each within its own outline — now it was the pulpit, now a statue, now a crucifix. Each object took on the vividness of a hallucination. The crucifix detached itself from the wall and leaned towards her, and for a long while she saw nothing but the heavy pendent body, the staring eyes, so that when the old man at her side let his head sink over on her shoulder and then woke up with a start she felt him no more than if they were two fishes touching in the sea. Bit by bit the incantations drew her in; sounds came from her mouth; prayers flowed between her and those troubled eyes that fixed hers. She swam into an ecstasy as rare as one of those perfect dances of her youth when she used to swing in a whirl of music, a swirl of bodies, a circling of lights, floated out of her mortal frame, alone in the arms that embraced her.

Suddenly it all exploded. One of the four respites of the night had halted the prayers. The massed pilgrims relaxed. She looked blearily about her, no longer disjunct. Her guts rumbled. She looked at the old man beside her. She smiled at him and he at her.

"My poor old knees are crucified," he grinned.

"You should have the skirts," she grinned back.

They were all going out to stretch in the cool, and now dry, air, or to snatch a smoke. The amber windows of the church shivered in a pool of water. A hearty-voiced young woman leaning on the balustrade lit a match for her. The match hissed into the invisible lake lapping below.

"The ould fag," said the young woman, dragging deep on her cigarette, "is a great comfort. 'Tis as good as a man."

"I wonder," she said, "what would Saint Patrick think if he saw women smoking on his island?"

"He'd beat the living lights out of the lot of us."

She laughed aloud. She must tell him that. . . . She began to wander through the dark crowds in search of him. He had said something that wasn't true and she would answer him. She went through the crowds down to the boat slip. He was standing there, looking out into the dark as if he had not stirred since she saw him there before midnight. For a moment she regarded him, frightened by the force of the love that gushed into her. Then she approached him.

"Well, Mr. Worldly Wiseman? Enjoying your boathouse bed?"

"I'm doing the vigil," he said smugly.

"You sound almighty pleased with yourself."

He spoke eagerly now:

"Jenny, we mustn't quarrel. We must understand one another. And understand this place. I'm just beginning to. An island. In a remote lake. Among the mountains. Nighttime. No sleep. Hunger. The conditions of the desert. I was right in what I said to you. Can't you see how the old hermits who used to live here could swim off into a trance in which nothing existed but themselves and their visions? I told you a man can renounce what he calls the Devil, but not the flesh, not the world. They thought, like you, that they could throw away the flesh and the world, but they were using the flesh to achieve one of the rarest experiences in the world! Don't you see it?"

"Experiences! The next thing you'll be talking about is symptoms."

"Well, surely, you must have observed?" He peered at the luminous dial of his watch. "I should say that about four o'clock we will probably begin to experience a definite sense of dissociation. After that a positive alienation. . . ."

She turned furiously from him. She came back to say:

"I would much prefer, Bobby, if you would have the decency to go away in the morning. I can find my own way home. I hope we don't meet again on this island. Or out of it!"

"The magic working?" he laughed.

After that she made a deliberate effort of the mind to mean and to feel every separate word of the prayers — which is a great foolishness since prayers are not poems to be read or even understood; they are an instinct; to dance would be as wise. She thought that if she could not feel what she said how could she mean it, and so she tried to savor every word, and, from trying to mean each word, lagged behind the rest, sank into herself, and ceased to pray. After the second respite she prayed only to keep awake. As the first cold pallor of morning came into the windows her heart rose again. But the eastern hills are high here and the morning holds off stubbornly. It is the worst hour of the vigil, when the body ebbs, the prayers sink to a drone, and the night seems to have begun all over again.

At the last respite she emerged to see pale tents of blue on the hills. The slow cumulus clouds cast a sheen on the water. There is no sound. No birds sing. At this hour the pilgrims are too awed or too exhausted to speak, so that the island reverts to its ancient silence in spite of the crowds.

By the end of the last bout she was calm like the morning lake. She longed for the cup of black tea. She was unaware of her companions. She did not think of him. She was unaware of herself. She no more thought of God than a slave thinks of his master, and after she had drunk her tea she sat in the morning sun outside the women's hostel like an old blind woman who has nothing in life to wait for but sleep.

The long day expired as dimly as the vapor rising from the water. The heat became morbid. One is said to be free on this second day to converse, to think, to write, to read, to do anything at all that one pleases except the one thing everybody wants to do — to sleep. She did nothing but watch the clouds, or listen to the gentle muttering of the lake. Before noon she heard some departing pilgrims singing a hymn as the great ferryboats pushed off. She heard their voices without longing; she did not even desire food. When she met him she was without rancor.

"Still here?" she said, and when he nodded: "Sleepy?"

"Sleepy."

"Too many chocolates, probably."

"I didn't eat them. I took them out of my pockets one by one as I leaned over the balustrade and guessed what center each had — coffee, marshmallow, nut, toffee, cream — and dropped it in with a little splash to the holy fishes."

She looked up at him gravely.

"Are you really trying to join in this pilgrimage?"

"Botching it. I'm behindhand with my rounds. I have to do five circuits between today and tomorrow. I may never get them done. Still, something is better than nothing."

"You dear fool!"

If he had not walked away then she would have had to; such a gush of affection came over her at the thought of what he was doing, and why he was doing it — stupidly, just like a man; skeptically, just like a man; not admitting it to himself, just like a man; for all sorts of damn-fool rational reasons, just like a man; and not at all for the only reason that she knew was his real reason: because she was doing it, which meant that he loved her. She sat back, and closed her eyes, and the tears of chagrin oozed between her lids as she felt her womb stir with desire of him.

When they met again it was late afternoon.

"Done four rounds," he said so cheerfully that he maddened her.

"It's not golf, Bobby, damn you!"

"I should jolly well think not. I may tell you my feet are in such a condition I won't be able to play golf for a week. Look!"

She did not look. She took his arm and led him to the quietest corner she could find.

"Bobby, I am going to confess something to you. I've been thinking about it all day trying to get it clear. I know now why I came here. I came because I know inside in me that some day our apple will have to fall off the tree. I'm forty. You are nearly fifty. It will have to happen. I came here because I thought it right to admit that some day, if it has to be, I am willing to give you up."

He began to shake all over with laughter.

"What the hell are you laughing at?" she moaned.

"When women begin to reason! Listen, wasn't there a chap one time who said, 'O God, please make me chaste, but not just yet'?"

"What I am saying is 'now,' if it has to be, if it can be, if I can make it be. I suppose," she said wildly, "I'm really asking for a miracle, that my husband would die, or that you'd die, or something like that that would make it all come right!"

He burst into such a peal of laughter that she looked around her apprehensively. A few people near them also happened to be laughing over something and looked at them indulgently.

"Do you realize, Bobby, that when I go to confession here I will have to tell all about us, and I will have to promise to give you up?"

"Yes, darling, and you won't mean a single word of it."

"But I always mean it!"

He stared at her as if he were pushing curtains aside in her.

"Always? Do you mean you've been saying it for six years?"

"I mean it when I say it. Then I get weak. I can't help it, Bobby. You know that!" She saw the contempt in his eyes and began to talk rapidly, twisting her marriage ring madly around her finger. He kept staring into her eyes like a man staring down the long perspective of a railway line waiting for the engine to appear. "So you see why there wasn't any sense in asking me yesterday why I come now and not at some other time, because with me there isn't any other time, it's always *now*, I meet you *now*, and I love you *now*, and I think it's not right *now*, and then I think, 'No, not *now*,' and then I say I'll give you up *now*, and I mean it every time until we meet again, and it begins all over again, and there's never any end to it until some day I can say, 'Yes, I used to know him once, but not now,' and then it will be a *now* where there won't be any other *now* any more because there'll be nothing to live for."

The tears were leaking down her face. He sighed:

"Dear me! You have got yourself into a mess, haven't you?"

"O God, the promises and the promises! I wish the world would end tonight and we'd both die together!"

He gave her his big damp handkerchief. She wiped her eyes and blew her nose and said:

"You don't mean to go to confession, do you?"

He chuckled sourly.

"And promise? I must go and finish a round of pious golf. I'm afraid, old girl, you just want to get me into the same mess as yourself. No, thank you. You must solve your own problems in your own way, and I in mine."

That was the last time she spoke to him that day.

She went back to the balustrade where she had smoked with the hearty girl in the early hours of the morning. She was there again. She wore a scarlet beret. She was smoking again. She began to talk, and the talk flowed from her without stop. She had fine broad shoulders, a big mobile mouth, and a pair of wild goat's eyes. After a while it became clear that the woman was beside herself with terror. She suddenly let it all out in a gush of exhaled smoke.

"Do you know why I'm hanging around here? Because I ought to go into confession and I'm in dread of it. He'll tear me alive. He'll murdher me. It's not easy for a girl like me, I can promise you!"

"You must have terrible sins to tell?" she smiled comfortingly.

"He'll slaughter me, I'm telling you."

"What is it? Boys?"

The two goat's eyes dilated with fear and joy. Her hands shook like a drunkard's.

"I can't keep away from them. I wish to God I never came here."

"But how silly! It's only a human thing. I'm sure half the people here have the same tale to tell. It's an old story, child, the priests are sick of hearing it."

"Oh, don't be talking! Let me alone! I'm criminal, I tell yeh! And there are things you can't explain to a priest. My God, you can hardly explain 'em to a doctor!"

"You're married?" — looking at her ring.

"Poor Tom! I have him wore out. He took me to a doctor one time to know would anything cure me. The old foolah took me temperature and gave me a book like a bus guide about when it's safe and when it isn't safe to make love, the ould eedjut! I was pregnant again before Christmas. Six years married and I have six kids; nobody could stand that gait o' going. And I'm only twenty-four. Am I to have a baby every year of my life? I'd give me right hand this minute for a double whiskey."

"Look, you poor child! We are all in the same old ferryboat here. What about me?"

"You?"

"It's not men with me, it's worse."

"Worse? In God's name, what's worse than men?"

The girl looked all over her, followed her arm down to her hand, to her third finger.

"One man."

The tawny eyes swiveled back to her face and immediately understood.

"Are you very fond of him?" she asked gently, and taking the unspoken answer said, still more pityingly, "You can't give him up?"

"It's six years now and I haven't been able to give him up."

The girl's eyes roved sadly over the lake as if she were surveying a lake of human unhappiness. Then she threw her butt into the water and her red beret disappeared into the maw of the church porch.

She saw him twice before the dusk thickened and the day grew cold again with the early sunset. He was sitting directly opposite her before the men's hostel, smoking, staring at the ground between his legs. They sat facing one another. They were separated by their identities, joined by their love. She glimpsed him only once after that, at the hour when the sky and the hills merge, an outline passing across the lake. Soon after she had permission to go to her cubicle. Immediately she lay down she spiraled to the bottom of a deep lake of sleep.

She awoke refreshed and unburthened. She had received the island's gift: its sense of remoteness from the world, almost a sensation of the world's death. It is the source of the island's kindness.
Nobody is just matter, poor to be exploited by rich, weak to be exploited by the strong; in mutual generosity each recognizes the other
only as a form of soul; it is a brief, harsh Utopia of equality in
nakedness. The bare feet are a symbol of that nakedness unknown
in the world they have left.

The happiness to which she awoke was dimmed a little by a conversation she had with an Englishman over breakfast — the usual
black tea and a piece of oaten bread. He was a city man who had arrived the day before, been up all night while she slept. He had not
yet shaved; he was about sixty-two or three; small and tubby, his
eyes perpetually wide and unfocusing behind pince-nez glasses.

"That's right," he said, answering her question. "I'm from England. Liverpool. I cross by the night boat and get here the next
afternoon. Quite convenient, really. I've come here every year for the
last twenty-two years, apart from the war years. I come on account of
my wife."

"Is she ill?"

"She died twenty-two years ago. No, it's not what you might think
— I'm not praying for her. She was a good woman, but, well, you
see, I wasn't very kind to her. I don't mean I quarreled with her, or
drank, or was unfaithful. I never gambled. I've never smoked in
my life." His hands made a faint movement that was meant to express a whole life, all the confusion and trouble of his soul. "It's just
that I wasn't kind. I didn't make her happy."

"Isn't that," she said, to comfort him, "a very private feeling? I
mean, it's not in the Ten Commandments that thou shalt make thy
wife happy."

He did not smile. He made the same faint movement with his fingers.

"Oh, I don't know! What's love if it doesn't do that? I mean to

say, it is something godly to love another human being, isn't it? I
mean, what does 'godly' mean if it doesn't mean giving up everything for another? It isn't human to love, you know. It's foolish,
it's a folly, a divine folly. It's beyond all reason, all limits. I didn't
rise to it," he concluded sadly.

She looked at him, and thought, "A little fat man, a clerk in
some Liverpool office all his life, married to some mousy little
woman, thinking about love as if he were some sort of Greek mys-
tic."

"It's often," she said lamely, "more difficult to love one's husband,
or one's wife, as the case may be, than to love one's neighbor."

"Oh, much!" he agreed without a smile. "Much! Much more difficult!"

At which she was overcome by the thought that inside ourselves
we have no room without a secret door; no solid self that has not a
ghost inside it trying to escape. If I leave Bobby I still have George.
If I leave George I still have myself, and whatever I find in myself.
She patted the little man's hand and left him, fearing that if she let
him talk on even his one little piece of sincerity would prove to be
a fantasy, and in the room that he had found behind his own room
she would open other doors leading to other obsessions. He had
told her something true about her own imperfection, and about the
nature of love, and she wanted to share it while it was still true. But
she could not find him, and there was still one more circuit to do
before the ferryboat left. She did meet Goat's Eyes. The girl clutched
her with tears magnifying her yellow-and-green irises and gasped
joyously:

"I found a lamb of a priest. A saint anointed! He was as gentle!
'What's your husband earning?' says he. 'Four pounds ten a week,
Father,' says I. 'And six children?' says he. 'You poor woman,' says
he, 'you don't need to come here at all. Your Purgatory is at home.'
He laid all the blame on poor Tom. And, God forgive me, I let him
do it. 'Bring him here to me,' says he, 'and I'll cool him for you.'

God bless the poor innocent priest, I wish I knew as little about marriage as he does. But," and here she broke into a wail, "sure he has me ruined altogether now. He's after making me so fond of poor Tommy I think I'll never get home soon enough to go to bed with him." And in a vast flood of tears of joy, of relief, and of fresh misery: "I wish I was a bloomin' nun!"

It was not until they were all waiting at the ferryboat that she saw him. She managed to sit beside him in the boat. He touched her hand and winked. She smiled back at him. The bugler blew his bugle. A tardy traveler came racing out of the men's hostel. The boatload cheered him, the bugler helped him aboard with a joke about people who can't be persuaded to stop praying, and there was a general chaff about people who have a lot to pray about, and then somebody raised the parting hymn, and the rowers began to push the heavy oars, and singing they were slowly rowed across the summer lake back to the world.

They were driving back out of the hills by the road they had come, both silent. At last she could hold in her question no longer:

"Did you go, Bobby?"

Meaning: had he, after all his years of silence, of rebellion, of disbelief, made his peace with God at the price of a compact against her. He replied gently:

"Did I probe your secrets all these years?"

She took the rebuke humbly, and for several miles they drove on in silence. They were close, their shoulders touched, but between them there stood that impenetrable wall of identity that segregates every human being in a private world of self. Feeling it she realized at last that it is only in places like the lake-island that the barriers of self break down. The tubby little clerk from Liverpool had been right. Only when love desires nothing but renunciation, total surrender, does self surpass self. Everybody who ever entered the island left the world of self behind for a few hours, exchanged it for what

the little man had called a divine folly. It was possible only for a few
hours — unless one had the courage, or the folly, to renounce the
world altogether. Then another thought came to her. In the world
there might also be escape from the world.

"Do you think, Bobby, that when people are in love they can give
up everything for one another?"

"No," he said flatly. "Except perhaps in the first raptures?"

"If I had a child I think I could sacrifice anything for it. Even my
life."

"Yes," he agreed. "It has been known to happen."

And she looked at him sadly, knowing that they would never be
able to marry, and even if she did that she would never have children. And yet, if they could have married, there was a lake . . .

"Do you know what I'm planning at this moment?" he asked
breezily.

She asked without interest what it was.

"Well, I'm simply planning the meal we're going to eat tonight in
Galway, at midnight."

"At midnight? Then we're going on with this pilgrimage? Are
we?"

"Don't *you* want to? It was your idea in the beginning."

"All right. And what are we going to do until midnight? I've
never known time to be so long."

"I'm going to spend the day fishing behind Glencar. That will
kill the hungry day. After that, until midnight, we'll take the
longest possible road around Connemara. Then would you have any
objections to mountain trout cooked in milk, stuffed roast kid with
fresh peas and spuds in their jackets, apple pie and whipped cream,
with a cool Pouilly Fuissé, a cozy 1929 claret, West of Ireland Pont
l'Évêque, finishing up with Gaelic coffee and two Otards? Much
more in your line, if I know anything about you, than your silly old
black tea and hot salt water."

"I admit I like the things of the flesh."

"You live for them!"

He had said it so gently, so affectionately that, half in dismay, half with amusement, she could not help remembering Goat's Eyes, racing home as fast as the bus would carry her to make love to her Tommy. After that they hardly spoke at all, and then only of casual things such as a castle beside the road, the sun on the edging sea, a tinker's caravan, an opening view. It was early afternoon as they entered the deep valley at Glencar and he probed in second gear for an attractive length of stream, found one and started eagerly to put his rod together. He began to walk up against the dazzling bubble of water and within an hour was out of sight. She stretched herself out on a rug on the bank and fell sound asleep.

It was nearly four o'clock before she woke up, stiff and thirsty. She drank from a pool in the stream, and for an hour she sat alone by the pool, looking into its peat-brown depth, as vacantly contented as a tinker's wife to live for the moment, to let time wind and unwind everything. It was five o'clock before she saw him approaching, plodding in his flopping waders, with four trout on a rush stalk. He threw the fish at her feet and himself beside them.

"I nearly ate them raw," he said.

"Let's cook them and eat them," she said fiercely.

He looked at her for a moment, then got up and began to gather dry twigs, found Monday's newspaper in the car — it looked like a paper of years ago — and started the fire. She watched while he fed it. When it was big enough in its fall to have made a hot bed of embers he roasted two of the trout across the hook of his gaff, and she smelled the crisping flesh and sighed. At last he laid them, browned and crackly, on the grass by her hand. She took one by its crusted tail, smelled it, looked at him, and slung it furiously into the heart of the fire. He gave a sniff-laugh and did the same with his.

"Copy cat!" she said.

"Let's get the hell out of here," he said, jumping up. "Carry the kit, will you?"

She rose, collected the gear, and followed him saying:

"I feel like an Arab wife. 'Carry the pack. Go here. Go there.' "

They climbed out of the glens onto the flat moorland of the Easky peninsula where the evening light was a cold ocher gleaming across green bogland that was streaked with all the weedy colors of a strand at ebb. At Ballina she suggested that they should have tea.

"It will be a pleasant change of diet!" he said.

When they had found a café and she was ordering the tea he said to the waitress:

"And bring lots of hot buttered toast."

"This," she said, as she poured out the tea and held up the milk jug questioningly, "is a new technique of seduction. Milk?"

"Are you having milk?"

"No."

"No, then."

"Some nice hot buttered toast?"

"Are you having toast?" he demanded.

"Why the bloody hell should it be up to me to decide?"

"I asked you a polite question," he said rudely.

"No."

"No!"

They looked at one another as they sipped the black tea like two people who are falling head over heels into hatred of one another.

"Could you possibly tell me," he said presently, "why I bother my head with a fool of a woman like you?"

"I can only suppose, Bobby, that it is because we are in love with one another."

"I can only suppose so," he growled. "Let's get on!"

They took the longest way round he could find on the map, west into County Mayo, across between the lakes at Pontoon, over the level bogland to Castlebar. Here the mountains walled in the bog-land plain with cobalt air — in the fading light the land was losing all solidity. Clouds like soapsuds rose and rose over the edges of the mountains until they glowed as if there was a fire of embers behind the blue ranges. In Castlebar he pulled up by the post office and telephoned to the hotel at Salthill for dinner and two rooms. When he came out he saw a poster in a shop window and said:

"Why don't we go to the pictures? It will kill a couple of hours."

"By rights," she said, "you ought to be driving me home to Dublin."

"If you wish me to I will."

"Would you if I asked you?"

"Do you want me to?"

"I suppose it's rather late now, isn't it?"

"Not at all. Fast going we could be there about one o'clock. Shall we?"

"It wouldn't help. George is away. I'd have to bring you in and give you something to eat, and . . . Let's go to the blasted movies!"

The film was *Charley's Aunt*. They watched its slapstick gloomily. When they came out, after nine o'clock, there was still a vestigial light in the sky. They drove on and on, westward still, prolonging the light, prolonging the drive, holding off the night's decision. Before Killary they paused at a black-faced lake, got out, and stood beside its quarried beauty. Nothing along its stony beach but a few wind-torn rushes.

"I could eat you," he said.

She replied that only lovers and cannibals talk like that.

They dawdled past the long fiord of Killary where young people on holiday sat outside the hotel, their drinks on the trestled tables. In Clifden the street was empty, people already climbing to bed, as the lights in the upper windows showed. They branched off on the long coastal road where the sparse whitewashed cottages were whiter than the foam of waves that barely suggested sea. At another darker strand they halted, but now they saw no foam at all and divined the sea only by its invisible whispering, or when a star touched a wave. Midnight was now only an hour away.

Their headlights sent rocks and rabbits into movement.

The heather streamed past them like kangaroos. It was well past eleven as they poured along the lonely land by Galway Bay. Neither of them had spoken for an hour. As they drove into Salthill there was nobody abroad. Galway was dark. Only the porch light of the hotel showed that it was alive. When he turned off the engine the only sound at first was the crinkle of contracting metal as the engine began to cool. Then to their right they heard the lisping bay. The panel button lit the dashboard clock.

"A quarter to," he said, leaning back. She neither spoke nor stirred. "Jenny!" he said sharply.

She turned her head slowly and by the dashboard light he saw her white smile.

"Yes, darling?"

"Worn out?" he asked, and patted her knee.

She vibrated her whole body so that the seat shook, and stretched her arms about her head, and lowering them let her head fall on his shoulder, and sighed happily, and said:

"What I want is a good long drink of anything on earth except tea."

These homing twelve o'clockers from Lough Derg are well known in every hotel all over the west of Ireland. Revelry is the reward of penance. The porter welcomed them as if they were heroes returned from a war. As he led them to their rooms he praised them, he sympathized with them, he patted them up and he patted them down, he assured them that the ritual grill was at that moment sizzling over the fire, he proffered them hot baths, and he told them where to discover the bar. "Ye will discover it . . ." was his phrase. The wording was exact, for the bar's gaiety was muffled by dim lighting, drawn blinds, locked doors. In the overheated room he took off his jacket and unloosed his tie. They had to win a corner of the counter, and his order was for two highballs with ice in them. Within two minutes they were at home with the crowd. The island might never have existed if the barmaid, who knew where they had come from, had not laughed: "I suppose ye'll ate like lions?"

After supper they relished the bar once more, sipping slowly now, so refreshed that they could have started on the road again without distaste or regret. As they sipped they gradually became aware of a soft strumming and drumming near at hand, and were told that there was a dance on in the hotel next door. He raised his eyebrows to her. She laughed and nodded.

They gave it up at three o'clock and walked out into the warm-cool of the early summer morning. Gently tipsy, gently tired they walked to the little promenade. They leaned on the railing and he put his arm about her waist, and she put hers around his, and they gazed at the moon silently raking its path across the sea towards Aran. They had come, she knew, to the decisive moment. He said:

"They have a fine night for it tonight on the island."

"A better night than we had," she said tremulously.

After another spell of wave fall and silence he said:

"Do you know what I'm thinking, Jenny? I'm thinking that I wouldn't mind going back there again next year. Maybe I might do it properly the next time?"

"The next time?" she whispered, and all her body began to dissolve and, closing her eyes, she leaned against him. He, too, closed his eyes, and all his body became as rigid as a steel girder that flutters in a storm. Slowly they opened their love-drunk eyes, and stood looking long over the brightness and blackness of the sea. Then, gently, ever so gently, with a gentleness that terrified her he said:

"Shall we go in, my sweet?"

She did not stir. She did not speak. Slowly turning to him she lifted her eyes to him pleadingly.

"No, Bobby, please, not yet."

"Not yet?"

"Not tonight!"

He looked down at her, and drew his arms about her. They kissed passionately. She knew what that kiss implied. Their mouths parted. Hand in hand they walked slowly back to the hotel, to their separate rooms.